Also by Jane Ashford

The Duke's Sons
Heir to the Duke
What the Duke Doesn't Know
Lord Sebastian's Secret
Nothing Like a Duke
The Duke Knows Best

The Way to a Lord's Heart
Brave New Earl
A Lord Apart
How to Cross a Marquess

Once Again a Bride
Man of Honour
The Three Graces
The Marriage Wager
The Bride Insists
The Bargain
The Marchington Scandal
The Headstrong Ward
Married to a Perfect Stranger
Charmed and Dangerous
A Radical Arrangement
First Season / Bride to Be
Rivals of Fortune / The Impetuous Heiress
Last Gentleman Standing
Earl to the Rescue

The
RELUCTANT
Rake

JANE
ASHFORD

sourcebooks
casablanca

Published by Sourcebooks Casablanca, an imprint of Sourcebooks
P.O. Box 4410, Naperville, Illinois 60567-4410
(630) 961-3900
sourcebooks.com

The Reluctant Rake was originally published as *The Reluctant Rake* in 1987
in the United States of America by Signet, an imprint of New American
Library, Inc. This edition issued based on the paperback edition published
in 1987 in the United States of America by Signet, an imprint of New
American Library, Inc.

How to Beguile a Baron was originally published as *The Irresolute Rivals* in
1985 in the United States of America by Signet, an imprint of New American
Library, Inc. This edition issued based on the paperback edition published
in 1985 in the United States of America by Signet, an imprint of New
American Library, Inc.

Printed and bound in the United States of America.
OPM 10 9 8 7 6 5 4 3 2 1

CONTENTS

THE RELUCTANT RAKE

ONE

SIR RICHARD BECKWITH EMERGED FROM HIS ELEGANT town house on a chilly spring evening wearing a black silk domino over his dark gray pantaloons and long-tailed coat of dark blue superfine. Any one of his friends would have been astonished to see him in this guise, still more to see him out of evening dress at nine o'clock. Had they known that a pocket of the domino held a black mask, they would have been dumbfounded.

None of Sir Richard's exclusive circle was likely to see him tonight, however. When he hailed a hackney cab and climbed in, he directed it to a part of London little frequented by the *haut ton*. If certain of its men from time to time made their way through these unsavory streets, they did not mention such excursions in polite society.

A cold mist rose from the greasy cobblestones, enlivened here and there by hoarse laughter and singing as the hack rattled past some gin mill or bawdy house. One victim of blue ruin went so far as to grab for the cab, hoping to jerk its occupant into an alleyway and fleece him. He missed his target, however, and fell flat in the garbage-filled gutter with a curse.

Through the ride, Sir Richard sat impassive, his regular features immovable as stone, his gray eyes cold. If his goal was amusement of the type his class usually sought in this neighborhood, he went about it with an odd implacability.

The hack pulled up before a broad, soot-stained building that turned a blank facade to the street. Its windows were obscured with bars outside and heavy draperies within. Wooden double doors, firmly closed, revealed only a carved peephole at eye level.

"You sure of that h'address, guv?" wondered the driver.

"Yes." Beckwith handed him a small coin, allowing him to see one of larger denomination in his hand. "Wait for me nearby. I'll call when I want you. There's a guinea for you if you come when I call."

The man stared at the money, greed warring with his desire to return to safer streets. "Right," he said finally.

Beckwith pulled up the hood of the domino and put on his mask, then knocked sharply on the wooden door with the head of his cane and waited.

The peephole opened, and a bloodshot blue eye surveyed him with suspicion. Abruptly, the hole closed, and the bolts were shot back, allowing the door to open a crack.

"I am here for the meeting," Sir Richard declared.

"Password," came a hiss from the dimness.

"Chaos," he answered, in a tone that suggested he found the word offensive.

The door swung open. Inside was a sharp contrast to the dirty street. A rich, red Turkey carpet covered the floor, and the narrow hallway boasted French wallpaper and gilt sconces. Though the individual in charge of the door was distinctly rough-hewn, the footman who indicated that Sir Richard should follow him would not have looked out of place in Grosvenor Square.

He ushered Sir Richard into a large room at the back of the building. It was furnished with the armchairs and side tables of a gentleman's club, but the inhabitants were not so familiar. Many wore domino and mask, like Sir Richard. Others had clearly cast off these disguises with their third or fourth brandies and were loud with the effects of drink. The buxom young women who served them endured their fondling and leers with good-humored impertinence, and a sharp eye for the banknotes that were continually being folded and thrust lingeringly into bodices.

The din was significant, and the air was heavy with the fumes of alcohol and candlewax and the clashing scents of pomades and cheap perfume.

Sir Richard found a vacant chair in a dim corner and sat down. When one of the serving girls came up to him, he ordered brandy, but he spoke to no one else. He had come with a purpose, his demeanor said, and he would allow nothing to distract him from it.

At last, there was a stir at the back of the room, and one of the other masked guests stepped from a chair to a tabletop there. "Gentlemen," he cried above the din. "Gentlemen!"

The volume of sound decreased somewhat.

"Gentlemen," said the man again. "We have a rare treat for you this evening. Indeed, I think I may safely say we have a unique entertainment in store. Its like hasn't occurred in our time, at least. I couldn't vouch for our grandfathers."

This elicited a roar of laughter and vulgar sallies from the crowd, which was beginning to gather around the table. Beckwith joined them; he had recognized the voice of the speaker, and his lips were drawn tight in a thin line.

"May I present to you," continued the self-appointed master of ceremonies, "Bess Malone." He jumped lightly down from the table and offered a hand to someone. In the next instant, a slender girl had stepped from chair to table and stood facing the audience.

She wore nothing but a thin, white cotton shift, as banks of candles behind her readily revealed. Her hair, jet black, tumbled over her shoulders in wild abandon. And when she raised wide eyes to the crowd briefly, they were shown to be vivid blue. Her skin was pale and dusted with freckles over the nose and cheekbones. She was exquisitely beautiful, and certainly not yet eighteen years old.

"Bess," declared the man, who had leapt upon another of the tables, "will go to the highest bidder tonight. And we expect the price to be high, don't we, Bess?"

The girl tossed back her hair, her breasts rising and falling with the movement and drawing ribald comments. She didn't look frightened, but neither was she at ease, particularly as the men began pushing forward and reaching up to caress her ankles and calves.

"Ah, ah, gentlemen," chided the master of ceremonies. "Bess comes untouched to her purchaser. Stand back and start the bidding."

"A hundred guineas," said a deep voice on the left.

"Two," responded a man in the front.

"Three," said Beckwith.

The master of ceremonies raised his head as if startled and turned to stare at Beckwith.

"Four hundred," said the first voice.

The bidding went on a full twenty minutes, one man after another dropping out reluctantly as the amount went above his touch. At last, only two were left—Sir Richard Beckwith and a nobleman of fifty or so in the front row, whose face was a map of debauchery and bitterness.

Silence spread through the room as the numbers mounted. When they reached fifteen hundred guineas, all conversation stopped. Only the quiet bids of the two stirred the smoky air, and the tension rose with each new offer.

At two thousand, the roué in front turned and stared pointedly at Sir Richard, gauging him. The older man's face looked devilish in the flickering candlelight. The room waited breathlessly to see what he would do, for most there knew him for a cruel and ruthless opponent. But after an interminable moment, he lowered pale lids, made a dismissive gesture, and walked away, signifying his withdrawal from the auction.

"Sold," said the master of ceremonies immediately, "to the gentleman in the rear, for two thousand guineas."

A sigh passed over the crowd as the tension released; then someone called for brandy, and the group began to disperse. A footman appeared at Beckwith's elbow to escort him to a small study off the front hall. The masked master of ceremonies and Bess Malone joined him there. "Sir," said the former, "my sincere felicitations. You have acquired a diamond of the first water."

Bess took Sir Richard's arm and pressed herself up against him.

"I assume you have clothing," said Sir Richard. "Put it on." The girl drew back, piqued. The master of ceremonies laughed. "Protecting your property? Or merely eager to depart for some more private place? I can't blame you for that. Hurry and dress, Bess." The girl ran out. "And now, sir, there is the matter of two thousand guineas."

Beckwith pulled a fat roll of bills from an inner pocket. "Who gets the money?" he asked.

But the other's eyes were riveted on the banknotes. "You carry such a sum on your person? In this part of London?"

"It is not my habit. Who gets this money?" He began to count it out, and the other man watched, fascinated. "Who?" repeated Beckwith with some asperity.

"Eh? Oh, half to the club, half to the girl."

"I see."

His tone made the other defensive. "It was her idea, you know."

"What?"

"Indeed. She came to, er, a member and proposed the plan not two weeks ago. I . . . He was taken aback, I may tell you."

Sir Richard laid the bills on the desk. The man snatched them up and fingered them as if they had the texture of velvet. "Two thousand," he murmured.

"I'll wait for the girl at the front door," said Sir Richard.

"What? Oh, to be sure. I'll have her sent to you there," was the reply. But the man's eyes did not waver from the money.

Sir Richard made his way back to the entrance, conscious, now that the business was concluded, of spreading whispers behind him. He hoped that they concerned his identity, and that none here knew him well enough to recognize him behind a mask.

At last the girl he had purchased appeared at the back of the hall and moved slowly toward him. Bess now wore a shabby dress of white sprigged muslin and a threadbare blue cloak, both garments clearly the long-ago castoffs of some more prosperous lady. But her dark hair remained unbound, and her eyes flashed as she examined him. Looking at her face, one forgot the clothes.

"Come," said Beckwith. "I have a hack waiting."

Someone in the room behind snickered, but Bess merely walked forward and took Sir Richard's arm, molding herself to his side and gazing up at the mask he still wore. Side by side, they went through the door the footman was holding open for them.

Outside, the mist had thickened, and the chill was even greater. Beckwith disengaged his arm and looked for his cab, hoping the driver had not lost his nerve and deserted him.

The jingle of harness and the sound of hooves on the cobblestones relieved him of this worry. The hack emerged from the mist and pulled up before the pair, the driver eyeing Bess Malone with amused appreciation. "A good night, then, guv?" he said.

Sir Richard merely stated his address in Mayfair and helped Bess into the carriage. In a moment, he had followed and shut the door, and the sound of hooves muffled by mist resumed.

Bess nestled close to her new protector, one small hand slipping over the buttons of his waistcoat. "Aren't you going to be rid of that mask, then?" she asked, in a lilt that called up visions of Ireland.

"We will talk when we reach my house," replied Sir Richard, removing her hand from his chest.

Bess straightened and eyed him. "Talk?" she echoed. "Aye, if you like. I'll be pleased to get acquainted before… what comes after talk. I've not done such a thing as this before, you see, and 'tis unnerving."

Beckwith merely grunted.

"Do you doubt me then?" flared Bess. "I swear I've never in my life…"

"No one has doubted you," interrupted Beckwith, and she subsided to watch his silhouette in the dim light filtering through the hack's window.

They made the journey in silence, broken only by Sir Richard's instructions to the cabbie when they reached the quietly elegant street where he dwelt. The driver steered into the mews at the back and deposited them before a narrow, slatted gate next to the stables before departing with the promised guinea.

Bess pulled her cloak closed and gazed about with disfavor. "Why do we come here?" she asked.

"I should think that would be obvious," replied Beckwith, taking a key from his pocket and unlocking the gate. "Follow me."

The girl glared at his back, but did so.

He led her along a narrow walk to a cobbled yard, then through the back door into the kitchen. The servants had gone to bed, and the fire was banked for the night. Beckwith turned to face the girl, pulling off his mask and letting the domino fall onto a wooden chair.

"Ah," breathed Bess, "a fine handsome man you are, too."

"Come here," said Sir Richard.

TWO

AT THE SAME HOUR THAT SIR RICHARD SET OUT ON HIS
surprising quest that evening, a stream of carriages before
the Earl of Leamington's Berkeley Square mansion paused
to allow a very handsome family party to alight. The
daughter first drew the eye, for she was a remarkably
lovely girl of twenty with smooth black hair and large,
pale green eyes strikingly set off by sooty lashes. She was
above medium height and slender, dressed in a white bro-
cade gown that proclaimed its cost even as it avoided all
extremes of fashion. Her parents were similarly clad—well
but conservatively—and rather older than most progeni-
tors of hopeful debutantes. Their faces were amiable, and
they clearly derived much pleasure from their daughter's
beauty and success.

They left their wraps and walked together up to the
landing where the Countess of Leamington and her newly
presented daughter waited to greet them. "Sir George and
Lady Devere. Miss Julia Devere," intoned the butler.

"Julia!" cried the countess, surging forward. "Allow me
to be the first to wish you happy. I'm sure I shan't be the last
tonight. Such a fine match! When I saw the announcement
in this morning's paper, I said at once to Alice, 'If only you
do so well, my dear.' Did I not, Alice?"

"Yes, Mama," murmured Lady Alice.

"Sir George, Lady Devere, you must be delighted," the
countess went on. "A positive paragon—wealthy, well born,
without a hint of that distressing unsteadiness so common
in the young men today. All London wondered where Sir

Richard Beckwith would find a wife to match his high principles, I vow. Until Miss Julia appeared, of course. 'Tis like a fairy tale."

The older Deveres, embarrassed by this effusion, muttered incomprehensible replies.

"Such a handsome man, too," continued the countess. "A fair match for Julia there as well, eh?" She turned twinkling blue eyes on Julia.

Julia Devere showed no signs of discomfort. Her answering smile was lovely and unselfconscious. "Thank you for your good wishes, Lady Leamington," she replied. "We mustn't keep you from your other guests any longer." And gathering her parents with a glance, she walked on into the ballroom.

Behind her, the countess shook her head. "That girl deserves her success if anyone ever did; she has the sweetest temper on earth. Take a lesson, Alice."

"Yes, Mama," murmured her daughter again, and they turned to greet the next arrival.

Lady Devere, on the other hand, was deploring the manners of the aristocracy. "I shall never understand it," she complained to her daughter. "Sometimes it seems that the higher their rank, the greater their vulgarity. I shouldn't dream of speaking so to Lady Alice, should she announce her engagement."

"Their ideas are different from ours," agreed Julia absently. Her thoughts were focused on the party ahead. She would be the center of attention this evening, she knew. Any newly engaged girl was the object of congratulations, and envy, and she had the added luster of having won one of the most eligible bachelors of the *haut ton*. She looked forward to the furor with some trepidation, but her main emotion was happiness. She had liked Sir Richard Beckwith from their first meeting, and everything she had learned about him since then had strengthened her regard. She knew herself to be very fortunate—to be creditably settled in life with a man she could wholeheartedly admire.

The Deveres were indeed surrounded by well-wishers as soon as their arrival was noticed. In the flood of congratulations and questions about the wedding, Julia missed the first set, and she was led into the second only after her partner pointedly excused her from a pair of talkative dowagers.

"That was very rude, Mr. Whitney," Julia told him as the waltz began.

"Rude? You accuse me of petty sins when you have broken my heart?" he retorted.

Julia laughed. "You know I have done no such thing."

"I shall never recover," protested her partner. "Where is the infamous Sir Richard tonight, by the by? I should think he'd be much in evidence, flaunting his triumph in our faces."

"He had business to see to. He won't be here."

"The cad. Leaving you alone to face all these congratulations. Don't you wish to reconsider your acceptance of him under these conditions?"

"No, Mr. Whitney. But I am beginning to wish I had not accepted your invitation to dance. Do be serious."

"Ah, you and Richard, always so serious. I do wish one of you would fly up in the boughs just once. A wild adventure, a tempestuous scene. Don't you wish for it sometimes?"

Laughing again, Julia shook her head. Mr. Whitney heaved a dramatic sigh and turned the subject.

The ball continued much in this vein for Julia. During

the supper interval, she was the center of a lively group of young people, and afterward she danced with a variety of partners. If she wished that one of these was Sir Richard, she did not let it show, and when one of her admirers went to fetch lemonade late in the evening, she awaited his return with a serene smile. She didn't even notice the arrival of two latecomers, one a young man whose handsome face was marred by chronic worry and the other the middle-aged roué who had bid against Beckwith an hour before. The two separated at the door, the latter stopping to scan the crowd, then moving with calculated nonchalance to a position just behind Julia, though partly screened from her by a curtained doorway.

"I must tell you the most extraordinary thing, Seldon," he said in a penetrating voice to an acquaintance he had taken in tow as he moved across the ballroom.

Julia's head turned slightly, and she started to move away as she recognized one of the most notorious libertines in London.

"What's that, Lord Fenton?" answered Seldon.

"Beckwith came to the Chaos Club tonight," was the reply. Julia froze.

"I don't believe it! Propriety Dick?"

"I tell you, he was recognized. And not only that, he laid down two thousand guineas to buy himself the loveliest little lightskirt I've seen in fifteen years."

"No!"

"I saw it myself."

"But he's never mounted a mistress. He's always deploring the morals of the *ton*."

Lord Fenton smiled slightly, his eyes on the rigid

shoulders of Julia Devere a little distance away in the ballroom. "Perhaps his decision to become leg-shackled gave him pause," he said very clearly. "That certainly makes a man think of what he's missed."

Julia moved away, returning to her parents, numb with shock. She had not been able to resist listening once she heard her fiancé's name, but what she'd heard was so unbelievable that she couldn't even think just yet. She fled instinctively to the protectors of her youth and sat down beside her mother. Julia's hands were trembling, and her skin felt icy; a void seemed to have opened inside her.

"You are very pale, Julia," said Lady Anne. "Are you feeling ill?"

"Only very tired," she managed to reply.

"All these congratulations are fatiguing. Shall we go home?"

Julia nodded emphatically, and her mother turned to speak to Sir George. As the three of them rose and looked for their hostess to say good-bye, Lord Fenton watched from across the room. His lined face showed both malicious satisfaction and an almost diabolical glee. He gazed about the ballroom as if wondering what he could do next to sustain the entertainment.

On the carriage ride home, Julia was silent. Her parents, chatting desultorily about the evening, noticed nothing amiss. When they reached the house they had hired for the Season, Julia stepped down first and went directly to her room, submitting to the ministrations of her maid mechanically and allowing herself to be put to bed without speaking a word. The maid, who was new to her service, fell silent also after her first few remarks were ignored and simply did her work as quickly as possible.

When she was at last alone, Julia gazed up at the canopy above her bed and allowed an unaccustomed tide of emotion to surge through her. Its strength was such that she had to clench her hands and jaw to keep quiet.

Julia Devere had been reared with loving, but strict propriety by middle-aged parents. Her principles were high, her ideas somewhat rigid, and her life up to this point had offered no upheaval that put these views to the test. With her engagement to Sir Richard Beckwith, it had appeared that this serene state would continue, unruffled.

Now, her certainty had been swept away with a suddenness that left her breathless. Even more unsettling was her reaction. Instead of calmly reviewing the circumstances and judging them by the measures she'd been taught, Julia was swinging wildly from scandalized condemnation, to hot anger, to hopeful disbelief. She'd never felt such turmoil. It was as if her mind had filled with a chorus of alien voices, and she was shocked to find that she could surprise herself this way.

Julia had been carefully educated in many subjects, but not in the lore of feelings. These, to her parents at least, were things to be kept under sedate control. A civilized person did not indulge. A proper young lady did not even acknowledge their existence. For the first time since early childhood, Julia failed to rein in her emotions.

Silently, she struggled with herself. Stories like Lord Fenton's malicious gossip circulated constantly among the *haut ton*, Julia knew. And though as an unmarried girl she was not told any of them directly, only the most unobservant or stupid deb failed to pick up scraps of information, and Julia was neither of these.

It was the connection of Richard with scandalous behavior that set her pulse pounding with a muddle of emotion—humiliation at the idea that Richard should find a mistress on the eve of their engagement and make her the butt of vulgar jokes, anger that he had deceived her about his character, amazement that she could have been so deceived, and overriding all else, an astonishing, fierce possessiveness that urged Julia to rise and fight for the man she intended to marry, and not to let some doxy steal him away.

The latter feeling surprised Julia most. If she had been asked earlier in the evening whether she loved Richard Beckwith, she would have replied, with a mildly reproving glance, that she admired and respected him, that she found in him her ideal of manhood, that she enjoyed his company and conversation. The hot emotion she felt now had no connection to any of those phrases. Julia wondered if she'd fallen prey to some kind of madness. There seemed no other logical explanation for the sudden, radical change in her character. Had some lunacy been growing in the hidden parts of her brain, she wondered, only to burst forth full blown now? But even as this fear surfaced, she dismissed it. She was furious, not insane.

She made a heroic effort to gain control of herself. She did not know that Lord Fenton's vicious story was true, a prim inner voice pointed out. Fenton was certainly not a trustworthy person. He had been pointed out to Julia at her first *ton* party as someone she should not know, and she had never even spoken to him in the course of the Season that was now waning. Was she, she asked herself, ready to take such a man's word about the conduct of Sir Richard Beckwith, whom she knew so well and trusted absolutely?

Of course not! She'd been distressingly unsteady, Julia realized, to allow this incident to overset her. It could not be true. And from what she had heard of Lord Fenton, it was likely to be a cruel jest. Julia flushed in the darkness of her bed, ashamed of herself for falling victim to such a hoax. Nothing had changed, she told herself; she would wake tomorrow to discover that Richard was the same as ever. And they would marry in six weeks as agreed and settle to a life much like her present one.

Thus reassured, Julia was finally able to close her eyes and fall asleep.

THREE

"Come here," said Sir Richard.

Bess Malone moved toward him across the silent kitchen, a smile curving her full lips. As she walked, she unfastened her cloak and let it fall to the brick floor.

Sir Richard made an impatient sound. "No, no. Sit down. There." He indicated one of the chairs that clustered about the wide wooden table.

Bess hesitated, frowning a little.

"And pick up your cloak," he added.

Petulantly, she snatched it up and cast herself into the chair, her expression sulky. Beckwith turned to poke the coals into life and add wood from the box beside the hearth. Then he faced her, hands clasped behind his back. "Now, then," he said, "we must decide what to do with you."

Bess's blue eyes went wide, and her dark brows rose.

"I think a position in some respectable household," he continued. "As a housemaid? Or perhaps you could serve as companion to—"

"Here, what are you saying?" interrupted Bess, now rigid with amazement. "You bought me fair and square. I don't—"

"I did so," explained Sir Richard, "to save you from the clutches of men such as Lord Fenton. You cannot have realized the fate in store for you. I will find you employment in some suitable—"

"No, you blinking won't!" exclaimed Bess, springing to her feet and glaring at him. "I want a house of my own and a carriage, and gowns and jewels and…a box at the opera!"

"What?"

"Are you deaf? Or daft? Why do you think I went to that disgusting place and sold myself to the likes of you? To make my fortune, that's why. I mean to be one of them ladies who drives herself in the park of afternoons and smiles when the gentlemen bow to her."

"You don't understand what sort of woman that is," objected Sir Richard.

Bess looked utterly exasperated. "Do I not? Did you think I was meaning a ring on my finger and standing up before the priest? I sold myself to be your fancy lady, and that's what I want to be. In proper style, mind! A regular high flyer."

"But I am offering to save you from such degradation. I can find you respectable employment, where you will not be forced to—"

"Respectable!" Bess spat the word. "Now, you listen to me, Mr.... You haven't even told me your name."

"Beckwith," he responded automatically. "Sir Richard Beckwith."

Bess continued to glare. "Let me tell you something about 'respectable employment,' Sir Richard *Beckwith*. I came to London six months ago to look for work. There was none at home, and my family was too poor to keep me. I found a place as a housemaid—rising up before dawn and lugging great, heavy water cans and scrubbing floors till my hands bled; falling into bed every night so tired I couldn't sleep, and not such a very comfortable bed at that. And the master of the house considering me his lawful property and catching me behind the parlor door for a bit of a touch. That's your respectable employment."

"But I could—"

"And so I left that post," continued Bess inexorably, "thinking I'd try something outside domestic service. I got a place in
a milliner's shop—a fine one, too. Just off Bond Street." Her
eyes flashed. "Well, it was nothing better than a fancy house,
let me tell you. The owner said since I was pretty, I should
work in the shop, and not sit in the room behind and sew
in the heat. She took care to present me to all the men who
came in, too. And none of them was shy in asking for what he
wanted." She glared. "It wasn't hats, either!"

Sir Richard started to speak, but she cut him off once
again.

"More than that, some of the ladies who spent their
money in that shop weren't the least bit respectable. They
dripped silks and jewels, though. So I made up my mind;
if they wanted to be buying *that*, I'd sell it dear. One of you
fine *gentlemen* was bound to have his way sooner or later, so
I decided to make you pay. I mean to get enough money to
support myself, and then I won't have to have any *employment* at all."

"You cannot understand what this means."

"No?" Bess smiled derisively at him. "I grew up in the
country, Sir Richard Beckwith. And I have nine brothers
and sisters. I understand very well. It's not such a great thing
as you gentry make of it, you know. And it's far easier than
hauling hot water cans."

Sir Richard was profoundly shocked. "You don't
realize—"

"It's *you* that don't understand," Bess insisted. "Look at
this house." She gestured at the walls around them. "You
have no notion what it's like to be starving or half-dead with

cold. You've never felt helpless and friendless and worn out with drudgery." She bared her teeth at him.

"I had a fine plan. I heard about that club, and I found one of the members and made him listen. I wanted a rich gentleman who would treat me fine and give me things. I'm quite ready to treat him fine, too." Bess looked at Sir Richard sidelong, then moved quickly and unexpectedly to twine her arms around his neck, pressing her body against him and stretching on tiptoe to fasten her lips on his.

Sir Richard's arms closed about her reflexively, to keep his balance at this onslaught. And something in him responded automatically to the sensation of a warm and willing girl pressing eagerly closer. His brain protested emphatically, however, and he was just about to push Bess away and scold her when the kitchen door opened and his young brother walked into the room.

For a moment, the scene was frozen, the two men staring wildly at one another. Then Richard thrust Bess from him and Thomas began backing hastily out of the room, blushing and muttering incoherent apologies.

Bess stood, arms akimbo, and glared, first at Sir Richard, then, following the direction of his gaze, at the younger Thomas. "Who's that?" she demanded.

"Just going," stammered Thomas. "Beg your pardon. Didn't realize…"

"Oh, for God's sake," said Sir Richard. "That is my brother, Tom. Tom, this is Bess Malone. You may as well come in."

"No, no," protested Tom hurriedly.

"Come," commanded Sir Richard. "This is not at all what it appears."

Bess stamped her foot on the brick floor.

Curiosity began to contend with the embarrassment on Thomas Beckwith's face, and he came a bit further into the room. As he looked from Bess's infuriated face to his brother's harried, self-conscious one, his bright green eyes began to twinkle, and he regained some of his usual nonchalance.

The brothers did not much resemble each other. Sir Richard had their deceased father's height and breadth of shoulder, along with his dark blond hair and cool gray eyes. Thomas was the image of their mother, with a delicate frame and brown hair. He had also inherited her sense of mischief, which surfaced now. "What's all this then?" he asked.

Bess had turned her back on both of them and gone to gaze angrily at the fire. Sir Richard briefly reviewed the events of the evening. As he spoke, his brother's green eyes grew wider. Before he was halfway through, Thomas was biting his lower lip to keep it from quivering with laughter. The thought of the staid head of his family in the situation he described struck Thomas as irresistibly funny. And when the end of the story came, and Bess's reactions were touched upon, he could stand it no longer. He burst out laughing so hard he had to sit down.

Both Bess and Sir Richard frowned at him.

"I'm sorry," gasped Tom. "I can't help it. The thought of *you*, Richard, in such a place. I can just see you rigid with distaste. And then being told by a chit of a girl that she doesn't care to be respectably employed. If I could only have seen it!"

"I thank you for your support," answered Sir Richard dryly.

"I'm sorry," said Tom again, gradually getting his laughter under control.

"I'm no chit of a girl," declared Bess.

Tom turned interested eyes upon her. "You don't look much over sixteen," he replied.

"I'm eighteen!" But Bess's eyes shifted from his.

"Of course you are," said Tom, his grin reappearing. "What are you going to do with her, Richard?"

Sir Richard Beckwith's temper snapped. "I haven't the faintest notion," he answered.

Tom went off in another gale of laughter, throwing his head back and folding his arms over his chest.

"Who's there?" called a feminine voice from the front hall. "Tom, is that you?"

Tom's hilarity was abruptly cut off, and his head swiveled toward the kitchen door. "It's Mama," he said.

"Of course it is," said his brother with a sigh. "Because everything that can go wrong this evening will, apparently."

"What shall we do?"

"Go and fob her off, since your noise has attracted her attention. I'll keep Bess here."

"Right." But even as Tom rose, the kitchen door swung open once again, and Lady Beckwith stepped through it, her bright green eyes lively with curiosity. She surveyed the tableau within for a moment, cocking her head as if trying to work out a sum. Her gaze finally came to rest on Bess.

"Hello, Mama," said Tom.

"You should go to bed," said Sir Richard at the same instant.

Lady Beckwith looked from one to the other of them. "Go to bed?" she echoed. "Not just yet, I think. Tom, have you been in some mischief?"

Her younger son looked deeply hurt. "I? Why do you assume it is I?"

"Because it always is," answered Lady Beckwith fondly.

"Not this time. This is Richard's scrape. He's bought a girl!"

"I beg your pardon!" Lady Beckwith's astonished gaze shifted to Sir Richard.

"Mama, I really do wish you would go to bed," he said. "I will take care of this."

"You cannot expect me to disappear docilely upstairs after such a remark," retorted his mother. "Is this one of Tom's jokes?"

"No. But he has put it, er, rather baldly."

Lady Beckwith examined both her sons. What she saw seemed to satisfy her, for the frown that had begun to mar her still beautiful face eased. "Is this the girl you have bought?" she asked Sir Richard.

Tom started to laugh again, and his brother glared at him. "I suppose I must tell you the whole," he said.

"I think you must," agreed Lady Beckwith.

"Oh, lord!" exclaimed Bess. She flung herself into a chair again. Tom nearly choked.

Sir Richard repeated the story, up to the point when he and Bess had reached the house.

"I see," said his mother as he paused. "Well, that was laudable of you, Richard, if a bit hasty. I don't quite see—"

"No," interrupted Tom, "and you won't either. Richard, you've left out the best part."

"Will you keep quiet," was the reply.

"What is the best part?" inquired Lady Beckwith, looking at both her sons in turn as if unsure whether to smile.

Tom pointed at Bess. "She don't want respectable work," he said. "She wants to be set up as…er, that is…" He faltered under his mother's cool gaze.

"I see." Lady Beckwith turned to Bess, who met her with defiance. "So, Richard, what do you intend to do?"

"He won't do anything," declared Bess, standing again. "Because I won't be staying around to be done to. I'm leaving."

"To go where?" demanded Sir Richard.

"Back where I came from, I suppose. Thanks to you! Ah, I'm that angry I could hit the lot of you."

"You mustn't go back," said Sir Richard. His mother glanced at him with sudden concern. "We will find some place for you. Some acceptable place."

Bess eyed him with suspicion.

"But where, Richard?" protested Lady Beckwith. "You cannot expect me to keep her here. I am as charitable as anyone, I hope, but it simply would not do."

"Of course not. At least, she must stay for one night. And then…"

Tom and Lady Beckwith gazed at him.

"I'll think of something!" he finished.

"You can't make me stay," said Bess.

"Can I not? What about my two thousand guineas?"

"Two thousand!" gasped Lady Beckwith.

"I'll return it," said Bess. "Throw it right back in your face, I will!"

"Yes? Including the half that was to go to the club?"

Bess ground her teeth. "You've ruined everything!"

"I will show you a place where you can sleep," added Sir Richard. "And tomorrow we will decide what is to be done."

"I'll run away," declared Bess.

"You will have no opportunity," was his reply. "Come along."

"*I'll* show her a room," put in Lady Beckwith.

"There's no need for that, Mama. This is my problem."

"Is it?" Lady Beckwith eyed him narrowly, but he returned her gaze without wavering. "Nonetheless, I should like to take her."

Sir Richard shrugged. "Very well."

Bess, who had watched this byplay with great interest, now glanced from Sir Richard to his mother with renewed speculation. Her rebellion seemed muted for the moment. She picked up her cloak and moved forward. "Good night, then," she said, brushing close to Sir Richard as she passed him.

Lady Beckwith's frown returned, but she said nothing, merely indicated that Bess should follow her.

"But, Richard," said Tom as the door closed behind them, "what *are* you going to do?"

"That is what I must now consider," his brother replied. "As yet, I have no idea."

FOUR

SIR RICHARD BECKWITH AND MISS JULIA DEVERE HAD arranged to go together to Vauxhall the following evening, accompanied by her parents and his family. It was to be an opportunity for all of them to become better acquainted, now that the engagement was a settled thing.

Julia looked forward to the outing with mixed feelings. She was eager to see Sir Richard and reassure herself about his character. She would know, she told herself, when she met him face to face whether the story was true. But she was also apprehensive. What would she do, she wondered, if it were?

Her parents were unaware of her dilemma; they never listened to gossip, and even if they had, there were many who found it more amusing to withhold such a tale from the principals, watching and snickering behind their hands as they carried on, oblivious to their notoriety.

As for Sir Richard, he thought of putting off the meeting. The problem of Bess hung heavy on his hands, and he felt beset from all sides. His brother laughed at him, his mother gently reminded him that she could not keep a girl who had sold herself before numerous gentlemen of the *ton* in the Beckwith household, and the inevitability of exposure nagged as well. The longer Bess stayed, the more certain it was that someone would discover what he had done and spread the news. Sir Richard had no idea that his escapade was already one of the juiciest *on-dits* in London. Yet a strong desire to see Julia outweighed all these concerns. When Sir Richard thought of her, he felt a sudden lifting of his anxieties. Visions of her serene smile cheered him, and in the end he decided to defer his decision for a few hours and keep the appointment.

Thus, of the group that gathered that night, only Sir George and Lady Devere were just as usual. The others met with varying degrees of self-consciousness and covert observation.

Lady Beckwith, with her greater experience, handled it best. She devoted herself to the elder Deveres and left her sons to entertain Julia.

Thomas, who retained something of the boy about him at twenty-two, lost his teasing humor in Julia's presence. It had not occurred to him before that the presence of Bess in their house might affect Julia; it did now, and he found it hard to meet her eyes.

The engaged couple were thus left generally to themselves. They greeted each other with suppressed emotion. Julia, seeing Sir Richard, was at once convinced that Lord Fenton's story was a cruel lie. She could not be so mistaken in his character. The happiness that welled up in her at this conclusion was difficult to contain; it kept breaking out in smiles and laughter and made her light-green eyes sparkle.

Sir Richard, too, felt happy. Everything about Julia pleased him, and tonight her well-ordered beauty and perfect manners seemed particularly captivating in contrast to the upheaval that had intruded into his life.

They came to Vauxhall by water, admiring the spectacle of colored lanterns among the trees from the boat and disembarking at the landing to join the groups strolling along the broad avenues. Sir Richard had taken a box for the evening, and when the older members of the party were settled there, he suggested a walk, and Julia quickly agreed. She took his arm, and they started off together under the benevolent gaze of her parents and the more uncertain scrutiny of the Beckwiths.

"A fine night," said Sir Richard.

"Yes. It is wonderfully warm."

"The moon is rising. There." He indicated a soft glow on the eastern horizon.

"A full moon tonight, I think."

Sir Richard agreed, and they strolled on in silence.

It was not, however, the silence of unease or lack of words. It was a delightful, comfortable silence that the two of them had discovered almost as soon as they met. Richard and Julia, together, somehow called up a private world that enclosed and nurtured them. When they were alone, this atmosphere rose about them and made each feel content and happy. The annoyances of daily life dropped away; they simply did not think of them. And when they did speak, they were in perfect agreement.

They walked on, each conscious of the other as their shoulders brushed or the pressure of Julia's hand on Richard's arm shifted minutely. He looked down at her, thinking how lovely she was in green. And as if he had spoken, Julia raised her eyes. Their footsteps slowed in unison for a moment, then continued as before. Neither was aware of the stares that followed them along the path, or the whispers and raised eyebrows they elicited.

"Here," said Sir Richard, steering Julia into a side path that wove between high flowering hedges.

"Oh, the scent!" she exclaimed. "Verbena. Isn't it exquisite?"

He nodded, and led her on. At the end of the path, they came to a tiny pillared temple with a domed roof, gleaming white among the lanterns. They stepped up and stood within it, the hum of the Vauxhall crowds seeming far behind them now.

"Look," said Richard, and Julia followed his gesture.

The moon had lifted above the horizon and hung huge and golden before them, seemingly close enough to touch. Its light was strong enough to throw shadows, and it felt almost liquid as it poured down over the fragrant bushes around them.

"Oh," breathed Julia. "I feel as if I had strayed into fairyland."

"Yes," murmured Richard. He moved slightly, and Julia turned to gaze up at him. Naturally, as if they had done it a hundred times, his arms slid around her waist and hers along his arms to his shoulders. Richard bent his head and kissed her softly.

The result startled them both. The kiss swept them up as it grew harder and more passionate. Richard, stirred to his depths, tightened his arms and pulled her close against his body. Julia, taken unaware by a flood of new feelings, yielded gladly, and laced her arms about his neck.

Time, sound, thought stopped as they clung. Their private world was suddenly extended in a direction neither had foreseen. Richard showered kisses on her cheeks and brows, and down her neck to her bare shoulders. Julia's fingers tightened in his blond hair.

The laugh of a woman in a nearby path separated them abruptly, and the tide of desire washed back upon itself. They stood apart, breathing quickly and gazing at one

another. Though as an engaged couple they had more lati-
tude than before, this had gone beyond the limits of propriety, and neither Richard nor Julia was accustomed to such
adventures. Too, their senses were still swimming, and their
surroundings retained an air of unreality.

"I...should beg your pardon," murmured Richard at last.
Julia shook her head.

He scanned her heart-shaped face, fully illuminated by
the moonlight, and was abruptly filled to bursting with happiness. He couldn't keep from smiling. "Well, that's good,
then," he added.

Julia bit her lower lip, then returned his smile. In the
next instant, they were both laughing, a little embarrassed,
but mainly giddy with joy.

Sir Richard offered his arm again, and Julia took it, though
this simple act was now wholly different than it had been earlier. They walked together back toward the boxes, from time
to time meeting each other's eyes and smiling again.

"Had a pleasant stroll?" asked Sir George Devere when
they arrived. Julia sternly repressed a giggle. "We ordered
supper. Will you have some ham, my dear?"

"Thank you, Papa," she replied, and sank into the chair
Sir Richard held for her.

Lady Beckwith surveyed them with anxious eyes. Unlike
the rest of her party, *she* was well aware of the unusual attention their group was receiving. The story of Richard's visit
to the Chaos Club was known, she was certain. And though
a small part of her was amused at this aberration in a son
she had sometimes found ever so slightly stuffy, a far greater
part was distressed and concerned. The Deveres were not
the sort to understand or overlook such a thing. Indeed,

though she liked Julia very well, and could see that her son was happy in his choice, she thought the girl would break it off at once should she hear of Bess Malone. And she would hear; some *well-wisher* would see to that. What could she do to save the situation? she wondered.

"Lady Beckwith and I have been discussing the wedding," said Julia's mother. "She thinks our idea of holding it in the country a good one."

"London weddings have become so common," agreed Lady Beckwith. She had grasped this plan at once, for it would remove the Deveres from town, and the gossips, most quickly.

"I should like to be married at home," said Julia.

"Let us consider it settled, then. Six weeks from now, in the country. We must start to work at once, Julia. We have a great deal to do." Lady Devere did not sound displeased at the prospect.

Julia met Sir Richard's eyes, and they exchanged a tender smile. Lady Beckwith, seeing it, groaned.

FIVE

THE FOLLOWING MORNING, IT WAS ONLY TOO OBVIOUS
that a solution to the problem of Bess must be found. She
flatly refused to spend another night in the attic bedroom next
to the housemaids where she had been placed. Moreover, the
upper servants clearly didn't believe that Bess was a cousin
of Sir Richard's gamekeeper, which was the story they had
been told. Lady Beckwith, knowing that the gossip of the
ton would spread rapidly to its servitors, insisted that the girl
must go before scandal broke over all their heads.

Sir Richard agreed. But he remained at a loss about
where to send Bess and how to settle her future. He'd taken
on this responsibility, and though the girl's refusal to enter
respectable employment had temporarily stopped him, he
did not think of abdicating it. Both his high principles and
his stubbornness prevented that. Still, he had wracked his
brain without result. He could think of no plan that would
satisfy both Bess Malone and the proprieties.

Finally, at breakfast that morning, when his mother
asked him yet again what he meant to do, he replied, "I shall
get her rooms, I suppose."

Lady Beckwith choked on her tea.

"Only until I can make some more permanent arrangement, of course, Mama."

"Why not simply give the girl some money and send
her on her way?" was the reply. "You have tried your best to
help her, and she refuses." Lady Beckwith was not an unfeeling woman, but the sight of her eldest son teetering on the
brink of ruin hardened her heart. If Richard threw away his

chance of happiness over this girl, she would never forgive him, she thought.

The object of her concern looked slightly shocked. "I cannot do that. I must see her creditably settled."

"Even if she doesn't wish to be?" answered his mother, goaded.

"She is in no position to judge." Sir Richard's tone was mildly reproving, and Lady Beckwith gave up. She had often in the past been grateful for her son's sense of duty; now, she wished that he did not so resemble his deceased father. If only he were more like Tom, she thought, or myself, we could laugh and forget this.

When Bess was informed that she would be given lodgings in town, she clapped her hands and gave a little skip of joy. "I shall need some fine new clothes as well," she declared.

Sir Richard frowned. "There is no question of that. You must understand—"

"I can't stay in London with only this one shabby dress," interrupted Bess. "It's a disgrace."

"That scarcely matters, since you will not be going out. You will not—"

"You mean to make me a prisoner?" Bess's blue eyes flashed, and she tossed her head. "I'll run away. I won't be locked up in some dingy room. No more than I'll be a housemaid. It's ruining my life you are."

"I am attempting to save you from ruin," retorted Sir Richard angrily.

"What do you know about it?"

They faced one another, both incensed, Sir Richard's gray eyes adamant against Bess's flaming blue ones.

"If I can't have new clothes and go about a little, I'll find some other gentleman to give them to me."

"This is blackmail!"

Bess shrugged.

Sir Richard turned his back and stared out the window. This had become more than a moral question; he refused to be bested by a chit of a girl. But he could see no way of forcing her to his will without the possibility of a greater scandal than the one he sought to avoid by removing her from his house. "Very well," he said through clenched teeth. "A gown or two."

Bess's frown gave way to a sunny smile, and she took a few steps toward him. "You can help me choose," she offered.

"No. I have in mind a companion for you who can do that."

The girl's dark brows came together again. "Companion?"

"A most respec—amiable woman who can show you the sights of London."

"I won't have her."

"Then you'll have no new clothes."

It was another standoff, but this time, after a long glare, Bess gave way. "If I don't like her, I'll run away," she added.

"But not, I assume, before your new gowns arrive."

She glared at him again.

"Be ready at two. I will escort you to your new lodgings at that time."

With a grimace, Bess flounced from the room.

She was ready at the appointed time, however, carrying a small case packed with nightclothes and other small things she had been given by the Beckwiths. But when Sir Richard would have taken her through the back premises to the stables, she balked. "I'll walk out the front door like a lady," she insisted. "I'm not one of your servants."

"You will do as you are told," replied Sir Richard, very conscious of listeners in the rear hall.

Bess darted to the front door, flung it open, and ran out. After an instant of enraged disbelief, Sir Richard followed her to the pavement. It took all his self-control not to shake her. Before he could speak, she had signaled a hack from the cross street, and the driver had turned toward them and started to pull up. Sir Richard grasped Bess's upper arm. "What do you think you're doing?"

"We can go in the hack." She struggled, and he pulled her against his chest, forcing her to meet his eyes. "I am in charge here. You'd be wise not to forget that."

Their eyes locked at a distance of only four inches, and Sir Richard held her immobile to reinforce his command. Neither looked around when the sound of hooves and carriage wheels again approached along the cross street.

And thus, neither saw Julia Devere go past in her parents' vehicle. She had directed the coachman to take this route, past the Beckwith house, with a thrill of shame-faced joy. After last night, she wanted a glimpse of his home to reinforce her pleasant dreams. She would not stop, of course. Julia knew this was silly, but she couldn't resist.

What she saw, however, was the man who had kissed her so passionately last night clutching another beautiful, black-haired girl to him, his face shining with more emotion than Julia had ever seen in it.

Julia shrank back in her seat and crouched low until the

carriage was well past his street. She struggled for breath, fighting a pain that filled her chest and constricted her throat. The after-image of the two of them would not be banished; it blazed in her mind, hurting her over and over. Her world seemed to be falling in ruins. And the worst of it, illogically, to Julia was that her rival was dark-haired, like her.

The same emotions she'd felt when she first heard Lord Fenton's accusations boiled up again, with far greater intensity. To them was added a bitter sense of betrayal. Julia was stunned when she thought of Vauxhall. That he could hold her so when he had this...paramour! She could not believe it. Yet this time, she had seen it with her own eyes. The fact could not be denied. She should break off the engagement at once.

With this thought came such overwhelming desolation that Julia pushed it from her mind. It was too soon to act, she told herself. She needed to recover. Reaching home, she flung herself down from the coach and up the front steps, startling the servants with her unaccustomed violence. In her room, she sat in an armchair, hands clenched, staring straight ahead, and gave in to the mad whirl of her mind.

"Get in," said Sir Richard curtly to Bess, pushing her toward the hack.

She snatched her arm from his loosened grip and complied.

Sir Richard gave the grinning driver the address and followed, his lips still tight with annoyance.

They made the short journey in silence. When the cab

pulled up again, he jumped out and paid the fare, leaving Bess to get out on her own. The hack left them standing outside a tiny narrow house, squeezed between two larger ones and obviously too small to be a desirable property. It was outside the fashionable area of London, but not so far as to be beyond the pale. Bess looked the structure up and down. "Not a prime house," she decided.

"I suppose you think you should have a mansion in Grosvenor Square?"

The girl grinned, her ill humor forgotten. "This'll do for now."

"Really? I'm so pleased."

Bess actually laughed, a pleasant sound, and Sir Richard's anger eased a bit. She was really little more than a child, he thought, and if her ideas were wrongheaded, her education was at fault. "Shall we go in?" he asked.

Bess trotted happily ahead of him, pausing beside the front door with an eager expression. This shifted to puzzlement when he rang the bell. "Your companion moved in this morning," he said in response.

Her scowl returned.

The lock scraped, and the door swung open to reveal a gray-haired woman of about fifty with a broad, ruddy face and sturdy frame. Lines in her face suggested that a smile was her natural expression, but the look she turned on Bess was wary. The girl eyed her with equal disfavor.

Sir Richard smiled. "Mrs. Hanlon, this is Bess Malone. Bess, a countrywoman of yours. I thought that would please you." He, at least, was pleased. He had devoted hours of thought to the choice of a woman to oversee Bess until he could find some permanent place for her. He had thought first of his old nurse, but she was rather frail these days, and certain to be shocked to her Midlands core by Bess's opinions and behavior. Sir Richard had then run through a mental list of pensioned servants and tenants on his estates in Hertfordshire, but none seemed suitable until he remembered Dora Hanlon. The widow of his former head gardener, Dora had come up to town to live with her sister upon her husband's death. She was fully capable of dealing with any tricks Bess might play, and unlikely to be shocked by her unorthodox views. She would also, Sir Richard knew, be glad of the wage he offered, and he was pleased to have the opportunity to give it to her in a way she would accept. The bargain had been struck at once when he called at her sister's cottage, and she had moved her things immediately.

"Good day," said Mrs. Hanlon in a lilt to match Bess's own. Bess eyed her silently.

"Come in, then." Mrs. Hanlon stood back, and they entered the tiny hall. "Will you take something, Sir Richard?"

"No. I shan't stay. I came only to bring Bess."

For the first time in Sir Richard's experience, Bess looked uncertain. "What will I do here?" she asked.

"We'll find plenty to do, my girl," answered Mrs. Hanlon. "The place is all over dirt. And there's meals to be cooked and pots to be scrubbed."

Bess's brief hesitation vanished in outrage. Hands on hips, she glared at Sir Richard. "I told you I would be no housemaid!"

"No, indeed. You will be working for yourself. Quite different."

"I won't!"

"Ah? And what of your new gowns?"

Bess clenched her fists and looked thwarted. Then, she seemed to think of something, and her blue eyes shifted craftily. "All right, then," she said.

Sir Richard was not deceived, but he had every confidence in Mrs. Hanlon. "I shall say good-bye for now. I'll call again when I have some suggestions for your future."

Bess shrugged. Sir Richard met Mrs. Hanlon's eyes meaningfully, and the older woman nodded. Reassured, he took his leave.

His relief was premature, however. Before dinner that evening, a footman came to knock on his bedroom door and report that a messenger from Mrs. Hanlon waited below. Sir Richard, in the midst of changing to go out, frowned. "What the deuce? Have him come up, John. I must dress or I shall be late."

"Yes, sir."

Sir Richard dismissed his valet and continued to tie his neckcloth. After a short interval, there was another knock, and the footman ushered in a good-looking young man with red hair and bright hazel eyes that took in every detail of his surroundings. "Who are you?" asked Sir Richard.

"Michael Shea, sir. Dora Hanlon's nephew. She sent me to you as she didn't care to leave the house, thinking the girl may come back."

Sir Richard's hands stopped moving. "Come back?"

"Aye. She's taken herself off."

"I placed Mrs. Hanlon in the house to prevent just such a thing."

"Aunt Dora's not a young woman, Sir Richard. You can't expect her to be climbing out of windows after some wild hellion and breaking her neck on the shed roof."

"Bess climbed out an upstairs window?"

"Aye. Quite a girl, she must be." There was admiration as well as censure in the Irishman's voice. "Mayhap you should let her be, Sir Richard."

Beckwith turned and examined Michael Shea closely. He looked to be about five and twenty, a few years younger than Sir Richard himself. His clothes were of a fashionable cut but not of the highest quality; he compensated with an air of jaunty confidence and ruddy good looks. His hazel eyes seemed ready to twinkle at the least excuse. "I am trying to help the girl, no more," answered Beckwith coolly.

"Well, I haven't heard the full story." Seeing that his lightly mocking tone was irritating Sir Richard, Michael Shea added, "And it's none of my affair, of course. I just carried Aunt Dora's message. I'll be going."

"How did you come?"

"In my tilbury." There was irrepressible pride in Shea's voice, and Sir Richard was indeed surprised to hear that he kept a carriage, however modest.

"I'll return with you, then. That will be quickest, and I can go on in a hack." Seeing Shea's expression, he continued, "Have you some other errand?"

Sir Richard was irritated about Bess, and some of this came out in his tone, which was clearly that of a baronet and landholder to the nephew of a servant. It was unlike him to speak so, but the circumstances were unusual.

Michael Shea stiffened, and his hazel eyes snapped with something other than mischief for a moment. But then he caught himself, shrugged, and grinned. "None that won't wait a bit."

Sir Richard felt a twinge of conscience. "Thank you." He

put on his coat, and they walked downstairs together, where Sir Richard gathered his hat and stick. In a moment, they were seated in Michael Shea's somewhat showy tilbury and moving briskly along the street. "A good-looking animal," said Sir Richard of the horse that drew them, trying to atone for his sharpness.

"Isn't she? As an Irishman, I do pride myself on my cattle."

Silence fell between them, two strangers of very different background and habits. Sir Richard complimented Shea once on a delicate bit of driving, but otherwise they said nothing until they arrived at the house where Mrs. Hanlon waited.

She was out the door at the first sound of their carriage wheels. "Sir Richard," she said, "I'm that sorry. I went to make tea, and the girl walked upstairs. If I'd had any notion she'd be climbing out the window, I'd have stayed closer by."

"You could not, of course," said Sir Richard, "though I warned you she was troublesome. Let us go in now and think what to do."

Michael Shea tied his horse and followed them, to Sir Richard's surprise. When the three of them stood in the front room, however, he was at a loss. He could not start a serious search for Bess. That would be both too public and futile, he felt. She could be anywhere in London. He didn't want to simply let her go in a dangerous city. Yet he was also conscious of relief at the idea that she was beyond his reach.

The other two were looking at him expectantly. Sir Richard cleared his throat and tried to settle his mind—then the bell at the front door pealed loudly, followed by a series of thumps that sounded like kicks on the panels.

They hurried to open it. As soon as Mrs. Hanlon shot the bolt, she was pushed back by Bess, who marched in, blue eyes blazing and black hair awry, her small hands clenched at her sides. "He spent my money!" she exclaimed. "He gambled it all away, the blackguard; it's gone! A thousand pounds, gone!" Her lower lip trembled, and it hung in the balance whether she would burst into tears.

Sir Richard's reproaches died in his throat. "The money from the club?" he asked.

Bess nodded, fighting tears with all her energy.

"Who lost it? Young Wearingham?"

"How did you know?" Surprise temporarily overcame Bess's outrage.

"I recognized him that night. It wasn't difficult. You and he arranged the thing between you, didn't you?"

Bess nodded again.

"You shouldn't have trusted him. He is well known to be far, far into dun territory."

"Lord Charles Wearingham, that'd be?" asked Michael Shea, who had been gazing admiringly at Bess. "Badly dipped." He shook his head. "I heard he dropped five hundred guineas at hazard."

"Mine!" cried Bess. "How dare he?"

"He's a gamester. In the blood. Can't help it." Realizing that the other three were staring at him, Shea subsided.

"But it was my money," declared Bess. "We had an agreement. He...he *stole* it."

"Did you think you could trust the men you met at the Chaos Club?" asked Sir Richard.

Michael Shea stared from Bess to Sir Richard.

"I met *you* there," she retorted.

Shea's hazel eyes widened further.

Sir Richard clenched his jaw, then took a breath. "I am still ready to help you. We will find you some—"

"Respectable employment!" Bess spat the words. "I'm sick of the sound of it. I don't *want* to be begging from the likes of you for a shilling or a new gown. I want to go my way and do as I please without starving or cowering in fear of my life." Bess's Irish lilt increased with emotion, and she looked magnificent in her rage. Michael Shea was obviously much struck.

So was Sir Richard, in a different way. His gray eyes, usually so cool, filled with compassion. "I understand you."

This seemed merely to enflame Bess further. "You? How could you understand? You've never had to beg for anything in your life." She whirled and threw herself at the stairs, racing up them so fast it was astonishing she didn't trip over her skirts. A choked sob was heard just before she vanished.

There was silence in her wake for a long moment. Finally, Sir Richard said, "I must go. But I will return tomorrow evening, and we will try to form some plan." Dora Hanlon and her nephew looked dubious, but Sir Richard took no notice as he bid them good night.

When the door had shut behind him, Michael Shea turned to his aunt. "What a spitfire," he said of Bess. "Tell me all about her, Aunt."

"She's nothing to do with you," was the reply.

"I know that. But we both love a good tale, don't we now?" He grinned, and Mrs. Hanlon's face softened.

"You're an incorrigible rogue, Michael. I never could resist you, but where will you end? That's what I ask myself, and so does your mother."

"I have my plans for that, no fear. Now, tell me about this Bess."

"Come into the kitchen, then, where we can shut the door. If she heard, she'd be down on our heads like a summer storm."

"She would that," replied Michael admiringly, following his aunt out of the hall.

SIX

SIR RICHARD WENT ON HIS WAY WITH RELIEF. HE found Bess singularly exhausting, and though he pitied her now and fully intended to help her if he could, he had been conscious of a renewed oppression when she appeared in the cottage doorway. Perhaps, he admitted to himself, he had made a mistake. He would of course see the matter through, but he rather wished he had never heard of the Chaos Club, nor overheard two of its members anticipating the scandalous auction. His outrage had driven him to the rescue; now, he couldn't quite see what to do.

Had he never heard of Bess, he thought, he might be devoting all his attention to Julia Devere and their plans for the future. The thought of Julia brought a reminiscent curve to his lips. She was everything he wanted in a woman. Where Bess was irritating to the point of madness, Julia was in harmony with all his wishes; where Bess was constantly rebellious, Julia was compliant without being spiritless; where Bess was a drain on one's energy, Julia seemed to renew it. And though both were undoubtedly beautiful, Julia's serene loveliness was far more to his taste than Bess's tempestuous beauty.

As his hackney pulled up before the Deveres' hired house, Sir Richard smiled in anticipation. How pleasant it would be, he thought, to spend the evening with Julia after coping with Bess's tantrums and complaints. Julia would not reproach him, even though he was nearly an hour late. He could not conceive of a reproach falling from her lovely lips. Memories of their last encounter rose in his mind, and his smile broadened.

Thus, Sir Richard was taken aback to receive a markedly cool greeting from his betrothed as he apologized for his tardiness. "A business matter kept me," he told Sir George and Lady Devere.

"What a great deal of business you have lately," said Julia in frigid accents. "Has there been some disaster on your estates?" Her parents glanced at her, startled at her uncharacteristic tone.

Sir Richard met her pale green eyes and blinked. They were icy, wholly lacking that soft glow he so loved. Moreover, he had not concocted a story to explain his lateness. He had not thought it necessary. "A, er, problem with a tenant," he replied.

"Really? What sort of problem?" Julia's gaze did not waver.

"Nothing that would interest you. A trivial matter."

"But I *am* interested in your tenants. I must be. And it can hardly have been trivial if it kept you from your dinner for a full hour."

Sir Richard was speechless, more because of the unexpectedness of the attack than its severity. He did not recognize this Julia, and that made him deeply uneasy.

For her part, Julia had been seething with rage for what seemed like forever. That he should keep her waiting, on top of everything else, was too much. And now she was sure he was lying, and that he had been with *her*. Julia was no longer, by this time, the gentle girl who had accepted Sir Richard's offer.

She had had a terrible twenty-four hours, swinging from rage to despair after her glimpse of her fiancé and his mistress. The turmoil she had experienced a few days earlier was nothing to this, for this was based on fact rather than rumor. Indeed, Julia was stunned to find herself at the mercy of a new personality, sprung full grown from some unknown corner of herself. She wanted Sir Richard, she found, and she wanted to destroy her hated rival. She also wanted revenge for the public and private humiliation they had brought her. The fierceness of these desires shook Julia deeply. And yet, there was a kind of exaltation to them, too. She had never felt anything so strongly.

"Let us go in to dinner," said Lady Devere. "They cannot hold it much longer." She took Sir Richard's arm, and he stared down at her placid countenance, wondering if she could be unaware of the tension in the room.

Julia, who had marveled over this same obtuseness in both her parents over the last few days, could have told him that the older Deveres had apparently become so accustomed to docile serenity in their daughter that they were incapable of seeing anything else. But she was not in a mood to give him any information.

Conversation during dinner was commonplace. Lady Devere chattered about wedding plans, and Sir George expressed his eagerness to return to the country. Sir Richard and Julia contributed little, and ate less, but their silence went unmarked.

For this family party, the two men did not linger in the dining room, but went at once to join the ladies upstairs. There, Julia's parents withdrew to the far corner and talked quietly together, for one purpose of the evening was to give the engaged couple an opportunity to be together. Not completely alone—the Deveres were too strict for that—but somewhat private at least. And as Sir George had jovially told his wife earlier, if Sir Richard should take Julia's hand or sit rather near her, he wouldn't be likely to object.

Both Richard and Julia had looked forward to such a chance. But tonight, all was changed. Julia sat stiffly in the very corner of the blue satin sofa, her eyes straight ahead, and Sir Richard watched her profile uneasily from the other corner.

"Is something wrong?" he asked. As soon as the words left his lips, he felt they were a mistake.

"Wrong?" replied Julia. "What could be wrong?" She meant this as a pointed hint, but as Sir Richard had no idea of her grievance, he merely frowned at her tone.

"Perhaps you are tired. Or have the headache?" he ventured.

"On the contrary. I feel perfectly well."

Silence fell. Sir Richard searched his memory for some offense he might have committed, for Julia certainly seemed offended. He could think of none. The possibility that she might have heard of Bess, far less seen her, did not enter his mind. Indeed, Sir Richard retained the illusion that his rescue of Bess was secret. An enemy to gossip himself, he had never experienced its power. And he hadn't counted on Lord Fenton's malice, which spread the story even more rapidly than was usual.

"I apologize again for being late," he said, grasping the only fault he could recall. "It really was unavoidable."

"No doubt." All Julia's self-control was required to keep her voice from shaking. Unavoidable because you preferred to be with *her*, she was thinking.

Sir Richard abandoned this topic and searched for one that should please her. "The plans for the wedding sound delightful," he went on. "I look forward to seeing the charming church your mother described. And a breakfast on the lawn should be pleasant."

"If it doesn't rain," responded Julia. She had no experience with sparring. She only knew that she wanted to disagree with everything he said.

"Naturally."

"*You* are glad it is to be in the country, I suppose."

"I think it will be splendid." He tried to inject enthusiasm into his tone, though he felt like saying he didn't care a rap where it was so long as she was happy.

"It will remove us from town." Leaving him free to disport himself with his paramour, she thought.

He frowned at her curtness. "The Season is nearly over," he replied.

"So convenient."

By now thoroughly puzzled, and beginning to be annoyed, Sir Richard leveled searching gray eyes at her. "In what way?"

Julia longed to tell him. But the whole weight of her training and the rules of polite society combined to prevent her. It was simply not possible to accuse one's promised husband of flaunting his mistress about London. The words froze on her tongue. Men did such things. So people said. Many men, right up to the very top of the social ladder with the Prince Regent. She hadn't thought it of Sir Richard. Julia's throat felt tight, and she had to swallow. It didn't matter. A lady was supposed to turn a blind eye to such habits. Her fiancé might even tell her so, should she dare to bring it up. At the idea, Julia's cheeks flamed with rage and frustration.

Sir Richard was transfixed by the glow this gave her pale skin. In a gown of soft rose silk, Julia looked particularly lovely tonight. He remembered holding her in his arms and longed intensely to do so again.

"It's sure to rain," said Julia savagely. Surely the elements would match her mood.

He blinked. "Then we will move the wedding inside, I daresay."

"No, it will be spoiled." It already was. How could he not know that?

"Surely there is ample space for—"

"It will be spoiled, I tell you. The whole thing will be utterly ruined." All Julia's pent-up emotion flooded into this irrational point.

"Julia, what *is* the matter?"

His use of her name thrilled her; it was still so new. But this involuntary response merely increased her hurt and anger. "I am concerned about our wedding," she snapped.

"But you are being totally illogical. There is no reason to think that…"

"I see." Julia rose, trembling and on the brink of tears. "I will spare you any further illogic, then," she added, and ran from the room before she broke down completely.

Her parents looked up, startled. Sir Richard stood and stared after her in bewilderment. It was as if, he thought wildly, Bess Malone carried some taint of irrationality which he had contracted and passed along to Julia. His whole world seemed to be going mad.

"What happened?" asked Lady Devere, hurrying over. "Is Julia ill?"

"She said not," he replied, "but she is certainly not herself."

"I'll go to her." She followed her daughter, and Sir George joined his future son-in-law.

"Females," he said. "Unpredictable creatures. Shall we go down to the library and have a brandy?"

Sir Richard demurred. He was too shaken to exchange polite nothings with Devere. He didn't even wish to see Julia, should she return. He'd had enough of feminine tantrums for one evening. He took his leave, with all the proper messages to Julia, and found a hack to carry him home. He had the brandy in his own library, shaking his head over the disorder his orderly life had fallen into.

He had only twenty minutes of quiet before his brother Thomas returned from a *ton* party and looked into the library on his way upstairs. "How wise you were to refuse Bridlington's invitation," he said. "The concert was a dead bore, and no one there but dowdies. Did you have a pleasant dinner with the Deveres?"

"Not really, no."

Tom came fully into the room. The concern that was never absent from his green eyes when they rested on his elder brother these days deepened. "Why?"

"Julia seemed out of sorts. She was quite unlike herself." Sir Richard did not usually speak to Thomas so frankly, but he was still puzzled and uneasy.

Thomas hesitated. He had great respect for Richard, who had been the head of the family since their father died eight years before. In many ways, he had been father as well as brother to Thomas. Yet in the present situation, Thomas thought he was misguided. The problem was how to tell Richard so. He decided on the direct approach. "Perhaps she has heard the rumors."

Sir Richard turned to gaze at him. "Rumors?"

His brother heaved a great sigh. "I declare, Richard, sometimes your deuced high-mindedness makes you blind as a bat. Of course, all London is talking of your visit to the Chaos Club and what occurred there. Other people aren't like you, you know. They love to exchange gossip; they ferret it out, and the more scandalous, the better."

"I was recognized?" said Sir Richard harshly.

Thomas shook his head at this question. "Naturally."

"But I was masked, cloaked."

"Only a man as honest as you could think that sufficient. Disguises are transparent in a place like that. The members all know one another; a stranger stands out a mile. And when it's someone they have met constantly—Richard, they knew you almost at once. Did you recognize no masked acquaintances?"

Of course he had. How could he have been so foolish as to imagine he was unknown? Where had his wits gone, these last few days?

"Not only that, you made an enemy of Fenton. You know what he is."

"A man who makes a mockery of the term *nobility*," Richard replied.

"Precisely. He's spreading the story with glee." Thomas considered, then added, "And a healthy dose of vitriol. Making it sound as bad as possible."

Richard digested this, his spirits sinking. "But surely no one would mention this to Julia," he protested finally, "an unmarried girl."

"*You* would not. I wouldn't. But there are people who'd *inadvertently* let it slip in her hearing. Her reaction would be so interesting, you see. And then there are others who would claim it was their *duty* to let her know."

"Damnable!" exclaimed Sir Richard.

"Perhaps. But very likely."

Richard began to pace the floor. "This would explain her behavior tonight," he muttered.

"She seemed offended?"

"Quite. But how could she believe malicious gossip? She knows me better than that."

"She's known you for two months, Richard. And who can say where she heard the story? Might have been someone she's been taught to respect."

Richard frowned.

Thomas decided to complete what he'd begun. "I think you should settle what to do with Bess as soon as may be, and remove her from London if possible. The talk will die down. And perhaps then you can explain to Julia."

"I shall not speak of the Chaos Club to Julia! I would not sully her ears with such a topic."

"How is she to discover the truth, then?"

Sir Richard shrugged and turned away. He would not admit to his younger brother that he was hurt and disappointed in Julia. That she would believe scurrilous tales about him, whatever their source, wounded him deeply. He had thought that after years of searching, he had found the woman he could both love and respect—the woman to share his life. He'd had no doubts of her; she was apparently not similarly constant, and this called everything into question. She put the false assertions of others above his own demonstrated integrity.

"Perhaps Mama could drop a word in her ear," ventured

Thomas cautiously, wary of the set expression on his brother's face.

"No. This is my affair. I will settle it."

"But, you know, Richard—"

"There is no more to be said, Tom."

His gray eyes had gone cold, a sign Thomas knew of old. It meant that it was no good talking any more. Richard would not listen. He bowed to the inevitable and said good night. Sir Richard did not follow him upstairs for a long time.

SEVEN

"But what's the harm in it, Aunt Dora?" said Michael Shea in a wheedling voice. "She can't stay shut up in the house all the day long. I've often heard you say yourself that a person must have fresh air. A turn about the park, then, and right back here she comes."

"I can't go out just now," protested Dora Hanlon. "I have a cake in the oven, and…"

"I'll take her," Michael assured her. "And watch her like a hawk, I will, I swear."

His aunt eyed him with suspicion. "What mischief are you up to now?"

His bright hazel eyes went wide and innocent. "Mischief?"

"I've known you since you were a babe, Michael Shea, and mischief is all you're ever at. Your poor mother…"

"Now, Aunt Dora, don't be starting that. Please. You know I treat her well. Who bought her the cottage, now, eh?"

"But how? Where did the money come from? That's what troubles her, and all of us."

Her nephew turned away, walking to the back door before facing her again. "Let that be," he replied in a quiet voice quite unlike his usual lilt.

Mrs. Hanlon met his level gaze for a long moment, then her eyes dropped. She moved heavily to the stove and picked up the steaming kettle with a cloth, carrying it to the table and beginning to make the tea she'd promised him when he arrived. Her deft, familiar movements bridged the silence between them. By the time the leaves were steeping, Michael had begun again. "A simple walk, Aunt," he said.

It took him twenty minutes, but he at last persuaded her to let him take Bess to the park.

"Ah, you can talk the leaves off the trees, Michael," she said at last. "Go, then, I never could refuse you anything you really wanted. But if you're not back in an hour..."

"Aunt Dora!" His voice was reproachful. "Didn't I say we would be, then?"

Mrs. Hanlon merely sniffed.

When Bess was told about the prospective outing, she was delighted, her pleasure marred only by the fact that she had no new gown to wear. Those she had been promised by Sir Richard had been forgotten in the recent furor, though not by Bess. She regretted them now, vociferously and at length. She came very near refusing to go in her shabby white dress, but the lure of the park finally prevailed, along with the loan of a shawl by Mrs. Hanlon so that she needn't disgrace herself in her threadbare blue cloak.

The two set out together at midmorning. Though they were strangers, neither was the least shy, and they were soon chatting happily about Ireland and their families there, and how they had come to London.

"I thought it would be so grand," confided Bess. "But it's mainly dirty and noisy and chock-full of impertinence. Sometimes I wish I had never come."

"It has its nice spots," he answered.

"But we aren't welcome in them." Then, struck by something in his tone, Bess scanned Michael Shea carefully for the first time. "What do you do in London?" she asked him. "Are you a clerk? Or a shop assistant?" She examined his clothes.

"Do I look like one of those?" he asked in return.

"N-no." Bess gazed up at him, puzzled.

Shea grinned, but did not enlighten her further.

"You must have some job," she continued slowly. "But why aren't you there now, at this time of day? It isn't a holiday."

He remained silent, and Bess became more intrigued. "Tell me," she begged, smiling enticingly.

"Let us say that I have a great deal of sympathy with what you said the other night," he answered.

"What I said?"

He grinned. "Shouted, then. About respectable employment."

"Oh." Bess looked down, remembering her tirade, then up again, examining his face with new interest. She saw only a handsome, rather impudent countenance that gave nothing away. "Why won't you tell me?"

"I might. Sometime. Here's the park."

They entered through a pillared gate and strolled along one of the gravel paths that wound through the green. Spring was far advanced, and there were flowers on all sides. "It is very pretty," was Bess's comment.

"You don't sound particularly keen."

"Well, it's all so...excessively tidy."

Michael Shea looked down at her, startled and impressed. "It is, isn't it? I've often thought the same myself."

"Have you? Perhaps it's because we're Irish."

"Aunt Dora wouldn't agree with that."

"No?" Bess considered what she had seen of Dora Hanlon. "I suppose not."

"You are a wonder, aren't you? And a beautiful one."

Bess opened her blue eyes wide. "Do you think I'm beautiful, Mr. Shea?"

"Ah, don't be giving me that innocent stare. You know you are. That's more than clear."

This time, Bess was the one startled. But before she could reply, she heard her name spoken behind them, and both of them turned.

They had come near one of the drives, and a mounted gentleman, dressed in the height of fashion, confronted them. He threw a leg over his high-bred horse and jumped down, removing his beaver hat as he did so. "It is Miss Malone, is it not? I don't think I am mistaken."

Bess gazed up into the lined face of Lord Fenton. "That is my name," she replied.

Lord Fenton smiled. "I thought so. We, er, encountered one another at the club several nights ago." His eyes slid to Michael calculatingly, and then back to Bess.

"Oh." It had not occurred to Bess that she might be recognized from the auction, and now she wondered why it had not. There had been many men present, and she had certainly not been disguised.

"I hope you have been…well?" Lord Fenton's gaze moved to Michael again, and he frowned a little.

Bess nodded. There was something unsavory about this older man. She found she was very glad he hadn't prevailed in the auction.

"And your companion. We have met somewhere, have we not?"

Michael Shea looked innocently bewildered. "I don't think so."

Fenton shrugged, dismissing him. "And where is your, er, friend from the club, Miss Malone? Has he abandoned you to another so soon?"

Bess drew herself up at his tone. He made commonplace phrases sound scurrilous. "No."

"Ah." The older man's cold gaze passed over each of them in turn. Bess's blue eyes burned; Michael Shea looked non-committal. "I mustn't keep my horse standing. I shall hope to meet you again, Miss Malone." Lord Fenton mounted gracefully and replaced his hat; with a nod, he rode on.

"Devil," muttered Bess.

"Only a minor servant of his, I think," replied Shea. And when she didn't answer, he added, "You might easily have ended up with a man like that, you know, rather than a gentleman like Sir Richard. In fact, I understand you nearly did, with that very one. What if Sir Richard hadn't taken it into his head to do a good deed? It was a stupid plan."

"How do you know anything about it?" demanded Bess. For some reason, she was outraged that this man should know what she'd done. Perhaps even ashamed? No!

"Sir Richard told my aunt a little, and I got that out of her. Very stupid."

"What do you know? You're a man." But having spoken to Lord Fenton, Bess was having doubts. The old nobleman made her queasy.

"A man has plenty of chances to sell himself," replied Michael Shea. "It's never a good bargain."

"Don't speak to me in that superior way. You have no right. You won't even tell me what you do. You're probably a criminal of some kind." Bess glared at him. "Of course, you must be."

He shook his head.

"What, then? Tell me, or I shall believe what I choose."

"You won't get me that way. I don't intend to tell you. Not just yet anyway."

"Thief! Murderer!"

Shea smiled, then laughed aloud. "Ah, you are a spitfire, aren't you?"

Bess pulled away from his arm and began walking swiftly back the way they'd come. He followed her and soon caught up, though he kept his distance, merely watching her slim figure and expressive face with amused admiration.

They returned to the house in silence, and found Mrs. Hanlon anxiously watching for their return. "You needn't come in," said Bess.

"Perhaps I want to speak to my aunt."

"Then go around to the kitchen!" Bess pushed through the door Mrs. Hanlon had opened for them and rushed inside and up the stairs.

"What did you do to her?" demanded Mrs. Hanlon.

"Me, Aunt? Why, nothing at all. I was the soul of politeness. I'll come to see you again this evening."

"No. Sir Richard comes then. And I don't want him to see you hanging about here. Indeed, Michael, that girl—"

Shea's face had clouded. "Tomorrow, then," he interrupted, and turned away to saunter down the narrow street. His aunt watched him go with a frown.

But Sir Richard's other concerns had pushed Bess to the back of his mind. He thought of nothing but Julia, and his appointment to discuss Bess's future was forgotten.

Indeed, the engaged couple were enduring very similar and sobering experiences. Both had been deeply offended in their highest principles, an area which each valued more than most people. In the past, when such a thing had happened, each of them had taken decisive action, cutting the connection with the person or group responsible. Julia and Richard had been perhaps a trifle rigid, a bit too proud of their own rectitude and quick to condemn others' slips. They began to realize this dimly now, because Richard longed for Julia despite his belief that she'd fallen short of his ideal, and Julia thought of nothing but Richard, though it now appeared to her that he was the sort of man she had always avoided and deplored. The resulting internal conflict turned their lives topsy-turvy; they had to face revolution within themselves as well as in their chosen partners.

Thus, when they met that evening at a ball, it was one of the most difficult occasions either had ever endured, exacerbated by intense public scrutiny from all sides.

They could not avoid each other; that would have fed the gossip like oil thrown on flames. Yet they could scarcely face each other without revealing even more to the avid audience, for neither was skilled at dissimulation. The result was a kind of silent torment they had never imagined.

They first had to greet each other as usual, under the eyes not only of the *haut ton*, but of their own families. The Deveres had not heard the rumors, but they had by this time gathered that something was wrong. Lady Beckwith was worn out with countering the innuendo and outright inquisitiveness of her friends, and Thomas was becoming positively belligerent.

They had to stand up together at least twice, and go in to supper in apparent amity, talking commonplaces and smiling as naturally as possible. Julia's eyes were hot with unshed tears the whole evening, and Sir Richard felt himself building to an explosion so all-encompassing that he feared for himself.

The worst was the waltz. When the music began, none approached Julia. It was taken for granted that she would stand up with her fiancé. Knowing this, he did his duty, and they moved onto the floor together and slipped into the half embrace.

The steps came easily; they were well matched and had danced so often, with such happiness. But conversation was another matter. No subject seemed safe in the midst of so many eager watchers. Yet silence would be noted, too.

"It is warm," offered Sir Richard after a while.

"Do you find it so?" asked Julia.

"Anyone must, I think. The room is quite hot."

"I myself rarely feel the heat."

"How convenient that must be for you in the summer months."

"Yes, it is."

Having by this innocuous exchange reduced one another to tight-lipped rage, they fell silent for a time.

"There is Mr. Staunton," said Julia then. "He looks quite handsome tonight."

Since Harry Staunton had been the most successful of his rivals for Julia's hand, Sir Richard recognized this as a calculated provocation. "That coat hides the slope of his shoulders admirably," he agreed.

"He is such a pleasant, *open* man," countered Julia. "One cannot imagine him stooping to the least deception."

"He barely has the brains to stoop under a low doorway," said Sir Richard savagely.

Both their faces stiffened; they gazed fixedly at Mr.

Staunton, who was nattering on to his partner in happy oblivion.

But Sir Richard had not abandoned the field. The word *deception* had enflamed him. "There is Lydia Devereaux," he continued. "I haven't seen her in some time. A very pretty girl, I've always thought; her expression is so *trusting*."

Julia nearly ground her teeth. That he should use such a word, after what she had seen, was unbearable. "I would call it vacuous myself," she replied in a languid voice. "She is too silly to have much discrimination."

Sir Richard's arm tightened involuntarily about her waist, emphasizing their physical closeness. This seemed a bitter mockery, and at the same time a disquieting mystery. For both of them enjoyed the sensation despite their anger. They resisted, scandalized, but the fact was that Julia reveled in the feel of his arm and longed to move even closer, and Sir Richard had to fight the impulse to pull her against him and kiss her so thoroughly that this nonsense about Bess would evaporate like dew in the heat of the sun.

Instead, the music ended, to their mixed relief and regret. Julia returned to her parents. The Deveres left the ball early, at her request, giving Julia ample time to indulge in furious, forlorn sobbing before she at last fell asleep.

When she was gone, Sir Richard remembered his previous appointment. Though it was nearly eleven, he drove homeward past the house where he had settled Bess, and when he saw a light, he stopped and knocked. Bess opened the door herself, warily.

"I'm sorry to be so late," said Sir Richard. "I had another engagement."

The girl stepped back to allow him to come in. "Mrs. Hanlon's gone to bed," she said.

"Ah. I won't stay, then." But he made no move to go. He didn't want to return home to his tumultuous thoughts. "Why are you sitting up so late?"

Bess shrugged. "I wasn't tired. And I wanted to finish my book."

Sir Richard couldn't hide his astonishment, and the girl smiled wryly. "Oh, yes, I can read. The priest taught me when I asked him, and he let me borrow books now and then. Dull as ditch water they were, too. But my mother got novels sometimes up at the Hall, where she...worked."

"I see. No doubt that is where you picked up the notions that took you to the Chaos Club. Romantic bilge."

"I didn't expect you would care for them." Bess sounded indifferent to his opinion.

"No, indeed. Novel reading is the source of much that is wrong with young people today. Particularly girls."

Bess made a disgusted sound. "How would you know? I wager you've never read one. Nor does that young lady you're engaged to, I suppose."

Sir Richard stiffened. The mention of Julia was like a lash on skin already wounded.

Bess misunderstood. "I'm not to speak her name, eh? She's not to be mentioned by the likes of *me*. She isn't to know that girls like me exist. I'll bet she does, though."

"Be quiet!"

"And from what I hear, many fine ladies aren't so sweet and pure. No indeed. Yours may turn out to be something quite different once she's married."

This suggestion, though ridiculous, grated on Sir

Richard intolerably after the evening he'd endured. He grasped Bess's shoulder. "I said, be quiet!"

"Don't tell me what to do!" She pulled away, but stumbled and fell against him. Their bodies pressed together, Bess's nervous eyes very close to his.

Sir Richard thrust Bess away so abruptly that she nearly fell. He was shocked at himself. He'd come close to striking her. He didn't understand that his fury had been roused by the situation with Julia, bursting out because it must. He thought he must be going mad. It had to be madness, to make him behave in a manner he despised.

"I…I'm sorry," whispered Bess, who had backed into the corner of the tiny hall, frightened by the look in his gray eyes.

Sir Richard raised his head and stared at her; Bess crouched and waited for she knew not what—a blow, a curse. She hadn't thought Sir Richard prone to this sort of outburst, but she saw now he was more like other men she'd encountered than she realized.

She was surprised again, however, for he simply turned and strode out the front door, leaving it open behind him. She heard the jingle of harness and then the snap of a whip. Hoof beats began and quickened to a furious gallop before they faded in the distance. Bess went to shut the door, carefully slipping the bolt. She fetched her reading candle and went slowly up the stairs.

EIGHT

"You don't seem to understand. I am not offering you a choice," said Lord Fenton to the younger man he faced across the shabby disorder of the latter's front parlor. "I want the address. Now."

"I don't care to give it to you," replied Lord Charles Wearingham. His youthful face was pale, but he stood very straight, his hand resting on the back of an ancient armchair.

Fenton's gray-flecked brows rose; they had a curious V-shape that made his seamed face diabolical in the dim early morning light filtering through the blinds. "No? That isn't very wise of you. It displeases me, and makes me feel that I no longer wish to hold your notes of hand."

"My...? How did you get them?"

"I bought them. From your customary moneylender. He seemed extremely glad to be rid of them. Do you suppose he doubted their quality? A distressing amount of debt, Charles."

Wearingham whitened further. Though he didn't move, he seemed to collapse in on himself. He was so deeply in debt that there was no chance of getting out, he knew that. Even a big win at the tables would likely only keep him from debtor's prison. And the devil of it was, he never did win. He'd lost the thousand guineas Beckwith paid for Bess in four days, when he'd been certain it was a sum sent by Providence to get him on his feet again. Now, he had taken to waking suddenly in the night, in a cold sweat of fear, unable to sleep again as his brain went around and around without discovering an escape. If Fenton called in his vowels, he was ruined. "Why do you want it?" he croaked.

"Perhaps I wish to call on the young lady."

"I don't know if she…"

"For God's sake, Wearingham, we're talking about a girl who sold herself to the highest bidder, not a duke's daughter. You say you know where she is. Tell me."

Wearingham hesitated for a moment longer, then grimaced and gave him Bess Malone's address.

Lord Fenton smiled. "Thank you." He turned to go.

"What are you planning?" Wearingham asked.

He was not vouchsafed an answer, and when the door shut behind his uninvited visitor, he let his head drop in his hands.

Lord Fenton returned home to make certain arrangements. Though these were somewhat unusual, the men he employed had done similar work for him in the past, and had few questions. They went on their way without comment and took up unobtrusive positions near the house where Bess Malone was staying.

And thus it was that when Dora Hanlon went out at midmorning with a market basket over her arm, a burly man approached the front door and knocked. After a moment, it was opened by Bess, who gazed at the visitor with some surprise. She was not given time to speak, however. The man pushed hard on the door, throwing Bess back against the wall, and stepped quickly inside. His colleague, who had come forward as soon as the door opened, followed suit and shut the door with a snap.

There was a brief pause, then the door opened again and the two men reappeared, supporting a limp Bess between them. They hurried her along the street and around the corner to a shabby livery stable, where a closed carriage with a team that had made the ostler gape awaited them, already harnessed. Bess was shoved inside and the doors secured; the two men mounted the box and whipped up the horses, driving quickly through the streets of London and out into the countryside, to a secluded cottage they had visited several times before.

When a footman informed Sir Richard Beckwith that Dora Hanlon had called at the back door and wished to give him a message, he experienced a disturbing sinking feeling. He had not gone near the house where he had placed Bess in a day and a half, and whenever he thought of her, a haze of embarrassment obscured his mind. Though he had done nothing wrong, he felt he had made a mistake. The good deed he had aimed at had not played out as he expected it would. In fact, it had become a threat to his lifelong happiness. And he hadn't figured out how to remedy this situation.

Mrs. Hanlon was visibly uncomfortable when she was brought before him. Her broad, pleasant face was creased with worry. "She's gone again," she said without preliminaries. "I went out to market, and she slipped away. I thought she'd made up her mind to stay, else I wouldn't have left her alone, Sir Richard."

Beckwith's first reaction was relief. Could he simply dismiss Mrs. Hanlon with thanks and forget Bess had ever existed? In the next instant he knew he could not. "She left no message?" he asked.

"No, sir. Nor took her things. The new gowns came yesterday late, and they're hanging in her room."

Bess would never have run away without these. "I'm sure she will be back, in that case, Mrs. Hanlon. You may as well go home and wait for her."

"Yes, sir." But the woman made no move. "I've a bad feeling about this," she added finally. "There's a smell about it."

Beckwith raised his blond eyebrows, and Mrs. Hanlon looked uneasy. "I know things sometimes, sir. It comes to me."

"I don't think this is such a time," was his reply. "Go back now, and send word when Bess returns."

Mrs. Hanlon dropped a small curtsy and went out, her face showing pique at his dismissal of her warning. Sir Richard turned to his papers, but his mind wouldn't stay on his work. He was restless and impatient. He longed to speak to Julia, he realized. More than anything else, he wanted to be reconciled with her. He wanted to think only of her.

He heard nothing more of Bess that day. But the following morning Michael Shea called early and was admitted before Sir Richard had risen from the breakfast table. When Beckwith joined him in the library, Mr. Shea was obviously impatient. "Bess has disappeared," he said at once.

Something in his tone annoyed Sir Richard so that he took his time closing the door and moving to his desk in the corner. "She has not returned?" he said then.

"No. We must start a search, though it may well be too late." Shea's voice was accusing, and his handsome ruddy face showed signs of deep agitation.

"Too late?" Sir Richard was not accustomed to being addressed in this way.

"Anything might have happened to her."

"Bess seemed able to take care of herself."

"Are you daft, man? That's just what she isn't. Selling

herself at the Chaos Club! If she hadn't had the luck to meet you there, Lord knows where she'd be now. We've got to find her."

Had he been less exigent, Sir Richard might have simply agreed. But he was unused to being ordered about by anyone, still less by Dora Hanlon's nephew. "If she has chosen to leave the shelter I attempted to provide—" he began.

"She doesn't know what she's about, man," said Shea. "Likely, she's fallen into the hands of some plausible rogue."

"Like you?"

"Not like me," said Shea through gritted teeth. "I would never—"

"She's run away before," interrupted Sir Richard.

"You're throwing her back in the gutter, then?" The other man's voice had gone cold.

"I beg your pardon?"

"You plucked her out on a whim, and now you're tossing her back. What do you care?"

Sir Richard's lips drew tight. "May I remind you that Bess rejected my help? I sought to do her a good turn, and she would have none of it. From the beginning. There is no question of 'tossing her back.' I resent your tone, Shea."

Michael Shea put a hand to his forehead. "You're right. I apologize. I was overhasty. But you will search for her, won't you? I've looked in all the streets around the cottage."

"I'll send some men out to inquire, but London is a big place." Sir Richard shook his head. "I don't know what else I can do."

Michael Shea hesitated, then gripped his cane so tightly his knuckles whitened and turned away. Sir Richard felt an uncomfortable pang of concern when he was gone. He gave the order for a search, and called for his horse.

Not twenty miles from Sir Richard's comfortable house, Bess Malone lay curled on a hard, narrow bed, drifting in and out of a frightening dream and moaning at intervals. In lucid moments, she would struggle to sit up and seek some avenue of escape, but the dream would surge back when she moved and push her down again.

There had been some drug in her dinner, she knew. She had been in a fine rage when she recovered from the blow her kidnappers had dealt her and found herself in a swiftly moving carriage with no way to get out. She had fought them with all her might when they forced her into this house. One of them wouldn't open his left eye yet a while after the scratch she had given him. But they were two big men, and she had been overwhelmed and locked in this windowless room, bare of anything that might aid her.

Still, when the knock finally came, Bess crouched, ready to spring on her captors once more. However, it swung open to reveal the nobleman she had met in the park, in full evening dress, and both his social position and the look on his face intimidated her. When he offered his arm and told her to come to dinner, she went. It wasn't until the second course that she began to feel odd and to realize that he had drugged her. This brought back her anger, and she had leapt up and accused him. He had merely laughed, and when she flew at him, stumbling a little from the drug, he had held her off at arm's length, his fingers biting cruelly into her upper arms, and laughed again. Like a devil, it seemed to Bess.

He enjoyed leaving marks on her pale skin, she realized. He liked resistance, too. He taunted her to encourage it. But at last, when it had come to the moment, he'd wanted her broken and docile, and she wasn't. So he called for more of whatever they had given her and forced her to take it in water. After that, everything dissolved in the phantasmagoria that still tormented her now. The second dose of the drug faded very slowly and erratically.

At last, in a more lucid interval, Bess heard a rattle and saw a tray being slid through a special hinged panel at the bottom of the door. It held coffee and bread and butter, and she fell from the bed trying to reach that delicious smell. Lying on the dirty wooden floor, Bess felt tears come. She wanted the coffee so, but she couldn't stand, or even crawl.

With a gigantic effort, she began to pull herself along the floor, inch by inch, dizziness threatening every move. It was hunger, she told herself fiercely, for she had lost her dinner soon after eating it. She would feel much better when she had eaten. And then she would think of a way to kill the despicable Lord Fenton.

It was a late spring day with a fresh breeze, and fashionable London had turned out in the park. Low-sprung barouches and high-perch phaetons dotted the landscape, along with riders and walkers. It was a pretty sight, though Sir Richard found his progress impeded by the necessity of responding to greetings and salutes from all sides. In his present mood, he found this dawdling gait frustrating, and he was relieved when he saw Julia Devere and her mother approaching in their elegant carriage. He pulled his horse's head around and moved toward them, his pulse speeding up in anticipation.

Julia's heart had begun to pound some minutes before, when she had noticed him across the grass. The sight of his broad shoulders and handsome blond head had first thrilled her, then made her miserable again.

Julia had been racking her brain for a plan since the ball and had come up with nothing. Her feelings hadn't changed. She was still angry and still determined to win Richard back from his hussy of a mistress. But she had no idea how to go about it. She had a vague notion that a woman such as her rival had many unfair advantages. She could offer entice-ments that Julia could not even imagine. She could lure him and bewitch him. Julia had no experience of such things and would not, she told herself haughtily, stoop to them if she did. Would she? What about kisses? She'd gladly offer *those*. But how to find an opportunity? She felt helpless, and yet absolutely determined to do something.

As Sir Richard greeted them now, all thoughts went out of her head. His presence increased her pulse and her outrage. That he could look just as before, after what had passed between them, seemed unbearable.

He chatted easily with her mother, but Julia could feel his eyes on her. Perversely, she turned her head away and watched the passing carriages. Let him speak, she said to herself; I shan't be first.

"You are looking particularly lovely today, Julia," said Sir Richard.

Julia glanced down at her gown of thin, white muslin

sprigged with two shades of green and trimmed with knots of green ribbon. It was new, and she had fallen in love with it the moment she saw it. "This dress makes me look positively hagged," she answered.

Both of the others protested. Julia shrugged, and wondered why she was being a fool.

Before the conversation could continue, they were interrupted by another rider who pulled up beside Sir Richard, greeted him, and nodded to the ladies. It was Lord Fenton.

Julia and Lady Devere turned their heads away, both now pretending great interest in the passing scene. Lord Fenton was not the sort of man they acknowledged, though neither had quite the temerity to order their coachman to drive on. He was, after all, an earl.

It was not Lord Fenton's habit to force himself on such a fusty group. He found people like the Deveres a dead bore. And up until recently, he had felt the same about Sir Richard Beckwith, until he had appeared at the Chaos Club and snatched Bess from under his nose. They were now, in Lord Fenton's mind, sporting rivals, and his desire to gloat overrode his customary discretion.

"Beckwith," he said with a false joviality. "Fine day."

Sir Richard, his mind wholly occupied with Julia, merely wished him away.

"Good to be outdoors," Fenton added. "I suppose you've been spending a great deal of time *indoors* lately." His emphasis of the word was unmistakably risqué, but the only member of his audience who caught it was Julia, sensitized by her hours of brooding in the last few days.

"And how is our mutual friend?" asked Lord Fenton.

Frustrated by his quarry's lack of response, he was becoming reckless.

The direct question finally penetrated Sir Richard's preoccupation. "Friend?" he echoed.

"Indeed. Such a charming young…person." Lord Fenton's tone was poisonous.

Richard blinked. He couldn't believe Fenton was speaking so. He had to get rid of the man before Julia caught his innuendo.

He was too late. Julia's pale green eyes were glittering with rage and humiliation, and her cheeks glowed with an unaccustomed brilliance. "We should be going, Mama," she said, as if no one else were present.

Lady Devere agreed, eager to leave the vicinity of Lord Fenton. She gave the order, and the barouche started to move forward.

Sir Richard's expression satisfied Lord Fenton. A thin smile crossed his face as Sir Richard pulled his horse's head around and followed the carriage.

"Julia," he said as he trotted along beside it, "I must speak to you."

Julia was choking with rage. She started to refuse, and then was overwhelmed by a wave of anger. "Very well," she snapped. "Stop, Edward." The coachman pulled up at the edge of the drive. "We will walk a moment," declared Julia, opening the carriage door unassisted. "I will be right back, Mama." She strode onto a graveled path.

Sir Richard could only swing down from his horse and hurry to catch up with her. Julia strode along the grass border as if marching on parade, her chin high, her eyes straight ahead.

"Julia…"

"I agreed to walk only because I must tell you something," she interrupted. "Our engagement is at an end."

"What?"

"I am breaking it off. I cannot marry you."

"But…" Sir Richard strove for composure. This was down to Bess, he knew, and he determined to tell her the whole story no matter how it might embarrass them both. "You must let me explain. I know you've heard gossip, but it isn't true."

"I saw you," replied Julia. She turned on her heel and rushed back to the barouche. Sir Richard caught up as she was climbing in again. "We can go home now, Edward," she said.

"We must talk this over," insisted Beckwith. "I will call."

"There is nothing to discuss. I shan't be at home to you."

"Julia!"

But the barouche had started moving. Sir Richard stood watching it wend its way among the press of vehicles, a cold like ice forming around his heart, oblivious to the stares of passersby.

NINE

SIR RICHARD CALLED AT THE DEVERES' AFTER DINNER that evening and was told they were out. As the upstairs windows were all dark, he was forced to believe this, but he was on the doorstep as early as possible the next morning asking for Julia.

"Miss Devere is not at home, sir," replied the footman.

From the look on his face, Sir Richard could tell that Julia was within, but refusing to see him. He considered knocking the servant to the floor and fighting his way to her, but even in his current state, he was not quite ready to take such a step. Instead, he said, "Is Sir George in, then?"

"I will inquire, if you would care to step into the study, sir."

He paced the small room for what seemed a long time before Julia's father appeared.

"Richard, my boy," was his greeting, with outstretched hand. "I've been trying to persuade Julia to come down, but it's no good. What have you two been quarreling about?"

He spoke so lightly and jovially that Richard took heart. Perhaps things weren't so serious after all. Perhaps his life's happiness was not being torn from him forever. He would tell Sir George the whole story, and let him speak to Julia. But when he met Devere's wide, china-blue eyes, he couldn't begin. Sir George would not approve of what he'd done. Indeed, he would not comprehend why Richard had thought of entering a place like the Chaos Club. He would vow that he was as willing to help the poor as anyone, but a girl who set out to sell herself? Sir Richard could see him shaking his head and pursing his lips judiciously.

"A misunderstanding," he said. "There was a girl. Julia thought… But it was nothing. I give you my word."

Sir George did purse his lips. "Now, my boy, I know Julia. Eh? Most even-tempered girl—child and young lady—I've ever seen. But here she is bursting into tears, insisting we leave for home this instant, railing at her mother and me one minute and refusing to speak to us the next. Doesn't sound like nothing. Eh? Not with Julia. Some women, yes. Act you a Cheltenham tragedy about an overcooked roast. But not my Julia."

"She is mistaken. She doesn't understand."

"Well, you explain whatever it is to me, and I'll put it right."

Sir Richard tried to think how to begin. With his outrage at the idea of a young girl being sold to some bored man of wealth?

"I should tell you," added Sir George when he didn't speak. "An old friend came to us with some story about you. We didn't heed it at the time, but now…" He looked grave. "Don't tell me it is true, Richard. I told our friend it was preposterous to think of *you* involved with some…girl of the streets."

And so it was, thought Sir Richard. That was why he had made such a mull of it.

"Won't you assure me it was a lie?" asked Julia's father.

"The story was distorted," he replied. "I was trying to help the girl. She had no idea what the Chaos Club—"

"The…" Sir George looked as if he might explode. "You are a member of that place?"

"Of course I am not!"

His tone was so emphatic that he pulled Sir George up short.

"I heard talk of what was to go on there, and I went to stop it. That is all."

"But this girl?"

"I set out to help her. To find her some...respectable employment." The phrase made Sir Richard want to hit something by this time. "She didn't care to be a servant. I was trying to find an alternative when she ran away. I had no other...connection with her whatsoever."

"Huh." Julia's father appeared to be thinking. "Well, I trust your word. Wouldn't want to try such a thing myself," he concluded finally. "I mean, plenty of unfortunates in other places, eh? Help some of them."

"Believe me, should a charitable impulse ever strike me again, I shall!"

Sir George sighed. "I'll see what I can do. Tell my wife, and let her speak to Julia. But I can't promise she'll listen. I've never seen her like this."

"If I could just see her."

Devere shook his head. "She won't come down. And I won't have her forced. Come back tomorrow, and we'll see."

"I can come this evening," urged Sir Richard.

"No. Tomorrow. Give her some time to cool down, my boy. Always best in these sorts of wrangles. Take my advice."

What could he possibly know about it, wondered Sir Richard bitterly, with his unruffled domesticity and his blameless life. But he couldn't argue any more with Julia's father. "Very well," he said.

"Good lad." Sir George clapped him on the shoulder. "It will all work out for the best, you'll see."

With something close to despair on his handsome face, Beckwith took his leave. He spent the rest of the day trying to run away from himself. But through a bruising ride on the north road, several tankards of ale at midday, and rather more wine with his dinner, his gloomy thoughts remained with him.

When night closed in and he retired to the library, he ordered brandy. His mother and brother were out, and the silence of the place weighed on him as it never had before.

Thomas came home some hours later and found his brother in a very uncharacteristic state of inebriation. He eyed him with concern. "What's wrong?"

"Nothing," replied Richard in a flat, dead voice. The brandy had finally stopped the endless rehashing of his dilemma in his brain, and he had no intention of starting it up again.

Thomas came in and sat down opposite. "I can see that there's—"

"I told you," roared Richard. "Nothing!"

Tom sat for a moment in stunned silence. His brother seemed a stranger all at once. He frowned as he watched Richard refill his brandy glass with a hand that wavered back and forth, spilling brandy on the tabletop. Richard didn't even like brandy.

Something dreadful must have happened. Thomas leaned back a bit, trying to appear relaxed, and poured himself a bit of brandy. "I saw something odd tonight," he said. His brother did not reply. "That Irish fellow who called on you, the one with red hair, I saw him at a gaming club with Lord Charles Wearingham."

There was still no response.

"Quite thick, they were. Wearingham had been losing again, of course. He always does lose. And the redheaded fellow was helping him drown his sorrows. What's his name, anyway?"

"Who?"

"Red-haired man who called here for you. Well set up. Clothes a bit flashy."

"Shea," muttered Sir Richard. "M-Michael Shea. Nephew of Dora Hanlon."

"Hanlon? The gardener?"

His brother nodded and gazed into his glass. He didn't want to think about Dora Hanlon.

"What can he have been doing in that club?" Thomas looked perplexed. "Roger Preston said he'd seen him around there before, too. Odd."

Sir Richard shrugged. He had no time for puzzles other than his own tonight.

Thomas yawned and stretched rather ostentatiously. "It's late. Shall we go upstairs?"

"You go on."

"Come along. You'll fall asleep on the table in a moment."

"I said—" But before Sir Richard could finish his sentence, a loud pounding began on the front door, reverberating in the hall like a giant's drum.

"Good God," said Thomas. "What the devil's that?"

His brother got unsteadily to his feet. "Go see." Tom caught his elbow to steady him, and they went to the door together. A half-dressed footman met them in the hall, pulling on a shirt. "Never mind. Go back to bed," said Sir Richard, his voice a little slurred. The servant stared.

"Go ahead," added Thomas, cursing their luck. The whole staff would be chattering tomorrow about their master's drunkenness.

The footman disappeared. Thomas went to the door and opened it slightly. Michael Shea pushed forward at once. "Sir Richard?" he said. "I must see Sir Richard right away." He came through the door and spotted him. "Sir Richard! Fenton has Bess. He's taken her."

Sir Richard Beckwith stumbled over nothing and slid to the polished floor of his own front hall.

It was a little while before the three men reconvened in the library, the brandy replaced by a pot of strong coffee made by Michael Shea. Thomas had tried to convince him to leave, but he refused so vehemently that Tom gave up and concentrated on restoring Richard to some semblance of himself. Shea watched this process with ill-concealed impatience and at the earliest possible moment, returned to his purpose. "Lord Fenton has her," he repeated. "We must do something. Get her away. Tonight. You know what sort of man he is."

"How do you know this?" asked Thomas, since Richard seemed to be still gathering his wits.

"I got it from Wearingham. I thought he might know something, because Bess had been to see him about her money. He told Fenton where she was." Shea pounded on the desk in frustration. "He said Fenton pressed him hard, the coward. Fenton's taken her, I tell you. She didn't go on her own." He leaned forward, his eyes blazing. "Do you hear me, Sir Richard? Bess was kidnapped!"

"I hear." Though not completely back to normal, Beckwith was much better.

"What are you going to do about it, then?"

Richard tried to make his mind function. "Lord Fenton asked for the address…"

"Not asked. Forced it out of Wearingham. And on the very morning Bess disappeared."

"Ah." Sir Richard's head was beginning to ache, and what he really wanted was for both of them to leave him alone. His loss of Julia filled his thoughts.

"If Fenton actually has taken the girl," said Thomas slowly. "We should do something. I've heard things about him that I don't like."

"Not half what I've heard," said Shea. "You don't move in the right circles. He's an ugly customer. He wouldn't be above getting rid of a girl when he was through with her."

"Killing her?"

The Irishman nodded.

Thomas looked grave.

"What are you suggesting, precisely?" asked Richard. "That we go to Lord Fenton's house and storm it? I won't allow Thomas to participate in any such thing." When it appeared that both of the other men would protest, he added. "Do have any idea where Bess might be?"

"I'll find out," replied Michael Shea. "I know people who could tell me, or at least send me to those who can. I'll see them first thing in the morning."

"Come back when you have," declared Sir Richard, pushing himself up from the table to indicate that the interview was over.

Shea departed. Thomas lingered in the library, hoping that his brother might now be ready to confide in him, but Sir Richard merely ordered him off to bed in gruff tones that offered no opening. With several looks back over his shoulder, Thomas obeyed. And Sir Richard Beckwith was again left alone with his thoughts.

TEN

WHEN SIR RICHARD CALLED AT THE DEVERES' EARLY the next morning, he was received by Lady Devere, and her expression did not promise good news. "Julia is still not herself," she told him. "Perhaps in another day or two."

"If I could just see her," he urged.

"No. I don't think she could bear it. She has begged me not to force her to meet you, and I have agreed for the present." Lady Devere did not add that both she and her husband were quite frightened by the mania that seemed to have seized their placid daughter. Wholly unused to emotional storms, they reacted by tiptoeing about the house and agreeing to whatever Julia demanded, in the hope that this fit would pass and their familiar daughter return. Another man, experienced in such upheavals, might have advised them that this approach was unwise. But Sir Richard was not that man.

"I explained to Sir George," he offered.

"Yes." Julia's mother turned her head away, embarrassed. "I told her, but Julia doesn't seem to listen just now. I think we must give her more time."

"If I could only speak to her—"

"No!" Lady Devere's nervous green eyes met his. "We can't… I'm afraid she might do something rash. She keeps insisting on leaving London. She has packed her things. We have told her it is impossible, but…" Lady Devere swallowed frightened tears. "I…I fear she might run away." To her, this seemed an incredible, shameful possibility. Three weeks ago, she would have laughed in the face of anyone who suggested such a thing about her Julia. But since then, the world had turned topsy-turvy.

The threat silenced Sir Richard, even though he felt as if some demon were turning a hot knife in his chest. "I'll call again tomorrow, then," he choked out between clenched jaws.

"Yes," replied Lady Devere eagerly, happy to be rid of him. "Perhaps she will be better then."

Sir Richard made his way home without any awareness of his surroundings. He didn't even hear the respectful greeting of the footman who opened the door for him, and he moved into the library like a sleepwalker, seating himself at the desk and putting his forehead in his hands. It was here that his mother found him some time later. Thomas had spoken to her, and her earlier worries had redoubled.

"Richard," she said, shutting the library door behind her. "Richard."

There was no response. Lady Beckwith went over to her son and put a hand on his shoulder. "Richard."

He started violently and jerked away, then sat back, breathing hard.

"I'm sorry, dear. I didn't mean to startle you."

"It's all right."

Lady Beckwith examined his face, as she had become accustomed to doing whenever they were together now. He looked ravaged. "Tell me what has happened," she demanded. "It is Julia, isn't it? She has heard the stories."

Sir Richard groaned aloud. "She has broken it off, Mama. The engagement is at an end. And she will not see me to talk of it."

His mother moved as if she would go to the Deveres at once. "Someone must explain to her that—"

"I have tried. I told Sir George. But Julia won't listen; she won't believe me." A spark of anger illuminated his misery. "I suppose I was mistaken in her."

"You were no such thing!" His mother's worry and irritation at the situation spilled over onto him. "Oh, what a muddle. I should have done something long ago, but you were so against it I put it off. And now you see!"

"What could you do?" he replied, grasping at straws.

"I can talk to Julia, and her mother. I can tell them everything."

"She won't see anyone."

"She will see *me*. I will convince her mother that she must." Lady Beckwith turned toward the door. "I shall leave at once."

Hope rose in Richard. "If you can put it right…"

"I shall!"

Lady Beckwith did not have much difficulty with Julia's parents. They were at their wits' end and welcomed any aid. But when she sat down in the drawing room with Julia and her mother, the atmosphere cooled distinctly.

Julia was not, as she had half expected, tearful and full of reproaches. She was like a maiden carved of ice. She sat in an armchair, as ordered, her hands folded in her lap, but she did not seem really present in the room. She listened to Lady Beckwith's story with no sign of emotion, and thanked her when she was finished for trying to be of help. "But it is no use," she concluded. "I have made up my mind. I am sorry." She had seen the girl in Sir Richard's embrace. She had incontrovertible proof that his interest in her was not purely charitable. That he had convinced them all that it was, and that he dared to push them to argue this lie, just made it worse. She had been a fool, she decided. She had completely misjudged him. He was like those London beaus she despised, like Lord Fenton even. The knowledge nearly crushed her.

For she had not ceased to love him. And there was a traitorous part of her that continually urged reconciliation. When Julia knew Richard was in the house talking with her parents, it pushed her to go to him and reinstate their engagement. It did not care what he had done; it wanted him.

What Julia thought of as her better self was at perpetual war with this other, and the conflict was exhausting her. She no longer had the energy to cry, and she was certainly beyond logical argument. It felt as if she was being torn apart, with no hope of succor, and her one longing now was to run away. Her parents had said she could not go home, but Lady Beckwith's visit decided her. She must. She would take her maid and a manservant with her, Julia thought, as well as the second coachman and post boys. Her parents could not think her unprotected among so many. As Julia bade a mystified and angry Lady Beckwith good-bye, she determined to leave London the following morning.

Sir Richard was pacing impatiently when his mother arrived home, but he saw at once that her mission had been unsuccessful.

"She would not be convinced," said Lady Beckwith with a puzzled frown. "It was as if she knew something that made her impervious to argument. What could it be, Richard?"

He shook his head and sank into the desk chair once again.

"She simply does not trust or love me." The anger he had once felt at this idea was dead. Only the wound remained, and the bleak vista of his future without Julia.

"Oh, Richard." His mother was cut to the heart by his tone.

"I shan't give up just yet," he continued in the same flat voice. "But I have little hope that she will come around. There is, as you say, some barrier between us now. I cannot break it."

"I'll call again, speak to her again," exclaimed Lady Beckwith.

"No. You have done what you could. I'll visit again tomorrow and make another attempt." He rose. "And now, I shall go riding."

"Richard, if only—"

He cut her off with a bitter laugh and strode out.

But when he made his way to the Devere house the next morning, a shocking sight confronted him. A post-chaise was pulled up before the door, and a pile of luggage was being tied at the back in preparation for immediate departure. Sir Richard, who had walked the short distance to work off some of his nervous energy, strode swiftly to the open front door. He collided with a middle-aged woman carrying a dressing case, but managed to retain his balance and steady her as well. When he straightened, he found himself face to face with Julia, who was rigged out in traveling clothes. Had he been ten minutes later, Sir Richard thought, he would have missed her. "I must speak to you!" he said.

"There is nothing to say. My chaise is waiting." Julia's voice cracked.

"And it will wait a little longer." He pulled her through an open door into the front parlor and shut it behind them. "I *will* speak to you!"

Julia turned her back on him and walked over to the

empty fireplace. "Apparently, I cannot prevent you without a vulgar scene."

Now that he was actually with Julia, Sir Richard wanted most to sweep her into his arms and kiss her until she admitted that this whole ridiculous series of events was a mistake. The impulse was so strong that controlling it held him rigid. Thus, when he spoke, the words were much more formal than he meant to be. "I have tried to explain things to you," he said. "Through others since you refused to see me. You stubbornly deny the truth of—"

"Truth! You *dare* to talk to me of truth?"

Sir Richard frowned. "Since I have told you nothing else, I do not see—"

"Stop it! I cannot bear it that you lie to me. I loved you! I thought you everything I could admire in a man. And then to find that you had deceived me so cruelly." Her voice broke again, on tears.

Beckwith stepped forward, hands outstretched. "But I have not—"

"I saw you!" cried Julia. "I saw you myself. It is no use denying it. Now let me go!" And pushing past him, she ran out the door, across the hall, and outside. Her maid had already gotten into the chaise, and the post boys were mounted. Julia clambered up and slammed the carriage door. "Go!" she cried. The driver obediently signaled the team, and the chaise began to move off as Sir Richard appeared in the doorway.

"Stop!" he shouted. "Julia!"

But the chaise picked up speed and moved on. He sprang down the steps and would have run after it, had he not suddenly noticed the gathering spectators. The Devere servants were peering from the hall; passersby had stopped and were gazing at him with amusement; an upstairs window opened and Lady Devere stared down with red-rimmed eyes. Beckwith cursed himself silently for leaving his horse at home, and strode rapidly off the way he had come. If Julia was going home, he thought, he would follow her there and discover exactly what she thought she had seen.

ELEVEN

WHEN SIR RICHARD REACHED HOME, CALLING FOR HIS horse to be saddled as he entered the hall, he found Michael Shea and Thomas awaiting him. "Come in here," said Thomas, pulling him into the library. "Shea has found her!"

"Found who?" he answered impatiently.

The others stared at him. "Bess," said Thomas. "Bess Malone. Is something wrong, Richard?"

"Yes, it is. And I haven't time for Bess just now. I must go out of town for a few—"

"You can't abandon her!" exclaimed Shea, his hazel eyes burning.

"You seem entirely capable of her rescue," Sir Richard retorted. "I leave it in your hands."

"I'm capable enough. But there's at least two ruffians in that cottage. I'll need help."

"I'll come," declared Thomas.

"No you won't!" Sir Richard was desperately impatient to get away, but he saw that he would have to deal with this matter first. "Find some of your own friends and go after her, Shea. Surely you can gather some men. I'll give you money to pay them if you like."

"The gardener's nephew can rescue the slum girl, is that it?" replied Shea bitterly. "Leave it to the servants?"

"That is not what I meant."

"Isn't it now? Well, I can't do it."

"And why not?"

"I don't want anyone else knowing what's happened to Bess, particularly not my own friends."

"I can see no reason why—"

"I don't suppose you can! But I intend to marry her."

Both the Beckwiths were struck dumb by the unexpectedness of his revelation.

"I imagine you have no objection?" added Shea defensively.

"No. I...simply had no idea," responded Sir Richard.

"Well, it's only a notion as yet. She doesn't know. I never got the chance to speak. But I will, if she'll have me. I'll take her off to France or Italy, I reckon. I've lived there off and on. I have my eye on a fine little gaming club in Paris. Just the thing for us. I'm like Bess, you know—don't care to live on anyone's wage."

Through his surprise, Sir Richard was realizing that this might be just the sort of thing Bess would like.

"So I don't want her story to get out. If I have to look for help, I'll be explaining over and over. It'd be talked of. *You* already know, and you won't gossip for your own reasons."

He would have to postpone following Julia, maddening as that felt. "All right," he said, "we will help you."

———————————

Little more than an hour later, they set out on horseback, following the instructions Michael Shea had squeezed from a Tothill Fields ruffian. Sir Richard was thankful to find that their way lay in the same direction as Julia's home, as he planned to go on there, after they had accomplished their mission.

They rode swiftly and in silence, all three thinking of what lay ahead. The journey was not long, and soon after midday they were approaching the area of the cottage. When it finally came in sight, they halted under a grove of trees to confer.

"You're certain this is the place?" said Thomas with a slightly nervous laugh. "I should hate to burst in on a rustic couple at their midday bread and cheese rather than a nest of villains."

"It is just as described to me," replied Michael Shea. His face had lost its ruddiness, and he looked set and pale.

"Let us watch for a short while and see," said Sir Richard.

They sat quietly on their horses gazing at the cottage through a screen of branches. A thin plume of smoke rose from the chimney, and the scene was deceptively peaceful. They saw no one.

Then, abruptly, Michael Shea muttered, "There's no garden!"

Thomas, startled, jerked his reins and made his mount sidle.

"It's no farmer lives there without a garden," he added. "And a few flowers at the doorstep. This is the place, all right."

As if to confirm his theory, the back door of the cottage opened, and a rough-looking man came out to lean on the fence and smoke a pipe.

"This is it!" exclaimed Shea in a hoarse whisper, and spurred his horse suddenly forward. The Beckwiths were only an instant behind him.

Shea rode furiously across the short space of rough ground beyond the grove and took the fence easily. The man standing there did not realize until too late that he was under attack. He merely gaped at the three riders up to the point when Shea bent over and grasped his collar, hauling him up against the side of his mount and reducing the man to choking helplessness.

Sir Richard, meanwhile, had leapt down and run for the cottage door. It was not locked, and he burst into the kitchen holding the pistol he had taken from his pocket. The man sitting at the table inside didn't have time to move. He sat frozen, his hands about a steaming mug, his eyes fastened on the pistol. Sir Richard waited thus while Shea hustled his gasping captive inside.

"The girl is here?" said Beckwith then. It was only half a question.

"What girl might you be—" began the man from outside, then gasped again as Michael Shea jammed a fist into his side.

"We don't want no trouble with you gentlemen," said the other man quickly. "We was just doing a job of work and collecting our pay."

"Work!" Shea spat the word.

The man at the table looked him up and down as if trying to place him. "Well, mayhap you can pick and choose. Harry and me…" He shrugged.

"The girl is here?" repeated Sir Richard.

"Aye."

"If you have hurt her…" began Shea.

"*We* ain't touched her, mate," was the ominous reply.

"Here is what you men will do," said Beckwith. "There are horses here?"

"One old nag in the shed. He took the others. Don't trust us with 'em." The man at the table gave a gap-toothed grin.

"You will take that horse and go on your way," continued

Sir Richard. "Don't come back. Tom, take the pistol and watch them on their way."

"If it's all the same to you, sir, we'll leave the nag," replied the other. "I don't care to have his horse with me when he finds out."

"He'll have our heads," croaked the other man, rubbing his neck where the collar had squeezed it.

"Well, now, Jem, it can't rightly be called our fault if three gentlemen come along with pistols and order us off," answered his colleague. "Still, I don't believe I'll go back to London just yet."

The other shook his head emphatically.

"On your way," said Sir Richard, gesturing with the pistol.

The two men went out and walked together around the cottage to the road. The Beckwiths followed them, then Sir Richard left Thomas with the gun and returned to the house.

Michael Shea was gone from the kitchen. Sir Richard hastily scanned the room, catching up a bunch of keys from a hook, then made his way through the empty front room and to the stairs. Shea was at the top, leaning on a closed door.

"She must be here," he said. "But she doesn't answer me, and it is locked. Help me break it down."

He sounded near the end of his tether. Sir Richard simply held up the keys and bent to try them. In the next instant, he had the door open.

The room thus revealed was dim, and at first they could see no one. Then Shea gave a cry and leapt toward the narrow bed. Bess was curled there, her arms crossed protectively over her chest. When Shea touched her, she cried out. He fell to his knees beside the bed and spoke to her, but she didn't seem to hear. "The devil," he hissed. "I'll kill him. The devil."

Moving closer, Sir Richard could see bruises on Bess's bare arms and on one of her cheeks. They were purple and glaring on her pale skin. He set his jaw and bent over her. "Bess," he said clearly. "Bess, we have come to take you away from here."

"What's wrong with her?" said Shea in a choked voice. "What's he done to her?"

Sir Richard gently explored Bess's injuries. When he touched her head, she muttered and pulled away. "A hard blow to the head," he concluded. "Perhaps when they first took her. And some drug. I think. Laudanum perhaps. Along with ill treatment, it has thrown her into a kind of delirium. We must find a doctor."

"We can't leave her here!"

"No. We shouldn't move her, but under the circumstances..."

"I'll carry her before me," was the fierce reply.

"We should have brought a carriage."

"It would have slowed us too much." Shea slipped his arms under Bess and rose to his feet, holding her tenderly against his chest.

"Shall I help you?" offered Sir Richard.

"No!"

They emerged from the dim room, and Sir Richard saw traces of tears on the redheaded man's cheeks. He turned away and ran lightly down the stairs, leaving Shea to follow more slowly with his burden and recover himself.

He found his brother outside, still watching the road.

"They've gone," said Thomas. "I'm certain they didn't double back."

"They were not paid to fight," replied Sir Richard. "Come, we are going now."

"Bess?"

"Shea has her."

"Is she…all right?"

Sir Richard merely shook his head.

It took a little while to get their group under way again. Bess was settled in front of Michael Shea, her head resting on his shoulder. She occasionally moved it from side to side and muttered incomprehensible phrases, but she had not regained her senses. Shea cradled her as if she were a rare treasure. Sir Richard rode in the rear. It would have been best, he knew, to leave Bess where she was and summon a doctor. But he did not want to risk meeting Fenton. Michael Shea would kill him. And even if he was kept from doing so, still this scandal would break over all their heads. If they left, Fenton could not be positive who had taken Bess. He might be sure in his own mind, but he could not accuse them. The men he had hired would stay out of his way. They weren't the sort to risk identifying their attackers and perhaps getting caught in the middle of the quarrel.

Now they just needed to find some place of safety where Bess could be restored to health and then spirited quietly out of the country with Michael Shea. The more Richard thought about this plan, the better he felt. Bess would not have to work as a servant. He could tell Julia that the girl was married and gone. And Fenton was thwarted without a public sensation. All would be well, if only Bess was all right. This brought back his worry in full force. He spurred his horse forward. "How is she?" he asked Shea.

"The same. We should be looking for a doctor." Shea's face and voice were showing the strain.

"Yes. Unfortunately, I don't know this country well. I suppose we must find a village and an inn."

"There's a carriage coming," called Thomas from up ahead. "It's in the cross lane. I didn't hear it until just now."

"In that cart track?" replied Sir Richard. "It can't be a carriage."

"It is, though. I saw it through a gap in the hedge. A post-chaise."

"Fenton!" hissed Michael Shea. "Where is your pistol?"

"He would scarcely be traveling post," objected Beckwith. But he was considerably annoyed. His hopes of keeping this matter secret were again in jeopardy. There was nowhere for them to hide; the road was bordered by open fields.

"Thomas and I will go ahead," he ordered. "Shea, you hang back. Perhaps we can send them on their way without exposing Bess."

They did this. The post-chaise emerged from the rutted lane with a drunken bounce, and the woman who was leaning out of the window said, "We are *still* lost? You told me you knew the way perfectly well. What are we to do?"

"Julia!" exclaimed Sir Richard.

TWELVE

"Oh, Richard, do you know the way back to the post road?" replied Julia, all grievances momentarily forgotten in her relief at seeing him. "We have been lost for nearly two hours, and I am so tired and dusty. None of the servants…" As she spoke, she gradually took in the group before her, and her voice trailed off.

Sir Richard was stunned by the ill luck of the meeting. Here was another incident he could not explain. He could not tell Julia Devere what had befallen Bess. It was not a story for female ears. Thomas Beckwith was equally frozen.

But one member of the party was not diverted. Michael Shea rode up to the carriage. "We cannot delay," he said as he went. "We must find help for Bess."

Julia gazed at him. She recognized Bess at once as the woman she had seen with Sir Richard, and she could not help but see the livid bruises on her face and arms. "What…?" she began. Then the awkwardness of the situation hit her, along with a belated recollection of her anger. She pulled her head back inside the chaise and wondered what she should do next.

"Go on with Shea," Sir Richard told Thomas. "I will catch up to you. I must speak to Julia."

His brother nodded, staring as if he wanted to ask what in heaven's name he meant to say, and started on. Sir Richard drew in a breath. "Come and walk," he said to Julia.

She shook her head, but he paid no attention. Swinging down from his horse and looping the reins over a handgrip, he opened the chaise door and held out a hand. "A walk will do you good," he added. "Take out some of the stiffness of the journey."

Seeing that she could not refuse without a scene, Julia allowed him to help her down. But she did not take the arm he offered. She merely walked beside him, at a little distance, along the narrow road.

"I am going to say something to you that perhaps I should not," Sir Richard began. "But I had already made up my mind that the proprieties must give way if they keep us apart. For that I will not have."

Julia made a sound, half-protesting, half-surprised.

"No," he said. "Hear me out. We have just taken the girl you know of from a house where Lord Fenton had imprisoned her. His hirelings kidnapped her five days ago. She has been cruelly ill-used. This rescue was made possible by a young man named Michael Shea, whom you just saw. He intends to marry Bess as soon as she is better. If she wishes it, that is. I think she will."

Julia had been gazing fixedly at the ground before her, shocked by what she heard. But now she looked up and met Sir Richard's gray eyes.

"Yes," he assured her. "It is Mr. Shea who cherishes tender feelings for Bess, not I. As I have been trying to tell you for some time."

"But I saw her in your arms!" Julia burst out.

"Impossible."

"I drove by your house. You were standing outside near a hack, and you…she… I saw you." Julia turned away, struggling with her emotions.

Frowning, Sir Richard cast his mind back. He knew he had not embraced Bess in the street, and at first he could not remember what she might have seen. Then, the circumstances came back to him, and he actually smiled a little. "In my arms," he said. "She was, in a manner of speaking. I was trying not to shake her until her teeth rattled. I have never known anyone who could put me in such a flame." He looked down. "Except perhaps one other."

Julia returned his gaze. "Can it be true?" she wondered aloud. But she knew it was. It explained all of the unbelievable contradictions that had plagued her and revealed that her own judgment, and that of those she trusted, was unflawed. The universe settled back into its former order, and Julia was abruptly flooded with joy. She needn't break it off with Richard, she told herself, and live the lonely life she had been forlornly contemplating during the journey. Everything could be as before. She met his eyes again, and smiled.

He pulled her into his arms, as relieved and happy as she, and held her against him for a long blissful moment. Then, consciousness of the watching servants and his unfinished task made him reluctantly draw back. "I must go," he said. "Bess must have help. We are headed toward the post road. You can follow that far."

"And go back to London?" replied Julia. But she said the words as a question to herself; and answered it. "No."

Beckwith looked inquiring.

"I shall go home as I planned, I think. I don't want to return to town now. After all that has happened, the quiet of the country will be welcome. My parents, and you, will be joining me soon." She smiled tenderly up at him.

"You had better write them the news, then," he suggested, with an answering smile.

"News? Oh! You don't suppose they have sent another notice to the papers? I told them to announce that the engagement was dissolved, but…"

"I think your mother meant to wait a while and see."

Julia nodded distractedly. "I'll write at once. Today. And send someone with the letter."

Sir Richard's smile widened. "I take it then that the engagement is *not* dissolved?"

Julia raised her chin at his teasing. "Perhaps it is!"

"Oh, no." He caught her against him again, his eyes fixing hers from very close. "I shan't let you get away from me again."

They were prevented from savoring this moment to the full by the sound of hoofbeats and the reappearance of Thomas further up the road.

"Richard!" he called. "Come quickly. Bess has had some sort of fit. She fell from the horse, and so did Shea. I don't know what to do for them."

Sir Richard ran at once to his mount and swung up. With a hurried, "I will come to you soon" to Julia, he pulled its head around and spurred it into a gallop, following Thomas back the way he had come. Julia stepped up into the chaise. "Follow them," she commanded.

The carriage bumped along the rutted road more slowly than the riders. By the time Julia reached the spot, all three men were kneeling on the ground around Bess, who lay on her back in the dust.

"There's nothing wrong with me," Julia heard Michael Shea declare as she jumped from the post-chaise again. "She startled me is all. She'd been lying so quiet that when she jerked about I lost my hold, and the horse threw us both. I was only stunned for a moment. But Bess. What of Bess?"

Julia joined them in looking down at her. Restless movement had replaced Bess's former limpness. She threw her
head from side to side and muttered. Her hands came up
to her face, then fell, and her whole body twisted in the
grass as if to escape some torment. Her skin was dead white,
and the bruises stood out against it cruelly. Julia, seeing her
much more clearly now, was shocked to the core. Such violence had never before intruded into her protected life, and
she had not imagined it existed.

"We must get her to an inn where she can rest com-
fortably," Sir Richard was saying. "And find a doctor. She is
obviously worse."

"Why didn't we bring a carriage," moaned Shea. "It
might have followed us. She can't be bouncing in front of
me any more."

"Put her in mine," said Julia.

All three men turned to look at her. They had been so
engrossed in their examination of Bess that they had not
noted her arrival. Now, Thomas Beckwith was embarrassed, Sir Richard surprised, and Michael Shea filled with
crazed relief.

"Whoever you are," said the latter, "bless you."

"Julia, I don't think this is wise," said Sir Richard. But his
voice lacked conviction, for he could see no other solution.

"We cannot leave that poor girl lying in the road," replied
Julia, whose attitude toward Bess had undergone a revolution. In her restored happiness, Julia felt a proprietary, pro-
tective interest in Bess.

"Indeed not!" exclaimed Shea, looking from Sir Richard
to Julia wildly.

"Julia Devere," Thomas muttered to him in a strangled

voice. "Richard's fiancée." Thomas was terribly worried that this encounter would be the final blow to his brother's engagement. Though Julia seemed to be taking it well, you never knew with girls, he had found in his rather limited experience. Too, she should not be exposed to such a situation; it was no place for a gently reared young lady. Yet he could see no way around using her carriage either.

"Come along," insisted Julia, turning back to the chaise and opening the door. "Put her in. Betty, move to the front seat."

As her maid obediently shifted and the men carefully lifted Bess from the ground and carried her to the chaise, Julia felt a sudden bubble of happiness expand in her chest. It was wholly inappropriate, unfeeling, but she wanted to laugh, and whirl in a mad circle with her arms outstretched. Her reconciliation with Richard had changed everything, she realized. Even her very real sympathy for Bess and shock at what had happened to her could not pierce this elation. She felt as if nothing could hurt her now.

When Bess was settled in the rear seat of the post-chaise, Julia got in beside her maid. "We'll return to the main highway," said Sir Richard through the window, "and stop at the first inn we see. You can resume your journey then."

Julia nodded, and the group got under way, the three men riding in front and the perplexed post boys bringing up the rear. They went slowly, to avoid shaking Bess up any further; more than once, Julia had to steady her on the seat.

When at last they reached the larger road and paused to confer, Julia caught sight of a sign post and exclaimed, "Why we are less than three miles from my home! And to think we have been wandering in that maze of lanes for hours. I should have recognized the country, but I never ride in this direction."

"Where is the nearest inn?" asked Michael Shea eagerly.

Julia frowned. "There is one at Moreley, but it is really only a tavern. Their rooms cannot be anything but attics. The closest good inn is more than ten miles."

"We will try the other, then," said Sir Richard. "Which way?"

Shea, who had ridden back to gaze worriedly at Bess, grimaced.

"No," answered Julia, her brows drawn together in thought. "It really won't do. She will be stifled there under the eaves. But I can't think of any other..."

"What about your house?" asked Shea. And when the others all stared at him, he met their eyes defiantly.

Julia was the first to recover. "Of course. She must come and stay with me. Dr. Phillips will know what to do for her."

"Out of the question," declared Sir Richard. "I won't permit it."

"There's no alternative, man," insisted Shea.

"There is the inn at Moreley."

"Do you want to kill her, then? Would that suit your purposes?"

Acutely conscious of Julia's maid and coachman, and of the avid post boys, Sir Richard could not reply as he wished to that he would not have Bess in the same house with Julia.

"You are overwrought, sir," said Julia, also thinking of the servants. "But this is clearly the best solution. I am sorry I did not think of it myself. Bess can stay with me until she recovers from her...accident. And then you can find her other quarters."

"God bless you, Miss Devere."

"Julia," began Sir Richard.

But she had turned to look up at the driver. "Do you know where you are now, Edward?"

"Yes, miss," replied the youthful second coachman. "I would have known before, only I thought we was further east."

"Let us go on home then." And Julia drew back inside the chaise before Richard could protest again.

In less than twenty minutes, they were turning in between tall stone pillars and riding down a tree-lined drive to Julia's home. This good-sized building, built of a lovely buff-colored stone, sat in a park through which ran a broad stream. On this warm late afternoon, the scene looked idyllic.

Their arrival set in motion a bustle of activity. Julia gave orders that a room be prepared for Bess, and she was carried upstairs to it and put to bed. A groom rode for Dr. Phillips. Julia's luggage was taken in, and the post boys paid off and dismissed. Through it all, Sir Richard waited for an opportunity to speak to her alone.

Finally it came. "Julia, this is unwise," he told her then.

"What else is to be done with the poor girl?" was the reply. "This inn…"

She shook her head. "It is really no place for a convalescent, Richard. You want her to recover quickly, don't you?"

"Yes! And leave the country with Shea."

Julia smiled. "Well, then?"

"I don't want her here with you."

"It can scarcely harm me to have her."

"But it is not proper," Sir Richard burst out.

Julia gazed at him. "It's odd, but I find that I don't really care. I've obeyed the rules of propriety all my life. Almost religiously, one might say. But it seems there are more important considerations." She gave him her hand.

Richard's heart swelled with love. "Still, we must make sure that the true story does not get out," he replied.

"I see no reason it should. The servants do not know who Bess is, and they will be told that she is an acquaintance from London who suffered a carriage accident on the road. Indeed, they already have been. We can hardly send Bess to a mean little inn after that."

"She may well disabuse them of that fantasy," he replied. "Bess Malone is…outspoken."

"She will have no opportunity. I'll watch over her myself."

"You!"

"Yes, Richard."

"She is not someone you ought to know," he said reflexively. He couldn't visualize Julia and Bess together. It went against every rule he had believed and upheld all his life.

"You know, Richard," said Julia gently, "had we not abandoned the proprieties at least for a little while, we should still be at odds, and the engagement broken off."

Richard hesitated, much struck by this. And before he could marshal further arguments, Thomas knocked and entered the room. "We must be on our way back to London, Richard," he said.

"I'm staying here." He smiled at Julia. "At the infamous Moreley inn."

"You can't." Thomas stepped further into the room. "I've been talking to Shea, and we agree that Lord Fenton isn't going to let this matter drop. He'll have a pretty good idea who got Bess away from him even if those ruffians of his don't talk. You and I must be in town behaving as if we'd never left. Besides, we don't want to lead him *here*."

The last point silenced Sir Richard. He struggled visibly with himself, then replied, "Very well. I'll come in a moment.'"

Thomas nodded. "Good-bye, Miss Devere," he concluded.

"Julia," she said with a smile, and he went out much reassured.

"I don't want to leave you with this all on your shoulders," said Sir Richard when the door closed behind Thomas.

"I'll manage quite well, you'll see. And I have my whole household to protect me."

"Julia."

In the next moment, she was in his arms, everything else forgotten in a kiss that went on and on and yet ended too quickly. The bubble of joy rose in Julia's chest again, and she tightened her arms around her beloved's neck.

"I'll return as soon as I can," promised Sir Richard when they at last drew apart. She nodded. "And I'll speak to your parents myself," he added with a smile.

"Oh! The papers. Yes, do."

"Be careful."

"And you."

Too full of feeling to say more, they walked together to the front steps, where Thomas waited with the horses. Julia watched him mount and waved as he rode off down the drive. As she turned to go inside again, she thought she had never felt happier in her life.

THIRTEEN

JULIA WENT UP TO CHECK ON HER PATIENT.

She found Bess much the same, muttering in a delirium and from time to time thrashing so actively she pulled the sheets from the bed. Julia was trying to calm one of these disturbances when a maid admitted the doctor. "Oh, Dr. Phillips, I'm so glad you're here," said Julia. "She won't keep still, and I'm very worried she may hurt herself even more."

Dr. Phillips, a round graying man with bushy eyebrows and twinkling blue eyes, came forward. "Let's take a look. A fall, the servants tell me?"

"Yes." Julia felt guilty deceiving him. She had known the doctor all her life and was very fond of him. Too, she feared that the half truth might prevent him from curing Bess. But she could not tell even him the real story.

Dr. Phillips had turned down the covers and was making his examination. His face grew more and more grave as he saw the bruises on Bess's pale skin. But he said nothing until he finished by gently fingering her head. Then he turned back to Julia. "A carriage accident?"

She merely nodded.

Dr. Phillips eyed her very seriously, then ran a hand across his chin. "Very well, if that is what you wish to say, I shan't contradict it. But…" He paused and shrugged. "The only serious injury is to the head. It has been struck very hard, and that is why she is in the state she is. Unfortunately, there is little I can do. She should be kept quiet and given barley water and other liquids; I'll leave a list with you. Otherwise, we must simply wait and allow her to recover."

"But she will?" asked Julia.

"I believe so. Head injuries are chancy things. But I have seen people recover from worse ones. Who will be sitting with her?"

"I will."

The doctor, who had been scribbling instructions on a piece of paper, looked up, surprised. "You?"

"Why not? I am very careful."

He frowned as if considering some problem and then replied, "You are here alone? Your parents are not returning from London?"

"Not for a while. But I am scarcely alone, with all the servants here." A girl less intelligent than Julia might have thought his question a non sequitur. But she could see how his mind was working. The odd circumstances of this case had accumulated until he began to worry about her. She wanted to reassure him, but there was nothing she could say.

"Humph," replied the doctor, handing her the notes he had made. "Well, you need only send for me, and I'll come around."

"Thank you." Julia smiled at him, hoping she looked confident and happy. "I'm sure we'll do well. Though you will call again and check on Bess, won't you?"

"Of course. Tomorrow."

"Good." Julia turned and walked with him down the stairs and across the hall to the front door. "I'll follow your instructions exactly."

She watched him climb into his gig and start off down the avenue, then turned back into the hall. At once the door to the parlor on the right opened and Michael Shea strode out, startling Julia considerably. "What did he say?" was

Shea's immediate question. "That *was* the doctor, wasn't it? Is Bess all right?"

Julia merely gazed at him, wondering what he was doing here and how he had remained without her being told.

Shea, reading these thoughts on her face, made a deprecating gesture. "Sorry. I didn't mean to surprise you. But I thought it best to slip in without announcement, so as not to cause talk."

"How did you get in?" asked Julia bluntly.

He grinned. "Your door isn't locked." The grin faded at once. "How is she?"

"About the same. But the doctor says she will recover." Julia was speaking to the concern she saw in his eyes. "You do not return to London?"

"No one will mark it if I'm gone," was the reply, tinged with bitterness. "Lord Fenton wouldn't know me if he stumbled over me. So, since it would do no harm…" He shrugged. "Can I see her?"

"She is just the same. She won't know you."

"Just a look."

Though she was still a bit uneasy about his presence, Julia consented and took him upstairs. Bess lay just as before, and Michael Shea took her hand and gazed down at her with a kind of furious anguish that touched Julia's heart. She slipped out into the corridor, leaving them alone together.

After a few minutes, Michael Shea joined her. "Ah, if only I could call him out," were his first words. "I could take such pleasure in putting a bullet through him. But he wouldn't meet me. He'd send his bullies to horsewhip me, more likely."

"Lord Fenton?" said Julia unnecessarily.

"Aye." They had reached the hall again by this time. "Well, I should be going. I'll call again tomorrow."

"You're staying here?"

"I am. In the inn you so despise." He managed a smile. "I've seen worse."

"But…"

"I'll not leave until Bess is better, so I hope you've no objections." His tone was polite, but adamant.

Julia wondered what he would do if she did object, but she didn't think of doing so. The look on his face in Bess's room prevented that. She felt suddenly akin to him. "You love her very much, don't you?" she asked softly.

"As I love life." Shea's hazel eyes grew distant. "Have you ever come upon your mirror image all at once, so that you're startled out of your wits for a moment, and then you recognize yourself and laugh? Meeting Bess was just like that for me—all in an instant. She's my other self."

Julia stared at him, touched and silenced by this poetic flight. Yet she had felt something similar herself. "I know," she managed finally.

Shea looked down as if he had forgotten she was there, and flushed a little. "Well then, I'll come along tomorrow," he said.

"The doctor will be back in the morning."

"Afternoon, then. I want to hear what he has to say."

Julia nodded, and they said good-bye. She watched, torn between amusement and concern as he slipped off on foot in the gathering darkness. Where had he left his horse? she wondered. And wouldn't some of the servants see him sooner or later? She would have to tell him to abandon secrecy or who knew what sort of wild story would arise.

Sir Richard and his brother reached London again in time for dinner. They had said little on their ride, and they sat down at the table in continuing silence.

"Where is my mother?" Sir Richard asked the butler as the first course was served.

"Lady Beckwith is dining at her aunt's this evening," was the reply.

Thomas made a face. "Poor Mama!"

"She asked me to inform you that she will see you at the Jordans' musical entertainment this evening."

"Thank you, Hodge," said Sir Richard.

"Music," Thomas groaned. "Do we have to go?"

"Yes," answered his brother, throwing him a significant glance.

"Oh. Right." They had to be seen in London, to give Lord Fenton no reason to suspect they had rescued Bess. And if Lady Beckwith was going to the party, all the *ton* would be there, her sons knew.

The two brothers accordingly dressed and went to the Jordans' at the appointed time. Lady Beckwith arrived only a little after them, and at once hurried over. "Where have you been all day?" she asked. "None of the servants seemed to know. What have you been up to?"

"We went riding in the morning, for an hour only," replied Sir Richard meaningfully. "And then took care of some business in the City. And so you should tell anyone who asks you."

Lady Beckwith blinked at his tone. "I should?"

"Yes, Mama."

"Very well." She looked from him to Thomas. "I shall demand an explanation, you know. But not now. Is everything all right?"

Sir Richard nodded. "Far more than that."

She raised her eyebrows, but an acquaintance joined them just then, putting an end to private conversation, and in a few minutes, the music began.

There was one interval in the performance, and the Beckwith brothers rose with alacrity when it came and made their way to the buffet. "Fenton isn't here," said Thomas in a low voice as they procured champagne.

"No," answered his brother. "Perhaps he had some other errand tonight."

"The cottage?"

"No doubt. But we can't talk of it here."

"He has been in town most evenings," persisted Thomas in a near whisper.

"Very late, you may have noticed. And that is precisely why *we* are boring ourselves with this second-rate concert tonight. Now, be silent!" He looked about the room. "Ah, there is Lady Devere. I have been trying to speak to her all evening." Sir Richard swiftly made his way to Lady Devere's side and bent to murmur in her ear. Her expression shifted from concern to surprise to pleasure, and by the time he had finished, she was smiling and nodding emphatically. It was not until just before the end of the interval that Sir Richard moved away from her, and he found that Thomas had been surrounded by a lively group of his friends. He turned toward the door of the refreshment room, and met Lord Fenton coming in.

"Ah, Beckwith," said the latter. "I wondered if I would find you here."

"Indeed?" Sir Richard raised his blond brows in polite surprise.

"I thought you might have gone out of town."

"Really, why?"

"Just a notion of mine. I thought you might be searching for something you had…lost."

Sir Richard feigned mystification. "Lost? I don't understand. Something I lost outside London? I have been in town for the entire Season."

"So you have. An eventful one."

"Every Season has its incidents."

"I refer, of course, to your engagement."

"Ah." Sir Richard did not like the turn this conversation was taking.

"The lovely Miss Devere is not here this evening?"

"No."

"Not ill, I hope?"

"No," said Sir Richard again. He realized that Fenton was twitting him on the awkwardness the stories of Bess should have created between Julia and him. Fenton had no way of knowing that this was now past. However, his thrusts hit home in another way, since Bess was now in Julia's charge. Sir Richard did not want Lord Fenton's attention on Julia. "Very busy with wedding preparations," he added, hoping to discourage the man.

"Ah." Fenton dropped this line. "Did you happen to see Atkinson today? I looked for him at Tattersall's and White's, but he wasn't about."

"I had business in the City," answered Sir Richard.

Fenton nodded distantly, as if he were not really interested. But Sir Richard could see that his eyes were sharp and vicious. He had discovered that Bess was gone, Beckwith concluded, but he wasn't certain how it had happened. His hired ruffians must have indeed fled. This was reassuring.

"Are you a vengeful man, Sir Richard?" was Lord Fenton's next remark. It did not seem to follow, but Sir Richard got the point.

"Vengeful?" He paused. "No, I don't believe I am."

"Really?" Lord Fenton made it sound as if this were rather pedestrian. "It is one of my besetting sins, alas. Vengeance."

"Indeed?" Sir Richard was all courteous lack of interest.

"When someone does me an ill turn, I cannot rest until I have evened the score." His eyes bored into Beckwith's, seeking to cow him.

"That must be wearisome," was his unshaken reply, "to be always totting up points to make certain you are even."

"On the contrary. It can be a positive pleasure."

Sir Richard made a politely disbelieving sound. "The music is beginning," he said. "If you will excuse me?"

"Of course." Fenton nodded as the other walked away. But he watched him with sharp suspicion until he disappeared through the doorway of the refreshment room.

"What did he say to you?" hissed Thomas when Sir Richard took his seat again.

"Only what might be expected."

"He knows?"

"Oh, yes. But only that she is gone. Now be quiet, for God's sake."

Thomas subsided, and Lady Beckwith glanced speculatively at them from his other side. Thomas would tell her the whole story, she knew, so there was no need to chafe.

FOURTEEN

BESS DID NOT RECOVER CONSCIOUSNESS FOR TWO DAYS, and those interested in her welfare found that the time hung heavy. The Beckwiths did not venture out of London, for Sir Richard had discovered on the day following the exchange with Lord Fenton that he was being watched by a rough-looking individual with a broken nose. Thomas was similarly blessed, and though he was eager to try slipping away from his watcher, Sir Richard forbade it as too suspicious. The thing that worried him most was the chance that they might lead Lord Fenton to Julia's house. The very idea made him shudder.

Julia, meanwhile, was concerned mainly about her own nursing skills. She had never nursed anyone before, and she feared she might forget some vital step or not notice a crucial change. Dr. Phillips reassured her on each visit, but when Bess remained unresponsive, she couldn't help but worry. Her fears were nothing to Michael Shea's, however. After the first day, he became convinced that Bess would die, and Julia felt as if she had two patients on her hands as she constantly reminded him of the doctor's optimism and pointed out that Bess was quieter and seemed in less distress.

At last, late in the afternoon on the second day, when Julia was alone in Bess's room reading by her bed, the stricken girl blinked several times, then opened her eyes and looked around. She made no movement, so that Julia did not notice the change and Bess was able to examine her surroundings thoroughly before she said, "Who are you?"

Julia started so violently that she dropped her book. "You're awake!" she cried.

Bess gazed at her in puzzlement, her eyes still slightly out of focus. "Am I?" she responded. "I don't remember..." She tried to raise a hand to her head and seemed surprised to find it hampered by the bedclothes. "I was in that cottage."

"Yes. Sir Richard and his brother got you out. But you were very ill, so they brought you here to rest." Julia recollected something. "Oh, Michael Shea, too." Realizing that she wasn't being clear, she paused to gather her thoughts.

Bess gazed around the room again. "Here?"

"I am Julia Devere," began the other again. "This is my home. You have been here two days. The doctor says you will be all right."

"But who *are* you?" repeated Bess plaintively.

"I am... Sir Richard and I are engaged to be married."

Bess's blue eyes widened in astonishment. "He brought me to you!" She struggled to sit up.

Julia reached out restraining hands. "The doctor says you should stay quiet. It's all right. There's nothing to worry about."

"I'm not worried," was the reply. "I'm..." She looked as if she couldn't find a word.

"It is a bit unusual," admitted Julia. She was rather enjoying the other girl's amazement; it was the first opportunity she'd had to impress someone with her daring.

"What did he tell you about me?" asked Bess.

"Oh, everything," replied Julia cheerfully.

Bess merely gaped.

"He had to, you see. I had broken off the engagement because of all the rumors flying about. And he wanted to explain. Then when I met you four on the road… Well, he just told me."

"No wonder he didn't want me for his fancy lady," said Bess.

Julia flushed at her forthrightness.

"You're not like any young lady I ever saw," she continued. "What are you going to do with me?"

"I? Why, nothing. I mean—"

"Because if you were thinking I'd be a housemaid or any such thing, I won't." Bess was recovering from her initial haziness now.

The thought of Bess as a servant in her house made Julia shiver. "I assure you I have no such intention," she said fervently. "Everyone here thinks you are an acquaintance of mine. I am merely trying to help you recover."

Bess examined the room again. "*You* have been nursing me?"

"Yes. You…talked quite a bit."

Now, Bess flushed. "About…about the cottage?"

Julia nodded, eyes on the floor. Some of the things Bess had muttered had shocked her to the core and filled her with outraged compassion.

"What happened to *him*?" asked Bess fiercely.

"L-Lord Fenton?" Julia stumbled over the name. "Nothing."

"They didn't kill him? Oh, if only I'd been awake."

"He wasn't there."

"What?"

"You must ask Mr. Shea for the story. He will be here to see you very soon. He always calls about this time." Julia smiled, thinking this would certainly cheer Bess.

"Michael Shea? What's he doing here?"

"Worrying over you. He could not go back to London under the circumstances."

Bess looked mystified.

"Your engagement," added Julia teasingly. "You cannot have forgotten that."

The other girl's mouth dropped open. "My engagement?"

"You and Mr. Shea. He said you were to be married and go abroad." Julia faltered under her blank stare.

"Married," repeated Bess, managing to get a hand to her head this time.

"They both told me so," replied Julia.

"Both?"

"Sir Richard and Mr. Shea."

"Well, they're both daft, then. Michael Shea never asked me, and I surely never took him."

The two girls stared at each other. At that moment, there was a discreet knock on the door, and it opened to reveal Michael Shea under the escort of a housemaid. "Mr. Shea," said the latter with a bob of a curtsy, and she shut the door behind him.

"Bess!" exclaimed Michael. "You're awake!" He would have rushed forward, but two accusing stares stopped him by the door. "Eh?"

"I've just been hearing about my wedding plans from Miss…er…"

"Devere," supplied Julia. "Indeed, Mr. Shea, I have been quite embarrassed. I had understood from you that—"

"Ah," interrupted Shea. "I see how it is." He moved further into the room. "The thing is, Bess, I hadn't the chance to—"

"I don't recollect giving you leave to use my name," retorted Bess.

Shea looked from one to the other. "I'm rightly in the soup now, aren't I? But how was I to know it'd be mentioned before I had a chance to speak?"

"You might have *known* when you told everyone in the place. I heard you tell the housekeeper yesterday," replied Julia.

"Well, she was chafing, you see. About me spending so much time up here practically alone with you, Miss Julia. So I had to tell her it was Bess—"

"She is *Miss* Julia, but I am Bess, I see," broke in Bess. She turned her head away. "Miss Devere, I am worn to the bone."

"Of course." Julia rose at once. "We should not have kept you talking this way so soon. Come, Mr. Shea."

"Aw, but look, Bess—Miss Bess."

"I really can't talk any more now," came the faint reply.

"Come along," repeated Julia, taking Shea's arm and guiding him out of the room. "The doctor says she must rest."

"Oh, Miss Devere?" came a thready voice.

"Yes?"

A hand from the bed gestured toward the door, and Julia shut it. Immediately, two bright blue eyes appeared over the covers. "I'm fair starving," said Bess in a perfectly normal tone. "Can I have something to eat?"

Julia smiled. "Certainly. I'll have a tray sent right up."

"But you won't tell Michael."

Julia laughed a little. "By no means."

"Good." The eyes disappeared again, and Julia composed her face and joined Mr. Shea in the corridor.

"She's all right, isn't she?" he asked anxiously.

"Rather shaken," was the solemn reply.

"Ah, I've made a mull of this, that's certain."

"Why did you tell us you were to be married when you hadn't even asked her?" wondered Julia.

"I had to convince Sir Richard. I knew he'd like the idea. And then, I don't know, it just kept slipping out. I thought she cared for me, I swear."

Julia took pity on him. "Perhaps she does."

"She said something to you?" His expression was eager.

"No."

His face fell.

"But you must have had some reason for supposing she would accept you."

"She's angry," he answered doubtfully.

"Of course she is. Any woman would be. But it may pass."

"You think so?"

"Quarrels are made up every day, Mr. Shea." Julia smiled, thinking of her own case and deciding she would help him. "But you must give it time. Call again tomorrow, and beg pardon."

"Yes. Yes, I will. Perhaps I'll ride up to London and buy her something. A bracelet, perhaps?"

"Hardly suitable," replied Julia, enjoying herself.

"No. I'll have to think. She has flowers. Fruit?"

"We have ample supplies from my father's succession houses." Julia did not see why this should be made easy for him.

"Ah. Well, I'll look about. Tomorrow at two?"

She nodded, and Mr. Shea took his leave with some haste. Julia was smiling as she went downstairs to give orders that a tray be sent to Bess and a message be carried to

Sir Richard in town. She had sent a bulletin that morning, but developments called for another.

When the food was ready, Julia went upstairs with the maid and sat down beside the bed again. At first, Bess concentrated on the meal, but after a while she sighed and sat back a little. "That was fine," she declared.

"And no wonder. You have had little but barley water and broth for two days."

"Four," said Bess curtly. "Is Michael Shea gone?"

"Yes. But he returns tomorrow at two. With abject apologies. And a gift, I believe, if he can find something grand enough."

Bess dimpled. "I deserve them."

"Undoubtedly. Do you like him?"

"Oh, yes. But I hadn't thought of marrying." Some of her indignation came back. "He never even mentioned it!"

"Outrageous."

"I don't know one thing about him, only that he has an aunt who is…a fine woman. I like her." Bess's tone had grown less strident.

"That's something," said Julia.

"I *do* like him. But why must men be such great dolts?"

Julia shook her head.

"To have him saying I'd marry him, without even asking, after…everything. I couldn't stand it."

She was thinking of Lord Fenton, Julia realized, and cringed.

"But it's *not* the same," Julia protested aloud, unable to stop herself.

"I know," agreed Bess. "It's just that after that…"

Julia nodded soberly.

FIFTEEN

MICHAEL SHEA VERY MUCH ENJOYED HIS EXPEDITION TO London the following day. He rose early and dressed in his best town clothes. During the ride, he imagined all the things he might buy for Bess, and on arrival he went directly to Bond Street, wandering among the best shops without trying to make a choice for some time. He envisioned Bess in a celestial blue satin gown lavishly trimmed with lace displayed in the windows of London's most exclusive modiste. He saw her in a series of fascinating hats, from a chip straw to a high poke covered with feathers. He most enjoyed the jeweler's, where he spent a good twenty minutes poring over diamonds and sapphires, having made up his own mind that these were the only jewels for Bess.

But he reluctantly left all these things behind, certain that Miss Devere, at least, would consider them unsuitable gifts. And as things stood, Shea wryly told himself, Bess would side with Julia Devere even if she wanted the things with all her heart.

Having come back down to earth, he found himself in difficulties. What could he buy, he began to wonder, that would satisfy both the proprieties and himself. He refused the paltry blandishments of flowers or sweets. After sapphires, they looked pallid. He examined the latest three-volume novels, but found the idea unromantic. As the morning wore on, he became concerned that he would find nothing, and the search grew more serious.

At last, a small, discreet display caught his eye, and he halted before a shop near the end of the street and eyed it. It might just do, he decided. Miss Devere might frown a little, but she would not absolutely veto his choice. With a quick nod, he strode into the shop.

When he emerged ten minutes later, Michael Shea was smiling. He walked back up Bond Street with a long package under his arm and total disinterest, now, in the offered wares. His one thought was to return to the country and give his gift. Thus, he did not notice Thomas Beckwith's start of recognition and wave from the other side of the pavement. It was not until the younger man actually touched his arm that he saw him and stopped, saying, "Hello, there," in a jaunty tone.

"What are you doing in town?" was Beckwith's terse reply. "Is something wrong?"

"Nothing at all. I came up to buy Bess a little something." He indicated his package.

"We agreed that we would not call attention to ourselves," replied Thomas. "That is why Richard and I have been kicking up our heels in town these past days."

"No one knows me," Shea pointed out with a tinge of bitterness. "I can go where I like if you and your brother take *care*."

The last was a reproach, and Thomas belatedly realized that he should not have stopped Shea so pointedly. He looked around for his constant companion, a small ferret-like man who seemed to imagine that his furtive slipping along the shopfronts was unobtrusive. He spotted him at some distance, peering at a display of riding gear. To Thomas's relief, he didn't seem to be paying any particular attention. "You're right," he admitted. "I was just surprised to see you. Is everything all right in the country?"

"As far as you're concerned, yes."

"What do you mean?"

"Bess is a mite put out with *me*."

Thomas Beckwith grinned. "Is she? No wonder you're shopping. I hope you've got something splendid."

Shea looked as if he were unsure whether to be offended, then finally grinned also. "I do."

"Good. I'll leave you, then. I don't think our encounter was noticed. Richard and I are still hemmed up here in London. Fenton has not given up his suspicions."

"The man's not stupid," replied Shea, his jaw hardening.

"By no means. We will come when we can. Tell Julia that Richard waits for her messages with some...eagerness." He grinned again.

"I will that. Good day."

Thomas nodded, and they parted, Shea striding along toward his livery stable and Beckwith continuing to his club. Neither looked back to see Lord Fenton emerge from a doorway quite near where they had been standing and stare intently after Shea. Nor did they see him walk quickly to a closed carriage waiting in the street and give orders to the driver before getting in. But the carriage began to move slowly down the crowded avenue in the wake of Michael Shea, and it paused as he entered the livery to retrieve his horse.

Shea was in a fine mood as he made his way back to the Deveres' country house. He balanced his package before him in the saddle and imagined to himself Bess opening it and discovering what he had bought. That would bring her around, he thought, though he intended to be lavishly apologetic as well. He had no real doubts that she would eventually listen to his suit. In the time they had spent together

in town, he had become convinced that she liked him as
well as he did her. He was so taken up with pleasant fan-
tasies that he did not pay any heed to the carriage behind
him even when the busy streets of London were left behind
and it was the only vehicle visible. It was not unusual for
travelers to take the road he followed, and thus no alarms
were set off in his mind. He might have been more wary had
he not come to think of himself as invisible, but too many
evenings passed in the gaming clubs had sealed this impression. The young scions of the *haut ton* were recognized and
deferred to everywhere, while no footman or serving maid
could so much as remember his name. This had caused him
some bitterness at the time, but lately he had been glad for
his anonymity, and perhaps lulled by it.

The journey passed quickly in pleasant visions, and
Shea reached his inn just after noon. After his early start,
his hunger was sharp, and he merely tossed his reins to the
ostler and went into the tap room in search of ale and suste-
nance, never looking back to see the carriage slow and halt
some distance off. Fenton leaned out the opposite window,
where he could not be seen from the building, and gave his
driver further orders. The man accordingly climbed down
and made his way to the inn, falling into conversation with
the same ostler.

"Name of Shea," was the driver's laconic remark when he
returned. "Been here a matter of four days. Rides off to the
big house every afternoon."

"The big house?" asked Lord Fenton sharply.

The man pointed. "A few miles further on. Belongs to a
family called Devere. Local nobs."

Lord Fenton's V-shaped brows drew together. "It can't be!"

"That's the name the hayseed told me, y'r lordship. Devere."

"He would not take her there," said Fenton to himself. "Impossible!"

The driver waited, recognizing now that his information was not being disputed.

"Drive to the house," ordered Fenton.

The other climbed back onto the box and got the vehicle moving again. They bowled past the inn at a spanking pace, and Michael Shea did look up from his luncheon. But he saw only a closed carriage like a hundred others and simply returned to his bread and cheese.

When they neared the Devere house, Lord Fenton rapped on the ceiling to bring the coach to a halt. "Go to the stables to ask the way," he told his driver when they had stopped. "And while you are there, bring the conversation around to the visitor in the house. Tell them you have heard she is a red-haired beauty, or some such thing. You will know how to go about it. I want to know when the girl arrived and what her position here is."

"Girl, is it?" answered the driver, securing the reins.

"Yes." Lord Fenton's eyes narrowed in his seamed face. "Can she actually be here? But where else? There is no trace." He turned to the other. "You'll know what to say."

"Aye," was the stolid reply, and the driver trudged along the road and in at the gate.

Lord Fenton waited, keeping well back in the carriage so as not to be seen.

"Black hair, not red," said the man when he returned. "And she's a friend of the daughter of the house, according to the grooms. Been ill, but getting better. Went out for a drive this morning to take the air. A likely looking lass, they say."

"I can't believe it," muttered Lord Fenton to himself. "What effrontery, to bring her here!"

The driver eyed him, then shrugged and spat in the dust beside the road.

"Back to London," declared Fenton then. "At once. I must think."

The man removed his hands from his pockets and remounted the box. He turned the horses with some difficulty in the narrow lane, but after that they made the journey back to town with good speed. By the time Michael Shea set out to call on Bess at two, Lord Fenton was nearly home again, and had already made his plans.

Shea was smiling as he dismounted before the Devere house and walked up the steps to the front door. His natural optimism had convinced him that Bess would have come around by now, and the long package he held increased his conviction. Too, it was a balmy, summerlike day, with hawthorn blooming in the hedges and primroses in the fields. It was hard to believe that anything could go wrong on such a day.

He was told that the young ladies were sitting in the garden, and was escorted along the front hall to a room at the back of the house, which had French doors opening onto a stone terrace. Here, two steps led down into a shrubbery, and on the other side was a rose garden. A table and chairs had been carried outside, and Bess and Julia sat in the sun reading. Shea paused a moment to enjoy the scene before interrupting them.

The roses were not yet in bloom, though some had fat buds that showed promise of red and pink and white. The bushes shone a glossy green, separated by neat gravel paths and encircled by a stone balustrade. In the foreground stood a wicker table and chairs with bright chintz cushions. Julia wore floating white and Bess a borrowed gown of pale blue stripe. They sat in the shade of a broad oak, with only the sweep of their skirts in the direct sunlight. The picture they presented made Michael Shea let out his breath in a sigh.

Bess's sharp ears caught this, and she turned at once. "Oh," she said, "it's you."

"'Tis," he admitted, coming forward. And before she could speak again, "I've brought you something." He presented the box.

Bess was temporarily silenced. She looked at the package, then at him, and finally at Julia, who smiled a little at the open mix of curiosity, desire, and wariness on Bess's face.

"Open it," added Michael Shea, pressing his advantage.

Bess couldn't resist. She untied the string and removed the lid. "Oh," she said as she pushed back layers of tissue to expose the contents. Slowly, she took out an exquisite sunshade of pale blue. The long slender handle was ivory trimmed with silver, and it was decorated with two blue tassels that swung delicately in the warm breeze. "Oh," said Bess again. She unfurled it, and raised it over her head, even though they sat in the shade. Smiling, she stood and stepped from beneath the tree's broad shadow, twirling the parasol above her head. It was precisely the color of her eyes, and she made a lovely picture against the background of rose buds and dark leaves.

"It's lovely," said Bess, coming back to her chair but leaving the sunshade up. "No one ever gave me anything so pretty."

"It is beautiful," agreed Julia.

"Thank you," added Bess, her voice soft. She gazed up at the sunshade again.

"You should have beautiful things," replied Shea quite sincerely. "You're meant for them."

Bess surveyed him. "You aren't thinking this is quits between us, I hope? I'm still angry."

Because the only reply that occurred to Mr. Shea was, "Of course you are," accompanied by a fatuous smile, he said nothing.

"You aren't thinking you've bought me off, are you now?"

"No!" He met her eyes. "Well, only a bit. Just taking the edge off, as you might say."

Bess burst out laughing, and Julia had to join her. The sheepish roguishness of Mr. Shea was irresistible. His answering grin, with its hopeful encouragement of their reaction, only made them laugh harder.

It was a little while before this merriment subsided. Then Bess said, "I suppose you think I'll marry you now?"

"Nothing of the sort," was his immediate response.

"I don't know one thing about you."

"You know my aunt," countered Mr. Shea. "And a fine woman she is."

Bess admitted it. "She doesn't think much of you. I've heard her give you the edge of her tongue more than once."

"Ah, that's just Aunt Dora's way. You don't suppose she meant it?"

Bess didn't suppose so. Indeed, she knew that despite Dora Hanlon's scolds, she was very fond of her nephew. She shifted her ground. "You can't expect me to marry a man when I don't even know his work. Are you a clerk?" She said it with unconscious disdain.

"What do you think?" was his offended reply.

"I think that's no answer at all."

"Shall I go?" offered Julia, thinking her presence might be preventing confidences. "I want to get some flowers for the house."

"No, no," said Shea. "I'm willing you should hear." He looked Bess in the eye. "I live by my wits," he told her. "At cards." There was defiance as well as pride in his voice.

"A gamester?" wondered the girl.

"No. I don't touch the dice or that newfangled wheel. I play cards, and I'm good enough so that gentlemen with money stake it to see if they can beat me." He looked a bit smug. "They can't. But nothing will convince them except trying. I've made a tidy bit of money, too."

"You mean, that's all you do? Play cards?" Bess seemed amazed, and Julia eyed her with concern, wondering if this revelation had shocked her. Julia herself was taken aback.

"I've plans," continued Shea. "I mean to go to France or Italy now the war's over and set up a small club. Everything of the best. Then, when I've learned the business, as you might say, perhaps I'll return to London."

"You make a lot of money?" wondered Bess.

He smiled. "I've begun to. It took some time to get in the better clubs. Not White's and such, you understand, but the gaming clubs. I'm beginning to be known, and I'm invited for a game now and then. But having my own house would be a different matter."

"Yes," said Bess eagerly. "I see that. And you take their money just by winning at cards?" She couldn't seem to get over this.

"There's no *just* about it," protested Shea.

"You're very good."

"I am that." He smiled, and Bess responded. "Would you care to stroll about the garden?" he asked. "If you'll excuse us, Miss Julia?"

Julia nodded, and Bess stood at once. Her anger seemed forgotten in her fascination with Shea's history.

Julia watched them walk along the gravel paths in animated conversation, under Bess's new sunshade, with mixed feelings. On the one hand, she was glad they were becoming reconciled. In her own newfound happiness, she wished everyone to be happy. She also felt a brief pang, for seeing them together reminded her of how she missed Richard. But she was also troubled by doubt. Was it really wise of Bess to consider marrying a man who planned to run a gaming hell? she asked herself. This was scarcely the kind of life one would recommend to anyone. And yet Bess had not been shocked, and Julia again reminded herself of their vast differences. It was possible to forget them briefly, but they did not go away. With a wry smile, Julia also admitted that she would prefer to see Bess go abroad. Though she now knew, and believed, that there had been nothing between her and Sir Richard, still her departure would be a relief, if only from the possibility of future scandal.

Julia picked up her book again with a sigh. It would be very good to have this matter settled, she thought, and to return to normal. She had a wedding to plan, and a future spreading out afterward that deserved all her attention just now. With a secret smile, Julia lost herself in pleasant daydreams.

Bess and Michael Shea talked until the lengthening shadows brought the servants out to fetch the chairs and table. "Come inside," called Julia then. "It is growing cool, and you haven't any shawl, Bess." The other two strolled over to join her. "We can sit in the back parlor near the terrace," she added.

"That's all right, Mr. Shea is just going," replied Bess, and Michael Shea looked down at her in surprise.

"Is he?" said Julia.

Bess nodded, closing her parasol with a snap. "He'll call again tomorrow afternoon."

Julia battled a smile. "Not morning?"

"Oh, no. Likely he has things to do in the morning."

They had reached the terrace by this time, and they entered the house through the French doors. "Well, er, good-bye, then," said Shea.

"Good-bye," responded Bess brightly. Julia bit her lower lip to stop it quivering. When she too had bid him farewell, Shea bowed and went out. Bess waited until they heard the front door open and shut before going off in peals of laughter, and Julia couldn't help but join in. They laughed so hard tears filled their eyes, and it took a little while for the spasm to subside. "I'll forgive him, all right," said Bess then. "But I didn't want to let on yet."

Julia nodded, dabbing her eyes with her handkerchief. "And will you marry him?"

Bess considered, cocking her head to one side. "I might. But don't tell him I said so."

"Of course not!" replied Julia, shocked by the suggestion.

SIXTEEN

As they rode in the park the following morning, Thomas Beckwith said to his brother, "You know, Richard, I believe my shadow is gone. I've not seen him today, nor anyone else who looks as if he's watching me."

Sir Richard nodded. "I think perhaps Fenton has given up. What he thought we would do while his hirelings dogged our footsteps, I cannot imagine."

"Well, he has apparently concluded we are not so stupid."

"Or found more efficient spies." Sir Richard looked around the park. He did not want to accept the latter possibility, for that would mean he must remain in London and keep up the pretense of his normal routine when he wished only to go to Julia. These last few days in town had been intolerable. But it really did seem that their watchers were gone. And after all, he reasoned, Lord Fenton must at some point conclude that they would not lead him to Bess. "I shall ride out tomorrow morning," he said aloud, "if there is no further sign of them."

"I'll come with you," responded Thomas. "I'd like to see how Bess is getting on."

"Bess? Or Michael Shea?"

His brother grinned. "Well, Richard, you have to admit it is amusing. When we received the message—"

"You made your feelings very clear," put in Sir Richard dryly. "And if you are going just to mock the man…"

"No. I want to see, er, whether Bess has come around yet."

Sir Richard made a noncommittal sound, but in fact, he

was also interested in this question. Bess's marriage to Shea had seemed a providential solution, and when he had heard from Julia how matters actually stood between the two, his heart sank.

"You won't leave me behind?" protested Thomas.

"No. You may come. But you are not to meddle and make things worse."

"I?"

Sir Richard snorted.

In the country, Bess and Julia had established themselves outside once again, reveling in the stretch of flawless weather. They read and sewed and talked, and since Bess had by now regained her normal health, walked about the park for exercise. When Michael Shea called that afternoon, Bess seemed so happy to see him that Julia left them alone and set off for a brisk walk along a path she often took. It led through a narrow gate in the estate walls and across the fields to the pond. One part of its banks, overhung by a massive willow, had long been a favorite spot of Julia's.

As she went, she kept her eyes down, enjoying the wild flowers that speckled the grass on either side of the path. And she thought about Bess. She would accept Michael Shea, Julia thought. The signs were clear. It was a happy conclusion to the whole muddle. They might even be married before the date set for her own wedding and safely settled abroad. This naturally led her thoughts to Sir Richard, and Julia spent a pleasant half hour sitting on the mossy bank, gazing down into the rippling water and thinking of him.

The sun was well down in the sky when she started home again, and she hurried, for she had stayed longer than she meant. Bess would have gone up to her room by this time, to rest before changing for dinner. She wanted to be home well before she came down.

As she came up to the wicket gate that led into the park, Julia was focused on getting home, and not paying much heed to her surroundings. She did not notice the sudden crack of a dry branch or a rustling in the bushes to her left. Only when her arms were roughly gripped from both sides and jerked behind her did she see the intruders, and before she could cry out, a cloth dripping with chloroform was pressed down over her face. Julia struggled briefly, but the fumes choked her and thrust her rapidly down into unconsciousness.

And thus, instead of a leisurely ride into the country the following morning, Sir Richard and Thomas Beckwith set off at a gallop at first light in response to a frantic message from Bess.

It was a grim journey. Thomas was afraid to speak to his brother, and the latter was using all his energy to control a tempest of emotion. Foremost was fear. It was because of him that Bess was in Julia's house; he should never have left her there. His imagination conjured an endless series of horrors that might have befallen his betrothed. Bess's note had been barely coherent, so he had no idea what had actually occurred. But Lord Fenton must be involved, he knew, and whenever he thought of the man, Sir Richard was swept by a killing rage such as he had never experienced before in his life. It shook him to know that he could take pleasure in choking the life out of a fellow human being with his own hands.

"There's the house," ventured Thomas, and they spurred their mounts yet again and thundered through the open gates and down the drive toward the front door. The place looked remarkably peaceful in the early morning light. Only a wisp of smoke from one of the chimneys showed that it was inhabited.

But as soon as they drew rein before the steps, the front door burst open and Bess ran out. "Thank God you're here!" she cried, and burst into tears.

Thomas leapt down and took the horses. Sir Richard gathered Bess and led her into the parlor nearest the door. For a minute, she could only cry, and he waited with mounting impatience for her to regain control.

"I'm sorry," she gasped finally. "I didn't mean to. But I was so glad…"

"Tell me precisely what happened," interrupted Sir Richard.

"I don't *know*! Except that Julia is gone."

He clenched his jaw and his fists.

"When? And how?"

Bess was taking deep breaths. "She didn't come to dinner last night," she said more calmly. "And when I went to find her, she wasn't in the house. She went for a walk. Something must have happened then."

"Something," echoed Sir Richard. "I presume you searched?"

"Oh, yes. The servants all went out. And Michael. But it was almost dark. They're looking again this morning." She twisted her hands in her lap. "I didn't know what to say."

"I'll deal with that," he said curtly. "Was anyone seen? Lurking about the place?"

She shook her head, biting her lower lip. "You…you think it's *him*?"

"What else? If Julia had had an accident, she would have been found by this time."

"But he wouldn't take Julia! Has he gone daft?"

Sir Richard shrugged and stood. "I must speak to the searchers."

Julia awoke in a moving carriage. The air was heavy and stuffy, and her head ached with a fierce intensity that made her close her eyes again at once. Her hands were bound behind her, and though the binding was not painful, it was efficient, as she found when she twisted her wrists without effect. She felt sick, and the bouncing of the carriage over a very bad road did not help. But the worst was that she did not know what had happened. In her half-conscious, drugged state, she couldn't remember what had befallen her; she could not think clearly.

She moved to brace herself better against the jolting and rest her pounding head on the upholstery. Then, she simply endured as the seemingly endless ride went on.

She must have either slept or lost consciousness again, for she woke with a start when the carriage pulled up. Her headache had not abated, and when she struggled to sit up, it made her dizzy. But she was determined to face her captors and hide her fear.

The door farthest from her opened, and lantern light streamed into the dim interior of the vehicle. It revealed a fashionably clad arm and, behind it, a face she recognized. "Lord Fenton!" cried Julia.

There was an instant of frozen astonishment, then the door slammed shut again.

"Idiot!" Julia heard Fenton's voice exclaim. "You have brought the wrong girl."

"What?" replied a rougher male voice.

"This is not the girl, you fool. This is a young lady."

"You told me a beauty, black hair. You said the minute she sticks her nose out the house, snatch her. How was I to know there was two of 'em, guv'nor? I did like I was ordered."

The door of the carriage opened again, more slowly, and Julia and Lord Fenton gazed at one another.

"You meant to take Bess," said Julia.

"Obviously."

"I demand you send me home at once," continued Julia, fighting headache and nausea.

"I should much prefer to do so, but it is impossible."

"Why?"

"Sir Richard Beckwith is, I understand, a superb shot. I have no wish to test his skill."

Julia's fear intensified. Though she tried not to think about it, memories of Bess when she had first arrived at the house kept surfacing. This man was terrible, she knew. "I won't tell anyone," she offered.

"Beckwith is also quite intelligent. I'm sure he has worked it out for himself by this time. Yet as long as you are missing, he has no proof. I must think." He shut the door again. Julia heard him speak to his companion, then the sound of retreating footsteps. She strained her ears, but heard nothing more. Moving awkwardly because of her bound arms, she checked both doors. There were no handles inside; she could not get out. She sank back on the seat and tried to penetrate the haze of pain and anesthesia to think what to do.

After perhaps half an hour, footsteps returned and the door opened yet again. This time, two unknown men took Julia from the vehicle and marched her across a dark courtyard to a good-sized house. She was escorted up two flights of stairs and left in a maid's room at the top of the building, where the windows under the eaves were far too small to allow escape. The room contained a shabby iron bedstead and poorer washstand. A scrap of dun carpet sat in the center of a dusty wood floor.

The men pushed her down on the bed and turned to go. "Won't you untie my hands?" exclaimed Julia.

They looked at each other. One shrugged, and the other returned to cut the ropes about her wrists. Julia pulled her hands in front of her and rubbed them as the men went out. She heard the key turn in the lock before their footsteps retreated along the hallway outside.

———————————

Sir Richard stood before a window of the Devere house staring blindly out at the idyllic country afternoon. The servants were still out searching for Julia, but he had satisfied himself by this time that they would not find her. Fenton had her, he was sure, and he was struggling with a desire to smash something or someone. Lord Fenton was, naturally, the preferred target, but in his present mood, almost anyone would do, and he fought to subdue his rage so that he could take some useful action instead.

The door opened and Michael Shea, Bess, and Thomas came in. Sir Richard turned at once, his gray eyes intent.

"I can find no sign," said Shea immediately. "I searched all night, and when people began to stir I inquired along all the roads leading from here. No one noticed a carriage or group of riders. It's as if she disappeared into thin air."

Beckwith clenched his fists and turned his back on them. The others exchanged worried glances.

"I'll keep trying," added Shea.

"And alert the world that she is gone," snapped Sir Richard, his voice throbbing with suppressed rage.

"I'm discreet," protested the other. "I tell them I'm searching for my brother."

"How did he find her, that's what I want to know. We were so careful not to come near." He jammed one fist into the other hand. The fact that he had not seen Julia in several days made things even worse.

Michael Shea and Thomas Beckwith looked at each other over Bess's head, then quickly looked away.

"There must be something more we can do," said Bess. "Someone must have seen a carriage, or heard it at least. We must keep trying."

"Of course," replied Sir Richard. "But this is not a populous neighborhood. He may have slipped away without attracting attention." His hands clenched again. "I shall get it out of Fenton, however." His mouth was a hard line.

"The scandal," said Thomas involuntarily.

His brother turned on him. "Do you think I care for that? When that devil has Julia!"

"No, no, of course not," muttered Thomas, wishing he hadn't spoken.

"Will you fight him?" asked Bess unhappily. Her burden of guilt seemed to grow heavier and heavier.

"I will use whatever means necessary to make him tell me where she is," was the answer. He picked up his hat from the sofa. "Thomas and Shea, remain here and continue to search. Something may yet come up."

"You're going back to London?" asked Thomas.

"Yes."

"Shouldn't I come with you?" Thomas felt that nothing disastrous could happen if he could keep his brother under his eye.

"I should prefer you to remain."

Thomas conceded to his implacable tone.

"You will, of course, send a message if you discover anything," added Sir Richard as he turned to go. "I will summon you if I need you."

When he was gone, the three looked at one another.

"We won't find anything," said Michael Shea. "I've spoken to all the people hereabouts."

"Julia might get away and come back," offered Bess.

The men greeted this hope with silence.

"This is all my fault!" she burst out then. "I should have left as soon as I was able. But I never thought—"

"No one did," interrupted Shea. "Don't be blaming yourself, Bess. It's Fenton who's to blame."

"But if I hadn't been here…"

"It doesn't help to think of that," said Thomas, meeting Michael Shea's eyes steadily. "We have to do something. Bess, perhaps you could see if anyone is in the kitchen now and order us some luncheon."

"How can you think of eating?" she protested.

"Please."

Bess sighed and went out. The two men looked at one another a moment longer.

"He must have seen me talking to you," said Shea then.

Thomas nodded. "He was having me watched as well as Richard. I suppose you were marked and followed."

"I saw no one. And I would have sworn that none knew me in London. Or at least none knew me as more than a face seen in a gaming club."

"Apparently, you were wrong."

They were silent again.

"I didn't have the courage to tell him," said Shea then. "The look in his eyes... I sheered off."

"Well, so did I," replied Thomas irritably. "And he's my brother. But we must make amends."

"How?"

"*I* don't know!"

"There's no need to rasp at me, I'm with you. I just don't see what to do."

The latch clicked, and Bess returned. "They're taking cold meat and fruit to the dining room," she informed them, "though how you can even think of food I don't understand. We must make a plan."

The two men looked at her.

"Have you no ideas?"

"We don't know where to begin searching," replied Shea. "He could have taken her anywhere in England."

Bess's face fell, then brightened. "Sir Richard will force him to tell," she said.

"And ruin himself," added Thomas heavily.

"What do you mean?"

"If he calls Fenton out, or even just confronts him in his house, the story will leak out. Such things always do. Fenton might well spread it himself. He's done it before. And then Julia will be ruined. If it becomes known that Fenton kidnapped her…" He grimaced.

"Good riddance to anyone who thinks so," said Bess fiercely.

"You may feel that, but Julia does not. Nor does Richard. They're accustomed to respect and admiration."

Bess bit her lower lip, staring at the floor.

"We'll think of something," put in Michael Shea heartily.

"*I* should make amends," answered Bess. "It is my fault she is gone."

"We needn't have brought you here," Thomas pointed out.

"Indeed," added Shea. "Don't you be getting any daft ideas, Bess Malone. You stay out of this. We'll get her back. Never fear."

Bess gazed up at him as if to protest. But seeing the fierce protectiveness of his expression, she did not speak.

SEVENTEEN

Julia was left alone long enough to explore her prison thoroughly and discover that possibilities for escape were limited to the door. Unfortunately, its lock seemed quite sturdy, and after fruitlessly trying to probe it with a hairpin, she returned to the bed and sat down to wait. As her headache and sickness faded, the fact that she had had no dinner or breakfast intruded insistently, but she ignored the pangs and bent her mind instead to her current dilemma.

This was frightening. As long as she had concentrated on details, she had been steady enough. But when she sat still and tried to think, she was terrified. She was at the mercy of the man who had so dreadfully mistreated Bess Malone, and none of her friends knew where she was. Julia began to shudder. She wrapped her arms around herself and breathed deeply, trying to control her fear, but it was of little use. She was trapped and unlikely to see her home or the man she loved again.

It was at this moment that footsteps approached along the corridor. Julia sprang to her feet and faced the door, pushing her nails painfully into her palms in an effort to control her trembling.

The door opened, and Lord Fenton stood there once more. He had changed his coat, Julia saw, for a garment more suited to the country. This brought outrage to her rescue and lessened her fear. She stood straighter. "Do you intend to starve me?" she asked before he could speak.

Fenton raised his eyebrows. He was not accustomed to

such tones in these circumstances, nor to women who faced him with haughty contempt. Tears or violence he had dealt with; this was new, and thus intriguing. "No," he answered. "You will be brought food." He stepped further into the room, closing the door behind him, and some of Julia's confidence evaporated. "First, there are things we must discuss."

Involuntarily, she moved back until the iron bedstead stood between them. She did not want to let him see her fear, but she could not bear to be near him.

"Our situation need not be awkward," he added in what he must have imagined were persuasive tones. "It is not what I planned, but it could be quite pleasant." Fenton gazed caressingly at the girl. Downstairs, as he had adjusted to the fact that a mistake had been made, Julia's loveliness had lingered in his mind and begun to work on him. Though he would not have kidnapped a girl of birth and breeding purposely, having her here under his sway excited him, and the limits society had set on his desires began to erode.

He smiled, and Julia shuddered. His ravaged, dissolute face was the antithesis of everything she admired, as was his character of all she respected.

"I offer you a great deal," he went on. "I am a man of wide...experience. I could show you pleasures you have not imagined." The tip of his tongue showed between his lips for a moment.

Recalling Bess, Julia felt sick. Her repugnance was so strong she couldn't even speak.

"We might even marry," Fenton said. "I require an heir sooner or later, and I have a certain position in the world."

"An infamous position!" snapped Julia, finding her voice at last.

"Perhaps I could redeem it with you." His smile was mocking.

"I would die before I would marry you!"

"Really? Women say such things, but they seldom mean them. Surely you would not let it go so far?"

Julia's blood froze. She had not quite faced it before, but if he could not allow her to go home, what was he to do with her? "You're mad," she gasped.

"On the contrary, I think it is a very clever solution."

"It would not be tolerated. My parents—"

"Would be grateful to see you safely married after this little...adventure." He gestured at the room around them. "It would be a nine days' wonder, of course. The *ton* would buzz with rumors. But we would put it about that you had changed your mind, as females are wont to do. I'm sure we could concoct a charming love story, and in a few months we should be just another feature of society. You would quite rehabilitate my reputation; some of my aunts would rejoice in the match."

"Richard," murmured Julia, knowing with a sinking heart that he was right about the world's reaction, even her parents'. They would see no other way to save a situation so far out of their conventional experience.

"Yes," Fenton agreed, "Beckwith is the problem. I fear you will have to speak to him yourself. But I shall be with you, of course."

"No!" cried Julia, her voice throbbing with anguish.

"I had certainly not intended to marry just now," replied Fenton, as if she had simply put some practical objection. "But I can see advantages." He looked her up and down in a way that made Julia draw back further. He moved toward her. "I shall enjoy seeing Beckwith's face. Yes, this is a far sweeter vengeance. But you will enjoy certain things as well, I promise you." He was suddenly beside her, and before Julia could slip past the bed, he had grabbed her wrists and forced them behind her back. He held them together in an iron grip as he pulled her against him, molding her body to his. Julia twisted this way and that, but she could not break his hold. She had trapped herself in the corner between the wall and the bed, and now he braced her there as he bent to fasten his lips upon hers.

This, at least, Julia could avoid, she twisted her head from side to side evading him. But Fenton merely let his lips slide down her neck to her throat and shoulder, kissing her again and again and pressing ever closer against her. The hard contours of his body were inexorable, and Julia's terror mounted as she continued to struggle wildly and without effect.

At last, his passion rising, Fenton loosed one of his hands, taking both of her wrists in the other. He reached inside the front of her gown caressingly, tearing it as the seams resisted his explorations. With a supreme effort, Julia got one hand free. Crooking her fingers into claws, she raked them with all her strength along the side of his face, catching the corner of one eye and leaving bloody trails behind.

With a cry, Fenton flung her away and clutched at his face. Julia struck the bedstead glancingly, then fell to the floor. In an instant, she was up and scrambling toward the door.

But Fenton was faster. He caught her arm as she was opening it and again threw her across the room. When he turned to stand over her, he was a dreadful sight, with blood dripping from the parallel gashes in his cheek. Julia crouched, awaiting a blow. But instead, horribly, Lord

Fenton slowly smiled. "A spitfire, eh?" he said, pulling out his handkerchief and pressing it to his wounds. "Splendid. From what I'd seen of you, I hadn't expected it." He reached behind him with his free hand and turned the doorknob. "I shall get this attended to and return better prepared," he finished, stepping back and out and locking the door behind him. Julia let her head sink on her knee and drew a shuddering breath that disintegrated into a sob.

Sir Richard stood before Lord Fenton's house and waited for someone to answer his knock. He felt a mixture of tension and anticipation. The next few minutes would certainly be difficult, but if they offered him a chance to face his enemy, they would be deeply satisfying as well.

A footman opened the door. "Lord Fenton," said Beckwith.

"I'm sorry, sir, his lordship is out of town."

Though this confirmed Sir Richard's fears, he did not show it in his face. Instead, he moved forward, forcing the young footman to retreat before him into the front hall. "It is a matter of the utmost urgency," he told the servant. "Can you give me his direction? I must communicate with him as soon as possible."

"Wait here," was the nervous reply, and the footman disappeared through a door at the back of the hall.

Sir Richard waited, but his hopes were fading. He had counted on surprising Fenton's location out of a lower servant. Their superiors would be far more likely to ask his business and fob him off with excuses.

After an interval so long that Sir Richard was about to go in search of someone, the young footman returned accompanied by, or rather supporting, a much larger, older man dressed as a butler. A reek of whiskey wafted ahead of them.

But when the pair came close, the butler straightened and attempted to stand alone, swaying as if in a stiff breeze. "Yes, sir," he said. "You was wanting?"

"I want Lord Fenton's direction," replied Sir Richard.

"Ah. That we do not have. No, sir. When his lordship goes off into the country—not visiting, you understand, but on his own hook—we are not given any direction." He hiccupped loudly and flushed a little.

"Damn it, someone must know where he is!"

The butler shook his head slowly from side to side. "We're not to know, y'understand."

Though infuriated, Sir Richard did understand. Lord Fenton did not want his servants gossiping about where he went and what he did there. He hired ruffians from the streets so that no rumors would reach the *haut ton*. Society might be fairly sure that his pursuits were unsavory, but they had no concrete evidence. If Fenton's hirelings gossiped, they did so in circles unfrequented by his friends and acquaintances.

But this left Sir Richard helpless, and Julia gone. He could not let it drop. "Perhaps if I inquire further," he said, and pushing past the two men, he went through the door into the back premises.

There, the opulence of the hall ended abruptly. Beckwith ran lightly down a narrow stair and found himself in the kitchen confronting an aged and very ugly cook and a maid whose swelling apron attested to an interesting condition seldom seen among servants. "Where is Lord Fenton?" demanded Sir Richard, hoping to intimidate them.

The maid gasped and held a carrot she had been peeling to her bosom. But the cook was made of sterner stuff. "Out of town," was her reply. "And what may you be doing down here? Is that Adams drunk again, then?"

Turning on his heel, Beckwith returned to the upper floor, nearly colliding with the butler and footman as he emerged. Then, deciding that he had already caused such a sensation that a bit more wouldn't hurt, he strode quickly through the house, upstairs and down. Fenton was not there. He hadn't really expected he would be. He was, a growing conviction assured Sir Richard, somewhere in the countryside with Julia as his prisoner. He longed to tear the man's house apart and throw his servants into the street. But the shadow of scandal dogged him even as he searched. He had gone as far as he could. Even now, whispers would start. They would probably concern Bess, but he could not take the risk of creating such an incident that more would be suspected. Even a whisper of the truth would come back on Julia.

His heart burning within him, Sir Richard left the house and returned to his own. All of his faculties were concentrated on how to find Julia. He did not even notice his mother's barouche draw up behind him as he rode around to the stables. But she watched him go with deep concern and sought him out as soon as he came inside.

"Richard, what is wrong?" she asked at once.

"Nothing to worry you, Mama," he answered.

"How can I help it when you look so…frightening and you won't even tell me where Thomas is." She came forward to clutch his sleeve. "Richard, has something happened to Thomas? You must tell me!"

"No! He is perfectly all right. He is visiting friends in the country."

"What friends?"

"Mama!" He nearly shouted it, and she drew back, startled. "I beg your pardon. But you must trust me. Thomas is well."

Lady Beckwith surveyed him. "But you are not."

He turned away. He had decided that he would not tell his mother, or Julia's parents, of the kidnapping unless it became unavoidable. He hoped to bring her back before they could miss her. He did this not only to spare them pain, but also to limit even more the chances of gossip. He did not imagine that any of them would spread the story, but the more people involved the more likely it was to become known. He had made Thomas swear not to speak of it to their mother. Now, he looked down at her with affection as well as impatience. "It is nothing you can help with, Mama. I will be better by and by."

"You told me all was well with you and Julia," she said, unable to let go.

"We are completely reconciled," he said, suppressing the pain that the sound of her name brought.

Lady Beckwith nodded. "But, Richard—"

"Mama, I swear that if you can help, I will call upon you. And you must be satisfied with that."

She hesitated, examining his face, then looked down. "Very well."

"I am going riding," he added, and left her standing alone, staring at the door he closed behind him.

EIGHTEEN

AT ABOUT THE SAME TIME, IN THE COUNTRY, BESS sought out Thomas Beckwith as he was leaving the house. "I must talk to you," she told him.

"Later. I am on my way out."

"No. It must be now."

He looked impatient. "We are searching to the west, Bess. Shea has already gone."

"I know he has; that is why I must speak to you now. I don't want him to hear what I have to say."

Thomas frowned. "I'm sorry, Bess, but looking for Julia is—"

"A waste of time! You've found nothing with all your questioning, and you won't. We must try something else."

Her tone made him angry. "Indeed? What?"

"That's what I am trying to tell you!"

Thomas fell silent, and they looked at each other for a long moment. "All right," he said then.

Bess looked down. "Come into the front parlor." When she had shut the door behind them, she turned and folded her hands before her, gazing at them as if for guidance. "Julia's gone because of me," she began. "If I'd never come here, she would be all right."

"It is not your fault," replied Beckwith, but automatically, in tones that suggested they had been over all this before.

"I mean, he was after *me*, not Julia," she continued. "So I can get Julia back."

She had his full attention now.

"I'll go to…him"—she couldn't bring herself to say his name—"and offer to take Julia's place. I stay if she is let go."

"Richard won't allow it," was Thomas's first reaction.

Bess sighed. "Very likely. So I won't tell him. Or Michael. But you must see it's the only chance to find her."

He was frowning. "I don't see. It would never work, Bess, even if I went along. Which I won't. He wouldn't release her; he would simply take you as well. I've been thinking. He can't just send Julia back, you know."

Bess gazed at him in disgust. "Any fool could see that," she declared. "But we'll find out where Julia is. He'll take me there. *You* follow and discover the place, then bring help."

"Oh." Thomas thought this over slowly. "I don't like it," he concluded finally.

"Nor do I," Bess assured him. "It makes me sick to think of seeing that man again. But it's the only chance."

"If you should get away from me," he objected.

"You must take care that I don't!"

Thomas frowned. While he very much liked the idea of finding Julia himself, and making amends for his slip in town, the plan repelled him. Using Bess as bait, to put it baldly, was not an idea he could easily accept. Yet their search had turned up nothing, and every moment that passed made the situation worse. "All right," he said at last.

"We'll go to town at once," replied Bess. "I'll go to his house, and you follow. You must take great care not to be seen."

"What if he is not there?" protested Thomas. "I've been thinking about that, you know, because of Richard. It's very unlikely Fenton has returned to town. When he found they had taken Julia, I expect he went to ground."

Bess merely nodded. "I know what to do."

"Indeed? What?"

"It doesn't matter. You just keep careful watch."

Thomas objected again, but Bess would only insist that they leave at once, and finally, he gave in. With only the flimsiest of stories to the servants, they set off on horseback for London well before Michael Shea was due back. Bess knew what his opinion of her plan would be, and she did not want to meet him.

They reached town early that evening, only three hours after Sir Richard's visit to Lord Fenton's house, and they proceeded directly there. Thomas warned that if they paused at the Beckwith residence, their plan would undoubtedly be discovered. He did not trust his ability to keep it from his mother and brother.

At Bess's insistence, they separated outside the fashionable neighborhoods, and she rode forward alone, with Thomas keeping out of sight behind. The looks she drew might have intimidated a lesser woman, or one with a less important mission. Bess ignored them so completely that she was not accosted.

At Fenton's house, she did not go to the front door. Rather, she slipped off her horse at the mouth of the alley that led to the mews and, after making certain that Thomas had seen her, walked quickly along it until she was at the back gate. There, she hesitated a moment, as one hesitates before plunging into cold water. Then, taking a deep breath, she went forward. Something she had heard during her imprisonment took her to the stables in the mews. She slipped through the gate and into a cobbled yard, across it, and inside the stable block. Immediately, she heard sounds.

"Searched the whole place, he did," said a rough, cracked

voice. "Shoved right into the kitchen. Gave old Ma Cramer a fright. But he didn't come out here." Liquid noises, as of a bottle being upended, punctuated this speech.

"So he didn't find out nothing?" asked another, deeper voice.

"Nah. None of them in the house knows."

"You be sure it stays that way."

"When have I ever blabbed?" was the surly reply.

Satisfied, Bess moved, stepping around the corner to enter a small, low room at the back of the stables. The two men sitting there with a jug between them leapt up, overturning their stools, and stared at her. But the nearer and younger of them recovered quickly and advanced. "Who might you be?" he demanded.

Bess returned the gaze with raised chin. "I'm the girl you were sent to snatch in the country," she answered. "You took the wrong one."

"Damme," exclaimed the old man in the background.

"Shut up," growled the older. "I don't know what you're talking about," he told Bess.

"Yes, you do. And I've come to strike a bargain with you."

"I don't—"

"You made a mistake," she interrupted. "But I can fix it. Take me to Lord Fenton. Sure, he'll be pleased that you've gotten it right this time."

The man stared at her, stupefied. "What's your game?" he asked after a moment.

"I want my friend let go," replied Bess. "I'll take her place."

He worked this out slowly, and a crafty expression crossed his face. "A trade, like," he concluded.

Bess nodded.

"Trade," cackled the older man. "More likely his lordship'll—" He was cut off by a shove of the table into his stomach and subsided with a grunt of pain.

"Say I agree," added the other, "and then your friends jump me as soon as I stick my nose outside."

"No. There's no one outside."

The man considered her. Bess could see that he did not believe her, but she could also follow his thoughts from the expressions that passed over his face. Her friends would not be interested in him, he obviously reasoned. They would want the girl and his lordship. There was a chance of a substantial reward and a clean escape before things got rough. And after all, he was only doing what he'd been hired to do—snatch the girl. He nodded to himself. "Right. You have a horse?"

Bess nodded again.

"Let's go, then," he turned. "And you. Keep quiet!"

"I ain't one to blab," repeated the old man.

Bess followed the man through the stables to his own mount, and then out into the alley again. She mounted at the block there, and they rode together along the narrow way and out into the street. There was no sign of Thomas, but that was as planned. Bess fervently hoped that he was in place and prepared to follow. Now that she was actually on her way to Fenton, she was frightened and reluctant. Thomas, waiting in another alley across the way, allowed them time to get well past, then slipped into position.

They rode through London in this way, Thomas in continual fear of meeting an acquaintance and being detained. He kept his hat pulled well down, however, and no such incident marred their progress.

Once out of town, Thomas's presence became more obvious, and he had to drop back further to avoid giving himself away. Had he but known it, Bess's escort was not taking any particular pains. This opportunity had fallen into his lap, and he was not on his professional mettle.

It was late by the time they approached the house where Lord Fenton was staying, and Bess and Thomas were both tired from a long day of riding. As she turned in at the gate, Bess gazed back in time to catch a comforting glimpse of him as he moved quickly behind a grove of trees. Then she bit her lower lip and went on to face Fenton.

Thomas urged his horse through the undergrowth and up to the low wall surrounding the house. This had to be the place, he told himself, but he wished he could be certain before turning back to get help. If only he could see Julia, he thought. But the windows of the house were empty and uninformative. At last, he shrugged and turned his mount. The horse picked up speed as it retraced its steps through the trees, and Thomas spurred to a gallop as soon as they reached the road again.

NINETEEN

BESS'S ESCORT TOOK HER AROUND TO THE BACK OF THE house and in at the kitchen. She was grateful for the delay, and had to remind herself fiercely of Julia's plight before she could step over the threshold. Inside, another man sat at the kitchen table with a mug between his hands. He looked up in astonishment when Bess appeared, then turned to her companion.

The latter grinned. "Another un," he said. "Where is he?"

The man merely indicated the front of the house with his thumb.

Bess shivered, but made herself move. They walked through a bare corridor past an uncarpeted stair. A door to the left stood open, and her escort gestured toward it. Bess took a deep breath and went in.

Lord Fenton stood before a long window, looking out into the darkness.

His back was to them, and his hands laced together behind. The mere shape of his head made Bess want to turn and run, but she held her ground while her companion first shuffled his feet, then coughed, to gain Fenton's attention.

"Yes?" was the impatient reply. "Haven't I told you not to come unless I call?" He turned, and was transfixed in amazement.

His hireling enjoyed the moment to the full, then said, "Is this the one, then, guv?"

Bess took in the set of enflamed scratches down his face and felt a little better.

"Where did you find her?" Fenton said finally.

"Well, now, actually, guv..."

"I found him," finished Bess. She had to take control of the situation, she felt, or lose it forever.

Fenton stared. He looked, thought Bess, like a man who had received a number of surprises in a short time. She felt an insane desire to giggle.

"I came because of Julia," she added, steeling herself to remain steady and meet his eyes.

He seemed to consider this. "You may go," he told the man, who went out with every sign of disappointment. Fenton turned to Bess again.

"I'll stay, if you let Julia go," she said. Even though she knew this was a ruse, the idea made her queasy.

"You came here alone?" was his reply, in a tone of utter disbelief.

Bess shrugged; she must do this very well, she thought, or he might escape before Thomas could bring help. "I knew none of them would let me come if I told them. They're all so upright."

He watched her face. "How did you find this place?"

"I heard you talking...before. You told one of the men that he should come to the stables if he ever had to contact you."

"So you went to Joe?" He sounded incredulous.

"Your stables, in London," answered Bess. She used every ounce of courage she possessed not to falter and ruin all.

Lord Fenton gazed at her a moment longer, but now that the initial surprise was past, he clearly wanted to believe that she was indeed in his power again. A smile had been emerging and vanishing about his lips, and his eyes were glowing with unholy glee. Along with the scratches that adorned his dissipated face, this made him terrifying. "A rescue, eh?" he said, and laughed a little.

Bess did not reply.

"Very gallant. Perhaps you would like to see the object of your efforts?"

"Julia?"

"Come along," said Fenton, obviously enjoying himself. Bess could almost see the plans blossoming in his mind as she followed him up the stairs and waited while he unlocked a door. He was thinking of two girls together.

He threw it open with a flourish and stood back. No one was visible inside. Bess stepped forward, and saw Julia standing rigid in the far corner of the small room, her fists clenched at her sides. "Bess!" she said in stupefaction.

"Are you all right?" was the quick reply.

Julia nodded automatically, too amazed to say more.

"You know one another," said Lord Fenton, shutting the door and leaning his shoulders upon it. "So very odd. But then, Beckwith has astonished me several times in the course of this affair."

"Let her go," blurted Bess, turning to face him in front of Julia. "She has nothing to do with you."

"But she does." Fenton's hand went to his wounded cheek. "She is to be my wife. And you…" He smiled. "You will be part of our household, perhaps the scullery maid. Yes, that is the place for you."

"It was me you meant to take," protested Bess. "I'm here. Let her go."

"You must realize that I cannot do that, even if I wished to," he replied. "No, we shall all remain here for a time, contemplating our future happiness and becoming even better acquainted." His eyes ran over the two women slowly. "The *three* of us," he added, as if testing a new, fascinating concept. "Yes. You are remarkably alike, you know, in coloring, though quite different styles, of course. Piquant."

They simply stared at him, Bess outraged and Julia uncomprehending.

"I'll have preparations made," he concluded. "Don't worry, it won't be long." With a disgusting leer, he went out, locking the door behind him.

"Bess, you shouldn't have come here," exclaimed Julia then. "But how glad I am to see you!"

"Are you really all right?"

Julia nodded once again. "You didn't come alone?" she asked with painful eagerness.

Bess started to reassure her, then stopped. Someone might be listening; she couldn't be sure. She gave Julia a sharp look.

Julia didn't get the message.

"You mustn't eat anything they bring," replied Bess instead. "He has probably gone to prepare some drug. He gave it to me before. We cannot even have water."

"Too bad," insisted Julia, trying to smile. "I am so very hungry."

"Why didn't I think to bring something?" wondered Bess. "A kind of picnic?"

The two women burst into wild laughter. The sound of it made them both stop short.

"What are we going to do?" said Julia then. Her voice trembled.

"We'll be all right," insisted Bess, but silently she hoped that Thomas was not far off.

Julia could think only how good it was to have someone with her. At times, alone in the shabby room after Fenton had gone, she'd been afraid she was going mad. Her sheltered life had not prepared her for such a trial, and though she did not break down before her captor, when he was gone she came close. Bess had some plan, she told herself. Someone—Richard, her heart cried out—was coming. She only need hang on a little longer, and with Bess here that would be much easier to do.

Thomas rode as he never had before in his life, bent low in the saddle, his spurs ever ready. More than one late traveler stared after him in astonishment or outrage as he raced back along the road they had taken from London.

He made the return journey in less than half the time it had taken earlier, for the city streets were now empty of most traffic. As he came into the more fashionable neighborhoods, he passed two acquaintances who stared after him through raised quizzing glasses and stored up the incident as a curiosity to retail at some dull party.

When he finally reached home, Thomas rode straight into the stable yard, nearly taking a spill on the slippery cobbles. The head groom emerged protesting, but Thomas merely threw him his reins and ran for the back door.

He encountered his mother in the front hall, pulling off her long evening gloves. "Thomas!" she exclaimed. "There you are. Where have you been?"

He put the question aside with a gesture. "Richard?"

"In the study, I think. But Thomas…"

He started to go past her, and Lady Beckwith got a firm grip on his coat. "Thomas!" she repeated. "Tell me what has happened. Now!"

He paused, impatient, and looked down at her. "Richard has said…?"

"Nothing! And I am *consumed* with curiosity." She smiled, but grew serious when he did not respond. "Thomas, what's wrong?"

"Mama, I cannot tell you. It is up to Richard. And I must speak to him now."

She released his coat and stepped back. "I can see that it is urgent. Is it about Julia? I only want to help, Thomas."

He nodded, then shrugged.

Lady Beckwith struggled with herself. Her younger son had never before refused to share a secret with her, and it was difficult to accept his silence. "I'll speak to Richard again later," she said finally.

"Thank you, Mama." Thomas reached out and squeezed her hand, then turned toward the study.

"Will you be staying home now?" Lady Beckwith couldn't refrain from asking.

"Not just yet," was the curt reply.

She watched him enter the study and shut the door with puzzled concern in her eyes.

Thomas found his brother slumped over his desk, forehead in hand. He looked the picture of despair, and Thomas was at once wrenched by the sight and elated that he could end it. "Richard," he said. "I have found her."

Beckwith's head came up. He gazed at Thomas as if his eyes would bore straight through him.

"A house in the country. Not more than an hour of hard riding. We must go at once."

Sir Richard stood. "How?"

"Bess helped me. She—" But before he could go on, the door burst open and Michael Shea exploded into the room. "She's gone!" he cried. "Bess is gone, too. Gods, I'll kill him this time. I'll kill him!"

TWENTY

"You will not be given the opportunity," replied Sir Richard Beckwith through his teeth. "Now, *where is Julia?*" His gray eyes bore into Thomas, and Shea automatically turned to look at him as well. The younger man took a step back. He had certainly not imagined telling his story to both of them at once, or under such dramatic circumstances. He felt as if he were facing two half-domesticated beasts who might spring on him without warning.

"In a house about an hour's ride from London. We should go at once."

"We shall," was his brother's reply. He rang the bell. "You may tell me how you discovered this on the road." A footman opened the door. "Have my horse saddled and brought around," he finished.

"And a fresh horse for me," Thomas added. He glanced at the newcomer. "Mr. Shea as well."

The footman nodded and went out.

"What about *Bess*?" protested Michael Shea.

"She's there too," answered Thomas, moving further away from the man. "That's how I found the place." Shea glared at him, and he hurried on before they could speak. "It was her idea. I was reluctant at first, but I couldn't think of any other plan. Bess went to Fenton's house and, er, got herself kidnapped. I followed and found out where Fenton is hiding. We must go back there as fast as we can. I promised Bess that."

His companions spoke at the same moment.

"You did not actually *see* Julia?"

"You let her go *back* to that monster?"

Before Thomas could respond to either question, Shea gave an inarticulate cry and lunged. He did not catch Thomas by the throat; the latter ducked sideways, and his grasping hands caught an arm instead. But this was enough to bring them both crashing to the floor in a tangle of limbs and curses.

Sir Richard moved like a cat. He got a hand into the back of Shea's collar and pulled. Shea, his wind cut off, fell back, and Thomas scrambled out of his way, keeping a wary eye on his opponent.

"Stop it!" said Sir Richard in a voice like a whiplash. Michael Shea relaxed in his grip, and he let him go.

"I didn't want to do it," said Thomas. "But I couldn't think of anything else, and we had to find Julia."

Shea straightened his neckcloth, rubbing his neck and breathing heavily.

"But Fenton is not at home," Sir Richard pointed out. "I looked for him there myself."

"Bess knew something. She went to the stables."

"Ah." He looked annoyed at himself rather than surprised.

"Shall we be on our way?" asked Shea, his voice a bit roughened by the throttling.

The door opened, and the footman reappeared, gazing avidly about the room. Clearly, the sounds of the battle had roused the household. "Your horses are waiting, Sir Richard," he said.

"Thank you. Come Thomas, Shea."

He opened a wooden cabinet at the side of the fireplace and took out two flat cases.

"Father's dueling pistols?" protested Thomas. "Those things go off in your hand at the least jar. We can't take them."

"I don't keep guns in town," was Sir Richard's grim reply. "And they will serve to kill a man."

In a matter of minutes, they were mounted and riding through the now deserted streets of London. "Now," said Sir Richard, "you will tell us the whole story, Thomas, leaving out nothing."

His brother proceeded to do so.

"Why did you not come to me?" asked Sir Richard when he had finished.

"Bess thought you'd refuse. Like Shea."

"She knew I'd never allow such a plan!" put in the latter. "When I see her, I shall…" His voice cracked, and his horse drew ahead in response to the involuntary pressure of his knees.

"I wish you had seen Julia," said Sir Richard, following his own train of thought. "What if she is not there?"

"I waited a little to try to catch a glimpse," responded Thomas. "But I didn't want to stay too long."

"She must be where Fenton is," offered Shea, bringing a frown to Sir Richard's brow. "Can't we go faster?"

"We have no plan yet," Beckwith pointed out coldly. "This will not be so easy as the last time. Fenton is there, and he no doubt knows we shall be coming after him."

"Bess was to tell him some tale," replied Thomas.

"The man is a blackguard, not a fool."

"So, how shall we go about it?" asked Shea, still impatient.

"Surprise is our best weapon," answered Sir Richard slowly. "Can we break into the house, Thomas?"

His brother considered, then nodded slowly. "It's

largeish, and they're using only part of it, I think. If we went to one of the far rooms…"

"Good. If we can get inside and silence the ruffians Fenton certainly has stationed there, we should be able to stage a quick attack and get the upper hand." His face showed deep satisfaction at the thought, and Shea's mirrored it.

For the first time, it occurred to Thomas to be concerned about Fenton. "You don't really intend to kill him, do you?" he asked. "I mean, I fully understand that you might feel like killing him, but…" He looked from his brother to Shea, then back again, and was not reassured. "I don't say he doesn't deserve punishment," he began again. "But you can't go about killing people. You'd have to flee the country."

"I intend to," Shea pointed out. "And besides, how is anyone to know what's happened? You said this was an isolated house. I'm sure that's why he chose it." The muscles of his jaw tightened.

"Anything may happen in a fight," was Sir Richard's only contribution, and Thomas had to leave it thus, though he was far from reassured.

They spoke little after that, and in due course, they reached the grove of trees where Thomas had concealed himself earlier. "The house is just beyond that wall," he told them. "You can see over it if you ride close."

"I think we shall leave the horses here," answered Sir Richard. "I suggest we walk around the wall and find the most deserted corner for our entry."

In the darkness, they had to move slowly among the bushes and weeds along the base of the wall. More than once, Michael Shea objected to the time this was taking, but

Sir Richard silenced him with curt inquiries as to whether he wished their rescue attempt to fail. At last they reached a point at the back of the house where they could see lighted windows on both the upper and lower levels.

"That must be the kitchen," murmured Sir Richard, indicating the lower one. "I assume his hirelings are there and… the rest above." He could not say Julia's name. The thought of her in that house with Fenton would drive him mad, he knew, and he suppressed it. "We must try the front corner opposite," he finished. "We can slip through the front gate."

They made their way there, stumbling more than once in the blackness. They slipped through the unlocked gate in single file and moved silently along the overgrown drive.

"Quiet above all else," whispered Sir Richard as they reached the edge of the unkempt lawn. "Try the windows."

They fanned out and began to test the windows along the ground floor.

At first, they had no luck. The house seemed securely locked, and they moved from window to window with growing impatience and anger.

"I could break the glass," hissed Shea finally.

"Too loud," was the immediate reply.

They moved on down the side of the building. A burst of male laughter reached them from the back of the house, and faces grew even more grim.

"Here's something," said Shea then, and beckoned. The Beckwiths joined him before a pair of French doors near the rear corner of the house. "The catches on these are a joke," he told them. "A child can force them." He took a slender knife from his pocket and slid it between the two doors. There was a delicate scraping sound, and then a sharp click.

All three men froze; it had seemed very loud in the silence. But the only response was another burst of laughter. With a silent flourish, Michael Shea opened the door and ushered them inside.

TWENTY-ONE

NOT MUCH MORE THAN AN HOUR BEFORE, LORD FENTON had returned with a loaded tray to the room where Bess and Julia sat. "I must beg your pardon," he said. "Things have been rather…confused, and somehow food was forgotten. But matters have been rectified." He put the tray on a small, unsteady table and, to Julia's surprise, went out again.

"Don't touch any of it," said Bess as soon as he was gone. "He'll have put in some of that devil's brew he gave me."

Julia nodded wistfully. There was soup on the tray, and it smelled wonderful. The bottle of wine had been opened and was obviously out of the question. "Can he have put anything in the bread?" she asked. "How could he?"

"We daren't find out," answered Bess, and Julia was forced to agree. But the hollow feeling inside seemed to intensify tenfold with food so close.

She turned away and went to sit down on the bed.

After a time, they heard footsteps returning and the key in the lock. Lord Fenton came in, scanned the tray, and frowned. "You haven't eaten."

"Do you think we're daft?" Bess asked him. "You don't drug *me* more than once."

His face indicated that he had assumed their naivete. An almost demonic expression crossed it now, but he didn't speak. He merely slammed the door again and locked it.

"Is the man mad?" wondered Bess.

"I have thought he must be close to it," replied Julia. "He can't think he will return to London and take up his old life after this."

Bess shook her head. There was no chance for further speculation, however, for sounds heralded the approach of more than one person this time. For a moment, hope lit Bess's green eyes, dying when the door opened to reveal not only Fenton, but his two hired ruffians.

"Hold them," said the former curtly.

Moving so quickly the women had no time to react, the men imprisoned them in a crushing grip. Julia could not break it, no matter how she struggled, and she could see that Bess was in the same predicament. Worse was the fact that the man held one hand over her nose and mouth, making breathing nearly impossible and revolting her with the smell of cheap gin.

Lord Fenton stood as if in the midst of a *ton* party and poured out two tumblers of wine from the bottle on the table. When both were full, he turned to evaluate his captives.

Julia fought to pull air into her protesting lungs, and failed. She began to feel dizzy and panicked and struggled even harder, but the man's arms were like steel bands.

"Ready?" said Fenton. And at some signal, he took two strides toward Julia, one tumbler in his hand.

At that instant, the grip on her mouth was released. Julia drew in a huge breath, limp with relief, and the entire glass was poured down her throat.

She choked, the wine burning and gagging. Desperately, she swallowed and swallowed to clear her throat, coughing and sputtering, tears streaming from her eyes. Inevitably, most of the wine went down, and she was too breathless to care.

Bess watched all this with wide eyes above her captor's

hairy fingers. She squirmed wildly as Fenton approached her with the other tumbler, but her struggles were weakened by lack of air. And when she, in turn, was allowed to breathe, she could not stop the reflex. Like Julia, she was forced to swallow the drugged wine.

While she was still recovering, Fenton made a quick gesture, and Julia and Bess were at once flung on the bed on top of one another. All the men then strode from the room, leaving them alone.

Julia sat up and helped Bess to do likewise as she continued to cough. "Are you all right?" she asked, her throat still raw.

Bess nodded, eyes streaming. It was another minute or so before she could speak. "Put your finger down your throat," she croaked then, and did so.

Julia watched as Bess tried unsuccessfully to get rid of the wine.

"I can't," she gasped finally, subsiding onto the bed. "My throat's too sore, devil take it."

There was a short silence.

"What will happen to us now?" asked Julia quietly. "I mean, how will it feel, the drug?"

Bess sighed. "You go sort of—far away, at first. As if you were watching everything from a long way off. It'll be hard to move. And then, after a while, you'll fall asleep."

"Oh." Julia felt detached already. She felt as if she had tried her utmost and failed; there was nothing further to do. Doom was descending.

"You must fight it!" insisted Bess fiercely. "Thomas is bringing help." There seemed no point in keeping the plan a secret now, and she could see that Julia needed some hope to cling to. In a burst, she explained the whole thing. "He should be back very soon," she concluded, "so you must keep fighting."

"Richard," responded Julia in a dreamy voice.

"Yes," agreed Bess, "he will be here soon, so you must not give up. When that devil comes back"—she paused in reaction to the surprise on Julia's face—"of course he'll be back. Why do you think he did this? So we can't fight him, the coward." Her scorn was withering.

The drug haze receded a little in the face of Julia's fear. "Now? Both of us?" she faltered.

"Aye, the filthy pig. But he'll find more than he's counting on." Bess's voice was sounding very slightly slurred. She rose. "Come and walk about. It'll help. I did it before." She took Julia's arm and pulled her to her feet. Side by side, they began to pace the boundaries of the small room.

"He gave us a lot," said Bess blearily, as she tripped over nothing. "Afraid of the two of us. Hah." She laughed harshly.

"Two against one," responded Julia in a sing-song, and giggled.

Bess shook her head violently, and then Julia's arm. "Fight it!" she repeated.

Julia bit her lower lip. "I feel so…fuzzy," she complained.

"I know, but don't give in." She turned her head abruptly. "He's coming."

The footsteps paused, and they heard the key yet again. In the next moment, Fenton was before them. He had taken off his coat and waistcoat and wore only a shirt and buff riding breeches above stockinged feet. When he saw them leaning on one another, he smiled. "Touching," he said, then grasped their arms and pushed them before him out into the corridor. "This way."

Julia tried to run, but her muscles were limp, and his grasp on her upper arm was like a vise. She tripped and would have fallen to the floor had he not jerked her upright again. She cried out at the pain in her arm, and Lord Fenton laughed.

Bess, flailing at him with her free arm and trying to bring her knee up to strike, had no more luck. She missed a step and pivoted clumsily on one foot. Fenton laughed again, and in a flash transferred his grip to their waists, pulling them close against him on each side.

He dragged them down the hall to another bedchamber, this one furnished with surprising opulence. A massive four-poster bed stood out from the far wall. On the threshold, he thrust them inside so hard that they both fell, turned, and locked the door behind him, reaching to place the key on a high shelf near the ceiling. By the time Julia and Bess had stumbled to their feet again, he was facing them, hands on hips. "What a lovely pair you are," he exclaimed. "So like, yet so unlike."

Bess launched herself at him, but her muscles had lost their usual suppleness, and she had to catch herself on his arm to avoid falling again.

"So eager?" asked Fenton, burying one hand in her black hair and twisting.

Bess cried out in pain, and the pins fell from her hair, bringing it down about her shoulders. She clawed at his hand without effect. Fenton reached into his pocket and pulled out a small knife with a curved blade. Julia, who could see it, gasped and ran to restrain his arm with both hands. She could not hold him with the drug sapping her strength, however, and he shook her off with another laugh.

Before she could move again, he had inserted the blade in the bodice of Bess's gown and ripped quickly downward, slitting the cloth so that the dress fell off her shoulders. He twisted his other hand again, eliciting another cry of pain, then flung Bess from him and turned to Julia. Bess fell, clutching her head, tears running down her cheeks.

Julia backed away, her hands held up in front of her, her eyes following his every move. If only she could think...but her mind was as useless as her muscles under the effect of the drug.

Her back touched the wall, and she pressed herself against it, looking from side to side in search of a weapon. But there was no such thing in the room—no candlestick, no fire tongs on the hearth. The small lamp was out of her reach. Fenton reached her with a sudden quick stride, and ripped her gown as he had Bess's. Julia caught the edges and held it to her, but the man grasped a sleeve, then pushed her back toward the center of the room, tearing the dress off and tripping her again with the uncut hem.

She fell more heavily this time, and lay there in her shift and thin stockings. Bess pulled her up with an arm about her shoulders. They sat gazing up at Fenton, who stood above them exultant.

"Take off the rest," he commanded them, "or I shall do it for you."

Bess stood as quickly as she was able and struck at him. He replied with a backhanded blow that flung her halfway across the room and left her stunned for a long moment.

"Do you wish to argue the point?" said Fenton in a tone that mocked by its smooth pleasantness. "I am quite willing."

He looked down at Julia. She half walked, half crawled to Bess and raised her gently, terrified that she might be badly hurt.

"All...right," was Bess's slurred response. She shook her head and blinked.

"The clothes," said Fenton. "Now."

Sitting up, Bess pushed her torn gown off her arms. "Got to," she said wearily to Julia. "Time."

Even in her fogged state, Julia understood that they must hang on until help arrived. Even so, she could not bring herself to follow Bess's lead. Her face flamed, and she crossed her arms on her breast.

Bess was removing her shoes. She saw this involuntary movement, and Lord Fenton's answering grin. "He likes hitting you," she told Julia, her voice somewhat clearer now. "Don't give him an excuse."

"I...I can't," Julia whispered.

Bess nodded. "You can, though." She eased off Julia's shoes and took her arm. Together, they rose shakily. "Come on. It'll be worse if he hits you."

"A practical approach," declared Fenton. He went to lean against the wall, one arm negligently on the mantle. His eyes moved slowly up and down their bodies.

Bess pretended to ignore him. She slipped off her stockings with her back to him and threw them on top of her ruined gown. Trembling and blinking back tears, Julia followed suit.

"The shifts as well," he commanded, his voice thickening with excitement. Bess froze, then started to pull her shift up. Fenton stared at the hem as it inched along her leg.

Julia ran for the door, or ordered her body to do so,

at least. But the drug was by now at full strength, and she stumbled to her knees after two steps.

Refusing to give in, she dragged herself the remaining distance and used the doorknob to pull herself upright again. At every moment, she expected to feel Fenton's bruising grip. He did not move to stop her, however, and Julia stretched her hand up for the key.

The shelf was out of reach. Strain as she might, she could not get her fingers over it. Lord Fenton laughed.

And then he was right behind her, pressing his body against hers, his breath hot on her neck. She felt the cold touch of metal, and her shift was ripped down the back and roughly pulled away. She cried out, and felt the impact of another body hitting Fenton and trapping her against the door panels.

Fenton twisted, his hands reaching high to deposit the knife beside the key and then whipping back to grasp Bess, who had thrown herself at him from behind. His free arm encircled Julia, and in the next moment he was propelling the two toward the bed.

He pushed them down across it. Julia instinctively tried to cover herself with her hands.

"So beautiful," breathed Fenton, pulling his shirt open and off.

There was a grinding crash, a hollow booming in the corridor, and a heavy thud on the door. With another splintering crash, the door burst open, and Sir Richard Beckwith entered, a pistol in his hand and Michael Shea right behind him.

TWENTY-TWO

FOR AN ENDLESS MOMENT, THE TABLEAU WAS FROZEN thus, the two rescuers transfixed with shock and fury. Then both moved at once, bearing down on Lord Fenton with murder in their eyes.

He was quicker, however. He jerked Julia to her feet and held her between his body and the pistols, one arm crooked about her neck and exerting a dizzying pressure. Julia hung limply against him, all her remaining energy concentrated on getting enough air. Unconsciousness hovered close, but she had not even the strength to raise her hands and pull at his arm. Nor could her nakedness embarrass her as she fought for her life.

"I'll kill her," hissed Fenton. "Believe me, I will."

"We can pull you down first," retorted Shea, and started to move.

"Can you?" He pressed harder, and Julia blacked out as Sir Richard shouted, "Stop!"

She recovered consciousness near the doorway. Lord Fenton still held her, but his grip had eased enough so that she could draw an inadequate, gasping breath.

"She's alive," said Michael Shea.

Julia blinked and focused bleary eyes on the room. Bess still lay on the bed, but she had pulled the coverlet over herself and was watching the scene with a wide, too bright gaze. Sir Richard and Shea faced the door, their pistols still in hand, but lowered now. Both looked furious, but Sir Richard's jaw was clenched, and veins stood out on his forehead with the effort he was exerting to remain still.

Fenton's hand shot up and retrieved the knife from the shelf by the door frame. He whipped it down and against the side of Julia's throat. "Stay back," he warned. "I can slice her jugular with this in an instant."

Michael Shea cursed vividly. "We should have moved before."

"I won't have Julia endangered," replied Sir Richard tightly. He looked at her, then away, as if the sight pained him physically.

"Exactly," said Lord Fenton, smiling without a trace of humor. "And the only way to ensure that is to stay where you are." He started to back into the corridor, dragging Julia before him.

On the bed, Bess pulled herself up like one swimming against a heavy current. She stared at the doorway. "Thomas!" she cried.

Fenton half turned, jerking Julia violently with him. His arm tightened, and blackness threatened her again. She felt something sting the side of her throat, and then was shaken by a deafening explosion before she slid helplessly into the void.

When Julia surfaced again, she was lying in bed in an unfamiliar room. She looked about it, trying to recall where she was and how she had come there. It was not home, nor the house in London. It was sparsely furnished, and the corners were not particularly clean, though the sheets that enveloped her seemed fresh enough.

Her head ached fiercely, and she was terribly thirsty.

Seeing a tumbler and jug on the table beside the bed, she reached out, and was immediately stopped by two things. First, she was so weak she could scarcely hold up her own arm, and second, she wore a man's nightshirt instead of her own lace-trimmed nightdress.

Memory flooded back. Julia's arm dropped to the bed, and she crimsoned with rage and shame. Where, she wondered, was Richard?

The door opened, and Bess's head appeared around it. "You're awake! Wait there."

What else could she possibly do? Julia wondered.

In a very short time, Bess was back with a tray which held a steaming bowl of soup, half a cottage loaf, and a pot of tea. Julia's hunger revived insistently at the rich scent, and her worries were temporarily forgotten as she began to eat.

When the bowl was half-empty, however, she looked up to find Bess smiling at her. "Where are we?" asked Julia without putting down her spoon.

"The same place. Lord Fenton's house."

Julia stiffened and straightened, nearly spilling the contents of the tray over the bed.

"He's gone," added Bess quickly. "There was nothing else to do. You couldn't be moved, and I was only a little better. They settled us here and brought Mrs. Hanlon to look after us."

"Mrs. Hanlon?"

"Michael's aunt. You'll like her. She made that soup." Bess's green eyes twinkled.

How could she be so happy? wondered Julia. She hesitated, then asked the question foremost in her mind. "Where is Sir Richard?"

"London. They had to go."

"Oh." Julia's heart sank. The memory of Richard's face as he came into the room where Fenton stood over them remained vivid among a jumble of confusion. Had he gone because he could not bear to see her?

"Because of Lord Fenton," added Bess, in response to her bereft expression.

Julia looked down at her soup. She didn't want it now.

"How much do you remember?" inquired Bess. "Shall I tell you the whole story? I had it from Michael yesterday."

"He was here?"

"Oh, yes. He can't do much. Sir Richard must attend to most of it. But, Julia, my plan worked." She looked very pleased with herself. "And that means it was the right thing to do, doesn't it?"

"I am certainly glad of it."

"There! Michael still refuses to see. But let me tell you the tale. Thomas fetched Sir Richard and Michael, as I told him to, and they rode here at once. Michael found a door he could open." She dimpled. "How he learned to do such a thing, he won't say. The three of them crept inside and went to the kitchen. They had pistols, you know, and had no trouble convincing those two hired bullies to do as they said. Thomas tied them up, while Michael and Sir Richard came up. Didn't they look splendid when they burst in!"

Julia winced, but Bess didn't notice.

"Well, I don't know what you remember after that, because the beast had you by the neck and kept squeezing." She looked inquiring.

"Very little," managed Julia, the sight of Richard's face too clear.

"Well, he tried to use you as a shield to get away. He was choking you, and then he got the knife."

"I remember that," said Julia shuddering. She put a hand to the side of her throat and discovered a small bandage there.

"He nicked you a bit," acknowledged Bess, "when I shouted 'Thomas' to distract him. Sir Richard was furious, but it worked, didn't it?"

"Furious?" echoed Julia, hope reviving.

"Well, what was I to do, then? Just lie there and let him go? Not likely! Anyway, he turned, and Michael and Sir Richard fired, and that was that."

"I remember a loud noise," said Julia.

"I should say it was loud. What a pleasure it was to see him fall bleeding!"

Julia had to smile a little at her vehemence. "Where have they taken him?" She straightened again. "He is not here?" The thought that Fenton might be recuperating in the same house was insupportable.

Bess stared. "Why, he's dead!"

"Dead!"

"Of course. They were in no mood to miss."

"I didn't think," replied Julia slowly.

"He cut you as he fell, but it was only a scratch. Though I thought for a while that Sir Richard would shoot *me* because of it. And then, of course, everyone was running about throwing blankets over us and swearing." She giggled.

Julia, who had felt warmed by her description of Richard's anger, was chilled again by the picture.

"After that, I fell asleep, too," finished Bess. "'Twas funny. Our brave rescuers come, and all we could do was sleep." She smiled at Julia, who could not respond.

"And now they have gone?" she asked.

"Yes. Well, they had to do something about the corpse, of course. And there was those two in the kitchen."

"Oh."

Bess looked at her. "You can't just kill an earl, even such a blackguard as he was. And they can't tell what really happened either. But Michael says Sir Richard is doing very well. He says he has unexpected talents for deception." She smiled impishly. "They're going to pay off the bullies and send them to Australia."

Though this sounded eminently sensible, Julia was not comforted. The fact that Richard had not come to see her compounded her shame at the way he had found her. Perhaps he would never be able to forget what he saw in this house, and all was at an end between them. He wouldn't wish to say so, after her ordeal; he simply stayed away so that she would take the hint.

"You are still tired," said Bess sympathetically, misinterpreting her silence. "You haven't finished your soup."

"No," declared Julia. "I want to get up." She held out the tray, and Bess took it. Julia threw back the bedclothes and looked down at the nightshirt.

"They couldn't get your clothes just yet," explained Bess. "Mine are here, and some new things. They're going to tell your servants some story, but they had to deal with Fenton first."

Tears filled Julia's eyes. Somehow, this seemed worse than all the rest, that she could not have any of her own things.

"You can put on one of my gowns," added Bess, looking worried and perplexed. "I left one for you." She hurried to the corner of the room, picking up a pile of clothes draped over a chair.

Julia turned them over in her hands. "What became of mine?" she couldn't help but ask, shuddering a little when she thought of her torn shift.

"I burnt them," replied Bess fiercely.

She looked up quickly, then nodded.

"Shall I help you?" offered Bess diffidently.

"No. I'll come downstairs in a few minutes."

Picking up the tray, Bess went out, and Julia slowly dressed in the unfamiliar garments. She must go at once, she thought. She could tell the servants something, and she needed her own things and people she knew well. The pain would be less there, she thought.

Thus, when she went downstairs and was introduced to Mrs. Hanlon, her first question was about transport.

"There's the carriage Sir Richard sent Mrs. Hanlon in," replied Bess dubiously. "But—"

"I must get home," argued Julia. "It will be hard enough to explain my absence as it is." Something occurred to her. "How long has it been?"

"Three days since you were taken. You slept a long time."

Julia nodded. "High time I reappeared." She froze suddenly. "My parents!"

"Michael says they don't know of this. Sir Richard prevented the country servants from sending to them. He told them you had a bad fall out walking, and some travelers picked you up and took you to an inn miles away. He convinced them you were being seen to."

Julia breathed again. "They will think me quite mad, of course, to have gone off without telling anyone, leaving my own carriage, but at least they may not suspect the truth. I will send the carriage back to you," she promised.

"Am I not to come?"

Julia looked down, feeling guilty. "If you don't mind, I should prefer to go alone." She didn't want anyone around to remind her of this experience.

Bess stiffened, then shrugged and turned away. "I'll tell them to bring the carriage."

"I can," protested Julia, feeling even worse.

"It's all right."

She went out, and Julia struggled with herself. But she could not bear to stay here. Too, the visits of Michael Shea would be too painful when she herself was alone. By the time Bess returned, Julia was composed.

"Ten minutes," said the other.

"Thank you."

They stood together in silence. To Bess, it appeared that Julia was withdrawing into the privilege of her class, and though she had told herself as she walked to the stables that this was only to be expected, Bess was still stung by the apparent rejection.

After a while, they heard the carriage and turned toward the door. Julia had nothing to take, so they went out as it was pulling up. "I'll send your gown back with the carriage," said Julia. "Is there anything else you want?"

Bess shook her head.

Julia was too miserable to make amends. She wanted only to run away. She climbed into the carriage and nodded to the driver that she was ready. He signaled the team, and they started to move. Julia waved, and tried to smile. Bess simply watched as the vehicle trundled down the over-grown lane and turned into the road.

TWENTY-THREE

JULIA CURLED INTO THE CARRIAGE SEAT AND GRATE-fully gave up pretending equanimity. It was a great relief to be alone. She could loose her feelings and think how best to face the future.

None of what had happened was her fault, an inner voice had been insisting for some time, and she listened to it now. That much was certainly true. She had had no hand in her kidnapping or what followed. But Julia's whole education and parental example had taught her to regard such things as shameful and not to be mentioned by decent people. She could not rid herself of the shame, though her mind argued otherwise. She could not imagine facing her parents and friends; *her* knowledge of what had passed would be enough to sink her.

And Richard—Julia shut her eyes tightly as the image of his face at the rescue rose again in her imagination. It was like a physical pain. Julia's very limited knowledge of men, imparted by her mother and the experience of one London Season, told her that Richard would never wish to see her again, that he would never be able to wipe out that picture. She didn't blame him; it would haunt her also. Perhaps it would make any happiness impossible. But the idea of a life stretching ahead without Richard filled her eyes with tears.

She reached home in the early afternoon and went through the exhausting process of explaining to the senior servants where she had been. Sir Richard's original story was weak, and she could see that it did not totally convince, but she could do no better. And fortunately, the household was soon absorbed in cosseting rather than questioning her.

It was wonderful to be surrounded by her own familiar things again. Julia ordered a bath and spent a long, luxurious time in the hot water soaking away the bruises, mental and physical, of the last few days. Her maid began to believe the story of an accident, Julia saw, when she undressed her and uncovered the signs of rough treatment.

When she had dressed in her own clothes and sent Bess's back with the carriage, Julia went out into the rose garden and sat there gazing out over the park and the fields beyond. It was a warm day, and the scent of the early roses was heavy and sweet. She sat still, her hands lying open in her lap, and breathed it in. She felt amazingly better, Julia thought, and she began to wonder if the drug she had been given had had lingering effects. Her terrible despondence now seemed excessive. Perhaps she was wrong.

These thoughts were interrupted by the sound of a carriage from the front of the house. Julia sprang up, half-eager, half-afraid, thinking of Richard. She longed both to run to the entry and to run away. The conflict kept her rooted to the spot until her maid appeared and said, "It is Sir George and Lady Devere, Miss. They're asking for you." Julia stared at her so fixedly that she added, "Are you all right, Miss Julia? Are you feeling ill?"

"No. No, I'll be right there. Tell them I'm coming."

The girl left, and Julia started to follow, moving very slowly and trying to formulate phrases with which to greet her parents. She was another person since she had seen them last, she realized. She had undergone epoch-making experiences and been changed by them. Would they see it at once? And how could she explain?

Her mother met her with outstretched arms and her usual smile. Sir George embraced her less effusively, as was his way, and inquired about the state of his stables. The ordinariness of it all dizzied Julia.

"But what is this garbled tale the servants give me about Sir Richard and an accident, Julia?" said Lady Devere finally. "You look perfectly well."

Julia tensed, and told her fabricated story again.

"But why weren't we told, summoned home?" was the indignant reply. "I cannot believe such a lapse. Sir Richard takes too much on himself."

"He knew I was all right," stammered Julia. "He...he didn't want to worry you unnecessarily."

"Acting quite the husband already," replied her mother, and seemed very pleased with the idea. "Still..."

"But if you hadn't heard, why are you here?" said Julia before she could speak again.

Her mother looked at her. "My dear, this is the day we always set to come home. You can't have forgotten."

It was, Julia realized, and the vision this opened up of life going on just as before, undisturbed by the revolution in her, was staggering. It made her feel at once small and unimportant, and vastly distanced from her parents and all of society. They would never even know, she thought. And although this was the goal she had striven for, it was also a gulf between them. They remained exactly the same; she would never be the same again.

Her mother sensed something, for she asked, "Are you all right, Julia? You weren't badly hurt in this accident, were you? You looked so well when we came in that I didn't worry. But now you are pale. Tell me all about it." She tucked her arm into her daughter's. "Come upstairs, and we will talk just as we used to."

Julia went, but a forlorn inner voice pointed out that nothing would be just as it used to be ever again.

Once her parents were settled, they had many more questions about Julia's supposed accident, and she was hard put to satisfy them about what had happened, the people who had supposedly rescued her, and why they had not been informed. Indeed, she most often had to resort to diversion. She would ask her father some question about the estate and make him forget all else. With her mother, it had to be the wedding. This was painful, but it was easier to endure her happy chatter about details than worried inquiries. The following evening, however, when Julia used this stratagem, her mother said, "Where is Richard, by the by? I should think he would have visited us. We scarcely saw him in town after you were gone." She smiled archly at her daughter. "But we expected to have him underfoot again here."

"I…I suppose he is busy," Julia stammered, repressing a pain in the area of her heart.

"With what? The Season is over."

"Perhaps…perhaps he went home to prepare his estates for a new mistress." This was an inspiration, for it sent her mother into happy speculation for quite half an hour. But it made Julia miserable. She hated deceiving her in this way, and the thought of Richard readying his house for her was so poignant she wanted to cry.

On the following day, Julia's second at home, her parents went out early to call on their neighbors and catch up on all the news of the neighborhood. Julia pleaded fatigue and was allowed to stay home. She established herself in the gardens once more, with books and a jug of lemonade. But most of the time, she simply stared out over the grass despondently. The future was a blank to her. She left the chair and strolled slowly about the park. She did not leave its walls; she was not ready to do that yet after what had occurred the last time. But the Devere acres offered enough variety and a pleasant feeling of safety.

She had stopped by the little pond near the west wall and was gazing into it, looking for the goldfish her mother had placed there, when she heard her name spoken softly. Julia looked up, and discovered Richard standing in the shade of a willow not ten yards away.

A tremor went through her. Julia felt as if she had been hit in every part of her body at once.

"Julia," he said again, coming forward. "Are you all right? I went to…the other house first and found you had gone."

He could not name it, thought Julia. Nor could she. "I wanted to be away from there," she replied in an uneven voice.

Sir Richard nodded as if he understood that only too well. "Forgive me for having left you in such a place. I was forced to. We had to move quickly, and then, of course, the arrangements took much longer than anyone wanted. It was only yesterday that I saw those two ruffians onto a ship."

A spark of hope had ignited in Julia, but she dared not heed it. "Ship?"

"Yes. Shea convinced them, how I do not know and do

not wish to, that they would be better off in a new country, with money to start afresh." As he spoke, Sir Richard watched Julia closely.

She nodded. "And…the other?" Lord Fenton's name lay unspoken between them like a wall.

Sir Richard looked grave. "We discussed a number of plans, but finally, we left him on Hampstead Heath. His death was blamed on footpads. There was a great outcry. And his nephew Gerard has succeeded to the title."

"Gerard Allingham?" asked Julia, surprised out of her apprehension. "I didn't know he was the heir."

"Apparently Allingham did not care to advertise the connection," he answered dryly. "He will certainly fill the position more creditably."

"Oh, yes. He is so completely unlike…"

"Exactly."

Silence fell, and lengthened, between them. Now it will come, thought Julia. He will say it. It will be over. She raised her eyes. His expression was stiff and strained. She gazed at the grass again.

"Do you wish me to go?" he asked then, in a voice so tightly controlled that tension flowed out from it.

Julia was wholly at a loss. This was not what she had expected.

"Go?" she repeated blankly.

"You left without sending any word. I thought perhaps…" He stepped forward suddenly and took her hands in an almost painful grip. "I failed you, Julia. What you endured… I will never forgive myself for not protecting you. I only hope you will not let it come between us."

She stared up at him. "I? I thought that *you*… When you

weren't there the day I woke, and you didn't come, I thought what you saw in that room had given you a distaste…" She broke off, unable to continue.

The memory of that moment rose almost tangibly between them. Each could see it in every terrible detail, and feel the churn of strong emotions. Neither had been trained to deal with anything like this. Just three months ago, they would have shrunk away from the mere hint of such a thing, repelled and unshakably condemning.

But those three months had brought a host of new experiences, a series of steps toward some new wisdom. "We will never be the same," said Richard, voicing this feeling.

Julia blinked, startled to have her own thoughts echoed so clearly. In that moment, she realized that he shared her sense of transformation. Unlike her parents, and almost everyone else she was likely to meet, he was not the same. He was the one person who could understand the revolution in her.

"The world is unchanged, but we are not, cannot be," he added, shaking his head as if this were difficult to accept.

"Yes," responded Julia.

"Except in one thing, I trust." He pressed her hands.

Julia met his gray eyes, which could be so cold but were now warm with emotion. Her fears and doubts dissolved, and the flood of relief and happiness was so overwhelming it brought tears.

"Julia?" said Sir Richard anxiously.

She shook her head and smiled, unable to speak.

He pulled her into his arms and held her close, cradling her head against his shoulder as if to guard and keep some terribly precious thing. Julia reveled in the love she felt from him, all the more wonderful because she had thought it lost. A memory surfaced from the time of their engagement. How little she had known then of love, she thought with amazement. She had seen it as some placid, pleasant thing to be assumed rather like a new gown or the latest fashionable phrase. Now, she knew that it was far more, holding heights and depths she was only beginning to explore. They would have a lifetime to do that, she told herself happily, together. She raised her head to look at Richard.

"You do still intend to marry me, don't you?" he asked, half-joking, half-concerned.

She laughed a little, and nodded.

"Good. That's all that matters." But he added, "What were you thinking of?"

"Love," she replied.

"Ah. There's more to it than we thought." Astonished once again to have her own idea echoed, Julia gazed up at him.

"And I find I'm very glad of it."

"I was thinking just that, exactly that!"

"Were you? Perhaps our trials have brought us into tune, like…"

"A violin and a pianoforte," finished Julia, and they both laughed.

Somehow, the laughter seemed to remind them that they stood very close. Richard's arms slipped from her shoulders to her waist, and Julia's curved about his neck. When they kissed, the gentleness and passion encompassed everything they had endured together. Their bodies fitted as if sculpted for one another, and their hands moved by shared instinct to cherish and enflame. When at last they drew apart, each was shaken and breathing quickly. "*When* is the wedding?" asked Sir Richard.

Julia laughed again. "Three weeks."

"Too long. We must move it up."

"I should like to watch as you tell my mother so."

"Umm. I suppose she would object?"

"'Object' does not begin to describe it."

"Ah. Well, we must wait, then. We will have to find ways to pass the time quickly." And he bent to kiss her lingeringly again.

TWENTY-FOUR

JULIA DEVERE BECAME LADY BECKWITH ON AN ENGLISH summer day that belied all complaints about the country's weather. The air was soft and balmy, weighted with the scents of roses and mint. Everything in the gardens blossomed as planned, despite the epic battles between Julia's mother and the head gardener. The guests, gathered from London and various corners of the country, agreed that they had seldom seen a lovelier bride, and Sir George offered champagne with exactly that combination of jovial openhandedness and poignancy that is expected of a father.

Certainly Julia and Richard were happy as they stood in the stone church to be married, then returned to the house for the wedding breakfast. Whenever their eyes met, they smiled so openly that some of the sharper wits of the *haut ton* began to point it out, rolling their eyes to show what they thought of such besottedness. Since Julia and Richard did not care, however, these satirists for once enjoyed themselves without spoiling anyone else's pleasure.

The only mystery was two wedding guests none of the others could identify. This was unusual because in Julia's and Richard's world, everyone knew everyone else, or could at least find an acquaintance to supply biographical information.

As the party progressed through toasts and trays of multicolored ices, however, it gradually became clear that no one knew the attractive young couple in the corner by the rosebushes. They were well-dressed and quiet, and the intrepid few who approached and presented themselves received a pleasant, but unencouraging reception and soon drifted away in the face of the man's monosyllables. The most that could be determined was that they were Mr. and Mrs. Shea and were acquainted with both Julia and Sir Richard.

When no more could be gotten from them, they were dismissed and ignored. No one noticed that they slipped away at the same time the bridal couple went to prepare for their departure. And no one missed them in the bustle of farewells as Julia's and Richard's carriage pulled away from the front door and started on its way to Dover. They would have been astonished to see that carriage slow and stop as soon as the house was out of sight, and the mysterious guests step out of the shrubbery that lined the drive and get in. But they had returned to the champagne and gossip by that time and had no hint of this curious development.

"A grand wedding," said Bess as she settled herself in the front corner of the chaise and the vehicle started up again. Michael turned his head quickly, and she added, "I'm not complaining. Ours was fine, too."

Julia smiled at the pair opposite. "Finer, in many ways. There were many times today when I remembered it and wished I could have had such a private, quiet ceremony."

Julia and Sir Richard had attended the Sheas in a small church nearby three days before, and signed the book as their witnesses after they were married by the parson. Only Michael's small family was there, and there could hardly have been a greater contrast between the two weddings. Yet the couple looked happy and satisfied.

"How long will it take to get to Dover?" asked Bess then.

"Most of the day," replied Sir Richard. "We will arrive in time for dinner, and your packet leaves early tomorrow."

"You're sure the trunks were sent to the right place?" she said, turning to Michael.

"Yes, Bess," was the answer, in a tone that suggested they'd had this discussion before. And that he'd said those two words often.

"I'm sorry. I never had a trunk before. I'd hate to lose it so soon."

The others laughed, and they all settled in for the day's journey.

Julia and Richard had arranged to make the first stage of their trip with the Sheas because it was difficult to let them go after what they had endured together. Though parting was inevitable, they put it off, for they knew it would also be final. It was most unlikely that the couples would ever see each other again. Bess and Michael were sailing for France, to settle in Paris and open the gaming club he had envisioned. Julia and Richard would take ship for Italy and spend three weeks there, then go on to Greece to examine some of the antiquities Richard had always wanted to see.

They talked intermittently of the future as they traveled, their plans very different, and when they arrived at the inn in Dover, they separated, promising to meet again in the morning at the dock to say farewell.

"I've ordered dinner here tonight," said Richard as the inn's servitors left their luggage in the rooms they had engaged. Julia's maid and his valet had traveled ahead, and would present themselves in the morning. "I didn't think we would want to eat downstairs."

Julia nodded. She felt shy, but only a little. In the last three weeks, she and Richard had become so close that it often amazed her. She hadn't known that such kinship was possible, and she was sometimes shaken at the thought that she might never have discovered it.

Sensing her mood once again, Richard came and took her in his arms. He held her close for a time, stroking her black hair in silence. Gradually, his hand slowed and stopped.

Feeling a change in him, Julia raised her head. He was looking down at her with a different intentness, and he immediately fastened his lips on hers in a kiss at once tender and demanding.

Julia pressed closer and slipped her arms around his neck. She had learned a good deal about passion in the last weeks, and she was eager to learn more.

The kiss went on and on. Richard's hands wandered over her body, rousing her as he had not done before and allowing his own desire free rein. His fingers were moving across her breast in a way Julia found intensely pleasurable when there was a brisk knock at the door, and they broke apart.

"Who the devil is this?" said Richard, striding to the door and throwing it open. Two servants stood in the corridor with laden trays.

"You ordered dinner, sir," one of them said.

He turned away abruptly, his face making Julia want to laugh. She did not, however, but merely indicated that the food should be brought in. Richard retreated to one of the bedrooms while a table was spread.

"They're gone," called Julia in a few minutes.

He reappeared, looking a bit sheepish, and she did laugh. After a moment, he joined her, and they went to the table in the bow window together. "I am hungry," he admitted.

Julia looked across at him, and he reached to take her hand.

They ate the crisp roasted chicken and vegetables with a very good wine Richard had chosen. Julia had three glasses before they had sampled the apple tart and risen from the table, far more than her usual ration. She felt giddy, as if bubbles of happiness were coursing through her and insisting on bursting out. She went to Richard and put one arm around his neck, urging him into a waltz.

"You're quite foxed," he said with amusement as they whirled about the parlor.

"I'm not!"

"I should not have given you that last glass of wine."

"I feel wonderful!" Julia stopped dancing and moved very close to him. "Wonderful."

"I'm glad of that," he murmured, and bent to kiss her again.

Their embrace was so arousing that they did not separate in the conventional fashion to don their nightclothes. Julia, her gown pushed off her shoulders and her eyes bright, undid the fastenings and let it fall to the floor. In one swift movement, she discarded her shoes and stockings, and her petticoat went in another. She stood before him then in her thin shift, her arms held out to either side in innocent abandon. His gray eyes hot with desire, Richard swept her up and carried her into the bedroom, shutting the door with his foot as he passed.

The day dawned foggy and cool, the halcyon summer weather gone. When Julia and Richard reached the dock, there was some question as to whether the packet for

France would go, and they stood with Bess in the chill, waiting for word. Soon, however, Michael returned to say that the captain of the vessel had no doubt the fog would dissipate. He had been told to get aboard, and he pulled Bess's hand through his arm.

The four of them faced each other for the last time. Though they were so unlike, their shared ordeal had brought them close, and none seemed able to put into words the sadness of parting. It was the clear end of one time, and though it was also the beginning of another, that lay in the future.

Someone called out from the boat. Bess moved abruptly, stepping forward to embrace Julia quickly and tightly, and then, after a tiny hesitation, Sir Richard. Michael shook hands with them.

"We'll think of you," said Julia. "Often."

Unexpectedly, Michael grinned. "Ah, we'll name our first after you," he said. "Julia or Richard, as the case may require."

They all laughed, and the Sheas went aboard. The packet cast off the dock. They stood side by side at the rail and waved as the boat slipped away, the strip of water between it and the land slowly widening. The fog began to obscure them. "Good-bye," called Julia. She heard a faint reply, and then the ship was only a vague outline. She blinked back tears.

Richard put an arm about her shoulders and held her against him.

"It is just so final," she said.

"I know."

"Usually, when you say good-bye, you know you will see the person again."

"Perhaps I will teach you to play hazard," he answered.

Julia looked up, startled. His face was perfectly serious, but there was a suspicious twinkle in his gray eyes.

"Then we can visit Shea's club together," he added, "and lose some money to him."

The picture was so absurd that Julia burst out laughing.

Richard smiled. "We can find them again," he said, "when we wish to. But now we have a boat to catch ourselves."

She nodded. "Italy."

They turned together and walked back along the dock, the fog slowly enveloping them as it had the boat for France.

HOW TO BEGUILE
A BARON

ONE

"It really does look *splendid*, does it not?" said eighteen-year-old Susan Wyndham, turning before the long glass to admire the flowing line of her pale green ball gown.

"Splendid," agreed her second cousin Georgina Goring, her twinkling gray eyes the only sign that this was at least the sixth time she had done so.

"I told you the ruffle at the hem would become me." Susan whirled to make the skirt bell out. "I am so glad I convinced the dressmaker to copy that pattern from *La Belle Assemblée*, in spite of her *ridiculous* objections. I do want to look stunning for my first ball."

Georgina, her expression wry as she thought of the turnup with the dressmaker, admitted to herself that Susan could hardly have looked ill. Her much younger cousin was exquisitely pretty, and had been since Georgina first met her at the age of six. Her hair was glowing red and her eyes sparkling green. She had the delicate figure of a Dresden shepherdess and the endurance of a navvy. If only, thought Georgina, her character was as perfect as her face, I shouldn't worry for a moment. She sighed softly. For Georgina, at the relatively young age of twenty-nine, had been put in charge of Susan's debut in society. Susan's mother was fully occupied at home with a brood of younger children—the result of her second marriage—and though there was great love between Anabel and her spirited daughter, the former was a confirmed country dweller and only too glad to delegate her responsibility. Susan's grandmother, Lady Sybil Goring, had happily taken it on, inviting the girl to her London town house and promising a variety of treats, but she had not been well lately, and a short visit by Georgina had been prolonged to allow Lady Goring to recover before resuming her social duties.

Georgina sighed again. Aunt Sybil *believed* herself within a few days of robust health, but the doctor's opinion was far different. It had been clear to Georgina for some time that she would be Susan's chief guide through the shoals of the opening Season. And this was doubly ironic—first because Georgina's own debut had been far from auspicious, and second because she was not at all certain she could control her young cousin, or even influence her.

Almost from birth, Susan Wyndham had been possessed of a lightning-quick temper. This had made her a difficult child, and it showed small sign of moderation, in Georgina's opinion, with the passage of years. The trouble with the dressmaker was only one example. Georgina had mediated a series of disputes since the girl's arrival less than two weeks ago.

In all other ways, Susan was charming, and her anger dissipated rapidly and completely, leaving her sheepish and apologetic. But in the first white heat of combat, she was formidable, despite her youth, and Georgina did not relish the prospect of chaperoning her among the *haut ton*.

There were many who would delight in rousing Susan, once her character was known, to discover how far she would go when angry, and Georgina shuddered to think of the consequences. Thus, her responsibility weighed heavily on her, obscuring any enjoyment she might have anticipated from the Season.

Of course, she expected little in any case. Georgina was

more at home in a country town than in a drawing room. She had learned something of the *ton*'s rituals during her own come-out ten years before, but her performance of them had been no more than adequate. She had arrived in London a bookish, overplump, and somewhat sullen young girl, resentful of the necessity to "come out," and though she had changed a great deal during those weeks, and even more in the years that followed, she was no more fond of town life. She wished, as she had many times in the last few days, that she could return to her quiet home. Though Papa had died four years ago, and she missed him, Georgina was content with her novels, her household tasks, and the round of visits and entertainments of country neighbors. That was the sort of society she loved, and in which she shone—a close-knit group of friends who shared both interests and experiences. Faced with Susan Wyndham, Georgina felt alarmingly like her clumsy young self, helpless in the grip of events and nearly certain the outcome would be disaster.

"Georgina," said Susan, her tone making it clear that she had spoken more than once. "What is the matter with you?"

Her cousin looked up, startled. "Nothing."

Susan surveyed her with pursed lips, deploring yet again Georgina's woolly-headedness. She did not understand how Georgina managed to get through a day without falling into the fire or walking in front of a moving carriage. Half the time when one spoke to her, she didn't hear, and when she did, the answers she gave were usually nonsensical. Only yesterday, as they'd been walking along Bond Street among the smartest shops, Susan had pointed out a ravishing bonnet and Georgina had answered, "She is his sister, I think, not his wife." It had turned out she was talking about a pair of complete strangers and paying no heed to Susan at all. Indeed, she often seemed oblivious of Susan, a trait which she found downright insulting. How unfortunate it was that Grandmama should be ill just now, Susan thought, not for the first time: for her own sake, of course, and also for Susan's. Georgina was a far less promising chaperone. Grandmama knew everyone and could have pointed out the notables and told their histories. Georgina would know hardly anyone. It was vastly irritating, and it might even, she worried, interfere with Susan's unwavering ambition to become a celebrated belle. Lady Goring was the picture of fashionable elegance and widely respected; all would notice her cherished granddaughter. But Georgina was unfashionable; there could be no two opinions about that.

There was nothing actually wrong with her appearance. She was of medium height, taller than Susan, and had a pleasing fine-boned frame. Her hair was a delicate pale blond and curled naturally into tendrils about her head, though it was *not* dressed in the latest mode, Susan thought. Her thickly lashed gray eyes were very striking, dominating an oval face with a straight nose and beautifully etched mouth above a determined chin. Susan freely admitted that Georgina had a way of moving, or turning her head slowly, that took one suddenly aback and revised one's opinion of her abruptly. At such times, there was an immense dignity and elegance in her carriage. If only she would make a push, lamented Susan silently, she could be quite fashionable. But no hint of Susan's seemed to reach her. Georgina went on wearing sadly simple gowns in the dullest colors. Her ball gown was a glaring example; it was of a washed-out rose and devoid of the simplest trim—not a ruffle or a knot of ribbon embellished its flow to the tips of Georgina's kid slippers. How could she expect to be distinguished in a garment such as *that*? wondered Susan with irritation.

She raised her eyes, met Georgina's gray ones, and had the uneasy feeling that her cousin knew exactly what she had been thinking. That was another trouble with Georgina. She saw through one in a way that Grandmama never did.

The corners of Georgina's mouth turned up a little, but she suppressed her smile. She was indeed fully aware of Susan's opinion of her clothes. But she disliked disputes, particularly with hot-tempered opponents, and she was too kind to point out that Susan's idea of elegance was rudimentary. Georgina prided herself on her taste, but the effect was too subtle for a girl fresh from the schoolroom and of a radically different temperament and coloring.

"We should be going," said Georgina. "The carriage is probably waiting."

"Oh yes," answered Susan, forgetting all else in her excitement over the coming ball. "I'm ready."

Smiling, Georgina indicated her wrap, and the two walked downstairs side by side, contemplating the evening ahead with rather different emotions.

Though the ball was one of the first events of the Season, it was also expected to be among the most brilliant. The Duchess of Millshire's eldest daughter was making her debut, and she was to be introduced with the greatest possible fanfare. The *ton* had been buzzing for weeks about the duchess's vast preparations, and none of the leading lights would be absent tonight. Indeed, Susan and Georgina were forced to wait nearly twenty minutes in Lady Goring's town carriage before the coachman could maneuver through the press of vehicles and deposit them at the pillared doorway. The delay raised Susan's impatience to fever pitch, and gave Georgina a sinking sensation, so that neither was at her best when they climbed the three steps and were admitted to the house by a liveried footman.

"Oh, do come along," said Susan, when Georgina was a bit slow in removing her wrap. "The dancing has probably started long since. We are missing everything!"

"I imagine, rather, that Lady Helen is still greeting guests with her mother," replied Georgina calmly, but she relinquished her cloak and started up the stairs.

The two ladies were indeed still at their summit, and Susan looked a little less sulky as they greeted their hostess and conveyed Lady Goring's regrets. And when they moved on into the ballroom, her annoyance faded in wide-eyed admiration of the decoration, for the duchess had spared nothing in decking her house for the occasion.

"Look there," exclaimed Susan as they walked. "That is a *fountain* in the corner, amongst those roses, and it is running!"

"I see it." Georgina was smiling.

Her cousin looked back. "You are laughing at me."

"I am not."

"You were. I suppose I sound hopelessly countrified. I must—"

"Look out," interrupted Georgina, who had noticed a group of guests approaching them from the side. Like Susan, they were engrossed in conversation.

But it was too late. Susan did not check, and the others had not seen. In the next moment, the girl had collided with a much taller young woman, and the two were forced to hang on to one another to keep from falling.

"I beg your pardon," began Susan.

"I'm sorry, I wasn't looking," said the other.

Then both fell abruptly silent and moved apart, staring. For they wore the same gown, down to the flouncing at the hem. The fabrics were a little different, but as the color was pale green, this scarcely signified. At first glance, the garments appeared identical, copied exactly from the pattern in *La Belle Assemblée*.

And this coincidence was made more startling by a superficial resemblance between the two girls. Both had vivid red hair and pale skin; both were strikingly lovely. And though the stranger's statuesque form and height contrasted strongly with Susan's delicacy, the difference merely accentuated the sartorial contretemps. The silence spread for quite five yards around them as people noticed the unusual tableau.

Georgina, seeing Susan's cheeks flame, opened her mouth to say something, anything, to ease the situation. But Susan was before her. "How dare you?" she said.

"What?" The taller girl had been looking slightly amused as well as disconcerted, but Susan's tone made her raise her eyebrows.

"Copy my gown," Susan hissed. As usual, her anger made her irrational. When it faded, she might well admit that this embarrassing misfortune was her own fault—for anyone might copy a fashion plate, after all. But just now she could see only the ruin of her plans to dazzle the *ton* and establish herself in society. She would be laughed at rather than admired. And the intolerable fact that this woman had her coloring, while a striking contrast in every other respect, only fed Susan's fury by spotlighting all the traits she had ever deplored in herself—her small stature, her tendency to fragility instead of curves, and the irritating air of innocence her features seemed to convey, when she wished to appear worldly and sophisticated. It was beyond bearing. At that moment, Susan would gladly have slapped the other girl's face.

"If we are to talk of copying," the newcomer replied, "I have had this dress since last Season. So you are the imitator." She couldn't resist the gibe, for the encounter had made her feel like a great clumsy giant confronting her image in miniature, and the sensation was far from pleasant. Though she could see the humor of the situation, its public character destroyed her impulse to laugh.

Susan's flush intensified, and her hands clenched at her sides. Any of her family would have quailed at these unmistakable signs.

"Isn't this too funny?" interjected Georgina, her voice sounding unnatural in her own ears. "I don't know when I've been so diverted." This was a feeble attempt, she knew, but something had to be done before Susan exposed herself before the whole of society.

"I should say, rather, exquisitely original," responded a deep baritone of such compelling magnetism that all three women turned instinctively. The man standing behind Georgina had not been part of either colliding group. He was also immediately identifiable to all but Susan. Even Georgina, whose knowledge of London society was small, could not mistake Randal Kenyon, Baron Ellerton. His physical appearance alone was distinctive. Tall, his well-formed person enhanced by various fashionable athletic pursuits, he radiated power and competence. And he was strikingly handsome as well, with deep chestnut hair and vivid blue eyes that seemed to take note of everything that passed before them. Indeed it was these eyes that transfixed the three women now; they were sparkling with intelligence and understanding of their dilemma, and with an amusement that somehow didn't offend. "However did you conceive such a stunning effect?" he added, suppressing a smile at their amazement. "You have certainly made a hit. I congratulate you."

Susan gazed up at him, her anger forgotten in astonishment and confusion. The other girl smiled slightly, her own amusement returning. Georgina simply stared. Her low opinion of the *haut ton* gave this intervention the quality of miracle. Why, she wondered silently, should one of the leaders of society exert himself on their behalf? For even she had heard of Baron Ellerton's vast fortune, his elegance, and his political influence. She could see for herself that he epitomized the Corinthian, his evening dress severely perfect, his manner supremely assured. Yet he had taken it upon himself to defuse a situation that was threatening to rouse a storm of malicious laughter. Georgina defined the *ton* by its malice; what could the man be about?

"I hope you'll pardon my intrusion," he went on, blue eyes dancing. "I could not resist complimenting you on your refreshing jest. Many women would have feared to try such a game, yet it is just the sort of diversion we need. Do you know that there are women, and men too, who would be livid to meet another in the same ensemble."

"No, Baron Ellerton!" exclaimed the tall girl in mock astonishment.

"I assure you." They exchanged a smile. "At least, Lady

Marianne, I am not guilty of pushing in where I am wholly unknown. Will you introduce me to your friends?"

"Er, Baron Ellerton, this is…" Lady Marianne turned to the others, perplexed. The baron's eyes twinkled anew.

But Georgina was too grateful to feel embarrassment. "Georgina Goring," she said. "And this is my cousin Miss Susan Wyndham."

Ellerton bowed slightly. "I have not seen you in town before, I think." And as he got a full view of Georgina, his manner shifted slightly. This was no silly chit, nor even a sensible girl, like Lady Marianne. Baron Ellerton took in the distinctive character of Georgina's gown and expression, and smiled in appreciation.

"No, we have come for the Season." Georgina responded automatically to his smile. She could see no mockery in it.

"I don't understand," declared Susan, her tone indicating that she was fully prepared to resume hostilities.

Georgina hastened to reply, "Lord Ellerton perceived your joke at once, Susan. He saw that you and, er, Lady Marianne had devised a scheme to amuse everyone. I'm certain they've all noticed by this time how clever you were." She put heavy emphasis on this last phrase, trying to convey a great deal more in her look.

Susan gazed around the ballroom appraisingly. She had feared being laughed at, but if these Londoners thought she had done it on purpose… She contemplated this prospect for a moment. She was quite eager to be *noticed*, as long as the scrutiny was favorable.

Three pairs of eyes watched the shift of emotion so visible on Susan's face—Georgina anxiously, Lady Marianne

quizzically, and Baron Ellerton biting his lower lip to keep
from laughing.

Susan took a deep breath. "Yes, well, it was a good joke,
wasn't it?"

Georgina couldn't restrain an audible sigh of relief.

"Capital," agreed Lady Marianne, then laughed.

"I can see that you two young women are very enter-
prising," added the baron. "You will be a definite asset
to society." He glanced at Georgina as if to share a joke
with her.

Susan looked up, truly seeing him for the first time now
that her rage had dissipated, blinked, and looked again. His
attractiveness and air of fashion seemed to register all at
once, and she took another breath.

"And now, if you will excuse me," he said. "I have promised to open the dancing, and I believe they are waiting for
me." With another small bow, he turned away. All three
women watched him approach their hosts and lead the
daughter of the house onto the floor to open the ball.

"What a complete hand he is," murmured Lady
Marianne.

This brought Susan swinging around again. "Who is he?"

"Randal Kenyon, Baron Ellerton, one of the acknowledged leaders of the *ton*," she replied. "And a true gentleman, as you saw. People will ask him about this incident,
you know, and what he says will be taken up and repeated."

Georgina nodded, her gratitude welling up again. How
would she have managed to smooth things over without his
help?

"You mean, if he says we did it on purpose, everyone will
believe him?" asked Susan.

"They will," answered Lady Marianne, "as they never would have if *we* said it." She smiled again. "And so, since we are to be talked of as great friends, perhaps we should become better acquainted. My name is Marianne MacClain. This is the start of my second Season in town."

"It is my first," responded Susan a bit grudgingly. She had not gotten over her envy of the other's poise.

"Well, you have made a fine start. Not every newcomer is noticed by Ellerton. I daresay you will be showered with invitations after this."

Susan turned to look at the baron once again, with this delightful prospect filling her head. He really was the handsomest man she had ever seen, and evidently a great catch. "Is he married?" Marianne shook her head. Susan smiled a little, then frowned as a dreadful suspicion entered her mind. "*You* are well acquainted with Lord Ellerton?" she asked.

Lady Marianne was also watching the dancers. "Not particularly. But I should not object to furthering my acquaintance."

"He helped *me*," snapped Susan, relieved.

"I beg your pardon?"

"Well, it must have been me. *You* were here last Season; he might have spoken to you anytime." Her tone implied that Lady Marianne had practically been left on the shelf.

"Susan!" said Georgina.

But Lady Marianne was smiling. "I had certain, er, other concerns last year."

"Lady Marianne MacClain," gasped Georgina. "You refused Lord Robert Devere!"

The other raised her russet eyebrows.

"I beg your pardon," said Georgina. "My aunt wrote me

about it. I thought I had heard your name, and it suddenly came to me…" She trailed off, once again conscious of her clumsiness with strangers.

"It doesn't matter. It is true, after all."

"Who is Lord Robert Devere?" asked Susan sharply.

Marianne looked around, then nodded toward the far corner of the ballroom. "There he is."

Susan looked, and saw a man as fashionable as Ellerton, though somewhat older and not, she thought, nearly so handsome. But it infuriated her that this confident girl should have actually received an offer from such a polished-looking nobleman, and rejected it! She felt bested again, a thing she hated above all else. "I don't see how that signifies," she said, tossing her head. "Lord Ellerton was clearly coming to *my* rescue." She looked at him again, calculating.

"I imagine he was simply amusing himself," corrected Marianne. "He is reputed to love oddities." She too directed a speculative gaze at the dance floor. "But he *was* very kind."

"To *me*," insisted Susan.

Marianne met her smoldering eyes, and her lips curved upward. "Well, we shall see about that, shan't we?"

Susan did not look away, for a long moment they faced one another like duelists. Then Susan nodded once abruptly. "Yes. We shall." And without taking leave, she turned and walked toward the row of gilt chairs against the wall.

"Oh dear," murmured Georgina. She looked from Susan to Marianne. "I beg your pardon. She did not mean…" She stopped, aware that Susan had meant various rude things.

Marianne MacClain laughed. "It doesn't matter. I know precisely how she feels. I daresay we really will be great friends in the end, as Lord Ellerton has christened us."

Georgina looked doubtful. "I hope so."

A young man came up then, full of reproaches. "Lady Marianne! I have been searching everywhere. You promised me the first set."

With a smile and nod to Georgina, she allowed him to lead her away. Georgina turned to follow her cousin, a worried line remaining between her pale brows.

TWO

LADY MARIANNE MACCLAIN SPENT THE FIRST PART OF the next morning alone in the drawing room of her family's town house wishing for callers. She was not a great reader, or indeed fond of any sedentary pursuits, and the lack of company soon began to wear on her patience. A year ago, such solitude would have been most unusual. Marianne could have been certain of the companionship of her mother and confident that her brother would appear at some time during the day. But both of these had married recently, her mother after a long widowhood, and now each was engrossed in personal concerns. Her brother Ian, Earl of Cairnyllan, was abroad visiting his new wife's father, the Duke of Morland, and her mother seemed to have become a different person since wedding a long-ago suitor. Marianne understood, and applauded, her mother's efforts to erase memories of her first, unhappy match, but it was unsettling to see one's mother behaving like a girl newly married. Though they still lived in the same house, Marianne often felt as if they had separate establishments. And there were moments when she came near to resenting her new stepfather, Sir Thomas Bentham, though in fact she liked him very much.

Thus, the sounds of an arrival in the front hall caused Marianne to jump up and run to the landing, straining to hear the exchange taking place at the door.

"I'm not certain Lady Marianne is in either," the butler was saying in the tone he reserved for doubtful callers.

"You mean everyone's out?" responded a youthful male voice. "Dash it, they had my letter a week ago."

The voice was unfamiliar. Marianne frowned as she tried to place it.

"Lady Bentham must have left instructions," insisted the visitor.

"Not to my knowledge, sir." But the butler sounded less discouraging.

"She and my cousin settled it all between them." The visitor sounded aggrieved. "I know no one in London. What am I to do? Kick up my heels in the street until Lady Bentham comes home?"

"If you will wait in the library, I will make inquiries."

The young man agreed reluctantly, and Marianne retreated to the drawing room as she heard the butler coming upstairs. In another moment he appeared. "I beg pardon, Lady Marianne, but a young gentleman has called. Or perhaps I should say, arrived. It seems that he is to stay with us." Hobbs looked reproachful. "I was not informed, or I should, of course, have ordered a room prepared."

"I don't know anything about it either, Hobbs." Marianne was intrigued. "Who is he?"

"His name is Brinmore, my lady."

She shook her head, perplexed. "I don't know anyone named Brinmore."

"He claims that Lady Bentham has corresponded with his cousin."

Since Marianne had overhead this, she was already puzzling over the connection. But she couldn't recall any mention of this man, or his family. It was an engaging mystery. "I suppose Mama forgot to tell me. She is...very busy lately." The butler ventured a commiserating look. Lady Bentham had always been gentle and absentminded rather than incisive, but since her marriage she seemed almost scatterbrained. "You had better bring him to me," concluded Marianne, concealing her pleasure in this unlooked-for diversion. "I'll find out what it is all about."

Hobbs looked doubtful. "Shall I send for your maid, my lady?"

"I don't think this young man can be dangerous. But if Mama comes in, send her up at once."

The butler hesitated, not quite approving this decision, then turned away. "Very well, my lady."

Marianne couldn't help grinning at his back, stiff with offended propriety. If their stuffy London butler, recently added to the household, had any notion how she had grown up in Scotland, wholly unsupervised, he would no doubt expire from shock.

Though she loved London and the amusements of the *haut ton*, its restrictions had been difficult for Marianne at first. Only her brother had ever tried to curb her before they left home, and she had resisted with all her strength, rightly concluding that the notorious excesses of their father had made Ian too strict. It had required personal experience, along with the far more understanding and tactful guidance of the woman who had later become Ian's wife, to show Marianne that certain restraints were necessary, and even desirable. She had come close to making a number of mistakes, but Marianne was remarkably levelheaded, as well as intelligent, and she had learned quickly and well. This Season would be far calmer than last.

A reminiscent smile curved her lips; what rows she and Ian had had. If anyone had told her that she would actually miss them... She shook her head.

Thus, the visitor entered the drawing room to find a very beautiful girl smiling pensively at the carpet. He was momentarily transfixed. Though liking to think himself at ease in any situation, Mr. Brinmore was in fact not yet one-and-twenty, and this was his first visit to the metropolis. Moreover, his dealings with the fair sex had not so far included a girl as lovely and fashionable as Lady Marianne MacClain. He swallowed, very conscious of her status as daughter and sister of an earl. "Er, hello."

Marianne started, brought back from a great distance. "Oh, I beg your pardon. How do you do? Come in." He moved a bit further into the room. "I am Marianne MacClain, you know. Hobbs tells me you've come to stay with us?"

Her tone was perfectly amiable, but Brinmore flushed. "I understood it was all settled, but no one here seems to know anything about it. I don't know quite what—"

"I think you had best tell me the whole story," interrupted Marianne, seeing his discomfort. "My mother is a little…forgetful sometimes. And let us sit down."

She did so, and Mr. Brinmore followed suit, leaning forward in his eagerness to justify his presence. "It all began with my cousin Elisabeth," he said. "She's great friends with the Fermors, in the country."

It took Marianne a moment to place the name. "Oh, yes, Sir Thomas's sister."

"Right." He looked relieved. "So when I thought of coming up to town, they determined to write to Sir Thomas and his new wife." Brinmore paused, as if uncertain how Marianne would take this reference to her mother's remarriage. She nodded encouragingly. "We knew no one else, you see, and I didn't like to come without any acquaintance."

"Of course not."

Brinmore looked further relieved. "Well, Lady Bentham replied that they, er, you, would be happy to make introductions. Indeed, she invited me to stay here." He looked slightly reproachful. "I have the letter in my bag."

"And when you arrived, no one seemed to know anything about it. How dreadful for you." Marianne shook her head sympathetically, but her vivid blue eyes were dancing.

"Well, it was," the young man agreed. Had anyone told him that Marianne was actually some months his junior, he would have scoffed. "If Lady Bentham has changed her mind, I can—"

"No, no. Mama simply forgot to mention it, I'm sure. I'll have the servants prepare a room. It won't take a moment." Privately, Marianne gave thanks for this addition to their household. Now, at least, she would have someone of her own age to talk with.

Brinmore rose as she did, uneasy. "I don't wish to put you to any trouble. Are you sure that—"

"Nonsense! I'll just tell Hobbs."

She went out, and he sank slowly onto the sofa again. This arrival was far different from the one he had imagined. He had seen himself sweeping into an elegant London town house with perfect aplomb, and greeted with gratifying deference roused by this assurance beyond his years. Instead, he'd felt like a clumsy schoolboy. Indeed, Lady Marianne reminded him strongly of his cousin Elisabeth, several years his senior and very much in charge of their household. It was almost too much.

"There," said Marianne bracingly, coming back into the room and startling him out of his reverie. "All settled. Now we can get better acquainted. Do you know you have not even told me your full name?"

Feeling an unaccountable trepidation, he said, "It's Tony. Anthony Brinmore, that is."

———————————————

Strangely enough, a very similar scene was in progress less than a mile away, in the town house of Lady Sybil Goring, where Susan Wyndham was confronting an open-faced young man with brown hair and blue eyes. Her approach, however, was more direct. "Well, I don't see why you've come. It was quite unnecessary."

The newcomer smiled, the shifting planes of his face suggesting a sunny temperament combined with familiarity with Susan's habits and a certain ability to deal with them. "Mama thought it a good idea, when she heard Grandmama was ill." His smile became a grin. "She thought Cousin Georgina might want some help."

"Nonsense!"

"We'll see what Georgina says." He continued to gaze at Susan with quizzical amusement, and after a valiant attempt at offended dignity, she finally let an answering smile show. In another moment, the two were laughing together.

"Well, but, William, it is too unfair," protested Susan after a while. "I have been a model of propriety since I arrived in town. That is, except for..." She paused, biting her lower lip.

"Just so," replied William. "I expect Mama thought you would benefit from the guidance of the head of the family."

"You?" She was torn between further laughter and outrage. "You are only three years older than me."

"Older than *I*," he corrected solemnly, though his blue eyes twinkled.

"Anyway," continued Susan, ignoring this, "Christopher is the head of our family."

"Not of the Wyndhams. As Mama's husband, of course he has our respect. But I hold the title and the estate." As he said this, his joking tone disappeared, and there was something impressive about the declaration despite his youth. It was obvious that he took his responsibilities very seriously, and was eminently capable of fulfilling them.

His younger sister was not impressed. "Sir William Wyndham," she mocked. "I wonder you don't have a long gray beard by this time. I shall write to Mama at once and tell her there is no need to take you away from your precious estate. We are getting along splendidly."

William shifted from one foot to the other. "I…wish you wouldn't, Susan."

"I won't be watched over like a prisoner!"

"Who said any such thing?" He paused, seeming a little embarrassed. "The thing is, I've a fancy to see something of London. I am of age now, and…"

Susan's green eyes glowed. "The country squire is giving in at last," she crowed. "I thought you hated the very idea of town. I thought you did not care if you ever attended an assembly at Almack's or saw the king."

"There *are* other amusements in London," he answered loftily.

"Oh, I see. Then you will not be accompanying us to any of the *ton* parties?"

"Dash it, Susan," he began, for clearly this was not his intention.

But she dissolved in laughter and ran forward to hug him. "I'm only bamming you. It will be splendid to have you here if you are not to be an odious watchdog. We will have such fun! It's too bad Nick is still at Oxford."

Her brother laughed again. "He's far happier there than in town. You know how he hates society."

"*You* changed your mind," she pointed out.

"I always liked our country entertainments," he countered. "Nick would far rather read a book."

For a moment they marveled silently at this aberration; then Susan shook her head and looked up. "Come and see all the invitations we've received just in the last week. I'm sure you can come with us to the parties." She looked him over. "After you buy a new coat, of course."

"What's wrong with my coat?"

"Oh, William," she said in pitying accents, and turned toward the hall. Instantly he caught up to her and tweaked at the ribbon threaded through her red curls. Unfastened, they tumbled down about her shoulders. Susan whirled to snatch the ribbon back. "You beast! It took me half an hour to tie it up."

"Perhaps *you* should get a new coif," he retorted.

Susan lunged as if to pull his cravat. William jumped back, but in doing so his heel caught on something, and he fell heavily to the carpet. His exclamation of surprise was nearly drowned out by a yowl, and both young people turned to watch a mass of ginger fur streak for the doorway.

"Susan, you haven't brought that damned cat to London?" exclaimed Sir William.

She merely smiled. He pushed himself up and stood, looking disgusted. "You'd think that creature would improve with age. He must be…what, nearly fourteen?" He shook his head incredulously. "But he's as mean-tempered as ever."

"Daisy is never mean to *me*."

"And why you insist on calling him Daisy—it's ridiculous."

Susan, who had acquired the cat at an early age, shrugged. "He's used to it."

"Well, we're none of us used to *him*," muttered her brother, examining his sleeve to make sure it wasn't torn.

"Come and see the invitations," she coaxed, taking his arm and urging him forward. After a moment, he yielded, and they walked out together.

Marianne MacClain's conversation was also just ending. The butler had come to say the young gentleman's room was ready, and Tony Brinmore had risen to follow him upstairs. But he paused in the drawing-room doorway, seeming uneasy. "There's one other thing," he said.

Marianne looked politely interested.

"I've, er…" He stopped, flushing.

Marianne wondered what could be the matter now. Her talk with their visitor had been halting. He was very like some of the young men she met at parties, awkward and tongue-tied in her presence. She found it rather wearisome. Tony seemed a pleasant-enough boy, but her visions of a replacement for her brother and his wife had dissolved.

"Actually, I've brought a dog," he blurted out.

"A dog?" she repeated, startled.

"Yes. I put him in the stables. He's so old now, you see,

that I couldn't bear to leave him behind. He would have fretted so, perhaps died. I've had him for years and years."

This made their guest seem younger than ever. Marianne smiled. "That's all right. He can stay in the stables."

Tony's face cleared. His relief was almost ludicrous. "Thanks."

"Not at all. I like dogs. You must show him to me later."

His anxiety returned. "Oh, well, he's not a purebred, you know. I daresay you may find him…that is, he may not be your sort of dog."

Marianne couldn't help but laugh. "We shall see. Now, go and settle into your room. Mama will be home for dinner, and you can meet her and Sir Thomas then."

This did not seem to lighten her guest's mood, but he nodded and turned to follow the long-suffering Hobbs.

THREE

THE COUNTESS OF CHEANE WAS THAT EVENING PRE-
senting an eminent Italian singer to society at a musicale,
and the *haut ton* was nearly all in attendance. Though genuine love of music was by no means widespread, the event
had acquired immense cachet during weeks of gossip fos-
tered by the countess and her friends. Thus, both Marianne
and Susan were able to assure the newcomers to their households that the evening was the height of fashion, and the
young men accompanied them with far more enthusiasm
than either would normally have shown for such an outing.

"Here we are," said Susan unnecessarily as they pulled up
before the countess's house. "Those are linkboys, William.
They light the way for the chairs."

"If you lean so far out, you will fall in the street,"
responded her brother shortly, not pleased to be lectured
on the ways of the town. Susan grimaced at him.

They went inside, and the ladies left their wraps. As they
climbed the stairs to the drawing room, William hung back a
little. "Do you think my coat is all right?" he asked Georgina
quietly. "Susan seemed to find it hopelessly countrified."

"It is not the latest fashion," agreed Georgina, knowing
that he would see this for himself soon enough and that
false reassurance would be useless. "But it is well made and
you look the gentleman."

He nodded. "That should be good enough for anyone."

"There is that girl," hissed Susan over her shoulder.

"What girl?" answered Georgina in a normal voice.

"Shh! The one from the ball."

234

JANE ASHFORD

There could be no mistaking this reference, and
Georgina looked up to find Marianne MacClain greeting
their hostess on the landing.

"That one?" asked William admiringly. "Are you
acquainted with her?"

"Shh!" repeated Susan. "Let us wait here until…" But
more guests came up behind them, forcing their group to
move up the stairs and reach the countess before Marianne's
party had left her. Indeed, the press was so great that the
two families were forced to walk into the drawing room
together.

Susan and Marianne exchanged nods, and might have
left it at that had it not been for William. Clearly struck with
Marianne's charms, he requested an introduction, and this
led to reciprocal presentations of Lady Bentham and her
husband, Georgina, and Tony Brinmore. Lady Bentham,
unconscious of any awkwardness, immediately suggested
they find chairs and to Marianne's amused consternation
and Susan's obvious outrage, they all sat down together near
the back of the room.

Lady Bentham was quite content to talk to her husband,
and Georgina offered an occasional remark in counterpoint
to their duet. William had taken care to place himself beside
Marianne, leaving Susan and Tony to occupy the end of the
row of gilt chairs.

"I understand this is to be a famous evening," William
ventured as soon as they were settled.

"Yes, indeed," replied Marianne with a smile. "You are
fond of music?"

"I? Well, tolerably fond."

"That's good. They say Signora Veldini can go on for

hours, once she begins. She is to do the aria from *The Marriage of Figaro*, you know."

"Is she, by Jove? How, er, splendid." William smiled unconvincingly.

Marianne began to laugh. "I don't believe you care for opera at all." As William began to protest, she added, "It doesn't matter. I don't myself. Indeed, half the people in this room will be dreadfully bored by the singing. More than half."

"But why do they come, then?"

"Why did you come?"

"Susan told me it was all the crack." He glanced at his sister accusingly, at the same time savoring the sensation of using a bit of fashionable slang he had picked up only in the last half hour.

"Oh, it is. Undoubtedly. And that is the answer to your question. Nearly everyone is here so that they may say they *were*. A great many *ton* parties are like that."

"A dead bore?" wondered William, half-suspicious that she was mocking him.

Marianne nodded, her blue eyes dancing.

His suspicion confirmed, William sat straighter, his face losing some of its eager openness. He looked suddenly older, and much more dignified. "I don't see why *you* bother to attend in that case," he replied.

Marianne opened her eyes very wide. "I didn't say *I* was bored," she retorted teasingly.

"Very true." William withdrew still more, his expression freezing and his eyes, which had been so ingenuous, hardening.

Marianne's smile faded, and her russet eyebrows drew together in puzzlement. She'd been playing the conventional game of flirtation. Why was he responding so coldly? It was almost as if he was offended. Too, she realized that her initial judgment of him had been incomplete. She'd thought him a typical country squire, awed by town trappings and fairly uninteresting to one who had already spent a season among the *haut ton*.

There was more to his character, she saw now. He had a sternness and an air of maturity that beyond his years. "I was only joking, you know," she was moved to say.

"Obviously," was the only reply.

Marianne's frown deepened. Really, he was prickly. But some spark of interest in him made her add, "As I would with anyone. It is a way they have of talking here."

He thawed slightly. "They?"

"Well, Londoners, the *ton*. I hardly count myself one of them."

"No?"

She was annoyed now, by his oversensitivity and the superior tone he took. But this very annoyance was intriguing. Marianne had met a variety of gentlemen since she came to town, from eager boys to blasé Corinthians, and this one was unlike any other. He seemed ready to enjoy the Season's amusements, but not to lose himself in them— neither bored nor dazzled. In an odd way, he reminded Marianne of her brother Ian. Yet that was ridiculous, she thought at once; the two were nothing alike. "No," she found herself saying, "I come from Scotland."

"Really, Scotland? I've always wanted to try the fishing there." William smiled—not sheepishly, but to show that he was more than willing to converse rationally on almost any subject she should suggest.

"It is good," answered Marianne, smiling back. She was, she found, relieved at the change in his mood. The two of them settled happily to discuss the north, gaining a more favorable impression of each other with every moment.

It was far otherwise with the couple on their right. Susan's first words upon sitting down were, "What a stupid place. We are much too far back. Why didn't Georgina object?"

Understandably, Tony Brinmore had no ready reply to this. He contented himself with a murmur that might be construed as assent and crossed one leg over the other in an effort to appear at ease. At first glance, Susan's elfin prettiness had attracted him, but it appeared that London girls were all intimidating, in one way or another.

Susan fumed silently for a few moments, but when her attempts to catch Georgina's eye failed, and she saw that William was not to be dislodged, she sighed audibly and turned back to the only available target. The appraising look she gave Tony caused him to shift uneasily in his chair. "Who are you, exactly?" she asked him.

"I…I beg your pardon?"

"I don't understand who you are," she repeated. "You are a connection of Lady Bentham's family?"

"No. Friend of Sir Thomas's sister. That is, my cousin is." Feeling this to be confusing, he added, "Name's Tony, Tony Brinmore."

"I heard your name," answered Susan. "So you're staying with Sir Thomas and Lady Bentham for the Season?"

He nodded warily.

"This is your first visit to London?" Susan was impatient, but she was also enjoying the sense that she was more at ease than he. Since entering society, she had suffered certain shocks to her self-esteem in this area.

"Yes."

"Mine also. This sort of thing is amusing, is it not?" She waved a hand to indicate their surroundings, thrilled by the world-weary tone she'd managed.

This was too much. "Have you been to a musical evening before?" inquired Tony aggressively.

"Well, I..."

"I suppose you know all about this"—he consulted the program sheet he had been given—"Signora Veldini? What's she like?"

"I have not actually..."

"No, I don't suppose you have. In fact, you know nothing whatsoever about it." He stopped abruptly and flushed at his own rudeness, then told himself that she had deserved it.

Susan Wyndham's green eyes were sparkling alarmingly. "I know more than you," she snapped. "I know, for example, that that neckcloth is wretchedly tied. It looks as if you crumpled it in your fist."

Tony drew himself up with a gasp, his flush deepening. She had hit a sore point; he'd had serious doubts about the neckcloth himself. But these were, of course, forgotten now. "I'll have you know this is a perfect Mathematical," he sputtered, using a term hastily recalled from a gentleman's periodical.

"Mathematical?" Susan sneered. "Don't be ridiculous."

Tony longed to give her a sharp setdown, but he also knew that he was on weak ground. He would go out and order a whole new wardrobe first thing tomorrow, he vowed. "Obviously you know nothing about fashion either," he replied loftily.

Susan began a scorching reply, but at that moment she caught sight of Baron Ellerton making his way along the back of the room to a chair three rows behind. Immediately, Tony Brinmore was forgotten. She followed the elegant figure of the older man, and eyed with rancorous curiosity the stunning brunette by whose side he settled himself.

Tony, conscious that he had lost her attention, followed her gaze. The sight of Baron Ellerton turned his anger to glum envy. Here, clearly, was a true man of fashion, and the contrast between his appearance and Tony's own filled him with despair. It was no wonder girls laughed at him, he thought. He had to find a tailor at once. Sir Thomas would know someone.

To Tony's relief, the countess mounted the low platform that had been erected across the end of the drawing room and called her guests to order for the beginning of the program. Susan was forced to turn back, and William and Marianne to drop what had by now become an animated exchange. Slowly the hum of conversation died, and the audience fell into an anticipatory silence.

Signora Veldini's voice was impressive; it filled the room with ease. Indeed, some of the countess's guests thought it overfilled, though few would have admitted it. Too, the statuesque Italian seemed tireless. Each mark of appreciation as she finished a selection spurred her to further efforts, and the audience's enthusiasm was clearly strained by the time their hostess again mounted the platform and announced the interval. The signora looked surprised and displeased, but the listeners rose at once, giving her no chance to protest that she was not yet at all tired.

"Who is this Figaro, anyway?" asked William as their

party moved slowly toward the refreshment room. "His marriage must have been a rum go."

Marianne laughed aloud, but when William frowned, she answered, "It must indeed."

"*I* think this party is rum," put in Tony Brinmore, who had overheard. "If this is the *haut ton*'s idea of amusement, I'm sorry I ever came to London."

William turned to agree, and the two young men sized each other up approvingly. They were similar in age and height, though they didn't resemble each other. Tony's hair was dark blond to William's brown, and his eyes a sparkling hazel while William's were blue. Too, Tony's frame was rangy rather than compact. But they were drawn together by the like state of their clothes. Surrounded by male elegance, and conscious of amused glances from more than one pink of the *ton*, they at once made common cause. William's concern was far less than Tony's, but he saw the other's discomfort with understanding. And their total agreement about the music further cemented the bond. Before the group reached the refreshment room, the young men had made a date to visit a tailor the following day, and were talking as if they'd known each other for years.

This left Marianne to chat with Georgina, for Susan was paying attention to nobody, her eyes fixed on the other guests.

"Did you enjoy the program?" Marianne inquired.

"Her voice is splendid," answered Georgina, "but I thought the selections poorly organized, and of course, she went on too long."

"You are a connoisseur, I see."

"I?" Georgina looked startled. "Oh no. I am fond of

music, and attend concerts whenever I can, but my tastes are uneducated."

"Indeed, anyone can see that," teased Marianne gently. "That is why you brought your music to follow along." She indicated the morocco folder tucked under the other's arm.

Georgina flushed a little. "I had heard she was to sing the aria, and I just thought…"

"You needn't act as if I'd caught you at something shameful. I admire your application. Do you sing?"

Seeing that she meant it, Georgina smiled. "I am a mere amateur."

"Oh yes, we have established that." The younger girl smiled again. She found Miss Goring's modesty endearing. "I wish I liked music more. My brother says I play the pianoforte as if I had no fingers, only fists. I began late in life, of course."

"You have other talents," offered Georgina.

"Do I? Perhaps." She smiled ruefully.

They reached the rooms where the buffet was spread, and the ladies sat round a table while the gentlemen went off to fill plates. Separated from her husband, Lady Bentham seemed to recall her social obligations, and she addressed some remark to each of them in turn, and introduced Georgina and Susan to several passing fashionables. She was just about to present another when Susan abruptly stood and moved a few steps away from the table. Startled, the others merely watched as she tossed her red curls and smiled brilliantly at an approaching gentleman—Baron Ellerton.

Whether he would have paused to speak to them was unclear, and irrelevant now, for he had no choice. He strolled back to their table beside Susan and greeted the other ladies with a pleasant smile. They had begun to exchange the usual comments about the performance when Susan blurted out, "Do sit down and join us."

Georgina couldn't restrain a grimace. Lady Bentham looked vaguely surprised, and Marianne's expression was a mixture of amusement, annoyance, and commiseration. The baron, unfailingly polite, agreed. "For a moment, perhaps." But he did not take the chair next to Susan, moving rather to that between Georgina and Lady Bentham.

Susan frowned, but the return of the other gentlemen with loaded plates put an end to conversation. As they were handing round their booty and finding chairs themselves, Georgina murmured, "I do beg your pardon."

Her voice was so low the baron barely heard, but he turned toward her, and Georgina's cheeks reddened a little as she repeated the apology.

"No need," he replied, smiling in a way that made Georgina's pulse quicken. He really was extraordinarily handsome, she told herself, trying to explain her uncharacteristic susceptibility. And, of course, one couldn't help thinking of his great position. But she'd encountered men with both these attributes before during her stays in London. What was it about this one, she wondered, that affected her so acutely?

It must be embarrassment over Susan's behavior. She'd never been in charge of another when going into society.

"Why be so very concerned about Miss Susan Wyndham's, er, enthusiasms?" he asked, still smiling.

"I must be. I am in charge of her, you see, and—"

"You?"

He needn't be quite so surprised, Georgina thought,

nettled. "I am well able to look after her." But even as she said it, she wished she'd held her tongue. She hadn't demonstrated any such skill tonight or at the ball where Susan had nearly lost her temper. Indeed, *he* had saved that situation while she stood by like a stone. She waited for a mocking setdown, which she undoubtedly deserved.

"I meant only that you are young to be in sole charge of a deb," he added. "And one who will most likely be, er, very lively." He smiled again, inviting her to share his mild joke and appreciating the play of expression across her face. This woman was unusual, he thought. On the one hand, she possessed a quiet elegance of dress and demeanor that suggested aloof disinterest. Had he not spoken to her, he would have merely admired the classically severe lines of her cream silk gown and her way of holding herself, and moved on. But in conversation she revealed a susceptibility and an endearing hint of uncertainty that was at odds with her cool beauty. She was, Ellerton thought, neither one thing nor the other, and he found the combination arresting.

Georgina gazed at him. He really wasn't mocking her, she saw with astonishment. Nor was he exhibiting the boredom and impatience she had expected to see in a very few minutes after he sat down. The expression in his eyes was interested and... She groped for a word. Measuring.

Georgina had not found much kindness in the higher reaches of London society. Indeed, her experience was just the opposite. In her own first Season, she'd been subject to enough sly raillery and careless setdowns to last her a lifetime; and though she'd changed a great deal since then, her expectations had not.

Had she considered the matter beforehand, Georgina

would have been certain Baron Ellerton was a supercilious, arrogant man, like many others she'd encountered, and that he would have no interest whatsoever in her. Now, faced with his actual behavior, she was nonplussed.

"I feel somehow as if I've made a blunder," he said in response to her silence. "But I'm not certain what it is. I was not, you know, impugning either your ability or Miss Wyndham's character."

"No, no. You were…" Georgina faltered, wishing desperately for some of the social address he possessed in such abundance.

"Commenting on things which are none of my affair?" he finished, smiling once again. "My friends claim it is one of my most distressing failings. They find my fascination with the human comedy incomprehensible."

Some of Georgina's awkwardness dissolved in curiosity. "The human comedy?"

He gestured at the people around them. "What else can one call it? Look at Rollin Enderby, for example." He nodded toward a gentleman two tables off.

"You mean the man with the nagging wife?"

He looked surprised. "You know him?"

Georgina cursed her wayward tongue. "No, but I…" She swallowed nervously. "You can see from the way he sits, and the way she is speaking to him."

Ellerton glanced at the Enderbys again, and then at Georgina, an arrested expression in his vivid blue eyes. This woman impressed him. "You can indeed. Is this your first visit to London, Miss Goring?"

She blinked. "No, I spent a Season in town some years ago. And I occasionally visit my aunt—Lady Goring."

"Ah. But we have not met."

"No."

"I wonder why?"

Georgina wondered why he should ask.

"But that is unimportant; we have met now," he went on before she could reply. "What do you think of Signora Veldini?"

Without thinking, Georgina repeated what she had said to Lady Marianne. Ellerton nodded appreciatively. "Indeed, discernment is as important to art as innate talent, is it not? Her voice is splendid, but she has no sense of pace or selection. I wonder at her great reputation."

Georgina nodded, amazed. He had clearly given thought to the subject, and his conclusions were very similar to her own. Again, he was behaving quite unlike her idea of a man of fashion.

Ellerton had by this time noticed the morocco folder, which Georgina had put under her chair. "May I?" he asked, bending to retrieve it. Before she could reply, he was flipping through the pages of music. His chestnut eyebrows rose. "Your score is in Italian."

Georgina flushed again. She had been called a bluestocking often enough, and in such insulting tones that she braced herself for a sneer. And she found to her astonishment that she particularly dreaded such a response from him. Moreover, it was monstrously unfair. Her studies were limited to music, for which her passion had grown as she matured.

"My compliments," he added with another smile.

Georgina searched his face for mockery, and did not find it. She couldn't believe he wasn't laughing at her. "I don't speak it," she responded hurriedly. "And I read it poorly—just for the music."

"You must be very fond of music, then." He was examining her face with interest. The more one conversed with her, he thought, the more one realized her beauty. She was not the sort of woman who could pose, statuelike, and be beautiful. Her appeal was more subtle and elusive, tied to her personality.

"Yes," answered Georgina quietly. Her heart was beating very fast—because she had expected a setdown, she told herself.

"You must educate me, sometime," Ellerton went on. "I prefer to understand as well as appreciate. In all things."

Georgina glanced up, surprised again, and the look she met in his eyes froze her tongue.

At this moment, Susan, irritated beyond measure by Ellerton's lack of attention to her, leaned forward and said, "It's nearly time to go back to our seats. Will you join us, Baron Ellerton?"

Her effrontery left the others speechless. But Ellerton merely smiled slightly and rose. "I beg your pardon, but I am promised to friends." And with a nod, he took his leave.

Susan opened her mouth to protest, and Georgina plunged in, leaning forward over her plate. "Do you like the lobster patties, Susan? Have you had them before? Oh, you are eating meringues, I see. They are delicious, are they not? We must ask the countess where she purchased them. Or perhaps she has a splendid cook. I do hope not, for I should so like to get some of these."

By this time, Baron Ellerton was well away, and the other members of Georgina's group were gazing at her in mild astonishment. None of them had ever heard her utter such a string of nonsense.

The moment of danger past, Georgina subsided, and talk again became general. But Susan ignored Tony Brinmore's feeble efforts at conversation and glared balefully first at Georgina, then at the retreating figure of the baron. "He hardly spoke to *me*," she said aloud, making Georgina wince. "And after I specifically *asked* him to join us." She paused. Georgina was relieved to see that only Marianne appeared to be listening. Susan's pretty face set. "The next time, he will notice me," she assured herself with a small nod. "He will indeed."

Grorgina pushed her plate away, hunger quelled. Marianne bit her full lower lip thoughtfully for a moment, then slowly smiled. The curve of her lips, Georgina saw with a sinking heart, precisely matched that of Susan's. In fact, in the brief interval before the two girls' attention was diverted, they looked more alike than Georgina would have thought possible.

FOUR

Two mornings later, on a very fine, warm day, Marianne encountered Tony Brinmore in the front hall of the Bentham house, on the point of going out. "Where are you off to?" asked Marianne, who was feeling bored.

"Oh, engagement with William Wyndham," he answered, hand on the doorknob.

This made him even more interesting. "To go where?"

"Nowhere you'd like." Tony opened the door, his impatience to be gone obvious.

But if he had thought to discourage Marianne by these methods, he was sadly mistaken. His resistance merely increased her curiosity. "Where?" she insisted.

Tony sighed heavily. "Wyndham heard of a balloon ascension on Hampstead Heath. We're riding out to watch. It ain't the least fashionable. You wouldn't care for it."

"On the contrary, I should like it above all things. I shall come with you."

Tony's dismay was so clear that she had to laugh. "Come now, it is not so bad as that. I assure you I shall enjoy myself. I attended a balloon ascension last Season, and it was wonderful. And I shan't get in your way."

This, thought Tony, was impossible. Having charge of a female would change the whole character of the expedition. And of all females, Marianne was perhaps the last he would choose. Inspiration struck him. "You can't go alone. It's just to be Wyndham and me, you know."

"I could take my maid. But I really don't think it necessary. You are an old friend of the family—or Sir Thomas's family, at any rate." This was weak, and Marianne hurried to divert him. "You won't refuse to let me come? You could not be so mean!"

Tony groped for a response. That was exactly what he wanted, but it did seem harsh and unfeeling when she gazed at him in that reproachful way, as if he was callous as well as rude. "It ain't an expedition for girls," he responded desperately. "I'm taking Growser, and we're riding, and—"

"I ride better than you, I wager," retorted Marianne, beginning to be angry. Why should he deny her this outing when she had been feeling so bored?

Tony felt trapped, but he didn't see any way out, or any that wasn't inexcusably impolite to the daughter of his hosts. "Oh, very well," he said grudgingly.

"I'll go up and change," replied Marianne with a broad smile. "I won't be a moment."

"Mind you aren't. Wyndham will be waiting. I'll be in the stables."

When Marianne met him there some twenty minutes later, Tony was holding the reins of both their horses and looking mulish. "If that's what you call a moment—" he began.

"Oh, don't be prickly. I'm here now. Shall we go?"

Marianne started to mount at the block, then paused as she noticed a strange animal waiting on the other side of Tony's horse. "What is that?"

Tony bristled. "That is Growser, and he is coming with us." His tone conveyed a great deal, and Marianne remembered what he'd said when he first arrived. She walked around to look at the dog. Growser was clearly of no particular breed. He was large and shaggy, brown, and, Marianne could see, very old. The hairs of his muzzle were white, and he moved with the economy of age. As she came closer, the dog looked to Tony for a sign, and receiving no demur, began to wag his short tail. His eyes, though nearly obscured by fur, were bright and good-natured.

She laughed and sank to her knees, rubbing Growser vigorously behind the ears. He wriggled in ecstasy and licked her face. Marianne laughed again.

Tony gaped, astonished that the formidable Lady Marianne would deign to notice Growser. But there could be no doubt her interest was genuine. Watching them, he smiled and thawed a bit toward her.

"Will he be all right running beside the horses?" she asked, standing again.

"Oh yes. He's still lively, though he is old."

"You said you've had him a long time, I remember."

"Nearly all my life." Tony braced himself for a joke. He'd often been teased about his attachment to such an unprepossessing animal.

But Marianne replied only, "My brother and I each had a puppy when I was small. My Sandy died three years ago, or I should have brought her to London."

Tony relented further. Perhaps, he thought, his judgment of Marianne had been prematurely harsh. However, he said only, "We should go."

She mounted, and they set off for the Goring house. It was not far, and they arrived to find William waiting for them in front. Tony started to apologize for their tardiness, but before he could speak, William said, "I'm sorry, Tony, but Susan found out where I was going, and she insists upon coming along. I couldn't persuade her that she won't like it, though I swear I tried my best."

Tony laughed and shook his head. "It seems we're in the same case, then." He indicated Marianne with a gesture.

William, who had been too full of his own concern to notice her until then, flushed and looked uncomfortable, wishing he hadn't been so vehement.

Marianne laughed aloud. "You poor things! But I dare-say it won't be half as bad as you think. We shan't bother you, and now that there are two of us, we can keep one another company." Only to herself did she admit a slight sense of relief that the proprieties would also be satisfied.

"I didn't mean…" stammered William. "That is, of course I am only too happy to have you come, Lady Marianne."

"You are too kind, sir," she responded teasingly.

He looked up quickly, then smiled at the ridiculousness of the thing.

"Is your sister ready?" asked Tony in resigned tones.

"Yes, I'll get her." William walked around the corner of the house toward the stable yard.

"Alas, Mr. Brinmore, the next time you must sneak out the back door in the dead of night," teased Marianne.

"I shall," he replied feelingly, then flushed at the rude-ness of this response.

The others appeared, already mounted, and Tony and Marianne moved forward to join them. Susan had clearly been informed of the other addition to their party, and she greeted Marianne with politeness if not with joy.

"It is rather a long ride," warned Tony, with perhaps a last lingering hope that the ladies would reconsider.

William and Marianne turned their horses' heads oblig-ingly, but Susan did not stir. "Is that your dog?" she asked Tony.

He looked belligerent. "It is, and he's coming!" He braced himself to squelch any objections. He had borne enough, he told himself.

"Well, then, I am bringing Daisy," Susan declared, starting to slide to the pavement.

"Susan, no!" exclaimed her brother.

Marianne and Tony exchanged a mystified look.

"If he's bringing that creature, I don't see any reason why not," she replied, starting toward the front door.

"They'll fight. He'll get lost, and we'll spend hours looking for him. He'll…"

"Nonsense!" declared Susan, and disappeared inside the house.

"Oh, Lord," said Tony, goaded beyond endurance.

"Who, or perhaps I should say what, is Daisy?" Marianne inquired.

William gritted his teeth. "Susan's cat. Daisy is to cats what Growser is to dogs, more or less."

"Indeed?" Marianne couldn't help but laugh.

"Except that he has the foulest temper of any cat I've ever seen."

"He?" wondered Marianne delicately.

But William merely nodded.

"By Jove, this is too much!" exploded Tony. "I plan a simple outing, with no fuss, and it turns into a deuced circus. What next, I wonder? An elephant? Growser don't like cats."

"Mr. Brinmore! How very disobliging of you," Marianne declared.

"It's all very well for you," he retorted savagely. "You can just sit there and laugh. But if Growser eats her rubbishing cat, *I'll* be responsible. And I can tell you I don't relish taking on Miss Wyndham. She'd cut me to ribbons."

William made an inarticulate noise compounded of agreement and amusement, and Marianne dissolved in helpless laughter.

As Tony turned to glare at her, Susan emerged carrying a basket from which protruded a ginger-colored feline head. Growser, who had been sitting patiently on the cobblestones, stood alertly.

"Oh, Lord," said Tony again.

Susan glanced at him with disdain, then walked directly up to the dog and extended her burden to within an inch of his nose. Daisy lifted his forequarters above the rim of the basket, and for an eternal moment the two animals contemplated one another. The three observers braced themselves for disaster.

Amazingly, it did not come. Daisy and Growser appeared to come to some sort of unspoken understanding; then Daisy subsided into the basket and Growser sank back on his haunches.

Even Susan was astonished. She had, William thought ruefully, expected to kick up a row. She probably would have enjoyed it.

"Upon my soul!" said Tony. "I've never seen anything like that in my life."

"Certainly not from Daisy," agreed William.

"Can it be because they are both old?" wondered Marianne, for it was obvious that Daisy was also well along in years. "Perhaps they are too experienced to…"

"Growser chased my sister's cat up into the hayloft not a month since," put in Tony.

"Well, whatever it is, it's deuced lucky for us," concluded William, and the other two nodded.

"William," said Susan, "are you going to help me mount, or not?"

They rode through the streets at a good pace, for they were now considerably behind the time Tony had set, and he urged them on with threats that they would miss everything. Growser, though he seemed suspicious of many of the denizens of London, had no trouble keeping pace, and Daisy observed the passing scene with cynical enjoyment from his privileged position before Susan.

They reached the edge of Hampstead Heath before noon and found the ascension well under way. The scarlet balloon lay on its side in an open meadow, and a group of men surrounded its basket with various mysterious machines. The bag was about half full, and swelling with each moment.

"Oh, I'm glad we arrived early," said Marianne. "Now we can watch them fill it."

"Early!" exclaimed Tony. "We've missed some of the best parts. I meant to help them lay out the bag on the ground."

"You have done so before?"

"Many times, at home. There's a man nearby who has been experimenting with balloons since soon after I went to live there. He says someday we will fly from place to place rather than riding."

"I shan't," said Susan positively. "How does it go up? I don't understand."

"They fill the balloon with heated air, which makes it lighter," replied Tony, "and it rises like a bubble in water."

William and Marianne exchanged a glance; this seemed a remarkably lucid and informed explanation.

"How could anything be lighter than air?" scoffed Susan. "Air is just…nothing." She waved her hand about to demonstrate.

"No, it isn't," replied Tony. "It's made of…well, different things. I don't recall exactly."

Susan shook her head, unconvinced.

"Well, how do *you* think they get up, then?" asked Tony, stung.

"I don't know that they do. I've never seen any such thing."

He gaped. "Are you telling me you don't *believe* balloons can fly? That is the stupidest thing I've ever—"

"Look," interrupted William to prevent an open quarrel. "That must be the man who is to go up."

"By Jove, it's Crispin!" exclaimed Tony.

"You know him?"

"Yes. He assisted at one of the ascensions at home. I must speak to him." Tony swung down and strode off before any of the others could speak.

"He might have asked us to come along," complained Susan.

"They don't want a crowd near the balloon," answered William. "Look, there's a little hill over there. We can dismount and still see everything. Come."

They moved to this vantage point and secured their horses among some trees behind the knoll. Growser, who had accompanied them, at once set off to explore, and as he did not seem inclined to stay out of sight for any long period of time, they left him to it.

"This is fine," pronounced William. "We can see everything quite well. We might even sit on the grass." He looked to Marianne questioningly.

She assented by doing so. The turf was dry and warmed by the morning sun, and even seated, their elevated position gave them a good view.

"We're too far off to see properly," complained Susan, still standing, Daisy's basket hooked over her arm.

"Nonsense," replied her brother. "It's much easier to tell what's going on from here. We can sort things out. Look, the balloon is beginning to rise from the ground."

They all watched as the great gas bag hesitantly lifted. Gradually, by fits and starts, it shifted from horizontal to vertical, floating above its wicker hamper.

"Oh," said Susan when it at last towered above them. She sank down beside the others and stared upward.

"Impressive," commented William.

"I'm always amazed when I see a balloon," agreed Marianne. "I wonder how anyone could have thought of such a thing. There seem to be so many intricate parts, and such calculations involved." She gestured toward the lacing of guy wires and ropes, the machinery on the ground, and the red sphere now flowering above them. "I can see how one might invent any *one*, but the whole?" She shook her head, and William nodded.

"Look," said Susan, pointing. "Mr. Brinmore is helping them." Tony was indeed working with the team of men preparing for the ascent, and he appeared to know exactly what he was doing.

They watched in silence for a while. The balloon began to strain upward on its ropes, as if eager to leave the earth. Daisy, whose basket had been placed on the grass before Susan, took advantage of their preoccupation to climb out and examine his surroundings.

At last, all seemed ready. The aeronaut clambered into the car, and his helpers moved back a bit, their hands on the ropes. Only Tony remained close, chatting with the man. The three on the hill stood again in sheer excitement; the ascent seemed imminent.

Without warning, a mass of shaggy, brown fur erupted from the wood behind the meadow and pelted toward Tony. Before anyone even saw to give warning, Growser had passed the circle of men and hurled himself on his master, in some mistaken effort, perhaps, to lend him aid. Tony, taken utterly by surprise, fell back under the onslaught, and Growser's momentum carried the dog on, right into the balloon's car. At that moment, by prearrangement, the men holding the ropes let go, and the balloon leapt upward.

They heard Tony's shout all across the meadow. His friends saw him jump wildly to catch one of the trailing lines, and fail. William rushed down to join him, but by this time the balloon was well out of reach.

"How dreadful," said Marianne. Gazing upward, her eyes shaded from the sun, she could just see Growser. The balloonist was apparently restraining the dog from leaping out of the car again. "We should have watched him more carefully."

"He should take care of his own dog," retorted Susan, and this thought leading naturally to another, she looked down. "Daisy is gone!"

Several minutes of complete disorder followed. Tony and William remained among the balloon crew, calculating the direction the vehicle was likely to take and its probable place of descent. Marianne and Susan scoured the nearby wood for the cat, Marianne growing more and more exasperated. Finally, when she heard William calling their names, she said, "He might be anywhere, even in a tree. We'll never find him. I'm going back to see what your brother means to do now."

"You can't just give up!"

"Can I not?" Marianne turned and picked her way back toward the meadow, holding up the trailing skirts of her riding habit and railing silently each time they were snagged on a branch or weed. It did nothing to improve her temper when, just at the edge of the trees, her hat caught and was pulled nearly from her head, leaving her hair in disarray.

Thus, when William greeted her by saying, "Whatever have you been doing?" she snapped, "Searching for your sister's wretched cat!" in a tone that left no doubt as to her opinion of wandering pets.

William looked puzzled, then simply pointed to the top of the knoll, where Daisy's basket still sat. In it, looking hugely self-congratulatory, sat Daisy himself. As Marianne watched, he began to clean his front paw, oozing virtue.

Marianne put her face in her hands and made an exasperated noise. Then, looking up again, she began to laugh. "Why haven't you wrung that animal's neck long since?"

"Susan wouldn't let me," replied William, unsurprised by the question.

"Well, you must find *her* now, and I do not intend to help you." Marianne strode determinedly to the little hill, sat down beside Daisy, and fixed him with a baleful stare. "You can bring her back here."

Hiding a smile, William set off in the direction from which Marianne had emerged. He'd scarcely left when Tony approached the knoll. "Where *is* everyone?" he asked in aggrieved tones.

Marianne did not care to discuss this. "What are you going to do? Growser will be all right, won't he?"

"As long as Crispin keeps him in the car. I'm going after him, of course."

"But how will you find him?"

"The direction and speed of the wind give one a pretty good idea where he will come down. And I shall follow the balloon." He spoke absently, most of his attention on the floating sphere, which would soon be out of sight behind the trees. "I must go. Will you tell the others, please?"

"Can we not help?"

Tony shook his head, still focused on the balloon, and went to fetch his horse. William and Susan returned as he was mounting up.

"We'll all go," insisted Susan when his plan was repeated.

"No," said Tony flatly, and it was clear that he would brook no argument.

"I should come, at least," added William, "but..."

"You must escort the girls home," finished Tony. "Besides, I don't need help."

William, who obviously very much wished to go, help or no, could not dispute this, though Marianne halfheartedly protested that they could return home on their own. In fact, she did not relish the idea at all.

Tony had turned his mount and started off when a high-pitched voice from behind them hailed Marianne. Turning, she scanned the crowd quickly, then answered, "Mrs. Gregg, how do you do?"

"Did you see the balloon? Such excitement. A dog jumped in; at least, I believe it was a dog."

Marianne nodded.

"Have you no carriage?" Mrs. Gregg seemed shocked by this. "But you cannot ride so far. Come with me. There is plenty of room."

Under any other circumstances, Marianne wouldn't have considered it. But she saw William's eager look, quickly suppressed, and resigned herself to the drive with a woman she did not much like. As soon as she accepted, William grinned delightedly, saluted her, and rode off before Susan could object, as he was certain she would. It was left only for the girls to tie their horses to the back of Mrs. Gregg's barouche and climb in.

"Why did you say yes?" hissed Susan furiously as they did so. "We might just as well have gone with William. Or ridden home alone."

"Shh," replied Marianne. "She will hear."

"I don't care if she does."

"Well, you should. Mrs. Gregg is one of the greatest gossips in the *ton*. She knows everything that goes on, and everyone listens to her."

This gave Susan pause, and she said no more as they walked around to the door of the barouche. They took the forward seat, as Mrs. Gregg and her female companion occupied the other, and Marianne staunchly resisted the former's attempts to shift her browbeaten friend to the less comfortable position. As soon as they settled, Mrs. Gregg signaled departure. "For I am promised to the Duchess of Devonshire for tea, my dears."

They talked at first of the ascension, Mrs. Gregg speculating about the disruption and the girls not letting on that they knew any of the participants. This subject exhausted, their hostess turned to contemplate her passengers. "You are two very famous young ladies now, you know," she said, her tone teasing but not benevolent. "Your trick of wearing the same dress to the Millshires' ball is causing all sorts of talk."

Marianne felt Susan stiffen beside her, and wished they had ridden home after all. "It was a good joke, wasn't it?" she said lightly.

Mrs. Gregg tittered. "Prodigious good. But you know the strangest thing? Though the story is that you are dearest friends, I swear I never heard Lady Marianne mention Miss Wyndham before now."

"Susan was in the country," answered Marianne as if surprised. "There was no occasion to mention her. I know how tedious it is to be always talking of absent friends with whom one's listeners are unacquainted."

"Very true," acknowledged Mrs. Gregg, who often did so. "Still, it seems queer." She looked from one to the other of the girls. "Wyndham. Now, that name is familiar. Where can I have heard it?" She made a great show of pondering this question. "I have it! Sybil Goring's daughter married a Wyndham. And was she not in town for the Season several years ago? Yes, that's it." She allowed a look of surprise to cross her sharp features. "Oh, my, yes. Well! You do have a great deal in common, don't you?"

"What do you mean?" asked Susan, sensing some slight to her mother.

Mrs. Gregg raised her thin eyebrows. "You *are* Anabel Wyndham's daughter?"

"Yes." Susan was truculent. Marianne tried to catch her eye, and failed.

"Well, Anabel jilted Norbury, you know. One of the most brilliant matches in England. It was a nine days' wonder. And then, of course, Lady Marianne did the same last season." She tittered again. "Not Norbury, poor man. He is long since married and, they say, sadly afflicted by the gout. But Devere. It comes to the same thing. Amazing." She paused, gauging the effect of her words on them. "And then both your mothers have married a second time. I always say that more than one marriage is, well, a bit excessive."

"It is certainly more than most can manage," replied Marianne dryly. Mrs. Gregg, who was said to have tyrannized over her late husband in the most shocking manner, was notorious for her relentless pursuit of another.

"The indulgence of calf love is so rare past a certain age," retorted the older woman. "And a trifle odd, don't you think?"

This time Marianne stiffened, at this clear hit at her mother. Both girls were by this time thoroughly incensed, a condition which drew them together.

Mrs. Gregg, seeing it, smiled a predatory smile. This was her invariable method. She had found that making people furiously angry often elicited the most interesting tidbits. They said things in the heat of rage that they would not have dreamed of uttering with a cool head. And it was obvious that Susan Wyndham, at least, was prime material.

Marianne realized it also, and with a supreme effort, she controlled her anger. There could be no satisfaction in lashing out at Lavinia Gregg. One's heated remarks would only be retailed to the *ton* and mocked. But how, she wondered, was she to convey this to Susan, who was clearly choking with rage. She racked her brain, but could think of nothing. Then, providentially, she happened to glance down. Daisy's basket had been placed on the floor of the barouche, between her feet and Susan's. It had been carefully closed, but now she nudged it with her toe. The lid moved a little.

Susan felt it, and also looked down. Marianne pushed the basket again, at the same time turning to gaze innocently out at the passing countryside. Susan looked startled for a moment, then slowly began to smile. The basket was concealed by their skirts, and neither of the others could see as she added her efforts to Marianne's.

Disappointed by their silence, Mrs. Gregg tried again. "There is something so, ah, ridiculous, about an older person mooning about in public, don't you think? Why, I—" Her voice rose to a screech as Daisy catapulted from his basket, enraged by the jostling, and snarled himself thoroughly in the ladies' mingled skirts.

"Oh dear," exclaimed Marianne, her voice shaking with suppressed laughter. "Susan's cat has gotten loose."

Daisy hissed and fought with tooth and claw to free himself from the mass of gown and petticoat, entangling himself still further.

"Ow, ow," squealed Mrs. Gregg. "It is biting me! Get it away!"

"Daisy, Daisy, stop it this instant," declared Susan, bending as if to free the cat, but in reality hiding paroxysms of giggles. Seeing her shaking shoulders, Marianne put a hand on her back to keep her down.

Mrs. Gregg's companion, hitherto totally silent, now began to scream at the top of her lungs, as Daisy worked his way deeper into the flounces. The coachman pulled up in consternation, and several passing riders paused and stared.

"Get it out! Get it out!" cried Mrs. Gregg again.

Marianne signaled to Susan with a pressure on her hand

that this was enough. At first, it seemed that Susan would not respond, but then she bent even further and managed to imprison Daisy in her own petticoat. Making soothing sounds, she began to extricate him from its folds.

Mrs. Gregg watched with tremulous horror. "I won't have it in my carriage," she declared. "That animal is obviously mad. It should be destroyed at once."

"I am so sorry, Mrs. Gregg," replied Marianne sweetly. "But he was only frightened, you know, at being caught. Susan will put him back in his basket."

"I won't have it in the carriage," she insisted.

"Oh?" Marianne looked around. "Well, we are nearly home. We'll ride from here, then."

Even in her outrage, Mrs. Gregg saw that this was going rather far. "I do not wish to force *you* out," she said.

"I quite understand. Come, Susan."

The girls climbed down, leaving their erstwhile interrogator feeling vaguely bested, and mounted from the barouche step. Bowing to Mrs. Gregg and her friend, and brushing aside another protest, they set off at a brisk trot.

"That was wonderful!" exclaimed Susan when they were out of earshot. She balanced Daisy's basket before her. "I thought I'd die laughing."

"Let us hope that when she tells the story we don't come off too badly," answered Marianne.

"I don't care a fig what she says."

"You should. You saw what a wicked tongue she has."

"The spiteful creature. I wish Daisy had truly bitten her—hard!"

"I expect he did. He bit *me*."

"And me." Susan giggled. "But it didn't really hurt. It was

a *splendid* idea. I should have said something really dreadful in another minute."

"I know."

Susan turned to look at her. "You're not so bad after all."

"I beg your pardon?"

"When we first met, I thought I'd hate you."

"My dear Miss Wyndham!"

"Well, you seemed so odiously superior. And there was the dress."

"Yes, there was that," responded Marianne dryly.

"But you're not stuffy and arrogant, really."

"Thank you very much."

"Indeed, I think we're rather alike." She meant this as a compliment, but it filled Marianne with dismay. "Mind, this doesn't mean that I'll give in over the baron."

"Give in? What do you mean?"

"We are still rivals there."

"Rivals?" Marianne was lost.

"Oh, don't pretend you don't understand me. But I shall fight fair."

"My dear Miss Wyndham—" began Marianne again.

Susan was diverted. "There is our street. Come, Georgina will be very cross with me for going out without telling her where."

She kicked her horse's flanks, and Marianne was forced to follow, still protesting. Susan ignored her, sliding from her mount almost before it stopped and skipping up to the front door. In the ensuing flurry of greetings, explanations, and arrangements for a groom to escort Marianne home, the subject was lost. But Marianne found she had much to think of as she made her own way home.

FIVE

TONY DID NOT RETURN HOME THAT NIGHT, AND
Marianne grew rather concerned, though she reassured her
mother and Sir Thomas. She rose and breakfasted early,
and by eight was sitting in the drawing room writing a letter
to her brother and listening for sounds of an arrival downstairs. But she found composition more difficult than usual.
Never a fluent letter writer, this morning she was unable to
concentrate on her page, more worried about Tony than she
would have expected. The outing yesterday had been unlike
any she'd had in London before. Indeed, she realized now, it
had been far more like expeditions she and her brother had
made as children in Scotland—a bit disorganized and hap-
hazard, filled with misadventures, and, she was surprised to
acknowledge, a great deal of fun.

Thinking of Tony and his dog, of William's criticisms
of his sister's cat, and of the very unusual Miss Susan
Wyndham herself, Marianne had to smile. This idea of
a rivalry between them was quite ridiculous; she didn't
understand exactly why Susan clung to it. Baron Ellerton
was unlikely to take serious notice of either of them.

Marianne had considered the idea of marriage a good
deal in the past year, as must any intelligent young lady
involved in the London Season. The festivities were so often
directed toward that one thing—to marry off the younger
generation of the *ton*—that it could scarcely be ignored.
And Marianne's own experience in refusing one of the most
eligible noblemen in England had brought the matter home
to her as no abstract imagining could do.

She wished to marry; she had no doubt on that score. But she was not at all certain what sort of man she would accept. Before she had come to town, sequestered in the wilds of Scotland, she had vowed to wed a thorough Londoner, who would guarantee her a round of gaiety from the capital to Brighton and Leicestershire. But when such a man had actually offered, she hadn't hesitated to refuse, despite the furor this caused. She had simply known that they would not suit. But this had left her perplexed about her own desires. What sort of life did she really want, having now tasted the pleasures of society?

This again called up the image of Ellerton. He was, on the one hand, everything she had dreamed of as a young girl—elegant, assured, a leader of society. Yet he was more, too. Marianne couldn't imagine Lord Robert Devere, whose proposal she had refused, taking the trouble to aid two near-strangers in a ballroom, or good-humoredly giving in to an importunate request to join a party in which he could have little interest. These were trifling things, she admitted to herself, but trifling things could be important. Was he the sort of man she had been unconsciously searching for? Smiling slightly, Marianne concluded that there might be something in what Susan Wyndham said after all.

Oddly enough, in Lady Goring's house not too far away, Georgina Goring was following a similar train of thought. This was odd not only because of the coincidence, but because Georgina almost never thought of marriage. Ten years ago, she had. Sent to town against her will, and far from successful among the *ton*, she had developed a severe case of calf love for the man Susan's mother had eventually wed. He'd been very kind to the difficult girl she was then, and she would have married him in an instant—no doubt to regret it bitterly later. But there had been no question of that, and she had soon realized it, with a good deal of pain. However, this period of intense emotion had taught her a great deal about people, which her isolated childhood had not, and it had changed her from a withdrawn schoolgirl to a thoughtful young lady. Indeed, she believed it had been a chief force in shaping her character, which she knew to be unusual. She looked back on it now with an odd kind of gratitude. Without that hurt, she felt, she would be far less than she was.

But it had discouraged her thoughts of marriage. She had met no other man she liked so well, and when she returned to her father's house, she found she was content there. She resisted her aunt's frequent invitations to spend further Seasons in town, and evolved her own pleasant routine at home. The death of her father had been hard, but it had not made her wish for any other life.

Yet she was not feeling as unhappy as she had expected, forced this Season to stay in town and reenter the social lists. She found that she looked forward to the ball they were to attend that evening, and to the other events that would come after it. And one of the chief reasons for this reversal, she had to admit to herself, was Baron Ellerton.

Georgina did not see how this could be. She prided herself on her common sense, and this side of her jeered at the notion that the baron might be interested in her when he had all society to choose from. Yet some hitherto dormant part of her persisted in calling up Ellerton's handsome countenance, pointing out the warm look in his eyes when he had joked with her, and daring to hint that perhaps

Georgina had simply never met the right man before and that this was her time.

"Nonsense!" she said aloud to herself, determinedly picking up the sewing she had allowed to fall in her lap. "I've never heard anything so ridiculous in my life. You are falling into a premature dotage. *And* acting just as you did at eighteen, when you 'fell in love' with a man who was kind to you but had no further interest." This silenced that unfamiliar voice in her mind, and Georgina flushed at the thought that she was merely repeating her earlier mistake.

Susan Wyndham, in her bedchamber upstairs, was prey to no such doubts. Her only thought, in fact, was for the gown she would wear to the ball that night, and its probable effect on the gentleman who was occupying so many feminine brains.

The ballooning party came together again for the first time at the ball. Tony and William had reached home late in the afternoon, too late for explanations, and they had agreed between them to walk to the ball, avoiding stuffy carriages. Thus, the girls were forced to wait until the two young gentlemen entered the ballroom to get any information. Fortunately, this occurred between sets, and Susan and Marianne immediately deserted the groups with whom they'd been chatting and descended on the newcomers. Georgina, who had heard the full story from Susan, strolled over more slowly, interested to learn the outcome.

"You selfish beast," was the first remark she heard, addressed to Sir William by his sister. "Why didn't you come and tell me everything at once? When Gibbs said you had come home and gone out again, I—"

"Do you want to hear it now?" retorted William, "or would you prefer to abuse me in front of all London?"

With a ferocious grimace, Susan subsided.

"Well, we got him back," continued William.

"Growser is all right?" asked Marianne, who had become rather attached to him in their short acquaintance.

"Oh yes." This was from Tony. "He's always getting into scrapes, and he is never hurt. I believe Crispin was worse off when we reached them. Growser would jump about, and the poor man looked quite green."

"Where did you find him?" asked Marianne. "It must have been quite a distance away."

Tony nodded. "The dratted wind carried them nearly ten miles, and Crispin was afraid to try to descend through it with Growser there. He had to wait for sunset. By the time he got down and we helped him secure the balloon, it was too late to come home. We stayed at an inn nearby."

"And slept half the morning," commented Susan acidly.

The two young men looked sheepish, and Georgina and Marianne smiled, thinking it very likely that they had celebrated the rescue of Growser by indulging rather too freely in the inn's libations. Both were a bit pale.

"We rode home pretty slowly," acknowledged William. He and Tony exchanged a conspiratorial glance. It was obvious that their budding friendship had been cemented by this shared adventure.

"Well, you missed Almack's," answered his sister. "We went last night."

"Remind me to buy Growser three pounds of steak," said William to Tony, who grinned.

Susan made an exasperated sound, but before her brother could bait her further, there was a stir at the door and Baron Ellerton strolled in, looking the picture of elegance and ease.

At once, all three women's attention shifted. Though they moved only slightly, it was clear even to Tony that their interest was elsewhere.

"Good evening, Baron," said Susan.

He nodded, smiled, and returned the greeting, including the others. Georgina and Marianne murmured acknowledgments. In the corner, the musicians began again.

"Oh, a waltz," exclaimed Susan. "Do you know, Baron Ellerton, I only last night received the sanction of Princess Lieven to waltz." She gazed up at him so meaningfully that Georgina had to repress a gasp. She might as well ask *him* to dance, she thought.

"I congratulate you," replied Ellerton, surveying the ladies with a slightly wider smile. They formed a striking picture—Susan exquisite and deceptively fragile in pale green muslin, Marianne magnificent in a blue exactly the shade of her eyes, and Georgina delicately distinguished between the two redheads in dove satin with an overlay of spidery gray lace.

"It is such an exhilarating dance," dared Susan. This time, Georgina could not suppress her intake of breath.

Ellerton, hearing it, met her shocked gaze with dancing eyes. Georgina's mortification eased as she realized that the baron was more than up to this contest. Indeed, he was completely in charge. "Some say so," he agreed. "If you will excuse me, I must claim my partner."

With a slight bow, he turned away, walking along the side of the room to the daughter of the Duchess of Lancombe, who welcomed him with a brilliant smile.

The ladies turned back to Tony and William, Susan clearly piqued, Marianne thoughtful, and Georgina flushed with embarrassment, both for Susan's boldness and her own ridiculous hopes.

"Fellow thinks he's top of the trees," murmured Tony to William.

"Umm," was the only reply. William was following the baron with his eyes, taking in the cut of his coat and the chaste austerity of his waistcoat. He'd been struck by the ladies' behavior. That even Georgina, whom he thought of as a kind of aunt, should forget his existence when confronted by Ellerton gave him pause. And Marianne's desertion piqued him so sharply that he began to reconsider his refusal to waste money on new clothes. He had discouraged Tony from replacing his wardrobe, urging him to what William thought more important outings such as visiting Manton's shooting gallery and Jackson's boxing saloon. But now he wondered if he'd been mistaken. Marianne's opinion was of increasing interest to him, and he didn't want to neglect any possible advantage, however trivial it might seem to him.

Tony was even more affected. He'd been worried about his clothes in any case, no matter what William said, and he had quite enjoyed being the object of several pairs of enthralled feminine eyes. The abrupt severing of this attention, and the obvious reason, put him on his mettle. "Must see that snyder tomorrow first thing," he muttered.

William nodded. To add to his chagrin, an unknown young man came up at that moment and claimed Lady Marianne's hand for the waltz. William, who had intended to do this himself, glowered as they went off to join the set.

Tony looked hunted. He had no wish to partner the spitfire Miss Wyndham, but politeness dictated that he dance, and custom urged that he not leave sister and brother to each other. Swallowing to find his voice, he heroically made his request. Susan accepted with scant grace, and they too departed.

"Georgina?" said William, ruthlessly pushing back his annoyance. He liked his cousin very well, and it was by no means a penance to dance with her, though it wasn't like dancing with Lady Marianne.

Georgina laughed, conscious of the trend of his thoughts. "You needn't, William. I shall go and sit with the chaperones, where I belong." She felt a pang as she said this, but she told herself fiercely that it was no more than the truth.

"Nonsense!" responded her young cousin. "You can't leave me standing here. I don't know any other young ladies, and they will all wonder what is the matter with me that you will not dance."

She laughed again. "Very well. We cannot let that happen. But when this set is finished, I will present you to some of them."

"Agreed," responded William with an answering smile, and they turned to join the set.

The waltz gave way to a country dance, and a cotillion, and a quadrille. Tony and the Wyndhams broadened their acquaintance with the aid of Marianne and those she presented. They went in to supper with a lively group and obviously were enjoying the evening, thought Georgina, sitting on the edge of the boisterous party. She herself was less content. She didn't feel much akin to young girls just out of the schoolroom and young men years younger than she; yet when she sat down with the chaperones, she felt equally out of place. She knew none of them well, and it was always clear to her that they wanted to gossip about matters they felt unsuitable for the ears of an unmarried woman. Whenever Georgina took a chair in their circle, the conversation died, and then began again, usually with a kindly inquiry about her family or her charge. Georgina felt distinctly in the way, and heartily sick of assuring them that Lady Goring was indeed on the mend, or that Susan was not the least trouble. The sweetly probing questions about Susan were the worst, for Georgina had the feeling that the older women shared her sense that Susan would do something outrageous before the Season ended. They awaited this event with avid relish. Their only amusement, so far as Georgina could see, was scandal.

Thus, Georgina was neither one thing nor the other, and she wondered as the supper interval concluded how she would get through an entire Season hanging on the fringes of two incompatible groups. If only Aunt Sybil would regain her health, she wished silently, she could return to her own good friends in the country. There, she didn't feel alien. Indeed, she knew she was admired and respected. But Lady Goring seemed the same each day when she visited her—bright-eyed and interested in all the news, yet still very weak.

Georgina followed her cousins back into the ballroom with these thoughts uppermost in her mind. As the music began once again, and the young people paired off for the dance, she looked about for a retreat. The chaperones were still at supper, their deserted corner a jumble of gilt chairs and blue velvet sofas. She did not want to sit there. Looking further, Georgina noticed that the long windows that marched down the far side of the chamber were recessed. Behind their draperies were shallow niches hidden from the crowd.

She edged her way around the walls, nodding to several acquaintances but not stopping, until she was in front of the first embrasure. The hangings were firmly closed, their hosts not being proponents of the advantages of fresh air. Glancing quickly about to see that no one was observing her, Georgina pulled a gilt chair through the curtains and let them swing shut behind her. Her heart was beating fast at this most unconventional act, and she stood very still for a long moment, awaiting discovery. But it did not come. After a while she took a deep breath and sat down, relaxing for perhaps the first time that evening.

As she recovered her composure, she leaned back in the chair and breathed deeply again. Her refuge was snug; the draperies brushed her left arm, and her right was almost against the cool windowpanes. She could see the back garden dimly, and the sounds of the ball were perfectly clear, though she was no longer, she felt, really a part of it. Her confidence growing, she pushed open a tiny slit in the curtains and watched the dancers whirl by. A guilty thrill ran through her. This surreptitious security was very appealing. She needn't worry whether people were staring and commenting on her social ineptitude, yet she could still do her duty to Susan.

Sheepishly content, Georgina watched one set give way to another, and another. The night waned, and she regretfully acknowledged that it was time to leave her hiding place and rejoin the crowd. Susan and William would be looking for her soon. She would, however, remember this scheme, she assured herself; next time, she might even try to bring a novel.

The last set struck up, a waltz, and Georgina rose and

prepared to emerge. But before she could do so, the curtain was pulled back slightly and Baron Ellerton leaned inside. "Will you dance?" he asked, as if there was nothing peculiar in finding a partner behind the draperies.

Georgina flushed scarlet, unable to answer for embarrassment. But the baron took her silence for assent and pulled her hand through his arm. Georgina walked onto the floor in a daze and followed his lead mechanically as he swung her into the set. Then, swallowing to ease her dry throat, she stammered, "I…I dropped my bracelet. I was searching for it."

Ellerton glanced at her silver-gilt ornament. "And you found it. My congratulations."

From his tone, Georgina could tell that he knew her excuse was a lie. She ventured an upward glance and saw that his blue eyes were dancing, but with mirth, not mockery. "Did you see me go in?" she asked in a small voice.

"Some time ago," he agreed, letting the smile he had been restraining appear. "I didn't wish to disturb you, but as this was the last set, I suspected you would be coming out."

Georgina gazed over his shoulder, flushing again. "What a fool you must think me. I…I just wished to sit quietly for a moment."

"Or a bit longer," he suggested mischievously.

She clenched her jaw. To appear ridiculous was bad enough, but to be unmasked by this man, who seemed never to make a false step or an awkward remark, was too much. His good opinion, she realized, would have meant more than the whole *ton*'s. She wished she'd never come to London.

"I beg your pardon," he added. "I shouldn't tease you. I know precisely how you feel."

She raised her eyes, embarrassment forgotten in astonishment.

Ellerton smiled again. "It that so surprising? Many people here must wish for a quiet retreat, at times. They simply haven't the courage to admit it, far less to act on the feeling." He gazed down at her with a mixture of amusement and admiration. "You acted on the impulse."

Georgina was not certain this was a compliment. "You're making fun of me," she accused.

"Not at all." He paused, then added, "Well, perhaps a little. If you could have seen your furtive look as you disappeared through the curtains." His smile encouraged her to share the joke. Slowly, reluctantly, Georgina began to smile also. The picture he painted was ridiculous.

"What do you suppose the servants will think when they find your chair?" he wondered.

Georgina laughed aloud.

"That's better." He guided her through an effortless turn. Georgina was abruptly conscious of his arm firm about her waist and his hand warm in hers. He was really very close. Her shaky composure disappeared again.

He seemed to sense her withdrawal. "I imagine they will put it down to an assignation," he continued. "A lovestruck swain awaiting his inamorata. Clandestinely, of course."

This did nothing to restore Georgina's poise—quite the reverse, in fact.

"Yes," he went on, "they will concoct a torrid history, I'm certain. I can almost hear them."

So could Georgina, with a vividness that made her wish for the first time in her life for a less lively imagination. The fact that she was enfolded in this man's embrace only made it worse. Couldn't he see how improper this talk was? Venturing a look, and meeting gleaming blue eyes, Georgina indignantly concluded that he did see—exactly. Some of her uneasiness dissolved in anger. "I don't find it so easy to think like a servant," she retorted.

"Good, very good," he replied. "A distinct hit."

She blinked at him.

"One is forced to extreme measures to break through your reserve, Miss Goring."

"My...reserve?" She was amazed. She had never thought of herself as reserved, merely awkward.

"What do you call it? You clearly have an interesting personality, but it is very difficult to reach. I thought you'd be more approachable if I caught you coming out of your hiding place."

"But you... Why should you care?" As soon as she spoke, Georgina wished the words away. She sounded hopeless. Not the sort of wit that the distinguished Baron Ellerton would find engaging.

He smiled again. "It's not often one encounters an unusual character." He indicated the dancers around them. "By and large, the *ton* is dull—the same gossip year after year, though the names change, the same round of parties and flirtations. And yet I'm something of a connoisseur of character. I'm always on the lookout for a refreshing view, a new outlook. I believe you have one." He didn't add that he also found her distinctively lovely. He didn't want her to think he was mouthing empty compliments, as did so many of the town bucks.

So she was an object of curiosity, thought Georgina resentfully. An oddity, whose strange behavior had piqued his interest. And perhaps, though he didn't say so, he pitied her as well. He must know that she didn't fit in in London. Perhaps he habitually befriended the awkward. She scorned his charity. "You're quite mistaken," she answered in a light tone. "I have no views whatsoever."

He was surprised at the coldness in her voice. Obviously she had misunderstood him. Gazing at her delicately etched features, Ellerton felt, for perhaps the first time in his life, at a loss. Observing and savoring the foibles of his fellow human beings was one of the joys of the baron's life. It did indeed, as he had said, prevent the boredom that an intelligent and thoughtful man might otherwise have felt in society. And he had thought that in Georgina he'd someone who shared his predilection, and had the necessary sharpness to practice it.

The combination of this possibility with her beauty and distinguished manner entranced him. He had not been flirting; he had been trying to share something important. He'd thought his tone showed this, forgetting to make allowance for Georgina's far narrower experience in society.

Now he had to make amends. With another woman, he would have known how. But precisely the qualities that drew him to Georgina made it impossible for him to predict her response. She was unique in his experience and, he realized, increasingly important to him. Feeling as clumsy as he had at sixteen, he groped for words. "I have offended you somehow. I beg your pardon."

Georgina looked up, startled. Her gray eyes met his vivid blue ones and held.

"I do not see exactly *how*," he added with a wry smile. "But I am very sorry. You are deucedly easy to offend."

"I am no such thing!" she protested, shocked at the accusation. Georgina thought of herself as unusually even-tempered and understanding.

"Yet I seem to repeatedly do so," he replied. "It does not happen with others."

"You are one of the *haut ton*," said Georgina, "and I come from quite another circle. Our habits are, er, very different."

"Mine being beneath contempt?"

"I didn't say…"

"It was obvious from your tone. So you despise me for my mode of living?"

"No!" Georgina was appalled. "It is rather you who…" She broke off abruptly.

He looked inquiring, and a little angry.

"London society despises all who choose to live otherwise," added Georgina carefully. "I have seen it over and over."

"And this is what you think of me?" His tone was curt.

"No. You have been… You do not seem… Oh, why can I never say what I mean?"

This last came out as a wail, and Ellerton's expression softened slightly. "We both seem to be having difficulty, Miss Goring. But may I at least assure you that I *meant* no offense?"

She met his eyes again. The sounds of conversation and music about them seemed to recede, and Georgina was acutely conscious of his embrace. Her heart pounded. Slowly she nodded.

"Perhaps I have gone a bit too fast," he continued. "Could we start again as friends?"

"Friends?" The word seemed to echo in Georgina's ears,

and she was not certain whether she felt glad or sorry. It seemed a pallid offer, yet his eyes suggested much more.

"On the way to becoming friends," he amended. "Never a bad beginning."

Hesitantly she nodded again. Ellerton smiled, and after a moment she did, too. Something seemed to tremble in the balance; then, to Georgina's intense disappointment, the music ended, and she was forced to step out of his arms.

In the next instant, Susan was upon them, looking thunderous, and Georgina's only thought was to get her away before the girl said something outrageous. She practically dragged her cousin out of earshot, and she was by no means certain the baron didn't hear Susan say, "*You* danced with him!"

Their ride home was unpleasant as Susan deplored this development and interrogated Georgina about what he had said and why he had stood up with her. Georgina refused to be drawn, however, finally forcing Susan to ominous silence. But though she retained her outward composure, Georgina's thoughts were far from tranquil.

SIX

THE FOLLOWING MORNING TONY AND WILLIAM WENT together to a tailor recommended by Sir Thomas Bentham, and by dint of Tony's insistence, and rather more money than either had thought of spending, contrived to receive their new clothing in a very few days. Thus, when a much-talked-of new play opened in the following week, the young men were able to attend decked out in their new finery. The females of their households were also present, in the first row of boxes, and had a full view of their sartorial splendor below.

"Well, I think Tony looks ridiculous," declared Susan when she had examined them both. Despite all Georgina could say, the four young people had fallen into using first names. "William looks fine, but Tony..." She shrugged and shook her head.

Georgina surveyed the two young men. Their taste had taken them in different directions. William had followed the Corinthian mode; he wore a dark blue coat and buff pantaloons with a plain waistcoat. His shirt points were moderate, and his neckcloth a fairly simple choice admirably executed. Georgina had complimented him on his appearance earlier in the evening.

Tony, on the other hand, had been seduced by the fashion of the dandies. His bottle-green coat was stiffened and padded into a kind of torture device, or so it seemed to Georgina. His waistcoat was a rainbow of color, adorned by a profusion of fobs. She knew he couldn't turn his head in his starched collar, for she had seen him rotate his whole body to look behind when William pointed out an acquaintance. Yet he looked pleased with himself, and Georgina thought that was probably the important thing. "He is striking," she replied mildly.

Susan laughed. "One cannot miss him," she agreed derisively.

Georgina sighed and went back to watching the arrivals. Susan had been more difficult than ever in recent days, and she was weary enough of her carping to make no effort at conversation. Her own concerns were more than enough to occupy her. Whatever Georgina had expected from this Season, it had not included inner turmoil. She'd been braced for a variety of problems, but so far, none of these had gone beyond her competence. Treacherously, the attack had come from within. Her own emotions had risen to trouble her, and she was helpless before this unexpected revolution. Susan's pranks paled beside it. Indeed, there were moments when Georgina remembered her fears for Susan with a kind of nostalgia. If only they were her principal worry, she thought at such times. Then, a certain handsome male face would form in her mind, and she would smile foolishly.

For her part, Susan Wyndham was feeling dissatisfied and rebellious. London was not nearly meeting her expectations. She'd envisioned herself as a reigning toast, surrounded by scores of admirers, the indispensable center of a glittering group. And she'd been certain this success would materialize as soon as she began to go about in society. Instead, she found she was merely one among many young ladies being presented. No one seemed to notice her special qualities. In particular Baron Ellerton, whom she had impulsively fastened upon as the object of her ambitions, paid her no heed whatever. No matter what she did to attract his attention, he either ignored or circumvented her. For Susan, this was a novel state of affairs. Her family had an exaggerated respect for her temper, and they'd allowed her more of her own way than was usual. Indeed, she was accustomed to being the center of attention, the one deferred to in making plans and decisions. She'd never considered that this was the result of her rages. She'd simply assumed it was the normal state of affairs. Now, in a much larger circle, among strangers, she found everything changed. No one deferred, not even William. He was out on his own most of the time, scarcely ever asking her if she wished to come or what she would like to do. And Georgina—here Susan's train of thought stumbled—Georgina was an odd case. She didn't exactly oppose Susan's will, but neither did she subordinate herself to it. It was almost as if she lived in some quite different world, in which Susan was irrelevant.

Naturally, this idea did nothing to improve Susan's mood. Something, she decided, had to be done. She would not endure a whole season as merely one of the masses. But when she tried to think what to do, she was at a stand. Though various schemes occurred to her, even she knew them to be outrageous. She had no desire to create a scandal—merely to make her mark.

Looking across the now crowded theater, Susan saw Marianne MacClain enter a box with her mother and Sir Thomas Bentham. She felt a pang of envy. Though she never would admit it, she admired Marianne; this was the chief reason for her insistence on their rivalry. It was a way of saying they were alike without the humiliating admission that Susan merely *wished* it was so. Marianne seemed so at ease among the *ton*, and she had an established place in it, of some consequence. All knew her as the girl who had refused a brilliant match. Susan would have given much for such a distinction. But she would not have said this aloud for worlds.

Susan straightened in her chair as Marianne, settled, began to look about the theater, nodding to acquaintances. Susan pretended to have been gazing in quite a different direction, and then to notice her, and bow. She saw William and Tony do likewise, with much more enthusiasm, and Marianne's gentle smile at their changed appearance. Once again, she was racked by jealousy. It was Marianne's ability to laugh at circumstances that filled her with blind rage that impressed Susan the most. Though her family would have been surprised to hear it, Susan wasn't proud of her temper. Sometimes she felt it was hardly even part of her; rather, it was like an inexorable tide descending from outside. Often she said and did things she regretted bitterly later, so bitterly that she refused to acknowledge the fact to anyone. It was less humbling to pretend she'd meant it all. But occasionally, as now, she faced the truth. Indeed, such moments had come far more often since she arrived in London.

The play began, interrupting Susan's train of thought. And since she'd never seen a play before, she found the spectacle too enthralling to interrupt with gloomy speculations. She sat forward in her chair, arms on the edge of the box, and gave the stage her rapt attention.

Tony was equally fascinated. Indeed, at the first interval, William had some trouble rousing him to visit the boxes. He had to shake his shoulder sharply, as mere words failed to reach him, saying, "Here, what's the matter with you? Are you ill?"

Tony surfaced with a jerk. "What?"

"I asked if you were ill," repeated William. "I've been talking to you for five minutes, and you just stood there looking like a mooncalf. Is it that little blond playing the daughter?" He grinned.

Tony bridled, indignant and embarrassed at once. "Nonsense. I was thinking, that's all. Are we going up to the boxes, or not?" He turned away before William could answer, but the latter, seeing his mood, had already chosen silence.

This restraint seemed to mollify Tony, for at the foot of the stairs he asked in a normal tone, "Where to?"

"I ought to pay my respects to Lady Bentham," replied William.

"You mean Marianne," corrected Tony, not averse to getting a little of his own back. "Oh, very well."

Lady Bentham's box already held two visitors, young men whom William eyed with suspicion. But they departed soon after, and the newcomers were free to take the extra chairs and await compliments on their new finery.

Lady Bentham asked whether they liked the play.

They agreed that it was vastly entertaining.

Sir Thomas wondered if this was their first visit to a London theater.

They acknowledged the fact.

Lady Bentham declared that she liked plays above all things, and her husband, in what Tony thought a disgustingly besotted voice, said that this was because she was so sensitive. With this, the Benthams retired into their customary absorption with each other, and Marianne burst out laughing.

Both young men turned to stare at her, frowning, but though she struggled, it was a moment before Marianne regained her composure. At last she managed, "I beg your pardon."

"What's so amusing?" asked Tony. He had a sudden awful fear that he looked ridiculous.

"Nothing! That is, your conversation with Mama."

"I must have missed the joke."

Seeing that William, too, was looking thunderous, Marianne suppressed her lingering smile. "It is just that Mama is distracted lately," she added, as if this explained everything.

The gentlemen puzzled over this briefly, but there seemed nothing they could say, and Marianne's next words drove all other thoughts from their minds.

"You have been to the tailor Sir Thomas suggested, I see."

"Yes," answered Tony eagerly. "What do you think?" He turned in his chair to give her a good view.

"You are...dazzling," said Marianne. "I have never seen such a waistcoat."

"Nor will you," he responded proudly. "The man said this piece of cloth was all he had. Arrived in a special shipment direct from Paris."

"Really? How lucky for you."

Something in her voice made him suspicious again, and he surveyed her for signs of mockery. "It's all the crack."

"I know," agreed Marianne solemnly. "I daresay you will soon be one of the leading lights of the dandy set. Have you met Oliver Grigsby?"

"At the ball the other night." Tony grew confiding.

"Actually, it was his coat that decided me on what to buy. I'd never seen its like."

Marianne nodded. "You must tell him so."

"Well, I don't know."

"But he aims to set fashions, Tony. He will be so pleased."

Tony pondered this. He had been much taken with the dandy set. Their dress and manners, so different from the older generation's, seemed to express a rebellion that matched his own impulses.

"There's Grigsby now," said William, looking down into the theater.

Tony followed his gaze to the group of budding pinks below. "Perhaps I will just speak to him," he said.

Marianne and William nodded encouragingly, and Tony rose and slipped out of the box with a bow to the Benthams.

Immediately, William had qualms. "I suppose it's wrong to push him on them," he said, watching as Tony emerged below and joined Grigsby's group.

"Nonsense. They're harmless."

"Are they?"

"Grigsby and his friends, yes. They are merely young men who enjoy shocking their parents and society with their eccentricities of dress. It lasts only a year or so. I think it is a public statement of independence."

"Do you?"

Seeing that he was smiling, Marianne raised her eyebrows.

"You sounded like a dowager giving her judgment of the younger generation," added William.

"I did not!" She drew herself up indignantly, then slowly smiled a little. "Perhaps I have heard someone else say that."

Her smile broadened, becoming sheepish. "Mrs. Grigsby, I think."

"A very sensible woman, evidently."

Marianne nodded, and they laughed together.

"And what do you think of *my* new clothes?" asked William then.

"In the very best of taste," she replied promptly.

"You don't think I am making a statement of independence?"

"I don't believe you need to."

Their eyes met, both a bit surprised. Marianne had not known she was going to say that, but once she had, she realized that it was true. William was not much older than Tony, but he was far more sure of himself. For his part, William was pleased as well as startled. Marianne's good opinion was becoming important to him, and he was happy to see that she did not classify him with Tony, whom she clearly viewed as a kind of amusing younger brother.

"Perhaps not," he agreed, holding her eyes. "Indeed, my effort may be just the opposite. My old coat possessed a little *too* much independence."

They laughed together again, each feeling a dawning warmth that intrigued and excited them. But at that moment the warning bell rang, signaling the end of the interval.

"Oh," exclaimed Marianne, her disappointment obvious.

William was pleased to see it, though he cursed all theater managers. He rose, then paused to look down at Marianne. "Perhaps I may call on, er, your mother one day?"

"Yes, of course." She smiled. "I'm sure she would be happy to receive you."

With an answering smile, William turned and strode

buoyantly out of the box. Despite the abrupt end to their conversation, he felt quite satisfied with the encounter.

If the second installment of the play seemed less engrossing to certain members of the audience, Susan and Tony didn't notice it. Indeed, when the second interval arrived, each was bewitched by the action on stage, and William again had to rouse his friend with a shake. This time Tony said, "By Jove, it is good, isn't it?"

William agreed, though with less fervor. "I'm going up to Susan and Georgina. Coming?"

"Umm? Oh, yes, I suppose I should. How do you think they do it, William?"

"Who? Do what?"

"Actors. I mean, one knows they're playing a role, but I'd swear they mean every word as they say it. It's astonishing."

This was not one of William's areas of expertise. "Well, they have an aptitude, I suppose. And they practice, of course. Rehearse, isn't it?"

Tony nodded. "It's astonishing," he murmured again.

There were no other visitors to the Goring box, and Susan seemed glad to see them. "Isn't the play *wonderful*!" she exclaimed to William as he sat down. "I never imagined it would be like this." Before William could reply, Tony seconded her enthusiasm, and the two at once embarked on a detailed review of the play's action and numerous attractions.

The others watched them, smiling, for a moment, then William said, "Do *you* like it?"

"Yes," responded Georgina. "I think it very well done."

"But you do not fall into raptures."

"Perhaps I am past the age for that."

William had been keeping a surreptitious eye on Marianne across the way, wondering resentfully who the three young men visiting her box might be and whether she was acquainted with all of London, but something in Georgina's tone drew his full attention. Georgina was looking tired, he saw as he surveyed her more carefully, and her gray eyes showed shadows of some unfamiliar emotion. "Is Susan running you ragged?" he asked quietly. "You mustn't let her, you know. You should ask me for help. I came up to town for that purpose, though I may seem to forget it." He smiled.

"It's all right."

"That I should forget? It isn't. Or do you think I cannot help? You might be surprised."

Georgina looked up, her brown study dispersed.

"I've been dealing with Susan almost all my life, you see," added William.

Georgina smiled. "And rather well, I imagine."

He shrugged. "Our brother Nick is better, really. He thinks it out. But I manage. You will ask if you need something, I hope."

She nodded, oddly warmed, and impressed by the inner strength evident in this young man. Whether by temperament or education, he had matured into a calmly capable, quietly compelling man. She could, she realized, rely on him; the thought was comforting.

"You blockhead!" exclaimed Susan, too loudly. "She meant nothing of the kind. She was trying to keep him from seeing that she loved him, so she pretended to be cold."

"Pretended!" retorted Tony, his voice just as penetrating. "She treated him shamefully, and you could tell she didn't care if he went off to Italy and died."

"*He* didn't care if she remained behind with her beast of a brother and was made to marry Runyon," Susan snapped. "He didn't mean to do anything about it."

"What could he do? She gave him no sign that he had a right."

"Oh, you are just like him. Any idiot could *see* that—"

"A bit softer, Susan," interrupted Georgina. Their dispute was attracting attention.

Arrested in mid-spate, Susan noticed it. "I was simply trying to explain the play to Tony," she replied with quiet hauteur. "He has misunderstood it completely."

"*I?*" Tony laughed, though he too lowered his voice. "We shall see who has misunderstood when it starts again."

"Yes, we shall," said Susan hotly. They turned their heads ostentatiously away from one another.

William and Georgina exchanged a smile. "Susan, you have not told us if you like our new coats," William pointed out.

But if he thought this placatory, he was mistaken. "You look very well," she replied. "Tony is a complete quiz."

The latter sputtered with renewed rage. "What do you know about it?" he managed finally. "A chit fresh from a country schoolroom. I shouldn't give a snap of my fingers for *your* opinion if you fell into raptures. Oliver Grigsby said I looked fine as a fivepence."

"Then he must be as silly as you are," answered Susan, with that air of utter conviction and infuriating superiority so familiar to her brother.

"He happens to be one of the pinks of the *ton*," responded Tony through gritted teeth.

"A dandy, you mean? Well, that explains it."

Tony looked as if he would cheerfully throttle her. William started to intervene, but the bell rang again, and Tony rose with alacrity to return to his seat. "Miss Goring," he said in his most polished accents, bowing to Georgina. He turned his back on Susan and left the box.

"Idiot," murmured Susan.

"Well, he isn't," William informed her. "And you were dashed rude to him."

"I was rude? What of him?"

"He didn't call you a blockhead."

"He called me a chit!"

Her brother merely looked at her. Gradually Susan's flush lessened. "He made me angry," she said in a subdued voice after a while. "I was so enjoying the play."

"So was he," William pointed out.

"But he was wrong!"

"I understand there may be two opinions on such matters—perhaps even more than two."

Susan tossed her head, started to speak, then changed her mind. "If you do not go, you will miss the end," she said.

William shrugged, smiled at Georgina, and went out. Thus, only Georgina saw Susan's shoulders rise and fall in a great sigh as she leaned forward to watch the resuming play. Georgina was, however, oddly heartened by this reaction.

SEVEN

THE FOLLOWING AFTERNOON, AT THE FASHIONABLE hour, Susan Wyndham set off to walk in the park, escorted by her maid and the cat Daisy. Susan was not in the best of moods. Neither Georgina nor William had been available when she made up her mind to walk—the former had gone out to Hookham's circulating library and the latter on some unknown errand of his own—and Susan unreasonably took this as a deliberate slight. Actually, her impatience arose out of the fact that she was accustomed to far more exercise than she got in London, for despite her fragile appearance, she habitually rode or walked a goodly distance every day. But she was not aware of this, and so blamed her family for their disregard of her comfort.

Once outside, however, her temper improved. It was a lovely afternoon, and she had put on a new gown of pale buff muslin sprigged with tiny, dark green flowers and a new chip straw hat. The matching sunshade she raised over her head filled her with deep satisfaction, and an admiring glance from a gentleman on horseback as they entered the park completed her triumph. She lifted her chin and smiled a little, and her maid heaved an almost audible sigh of relief.

Susan chose a path that ran beside the main avenue of the park, where fashionable carriages moved in a dignified cavalcade to allow their passengers to bow to one another and exchange occasional remarks. She kept a sharp eye on these vehicles, hoping to see an acquaintance, but only twice did she spy a known face, and on the second occasion the rider did not notice her.

This ruffled Susan's temper again. It was exactly as she had concluded at the theater, she told herself irritably: she wasn't well enough known to make a hit. Grandmama had promised a ball in her honor, but since she had fallen ill the plan had not been mentioned. Georgina was clearly incapable of carrying through, and even Susan was a little daunted at the idea of supervising such an undertaking. Yet her introduction to society so far had been definitely disappointing. Susan watched the passing stream of carriages, filled with elegant people whom she did not recognize, and she felt suddenly isolated and excluded. She was prettier and more interesting than any of those women, she thought petulantly. Why should they have every advantage and she none at all!

With this very unfair observation, Susan turned homeward. She was not consciously aware of the need to relieve her pent-up feelings in some outburst, but she knew she strongly wished to talk with William or Georgina.

It was at this moment that Susan saw Baron Ellerton approaching from the direction of the park gates. He was driving an impeccable high-perch phaeton drawn by the most magnificent team of chestnuts Susan had ever seen, and he handled the spirited animals with negligent grace. Without pausing to think, Susan stepped forward, nearly into the carriageway, smiled, and raised her hand. When it seemed as if the baron would simply bow politely and drive on, she moved even further forward, eliciting a warning exclamation from her maid. Susan continued to smile.

Ellerton pulled up with a mixture of annoyance and amusement. The Wyndham chit was certainly determined, he thought as he brought the phaeton to a halt beside her.

He'd never encountered such a strong will in such a deceptive package, but if she thought to get the best of him, she would be disappointed. The baron had been a target for countless marriage-minded young ladies and gimlet-eyed mothers in the fifteen years he'd been on the town, and he had profited from this experience. "Good day, Miss Wyndham," he said coolly. "A fine day for a stroll."

"Oh, I'd much rather be driving," replied Susan brightly. "*Would* you be so kind as to take me up for a spin round the park, Baron Ellerton? I have never ridden in a phaeton in my life." She gazed up at him with large, innocent eyes, just as if this was not an outrageous request. Both her maid and the middle-aged groom who sat beside the baron had gasped.

Ellerton could deal with simpering, flirtation, even tears, with the greatest ease, but Susan's flat demand—for it amounted to that—could not be turned aside without absolute rudeness. Because of the chit's connection to the fascinating Miss Goring, Baron Ellerton found himself reluctant to give her a sharp setdown. His handsome face stiff with annoyance, he answered, "Very well, Miss Wyndham. You may get down, Hines."

Any other young lady in London would have cringed at his tone, and hastily withdrawn her suggestion, but Susan merely turned to her maid and said, "You may go, Lucy. I daresay the baron will escort me home later."

Lucy opened her mouth and closed it like a beached fish.

"Oh, and I will take Daisy's basket. He loves carriage rides."

The maid, knowing this to be untrue, paled and tried again to object. But Susan paid no heed. She took the basket from Lucy's nerveless fingers and accepted the groom's aid

in climbing up the vehicle's steps. Only when the phaeton
was moving away did the maid regain her powers of speech,
responding to the groom Hines's "Well, I never!" with a
half-hysterical catalog of the vicissitudes of her post. Hines
was forced to support her on the journey home, giving her
gratefully into the hands of the Goring cook, who had wit-
nessed such scenes before.

"This is splendid," declared Susan as she settled herself
in the carriage. She set Daisy's basket beside her feet and
adjusted her dark green shawl about her shoulders. The
view from the phaeton's high seat was impressive; she felt
far above the people sauntering in the park, whom she had
numbered among just moments ago.

The complacency in her expression goaded the baron,
and now that there were no listeners, he felt able to remark,
"You know, Miss Wyndham, it is not usual for a young
lady to command a gentleman with whom she is barely
acquainted to take her up in his carriage."

"I know," agreed Susan. "But I didn't think you would
ask *me*, and I wanted to come."

Once again, Ellerton found himself silenced by her
bluntness. One side of his mouth quirking up at the ridiculousness of it, he began, "Nonetheless—"

But Susan did not want to hear his admonitions. "And
everyone will see me and talk of it," she interrupted happily.
"It is quite a mark of distinction to be driven by you."

The baron was not unaware of this. "A mark of distinction is customarily *bestowed*, Miss Wyndham," he answered
dryly, "not, er, seized."

"Yes. But you have no idea how difficult it is to make an
impression here in London. There are so many girls coming

out, and even though they are mostly the merest nothings, one is classified with them and ignored. I want to make a splash!"

"Do you?"

"Oh, I don't wish to do anything scandalous." She turned wide green eyes on his face. "But I *should* be a famous belle, Baron Ellerton."

Taking in her passionate determination, Ellerton found his annoyance fading into curiosity. Irritating, Miss Wyndham certainly was, but she was also unusual, with a far stronger will than most young ladies Moreover, she had a point. Although there were many factors involved in the creation of a reigning toast—money and rank as well as beauty and personality—a strong character such as this girl clearly possessed could tip the scales. Ellerton discovered an interest in her future career, though no desire to take an active role in it. Indeed, the thought made him shudder. But he would enjoy observing her tactics. At the moment, however, he had a more important mission. "Perhaps," he conceded. "But I will not be used in your campaign again, Miss Wyndham. I give you fair warning, the next time you put me in such a position, I shall be rude, as I was not today."

She did not pretend to misunderstand him. "I'm sorry. I won't do it again."

The baron glanced at her face. She was grinning mischievously but seemed sincere. "See that you don't," he finished.

Susan nodded. "Now that that is settled," she added, "could I take the reins for a little while?"

Ellerton stared at her as if she'd gone mad.

"I am a famous whip," she assured him. "I drive a great deal in the country. I've even handled a team."

"No one drives my horses but me," he replied in his most repressive accents.

"But I—"

"Miss Wyndham! We have just discussed your behavior. I tell you now that this is absolutely beyond the line. You cannot drive my cattle!" To himself he was marveling at her effrontery. No *man* in London would have asked this, but she did so without the least sign of constraint.

Susan's elfin features set in lines that would have warned anyone better acquainted with her, and she began to look about the park as if plotting strategy. Actually, she didn't understand the gravity of what she'd asked. Her brothers had let her try their horses. William was a bruising rider but lacked finesse in driving, and Nicholas preferred scholarly pursuits to a neck-or-nothing gallop. Their teams were far gentler than those Baron Ellerton bred, leaving Susan with an inflated idea of her own competence. To her, Ellerton's refusal seemed simply a punishment for her earlier behavior. "I suppose I should be going home now," Susan declared in a deceptively mild tone as they approached the gate of the park once more.

"Certainly," the baron agreed, only too pleased to cut his drive short if it meant ridding himself of her. He maneuvered around a dawdling barouche and turned into the street.

Susan leaned over and fingered the lid of Daisy's basket. As she opened it a crack, the cat's broad ginger head thrust out, his yellow eyes glittering with malice. Daisy was not fond of carriage rides, but if forced to ride, he much preferred sitting up where he could see, or at the very least being free to move about. Shut in his stuffy basket, which he at all times hated, and bounced about by the vehicle, he'd been roused to a towering rage. At the first sign of rescue, he was out of the container and standing rigid on the floor of the phaeton. Susan, who might have been expected to know his predilections, merely gazed at him speculatively.

"Your cat must stay in the basket," ordered Ellerton, glancing briefly down, then up again. The busy London streets required his attention.

With the look of a dispassionate experimenter, Susan advanced one kid-shod foot to prod Daisy's stomach sharply.

The cat went up like a rocket, teeth bared, claws outstretched. The latter sank into the immaculate yellow pantaloons that sheathed the baron's knee and held there while Daisy yowled defiance.

Ellerton swore, his hands dropping for a startled instant. The team increased its pace, barely skirting an overladen cart slowing before a greengrocer's. "Get that creature off me!" he commanded through gritted teeth.

Susan bit her lower lip. "Oh dear," she said in an insincere voice.

"I said..." Daisy reached the baron's thigh, paused, digging in his claws, then leapt for his chest. Ellerton gathered the reins in one hand and sought to capture the animal with the other.

"Look out for that gig," cried Susan.

The baron attempted to pull up the phaeton, collar Daisy, and glare furiously at Susan all at once. The cat, fighting, as he thought, for life, limb, and freedom, wrapped himself about Ellerton's neck and tried to shred his very elegant neckcloth. The baron cursed fluently.

Susan, seeing the opportunity she'd been waiting for, seized the phaeton's reins from its owner's momentarily slack grasp, slapped them across the team's glossy backs, and laughed as the carriage began to race through the cobbled streets.

The baron shouted something incoherent, but Susan's unexpected move had thrown him back in his seat and driven Daisy to a frenzy of rage. As Ellerton tried to regain his balance, the cat swarmed about his face, hissing and scratching and requiring all his attention.

Susan realized almost at once that she'd made a dreadful mistake. The baron's team was more powerful than any she'd driven before. Indeed, it took all her strength merely to keep hold of the reins. Any thought of controlling the chestnuts had to be abandoned. The phaeton raced at a dangerous speed through the streets, eliciting angry shouts and leaving a wake of shaken pedestrians and, in at least one case, scattered vegetables. Holding on with all her might, Susan soon began to be truly frightened. She dared a glance at the baron. He was trying to corral Daisy, who was fighting back with all his strength. "Daisy, stop it!" she cried. But the cat was too far gone to hear by now.

They hurtled out into a broad highway, the team turning of its own accord and racing along it. Susan's wrists and forearms ached, and the wind of their passage had whirled away her beloved sunshade and pushed back her hat to dangle from its ribbons. The buildings were thinning, she noticed. They must be near the edge of town.

With a jerk, Ellerton got both hands round Daisy's squirming body and threw the cat from the carriage into a tree beside the road. At once he turned to grasp the reins, and Susan gave them up without protest. Indeed, she was only too glad to relinquish responsibility for their disastrous race.

But this new disturbance was too much for Ellerton's high-spirited team. Never in their pampered lives had they endured such treatment. They'd always been driven with impeccable skill and received in the city streets or country lanes with deference and admiration. These violent jerks on their guiding lines and shouts and curses from all sides had upset their high-bred equilibrium. As the baron strove with all his strength to pull them up and stop the phaeton, they rebelled, galloping even faster than before.

Seeing blood beginning to fleck the froth at the corners of the horses's mouths, Ellerton eased his grip, letting them run. "I won't ruin them," he snapped at Susan. "They will have to run it out."

She simply nodded, white and ashamed, but less frightened now that he'd taken over.

The chestnuts strained in their harness for nearly fifteen minutes, pulling the tossing phaeton through ruts and dust, heedless of anything but their need to flee. Ellerton held the reins with iron wrists, gradually reestablishing control and very slowly moderating their pace. They were outside London when it at last appeared that he would be able to stop the carriage, and he felt free to glance at Susan and open his mouth for a blistering setdown. At that moment, a pair of sparrows erupted from the bushes at the right of the road and hurtled across under the very noses of the leaders. The chestnuts shied violently, and one of them reared, then plunged into the foliage. The phaeton rose perilously on one wheel, hanging there for an endless instant, then slammed to the ground, flinging both passengers from their seats into the leaves.

Susan landed on a thorn bush, the breath quite knocked out of her. As she strove for air, thorns prickled her from all sides, but the pain was nothing to her apprehension about what the baron would do to her when he found her. He was furious, and she had to acknowledge, he had every right to be. Her dreadful temper had gotten the better of her again.

Susan considered trying to crawl away through the bushes and make her own way back to London, but her sense of responsibility at last forced her to struggle out of the thorns, leaving a good many scraps of sprigged muslin behind her, and return to the road. She saw the phaeton at once; it lay on its side and would not move again without repair. The team was still harnessed to it. They were standing still, sweating and trembling in the traces. She should try to cut them loose, Susan realized, but when she ventured closer, the more nervous leader shied again and looked as if he would lash out with his hooves. Better leave them to the baron, Susan thought, backing away again. And she frowned as she looked for him. Surely he would have gone directly to his horses?

Frightened again, Susan returned to the bushes and began to search, calling Ellerton's name. There was no response, which shook her further. She plunged through the undergrowth, oblivious of lashing branches and thorns, until at last she came upon him, on his back under an elm, white and unmoving.

With a cry, she sank to her knees at his side. There was a great gash in the side of his forehead. It had bled all down the side of his face and dyed the fallen leaves beneath him crimson. Too, one of his legs lay at an odd angle.

Some girls might have fallen into a fit of the vapors then and there, but Susan was made of stronger stuff. She had seen a number of hunting accidents, and knew something about treating such injuries. Cuts to the head always bled heavily, she knew. Nonetheless, her hands were shaking as she groped in the baron's pocket for a handkerchief to bind up the wound. She felt for his pulse, conscious of an almost unbearable relief when she found it, and ran her hands along the bent leg. Ellerton groaned when she touched it, and she snatched her hand away.

"Baron Ellerton," she said urgently. "Baron!"

He groaned again but did not wake. Susan sat back on her heels, still trembling, and wondered how best to find help. She would have to leave him, she decided, while she walked along the road to the closest house or village. She ran back to the phaeton, and after a rapid search, found a rug, which she hurried to spread over him. The horses shied again as she passed. Then, hair wild and bleeding from numerous thorn pricks, Susan set off toward town.

EIGHT

AT NEARLY THE SAME TIME, GEORGINA GORING WENT in search of Susan's brother. She found him in the library, dozing over a book in the hour before dinner. "William," she said softly, and he started awake.

"Uuh! What? Oh, Georgina." He straightened in the brown leather armchair.

"William, do you remember you said I should ask for your help if I needed it?"

Her tone made him rub the last drowsiness from his eyes. "Of course. Is something wrong?"

"I hope not." She hesitated. "I'm worried about Susan."

He groaned. "What's she done now?"

Georgina sighed and sank down on the sofa nearby. "Perhaps nothing. But I can't help but be concerned." She told William the maid Lucy's story. "It is nearly two hours since then, and she is not back," she finished. "I don't know what can have happened."

Some men might have doubted the baron's motives or suspected him of treachery. William Wyndham exclaimed, "She has kidnapped him!" and put his head in his hands.

Georgina was torn between laughter and outrage. "William! Why should she do any such thing?"

"Why does Susan do anything?" he retorted, raising his head again. "He probably gave her a well-deserved setdown for pushing herself upon him, and she decided to make him sorry."

This sounded disturbingly plausible to Georgina. "But how could she—"

"Susan would find a way," interrupted William positively.

Once again, Georgina could not muster convincing arguments, and her spirits fell even further. She had failed in her duties as a chaperone, she thought, just as she feared she would. But she also felt a spark of resentment. That Susan should disappear in the company of Baron Ellerton seemed to her unfair, though she would have been hard put to explain what exactly that meant. She pushed these thoughts aside. "We must look for her," she told William.

He nodded wearily. "I'll get my horse and ride through the park. Of course, they can't still be there."

"I'll speak to Lucy again. Perhaps she will remember something Susan said, or..." She trailed off, and they gazed at one another, each feeling that their suggestions were weak. Then William shrugged and went out.

The maid had no more information, and William returned as the sky was darkening toward evening with no news, though he had ridden along all the streets leading to the park and even gone to inquire at Baron Ellerton's house. He had been turned away with some hauteur by the butler, whose icy reserve was such an effective mask of his concern that William never suspected it.

"What shall we do now?" he asked when he and Georgina had left the dinner table, having eaten very little.

She rubbed her eyes. "I don't know. I suppose I must speak to Aunt Sybil, but..."

"It might make her worse. I could go and fetch Christopher, but that would take three days." He frowned.

Georgina found his confidence in his stepfather touching, but unhelpful. "No, we have to think of something ourselves," she concluded.

They looked at each other, their feelings very similar. Georgina was scolding herself for her inadequacy as a guide to Susan, and William was deploring his poor showing as head of the Wyndham family. Both had a strong sense of responsibility and a hatred of failure.

"I *could* go back to the baron's house and tell the truth," ventured William, sounding far from eager.

"No. We must keep this a secret as long as we can. I even managed to fob Lucy off, for a while. It mustn't get out."

"What mustn't?" inquired a cheerful voice from the drawing-room doorway, and they turned to find Tony Brinmore and Marianne MacClain standing there.

Their surprise and chagrin were so obvious that Marianne said, "A footman let us in, and told us you were here. We were passing by on our way home from the Wigginses', and Tony wanted to speak to William."

"What mustn't get out?" repeated Tony, throwing himself into an armchair and gazing at William with cheerful curiosity.

"Tony, we should go," responded Marianne.

He looked startled. "We just got here. What's the matter with—?"

The maid Lucy rushed in, wringing her hands. "Oh, Miss Georgina, the cat's come home," she cried, oblivious of the presence of visitors. "All dusty and draggled, he is, with a cut on his leg. It's footpads, or highwaymen, I'll lay my life. Miss Susan's killed. Or worse!" She began to blubber noisily.

"You mean she took the cat with her!" exclaimed William, astounded.

Lucy was incapable of speech. Georgina closed her eyes and prayed for strength.

"What's Susan done now?" asked Tony, clearly intrigued and amused.

Marianne tugged at his arm. "Tony, come. We're in the way here."

He shook her off. "Nonsense. William needs my help."

Marianne looked at Georgina, who had gone to deal with Lucy. "I do beg your pardon," she said.

Georgina simply shook her head. She succeeded in quieting Lucy enough to guide her out of the room and down to the kitchen, where the cook again took over ministrations. When she returned to the drawing room, she found William completing the tale of the day's events. "So we don't know where she's gone. But now that I hear about Daisy, I have a good idea."

"Where?" Georgina exclaimed, too eager to scold him for spreading the tale.

William turned. "Ellerton's killed her," he replied matter-of-factly. "Throttled her and left her under a bush in the park. Daresay he tried for Daisy, too, but that animal is devilishly clever."

Tony burst out laughing. Marianne, throwing him an indignant look, went to Georgina. "I am terribly sorry. I..."

"It's all right. I know you won't talk of it." Georgina turned to Tony. "And if you do, you will—"

"What do you take me for?" Tony was still fighting a smile. "I mean to help."

With a deep sigh, Georgina went to sit on the sofa again. Marianne joined her. "I don't see what any of us can do. We don't know where to search."

"Perhaps the cat can lead us to them," suggested Tony, grinning.

"Oh, stop it!" responded Marianne. "This is no joking matter."

"Do you suppose there's been an accident?" wondered Georgina. "Lucy said it was a high-perch phaeton. They don't look very safe."

"Ellerton is one of the finest whips in the country," said Marianne. "I can't imagine him taking a spill."

"Susan would," declared William. "And she'd be wild to take the ribbons."

"Ellerton would never allow it," Marianne assured him. "No."

They sat in glum silence for a while, each trying to think of some plan, and none succeeding. Georgina was growing desperate when the butler entered with an envelope. "For you, miss," he said. "A boy just brought it."

They all clustered around as she opened it and scanned the message. "Oh, my God!" said William then, collapsing into a chair.

"She's killed *him*," crowed Tony. "Or half-killed him, anyhow."

Marianne was silent, but Georgina crumpled the paper in her fist and said, "I must go to them at once," her voice shaking.

No one disagreed, but Marianne surveyed the other woman with deep concern. She could see that Georgina was dreadfully upset, and she understood at least some of the reasons. "I will go with you," she offered.

"We'll all go," said Tony, not quite able to hide his excitement at the adventure. "You'll need someone to, er, run errands and, er, that sort of thing."

In the end, despite William's protests and Georgina's

firm denials, they all set out together, Marianne and Georgina in Lady Goring's carriage and the young men riding. By the time they had gathered their things and sent word to Marianne's mother, it was full dark, and they had to travel very slowly. Gradually, even Tony's high spirits were dampened by the dismal drive, and conversation dropped to nothing.

Susan had long since decided that this was the worst day of her life. After leaving the wrecked phaeton, she walked nearly half an hour before reaching a cluster of buildings. And when she came among them, she saw to her chagrin that they belonged to one of the main posting houses on the road out of London. The place bustled with ostlers, waiters, and elegant travelers, and she drew a great many curious looks as she made her way inside, her tattered gown and tangled hair making her feel horribly self-conscious. With every step she expected to be recognized and questioned by some London acquaintance, but mercifully she managed to find the innkeeper and tell her story without being remarked.

At this point, she began to appreciate her luck, for the landlord at once delegated three of his large staff to take her back to the phaeton and help her bring Ellerton to the inn. He sent another for the nearest doctor. Amidst this whirlwind of activity, Susan at first felt dazed, then grateful to have some of the responsibility lifted from her shoulders.

When she had guided the men back to the location of the accident, they found that a small huddle of onlookers had by this time collected. As two of these were examining the equipage with furtive greed, Susan was unexpectedly thankful for the horses' difficult temperament. They had clearly kept everyone away from the phaeton. "He's in here," she told the men, and they pushed through the foliage to the baron, who lay as she'd left him, still unconscious.

"Be careful of his leg," she warned as they transferred him to an improvised stretcher. "Oh, shouldn't he have wakened by now?"

"He do look bad," replied one of the men, an ostler. "That were quite a spill you took." His tone was almost admiring, but it did nothing to comfort Susan.

They laid Ellerton in the wagon they'd brought, and the ostler went to deal with the team. "They are in a bad temper," warned Susan, but he merely gave her a gap-toothed grin and began to murmur to the animals. By the time the wagon was turned and ready to depart, he had gotten close enough to stroke the noses of the leaders.

"I'll have to lead 'em back," he called. "Axle's broken. I'll cut 'em loose and be along directly."

The wagon driver nodded, and they went slowly back to the posting house. Susan sat in back to watch over Ellerton, but though he groaned once or twice when the wheels jolted over something in the road, he did not come round.

By the time they had carried him up to one of the inn's bedrooms, the doctor had arrived. Susan was ordered from the room and forced to wait in a parlor downstairs while he made his examination. Here, for the first time able to relax a little, she nearly gave way to tears. This time her wretched temper had gotten her into a scrape that she might not escape unscathed, she thought miserably. She had meant no harm—or not much, at least—but she had again allowed her fury to take over. What if he died? What would she do?

Shuddering, she wrapped her arms around her chest and went to stand by the window, staring unseeing out at the approaching dusk. Her supposed admiration for Baron Ellerton was forgotten in worry for herself; he was to her at that moment less a man than a symbol of her own mistakes and stupidity. If he is all right, she told herself fervently, I promise I will change. I will never do such a foolish thing again as long as I live.

"Miss?" said a deep, scratchy voice from the doorway.

Susan started and turned. "Doctor! Is he… How is he?"

"Not good." The doctor came further into the room. He was a dark, competent-looking man of about forty. "His leg is broken, as you thought, as well as two ribs. But it is the blow to the head that worries me. He obviously struck something very hard when he was thrown from the carriage. He still has not regained consciousness."

"Does that mean… Will he…?" Susan's mouth was very dry, and she found she could not ask the crucial question.

"I cannot tell anything for certain until he wakes," answered the doctor seriously. "You must send for me as soon as he does. I will come back in the morning in any case."

She nodded, numb.

The doctor eyed her, pity and uncertainty in his brown eyes. "Is there someone you can send for? You should be in bed yourself. Are you sure you're all right?"

"Perfectly." She didn't look it as she gazed abstractedly about the room. She would have to write to Georgina and William, she thought.

"You are... That is, the gentleman is a member of your family?"

"Oh, no. We were just...out driving."

"I see."

His tone made Susan focus on him again. "The horses were frightened and bolted," she added. "We...he said they must run themselves out. We came from London." The doctor's expression told Susan how improbable this sounded, but she refused to tell a stranger about her dangerous prank. Gathering the shreds of her dignity, she continued, "Thank you very much for your help. I must write to my family now."

This seemed to relieve him somewhat. "Good. I will see you in the morning, then." His cheeks reddened slightly. "Or, that is, I will see the gentleman, and whoever stays with him. My name is Mason, by the way." He paused, waiting for Susan to give her name.

She balked. This escapade would cause storms of gossip if word of it got out. "Thank you very much for your help, Dr. Mason," she answered dismissively.

He stiffened a little, then bowed and went out.

Susan put her face in her hands and stood very still for a long moment, then straightened and moved to the writing desk in the corner of the parlor. For the first time in her life she longed for William's down-to-earth advice. He would be furious with her—rightly, she admitted—but he would stand by her and do whatever he could to help her out of this tangle. As would Georgina, Susan realized. Though her hand trembled as she scribbled a note to them, she was also filled with a warm flood of relief.

NINE

GEORGINA AND THE OTHERS ARRIVED AT THE POSTING house later that night. Susan had gone up to her bedchamber, but she had not undressed, being certain sleep was impossible. Thus, when Georgina tapped very lightly at the door, she answered at once, and immediately flung herself into Georgina's startled embrace. "Thank heaven you have come! I feared you would wait until morning. I have gone nearly distracted trying to think what to do."

Georgina patted her back comfortingly and waited a moment to let her regain her composure. Then she said, "How is Baron Ellerton? And what happened, Susan? Your note said only that he was injured."

Susan stepped back a pace and hung her head. "He is very bad. The landlady is sitting with him now. It is all my fault, but I am sorry!" This last rose into a wail.

"But what happened?" Georgina was sympathetic but impatient.

"I saw the baron in the park," began Susan in a small voice.

"Yes, we know about that. Lucy told us. But I think we had better go down to the others. That way you needn't tell the story but once."

"What others? Is William with you? Of course, he would be."

Georgina nodded. "And Lady Marianne MacClain and Mr. Brinmore."

Susan stared at her, appalled.

"They called just as we received your letter," added

Georgina, conscious that Susan had some right to be upset. "They came upon us before we realized, and heard part of the story. Then Lucy grew hysterical, and...there was nothing for it but to tell them the whole."

Susan recovered from her frozen astonishment. "I cannot possibly face them, Georgina. I won't go down!"

"They have been very kind," protested the other. "They want to help."

"Help! Marianne will gloat over my foolishness. She probably came only because of the baron. And Tony will laugh himself sick. I will not see them!"

"Nonsense!" insisted Georgina. "All of us are here to help. Come." She took Susan's arm and attempted to lead her, but the younger girl pulled away. It was nearly twenty minutes before she could be convinced to descend to the parlor where the others waited, and even then she did so with no good grace.

Tony and William were lounging on a sofa when they entered, half-asleep. Marianne sat opposite, looking tired but determinedly alert.

"Hello," said Susan, stepping into the room ahead of Georgina. "Isn't this the most ridiculous muddle? But you needn't all have come out here. Things are nearly under control again." She took the remaining armchair and looked from one to another of them, smiling.

Georgina couldn't help but gape. Susan seemed a different person from the frightened young girl upstairs.

"What the deuce have you done, Susan?" asked William, "Is Ellerton badly hurt?"

His sister looked solemn. "Yes, I fear he is. I have been very foolish." But her tone showed none of the anguished contrition she had exhibited only minutes earlier. "I tried to drive his team, you see, and—"

"Ellerton allowed you to drive his horses?" interrupted Marianne, amazed.

"Well, no." Slowly she told them the story. She would have preferred to omit certain details, but the others asked questions which forced her to reveal them. There was no other explanation for what had happened.

At the description of Daisy's attack, Tony choked. "That hellish animal is all right, by the by," said William. "He found his way back to the house."

"Did he?" Susan was diverted from her tale. "How clever he is." She avoided Marianne's outraged gaze. The latter was stunned that Susan had used her previous ploy in this way.

"Too clever by half," growled her brother. "What happened then?"

She described the accident and its aftermath. "The doctor will call again in the morning," she concluded. "He hopes the baron may be better then."

This reduced them to glum silence again. Ellerton's precarious state weighed on all their minds.

"So, what are we going to do?" asked William. Instinctively he looked to Georgina, though he would have denied any claim that he expected her to save the situation.

"We must see what the doctor says," she answered, looking fatigued and distressed. "And we must see that he is well nursed, of course. We will have to send word to his family." She turned to Marianne. "Do you know them?"

The girl frowned. "I don't think he has any close relations. I have never heard of any."

"Well, we will inform his household. They will know."

"But what are we going to tell them?" wondered William.

This was the difficult question. They all contemplated it for a moment.

"We can't give out the true story," he added then. "It would create a scandal." He glared at Susan, who avoided his eyes.

Georgina pondered. "We will let it be known that Baron Ellerton has had a carriage accident," she said. "Susan will not come into it. And we will see that he is cared for." She paused. "If he has no suitable family, I will nurse him myself."

"You?" William was surprised. "Susan should do it, if anyone." But he eyed his sister doubtfully.

"I doubt that nursing is one of her talents," responded Georgina, and no one disagreed. "It is, however, one of mine. I nursed my father through his last illness." She did not add that the thought of allowing anyone else to care for Ellerton annoyed her intensely. "The rest of you will return to London and go on as before."

"You cannot stay here alone," objected Marianne.

"I will send for my maid. And I imagine some of Ellerton's servants will come to help. I shan't be alone."

"But it isn't fair."

Georgina shrugged.

"I shan't be able to go out without you to chaperone me," pointed out Susan. She felt that this might annoy them, yet it was important to her.

"William can escort you," said Georgina.

"But…"

"You can go about with me, if you like," offered Marianne, her tone barely warm. She was not feeling in charity with Susan Wyndham.

"Good," replied Georgina, as if all were settled. Susan looked skeptical.

"But how will we explain your absence?" asked William. "*And* your presence here? If we have Ellerton's servants, they will spread the tale."

This caused another silence.

"It is easy enough to tell people I have been called away," said Georgina meditatively. "We must tell Aunt Sybil and your mother the truth, of course." She paused. "Ellerton's servants will not know me."

"But travelers passing through this inn may," put in Marianne.

"Umm. Well, I will simply have to keep to my room."

"Ellerton'll have visitors," protested William. "This won't work, Georgina. I say we just leave it to Ellerton's people."

She shook her head. "I learned with my father that one must be on hand oneself."

"Tell them you stopped at this inn on your way, er, somewhere, and found Ellerton here. Took pity on him," suggested Tony, who had contributed nothing so far. "No one else to watch over him, so you stayed."

"That would never work," scoffed Marianne.

"Why not?"

They all contemplated the idea for a moment.

"It *might* do," admitted William. "You could repeat what you told us. Say you had a particularly poor specimen of a nurse with your father—"

"Which we *did*," interjected Georgina.

"And you couldn't just leave him." William seemed to warm to his story as he went on.

"You tried to send for his family, but there was no one to come," contributed Marianne.

"Very awkward, of course, but what could you do?" finished Tony, very proud of his scheme.

For some reason, the possibility that her plan would work filled Georgina with joy. "That should pass muster. There will be talk, naturally, but..."

"It is unfair that they should talk about you rather than me," objected Susan, her conscience pricking her through her relief.

"It certainly is," agreed her brother, "but I see no way around it. And it won't be that same sort of talk. Besides, Georgina is..." He stopped and flushed.

"Ten years older than you," finished Georgina calmly. "Quite on the shelf, in fact. I daresay the gossip will die down almost at once."

None of them disputed this, but all four looked uncomfortable.

"Well, now that is settled," Georgina continued, "we should all try to sleep. There will be a great deal to do in the morning. William, did you speak to the landlord about rooms?"

"Yes. That's all right."

"Splendid. Let us go up, then." She turned, and Tony rose to follow, but the others hesitated.

"I say, Georgina," blurted William, "this is really good of you. I don't know how... Isn't it, Susan?" He scowled at his sister to hide a softer emotion.

Susan nodded vigorously.

"Indeed, it is...thoroughly admirable," agreed Marianne.

"Stuff!" replied Georgina, and walked out into the hallway.

None of them slept particularly well, and in the morning there were notes to be written and arrangements to be made. Georgina took some trouble over the composition of her letter to Baron Ellerton's household, knowing that whatever tale she told was likely to be circulated throughout London. "You will be responsible for speaking to our own servants," she told William when she gave it to him. "Their knowledge is garbled and incomplete, but they should be asked not to speak of the incident in the park."

"Of course," said William.

"Susan, here is a list of the things I shall need. You can pack them up for me and send them down with Lucy." It had been decided that Susan and Georgina would exchange maids, to remove Lucy from London and the temptations of gossip.

"We'll all be at your service for errands and the like," offered Tony. "You need only send word."

"I shall." Georgina smiled. "And now, you should be on your way. That note should be delivered as soon as possible."

The carriage had already been ordered. The four young people gathered their things, and Georgina walked with them to the wide front door. Outside, Tony and William mounted up, but the girls lingered.

"I feel as if we're abandoning you," said Marianne, holding out her hand. "Are you certain you don't want one of us to stay?"

"Completely," responded Georgina. "It would not do." She smiled. She had been greatly impressed with Marianne's calm good sense and ready sympathy through this episode.

Susan might actually be better off under her tutelage, she had decided.

"If you change your mind, you need only write," said the other.

Georgina nodded, still smiling, and Marianne turned to climb into the chaise.

This left only Susan. "I feel dreadful," she said in a low voice. "You are paying the price for my folly."

"You may make it up by falling into no more scrapes," replied Georgina.

"I shan't. I shall be a model of propriety."

This made Georgina smile again. "Don't promise what you cannot fulfill. I will be content if you are merely a little prudent."

Susan bridled, then grinned, her elfin face lighting with mischief. "Very well. I think I can manage that."

Georgina laughed. "Good! Now, go."

Susan got into the carriage, and the party set off. Georgina stayed to wave, then turned back to her duties. She felt a curious sense of relief to be rid of her family and friends. Though she would not have said it aloud, she found she relished the idea of solitude, with worthwhile work to do. It was much more to her taste than the gaieties of the Season. She did not explore her emotions beyond this, and thus was not required to consider the pleasure she took in the thought of caring for Baron Ellerton. She was terribly concerned for him. She had visited his room twice during the night, and each time the landlady had shaken her head and whispered that he had not come round. Georgina's anxiety was at least partially eased by the knowledge that she would be doing her utmost to help him.

Dr. Mason arrived soon after this, and Georgina received him just outside Ellerton's room. When she had introduced herself and explained that she would be nursing the patient, the doctor was relieved. This clear-eyed young woman seemed much better suited to the task than the shaken girl he had met yesterday. "You are a member of his family?" he asked.

"No. Unfortunately he has none. I am a friend who happened to be traveling and found him here. I have had some experience with hired nurses and will not leave him to them."

"Ah, you have worked in a sickroom yourself, perhaps?" he was examining her measuringly.

"My father's. And I will have the help of my maid and, I think, some of the baron's servants."

"Baron, is he?" Mason nodded. It had been obvious to him that his patient was distinguished. It was also obvious that he was not being told the whole story, but he was not surprised by this.

"Baron Ellerton. And my name is Georgina Goring. Will you examine him now? I am very worried."

"Of course." Dr. Mason disappeared into the bedchamber, impressed anew with Miss Goring's capable air.

His expression was less cheerful when he came out again, and in answer to Georgina's inquiring look, he shook his head. "I don't like it. I wish he would wake. I can make no final judgment on his state until he does."

"Is there no sign when that may happen?" Her voice trembled slightly.

"No. In some of these cases..." He hesitated.

"What?"

Dr. Mason shrugged. "Sometimes, a person taking a blow to the head never wakes. He simply…fades away."

"That will not happen to Baron Ellerton!" exclaimed Georgina. The doctor raised his eyebrows at her vehemence, and she quickly added, "Is there nothing I can do to help him?"

"Try to make him drink. Speak to him now and then." She nodded as if memorizing these meager instructions, and the doctor wished he could offer more. "I'll call again this afternoon," he finished, putting on his hat. "Send for me if there is a change before that."

"I will."

Mason took his leave, and Georgina slipped back into the bedchamber that was to be the focus of her existence for an indefinite time. The blinds were half-drawn so that it was dim. A single candle stood on the bedside table, screened so as not to shine in Ellerton's eyes. He lay as he had ever since Georgina arrived, on his back, unmoving, his breath now shallow, now rasping. She moved closer and scanned his chalk-white skin and bloodless lips. The innkeeper had removed his clothes and put him into one of his own nightshirts last night when the doctor set the broken bones. Since then, there had been no change. She leaned over him. "Baron Ellerton," she said in clear tones. "Baron, can you hear me? Wake up."

There was no reaction. His eyes remained closed, and he neither moved nor made a sound, though occasionally in the night he had groaned. With a sigh, Georgina settled herself in the armchair drawn up on the other side of the small table. It was frustrating not to be able to do more, but she would follow the doctor's instructions and wait. She refused to allow the smallest doubt of his recovery to enter her mind.

The morning passed slowly. Georgina read one of the dog-eared periodicals a traveler had left behind at the inn and looked forward to the arrival of her own things. Then, at least, she would have books and sewing to fill her time. She ate luncheon downstairs, the landlady again sitting with Ellerton, and was starting upstairs once more when the sounds of an arrival drew her to the parlor window in hopes her luggage had come.

It had not. She had never seen the very elegant traveling carriage drawn up outside, and she was about to turn away when her attention was caught by its occupant, who was just climbing down.

He did not look like the vehicle's owner. He was a small, bandy-legged man with sandy hair and brows and a suit of severe black. His expression was ludicrously haughty. He gazed at the emerging innkeeper as if he were some particularly contemptible breed of insect. "Take me to Baron Ellerton's chamber at once," he commanded, in such ringing tones that Georgina heard him perfectly. Nonplussed, she hurried out to the corridor to intercept him.

"Here's the lady," said the innkeeper with patent relief when he saw her.

The newcomer turned and looked Georgina up and down. He was not precisely insolent, but she felt that he gauged the cut of her gown and elegance of her coif to a nicety. "Miss Georgina Goring?" he inquired.

"Yes?"

"I am Basil Jenkins, Baron Ellerton's man. I have come to take him home."

It took Georgina a moment to realize that this was the baron's valet. She had had no experience with the superior gentleman's gentleman, and thus was unprepared for his manner. But she recovered quickly. "He is far too unwell to travel," she answered. "The doctor scolded them even for bringing him the short distance to this inn."

"Indeed? Perhaps I could see for myself?" The man's tone suggested that he put little faith in the judgment of hysterical females, but Georgina found this amusing rather than offensive, particularly as she knew she was right. With a gesture, she invited him to follow her upstairs. And she did not speak again until Jenkins had seen the baron and returned to the hall outside his room.

"You see?" she asked then.

He nodded, his imperturbable facade gone. Seeing his genuine concern, Georgina added, "I hope you will stay and help me nurse him. My maid will also do what she can."

The valet drew himself up. "I shall do whatever is necessary, miss. You were very right to send for me, but there is no need for you to remain."

"You cannot sit with him every minute," retorted Georgina, stung. "You must sleep sometime."

"I'm sure the landlady will—"

"I intend to stay," she said flatly. "I have some experience in a sickroom, and I mean to use it."

Jenkins eyed her with a mixture of suspicion and annoyance. "And just what do you have to do with it, if you'll pardon my asking, miss? I don't recall hearing your name before you were so kind as to write."

Georgina stiffened, feeling herself on weak ground. "I am a friend of the baron's," she said.

"Are you now?" His gaze grew speculative, and Georgina nearly quailed under it.

But her instinctive dignity came to her aid. "I am," she replied coolly. "And I don't intend to discuss this matter further. You will want to see about a room for yourself and have your things brought up."

"The baron's things," he corrected.

She inclined her head majestically and swept past him and into Ellerton's room once again. But even as she heard him move away outside, her heart sank. It was clearly to be a battle for control of the sickroom, and she hated such brangles above all things.

TEN

FROM THIS POINT ON, NOTHING WENT AS GEORGINA HAD expected. She had unconsciously had a vision of herself moving efficiently around a darkened sickroom ministering to Ellerton, and perhaps later talking with him and amusing him through a boring time of recovery. Instead, wherever she turned, there was Jenkins, bringing a fresh jug of barley water, smoothing clean towels with complacent skill, unpacking the baron's things, or applying a cool cloth to his brow. Georgina felt useless, and increasingly annoyed. She suspected that Mr. Jenkins knew this, and enjoyed it, which made the situation worse. By the end of the first afternoon, she saw that she would have to make some stand or lose control entirely. Steeling herself, she poured out a cup of barley water and began to coax Ellerton to drink a little. Though he remained unconscious, he had once or twice been induced to drink.

"He won't take anything," whispered Jenkins from the corner where he was laying out Ellerton's toilet articles. "I tried him a moment since."

Georgina stayed where she was. "The doctor left orders that I should keep up the effort," she answered with a slight but unmistakable emphasis on the pronoun.

"Before *I* arrived," conceded Jenkins.

Georgina, having no success, straightened and put the cup aside. "Indeed. I am only glad I was on hand when the baron had no one else."

"Very fortunate," said the valet, with something very close to a sneer. "Though hardly necessary any longer,

now that his *proper* attendants have arrived." Two more
of the baron's servants had come in the late afternoon, to
aid Jenkins, now that it was apparent Ellerton could not be
taken home.

"*Properly*," replied Georgina, who was by this time more
irritated than she could recall being in the course of an
even-tempered life, "he should be nursed by the females of
his family. It is too bad there are none, for such a task really
requires a woman's special talents."

Jenkins drew his small frame up. He was obviously put
out both by her opposition and the fact that he had no ready
riposte to this remark. But a muffled sound from the bed
caused them to drop their argument and turn.

Ellerton's eyes were open, and he was watching them.
As Jenkins hurried closer and Georgina bent to speak, he
muttered, "Good God," and let his eyelids droop.

"Baron Ellerton," said Georgina. "How do you feel?"

"Let him be," objected the valet. "He needs his rest."

"The doctor said he could not tell his condition until he
woke," snapped Georgina.

"I kept dreaming of that fiendish cat," murmured
Ellerton in a thready voice. "Is my leg broken?"

"Yes," said Georgina.

"Umm. And ribs, I think." He moved very slightly, and
grimaced. "What of the horses, and the phaeton?"

Georgina, who had not inquired deeply into their fate,
was forced to draw back, chagrined.

"The team will be all right, Hotchkiss says," volunteered
Jenkins eagerly. "They were pretty thoroughly blown, but he's
taken them back to London and is looking after them. The
phaeton's broken a wheel and axle and the paint's spoiled."

Ellerton nodded, as if this was no more than he expected, and closed his eyes again. But after a moment they snapped open to focus on Georgina. "Miss Wyndham?"

"She's all right. She wasn't hurt."

"Ah. Unsurprising. What are you doing here?"

"Just what I was asking before you woke, my lord," blurted Jenkins. "Now that I've come to look after you, I'm sure there's no need for the young lady to remain."

"Susan sent for me," answered Georgina, her gaze steady on the baron.

Jenkins's glance grew sharp. "I thought you told me you were traveling and happened upon his lordship here?"

Ellerton took in the situation at once. "Very kind of you," he said in a stronger voice. "I'm grateful."

The valet looked from one to the other. "But she needn't stay now, eh, my lord?" he repeated.

Starting to agree, his master met Georgina's clear gray eyes once again. In his weakness, he felt a strong desire for her company. "She *need* not, of course. She has done far too much already. But I admit I should be glad if she stayed."

Jenkins was dumbfounded. Georgina smiled. "I should be happy to do what I can," she murmured.

Ellerton smiled fleetingly as well; then his meager strength gave out and he drifted into a light slumber.

After this, there was nothing more Jenkins could say. Through the doctor's call (and profuse apologies for its lateness), Mason's more optimistic assessment, and preparations for dinner, he was generally silent, merely muttering to himself from time to time and venting his feelings through sharp commands to his fellow servants. Georgina had to smile more than once, but she was careful to hide her reaction, knowing that it would only make things worse. She had nearly concluded that the valet was vanquished when, as they sat together in the sickroom later that evening, he said, "My lord's accident will break a deal of hearts in London." He spoke absently, as if to himself, but his words were perfectly audible to Georgina. "He's popular with the ladies, he is," Jenkins continued. "And no wonder, I always say. But it's amazing the lengths they'll go to put themselves in his way. Why, I recall one—a countess she was, and so lovely it made your eyes ache—pretended she'd hurt her ankle outside our front door. Had herself carried in to the drawing-room sofa, and stayed the whole afternoon. His lordship wasn't fooled, of course." He paused reminiscently. "And then there was the young lady from the country who claimed she was a cousin. Called his lordship 'dear cousin' so often I thought he would give her a setdown. But he's always polite, my lord is. Never speaks ill of a lady, or to her, though he manages to thwart all their little schemes anyhow. A downy one, and no mistake."

He paused, and Georgina knew that he was glancing sidewise to see what effect his remarks had had on her. Her cheeks were flushed. She couldn't help that, for it had been only too clear that he was classifying her with these women who ran after the baron. But she sat straight, her chin high, and refused to give him the satisfaction of seeing that she was embarrassed. Ellerton could not believe this, or he would never have sanctioned her stay.

"No, his lordship's taste in women is somewhat different," continued Jenkins musingly. "His latest, now, she *is* a caution. All that black hair and those dark eyes. And a temper!" He chuckled as if recalling some incident. "I suppose it helps her on the stage."

Georgina grew even more rigid, and at the small movement she made, Jenkins clasped his hands together and pretended horror. "Miss! I beg your pardon. I quite forgot you
were there. Talking to myself, I was, as I often do when I'm
waiting up for his lordship. I'm not accustomed to having
another person in his bedchamber, you know." He made
this sound scandalous.

Georgina rose, routed. "I'm going to bed," was her only
reply. "I will take your place first thing in the morning."

The valet had stood when she did. "I do hope you will
forgive me, miss."

Georgina turned back to look at him, her understanding of his purpose clear in her eyes. To his credit, Jenkins
quailed a little. Without answering, she went out.

But when she had put on her nightdress and gotten into
bed, Georgina could not dismiss the man's tales from her
mind. Indeed, they had conjured up, only too vividly, visions
of the many young ladies who had pursued Ellerton, subtly
and blatantly, and of the few he had granted his favor. The
latter in particular preoccupied Georgina. She knew very
little about such women, but Jenkins had painted a compelling portrait. Georgina's active imagination required no more
to weave a series of scenes that greatly depressed her spirits.

More embarrassing was the valet's equation of her with
the girls who had thrown themselves at Ellerton's feet, some
literally. Jenkins clearly thought her another of these, and
her wish to nurse the baron merely a scheme to capture
his attention and stay by his side. Rehearsing his remarks
made Georgina blush anew, for she saw that many would
agree with him. Though it is completely untrue, Georgina
thought fiercely. But some part of her remained uneasy.

Feeling that she must understand her motives completely, Georgina asked herself why she was determined to stay on at the inn. Jenkins was correct in arguing that he and the baron's other servants could care for him adequately. Was she acting as those other women had?

She was trying to help, she insisted, and to shield Susan from the possible consequences of her foolhardy behavior. But the annoying skeptical voice in her mind replied that her help was not necessary.

Yet *she* would not wish to be left alone at an inn, injured and weak, with only servants, she told herself. And though Jenkins seemed very capable, he showed no signs of having nursed a sick man before, as Georgina had. Moreover, Ellerton's condition was Susan's fault, and it was only right that the family make some amends. Susan could not, so Georgina would. The only unfortunate thing was that she could not explain this to those who would undoubtedly find her presence startling.

Trying to feel virtuous at her adherence to duty, Georgina turned over for perhaps the twentieth time and ordered herself to sleep. She would be no good to anyone tomorrow if she did not. But a part of her remained unsatisfied, and each time she closed her eyes, a procession of women passed before her mind's eye—demure, laughing, boldly vivacious, and all beautiful and utterly self-assured. Nothing, thought Georgina despondently, like herself. Baron Ellerton could have no interest in her. She recalled his remarks about her odd character.

"Then no one will link you with those women who pursued him," said Georgina aloud. "It will not occur to them!" And pulling the bedclothes up over her chin, she commanded herself to sleep.

It was apparent the following morning, with Georgina's maid settled in and all her things unpacked, that she had one advantage at least in the sickroom. She could establish herself in the armchair with her books and her sewing and easily hold the field, while Jenkins, who failed to depart with the coming of daylight, had to find reasons for his presence. The fifth time he adjusted the baron's pillows, eliciting an impatient sound from Ellerton, Georgina had to hide a smile. She understood some of the valet's feelings at finding a stranger in charge of his master, but she would not have been human had she not enjoyed her small triumph after last night.

At one, when Georgina went downstairs for luncheon, she was greeted by her four young friends, who had ridden out to visit her and inquire whether she needed anything. "How is he?" was the first remark, voiced by Marianne but obviously a general concern.

"A little better. He woke last night for a while, and has been awake most of this morning. The doctor thinks he will be all right, though weak for a time."

Susan looked distinctly relieved.

"Have his servants arrived to help you?" asked William.

Georgina nodded, and her expression was so wry that Marianne inquired further. "It is his valet," replied Georgina. "He is…difficult."

No one but Marianne appeared to find this of interest, or comprehensible. The other three, assured of Ellerton's improvement, had turned their attention to ordering luncheon. "I understand that the personal attendants of men of fashion are often so," said Marianne quietly. "Their work requires such fussiness."

"I think he is simply jealous," responded Georgina.

"Ah. Not accustomed to interference in his arrangements." Marianne nodded.

The other was surprised, and grateful, at this ready comprehension. "Exactly. He wishes Baron Ellerton to rely on no one but himself, I think. He seems much attached to him."

"Perhaps he is a family retainer. I hope you are not finding things too unpleasant?"

"Oh, no."

"You could, I suppose, leave everything to his servants now." The look that passed over Georgina's face at this suggestion made her hurriedly add, "Though I'm sure Baron Ellerton would find that less pleasant."

"I think we owe him some return, after Susan's foolishness." Georgina's tone was unnatural, and she dropped her eyes.

"Of course." But Marianne eyed her with new concern. She had been pleased to find that Susan Wyndham had put aside all thoughts of Ellerton after their disastrous adventure. Indeed, she had laughed with the other girl this morning over the ridiculous idea of their rivalry for his attentions, a rivalry that had been wholly the creation of Susan's imagination. And they had agreed on the unlikelihood of the baron's being smitten with either of them, Susan because he now seemed much less appealing and Marianne from a more realistic perspective. The latter was discomfited to see signs of attraction in Georgina, whom she had thought so sensible and likable. Marianne's immediate impulse was to warn her, though she could see that this would not be welcome. She did not wish to let Georgina be hurt. Yet it was obvious that her advice was neither sought nor desired. And speaking might well prevent any future talk on the subject. Undecided, she kept silent.

"Georgina," said Susan then. "Do you want cold ham or cold beef? *I* want ham."

"But I thought we agreed," began Tony hotly.

"Why not have both?" offered Georgina.

The two young people seemed much struck.

Smiling, William Wyndham came over to join her. "We are in for a feast, I think. They are ordering whatever either of them wants."

"We'll make them pay, then," replied Marianne, and the two exchanged smiles.

"But what can we do for you in town, Georgina?" he continued. "That is why we came, after all."

"I have all I need just now. I will call on you when necessary."

"See that you do."

"How are things in London? Did Aunt Sybil and Lady Bentham take your news well?"

"Grandmama was agog," laughed William. "I believe she would be here now if there were any means of fitting her bed into a carriage. Do you think she has a *tendre* for Ellerton?"

Georgina's answering smile was stiff, and Marianne spoke before William could notice it. "Mama, on the other hand, scarcely heard what I said, I think. But she is happy to have Susan accompany us when we go out."

"Poor woman," said William. "She has no idea what she is taking on. But you may count on me to support you."

The look that William and Marianne exchanged then made Georgina frown thoughtfully.

"Are you coming to the table?" complained Tony. "I'm half-starved."

"You're always half-starved," William retorted, but he turned to usher the ladies to their chairs. "Anyone would think your parents never fed you."

"I'm an orphan," responded Tony with mournful dignity, "with no one in the world to watch over me." His hazel eyes sparkled with reproach.

"Except an immensely rich cousin who dotes on you, from all reports," laughed William, "and a worshipful older sister."

"Worshipful!" Tony appeared amazed and revolted. "Someday I shall present you to Amanda, and you will see just how worshipful she is. Why, her husband—"

"*I* am going to eat," declared Susan, picking up her fork. She had been seated for some time.

Abandoning his argument, Tony hastened to join her, and they were all soon engrossed in the landlord's fine cold meats and fruit. Georgina was surprised to enjoy herself, and it was clear that the other four were having a splendid time. Indeed, sitting back to watch them for a moment in the midst of the meal, Georgina felt a pang of envy along with her pleasure in their happiness. They all seemed so carefree, their lively laughter unmarred by concerns more serious than which party they would attend that night. Yet when the time came for them to depart, and she returned to Ellerton's sickroom, her envy faded at once. Jenkins had at last gone to get some sleep, and Georgina and the baron talked quietly together at intervals. When Ellerton dozed, she read or sewed, and throughout the afternoon she was filled with a warm contentment.

ELEVEN

THE JOURNEY BACK TO LONDON WAS NOISY. SUSAN AND Tony couldn't seem to speak to each other without quarreling. They began on departure from the innyard, disputing the merits of Tony's mount, and continued through every foot of the ride, bickering over the chance of a shortcut, the probable hour of their arrival home, and a thousand other things. William and Marianne gradually fell back, putting enough distance between them so that they could hear only the constant rhythm of argument, not the specifics.

"They might be brother and sister," said Marianne with a smile.

"Susan never argued with *us*," corrected William. "She commanded, and we obeyed. Or didn't. And then there was a fearful row. But not like that." He nodded toward the two ahead. "They seem to be enjoying themselves."

Marianne agreed, impressed by his perspicacity. "That sounds like my brother. He was always commanding, too, though I seldom listened." She smiled again. "At least until he married Alicia."

William smiled back at her. "And then you listened?" he teased.

"Then he stopped being so silly." They laughed together.

"So you don't care for commands?" he added.

"Not much."

William watched her profile as they rode along the grassy lane that Susan and Tony had insisted was a quicker way back to London. Marianne looked resplendent with the sun lighting her red hair to molten copper where it curled from beneath her hat and the lines of her body clear in her deep blue riding habit. William had never met a girl who attracted him more. He wanted at the same time to learn everything about her, and to throw caution to the winds and sweep her into his arms.

Marianne felt his gaze, but did not turn at first. Her own feelings were less certain than William's. She knew she liked him, and she was intrigued by his air of maturity and assurance. In London, to which her experience of the male sex was generally limited, men seemed either callow and stammering or arrogantly self-assured. Marianne had thought until Lord Robert Devere offered for her that she favored the latter, who most resembled her beloved brother, but now she wasn't sure. And William was a third sort of man. He had assurance without a trace of arrogance. She turned her head and met his admiring look. Their eyes were nearly the same color, she realized.

Their gaze held for a moment that seemed to stretch far longer. Wordlessly they communicated their special interest, each thrilling to the knowledge that the feeling was mutual. Their surroundings receded into a humming blur.

"William!" called Susan urgently from just ahead. "Hurry. There's a storm coming."

Both William and Marianne started visibly and turned to her. Susan and Tony had pulled up and were much closer than before, though they didn't appear to have noticed anything unusual. Susan was motioning them forward. "Come on!"

Glancing up, they saw at once that she was correct. As they talked, a line of dark clouds had raced in from the east, and a heavy shower was imminent. When Susan saw that they understood, she immediately turned her horse and kicked it into a gallop, hoping to outrun the rain. Tony was hot on her heels.

"We won't make it," judged William.

Marianne was looking for shelter. "No."

"And they led us into this cursed lane where there are no houses at all."

She nodded, then abruptly laughed. "I'll race you." And before he could reply, she was off.

William lost a valuable moment looking after her. Then he recovered and set his heels to his mount.

The four of them thundered down the empty lane, Susan and Tony well to the front, Marianne next, and William gaining on her. Susan's laughter floated back over the grass, and when Marianne glanced over her shoulder, she was grinning.

A bolt of lightning made them urge their horses on, and the animals needed no further encouragement when thunder followed. But their speed was in the end to no avail, for they hadn't reached the end of the lane when the skies opened. A torrent poured down, soaking them in the first minute. The rain fell so heavily that it seemed there was no space between drops, and it was difficult to see more than a few feet ahead. Shocked by the sudden onslaught, Marianne slowed her horse to a walk, and William soon drew up alongside. Susan and Tony, invisible in the storm, apparently continued to gallop, for their excited whoops gradually faded with distance.

Marianne breathed in gasps. The rain pounded at them, and it had started so abruptly that she was still breathless with the shock. She glanced at William; huge raindrops were striking the top of his head so violently that they sent up tiny circles of spray, and water was pouring down his face so that he had to keep blinking and sputtering. She tipped her head a little more forward to better take advantage of her hat brim and to hide a giggle. "Where is your hat?"

"What?" The roar of the storm kept him from hearing.

"Your hat!"

"Oh. Gone. This confounded rain knocked it into the ditch, and I decided it wasn't worth getting down." He stopped, coughing, then added, "We've got to get out of this."

Marianne merely nodded. She found it difficult to converse at a shout.

William kicked his mount to a reluctant trot, and they moved forward more rapidly again. Susan and Tony had disappeared.

It was nearly impossible to see anything in the heavy downpour. Indeed, at moments they feared to stray off the ill-marked lane. But occasionally the rain seemed to part like a curtain and afford glimpses of the country. In one of these, Marianne saw something. "Look there!" she shouted, pointing. But by the time William had turned, the view was obscured again. "I saw a building," insisted the girl. "Off that way, perhaps twenty yards."

"Are you sure?" cried William.

At Marianne's decisive nod, he turned his horse's head to follow hers. She negotiated the shallow ditch at the side of the road and began to push through the bushes beyond. At any other time she would have avoided the dripping vegetation, but she couldn't get any wetter. Almost at once, they came to a narrow path, just wide enough for a farm cart, and in a short time reached a small, dilapidated barn at the edge of a field.

William jumped down and tried the door, which, mercifully, was unlatched. He pushed it wide, and Marianne rode in, William leading his mount just behind. Inside, it was musty but dry. Marianne slid from her saddle and gave a great sigh of relief. It was wonderful to be out of the rain. Standing beneath a roof, listening to it pounding above, filled her with an exquisite feeling of coziness, despite her soaked garments.

William led their horses to the far corner of the barn, where a few wisps of hay tempted them. "No use rubbing them down," he concluded. "We'll be going on soon."

Marianne unpinned her hat and pulled it off, a spray of droplets fanning out from the feather that had once adorned it and now drooped soddenly along the brim. She shook her head, and her red hair escaped its binding and fanned out across her shoulders, part drenched and part dry where it had been protected by the bonnet.

William had to stifle a gasp. With her radiant hair all down around her face, Marianne was more beautiful than ever.

Unaware of his reaction, she put the hat down and bent to try to wring the water from her skirt. The long sweep of a riding habit was always cumbersome on the ground, but wet, it was impossibly weighty. "We should shut the door, don't you think?" she said without looking up. "It is beginning to blow in."

As if physically prodded, William sprang toward the door and closed it, then turned to stare at Marianne again. He couldn't help it.

"Water is dripping off your coat tails," she said, laughing a little as she pointed at them. "You should try wringing, though I'm not having much luck." When he didn't move, she raised her eyes to his face, and what she saw there stifled speech. Marianne was suddenly conscious of the way her wet habit molded to every curve of her body, and of her hair in wild disarray about her face. She flushed vividly and abandoned her efforts to dry her skirt. Its waterlogged folds dragging over the dirt floor, she moved to the horses, hiding her scarlet face by turning her back. "How are you, Willow?" she asked her mount. She put a hand on the mare's shoulder, and it twitched. "It's all right," she murmured.

Under control again, Marianne turned. "We can't keep them here long; they'll take cold."

William, too, had sternly repressed his emotions. "And we shall contract a desperate chill." He went to look through the narrow opening he had left in the door. "It is letting up a bit, I think." But he didn't sound convinced.

"It can't go on raining this heavily for long," responded Marianne. "And perhaps Susan and Tony will discover a carriage and come back for us."

William nodded, trying to look optimistic. But his knowledge of Susan suggested it was far more likely she would settle herself in some comfortable shelter and wait for them to arrive. The proprieties of the situation would never occur to her, he thought bitterly.

An awkward silence fell, the first in the history of their acquaintance. Before, it had seemed they always had something to say to each other; now, suddenly, they had nothing. Every remark that Marianne thought of, and prepared to voice, seemed unwise or inane. She wanted to speak, to show William that she was perfectly at ease and thought nothing of the necessity of their remaining together here for

some time—indeed, that she was quite pleased to do so—
but the English language seemed inexplicably full of pitfalls,
when a few minutes before it had been innocent.

William scarcely noticed her silence. He was wrestling
with far more compelling problems. He had nearly pulled
her into his arms, he thought guiltily, and he still wanted to.
It was out of the question, of course. Marianne was under
his care and in his power; he couldn't take advantage of this
accident to force himself upon her. Yet whenever he looked
at her... He savagely cut off this line of thought. "Perhaps
we should just ride on," he said, his tone so harsh that
Marianne blinked. "We can't get any wetter, after all, and it
may go on raining for hours."

"You don't think—?"

"I have said what I think!"

She stiffened, offended at the snap in his voice and
unable to see what was causing this sudden unpleasantness.
"I should prefer to wait awhile," she answered coldly.

Irrationally, William felt as if this made everything her
fault. Couldn't she see the difficulty? "It is...unsuitable," he
replied.

At this, and recalling the look in his eyes a few moments
before, Marianne did see. She flushed slightly again, at the
same time amazed at herself. She was no simpering milk-
and-water miss, afraid to be left alone with a man for an
instant; she never had been. What was it about Sir William
Wyndham...? She raised her eyes and met his, dropping
them again at once. "Perhaps you're right," she said shakily.

William, inexplicably, felt disappointed. But he strode at
once to the horses and turned them toward the door. After
quickly checking the harness, he looked at Marianne.

"You'll have to throw me up," she added in a voice that she scarcely recognized as her own. "There's no block, and my skirts..." She gestured helplessly.

"Of course." William might have been speaking to a stranger, one he did not find particularly amiable. His cool courtesy was discouraging. Standing beside her mare, he laced his fingers together and bent to allow her to step into them, his eyes resolutely on the floor.

Marianne put a hand on his shoulder and slowly raised her boot. For some reason, she felt like crying. William grasped her foot and prepared to throw her into the saddle as she tensed for the jump.

In the next instant, they both moved, but Marianne's riding boot was slicked with mud from its soaking and movement about the dirt floor, and the floor itself was slippery with the water they and their animals had brought in. William slipped, and Marianne's foot slid in his hands, and the two went down in a confused heap together, entangled in her heavy skirts.

"I...I beg your pardon," gasped William, struggling to sit up and finding himself trapped by sodden cloth. He pushed out with his arms, and discovered that they were entwined around Marianne's waist.

"It wasn't your fault," she responded, and twisted to kick her feet free of the folds of her dress. This brought her face to face with William, hardly two inches away, and made her vividly aware of his arms about her and the feel of his body along the length of hers. He was warm against the chill of her wet clothes. "It was slippery," she added on a gasp.

Their eyes locked, and all thoughts of propriety went out of William's mind. He knew only that he held this lovely girl close, as he had longed to do, and that she did not seem revolted. Indeed, her look held tremulous signs of encouragement. He bent his head and fastened his lips on hers. Marianne, equally rapt, wound her arms about his neck.

The kiss seemed to go on forever. They forgot that they were lying on a muddied dirt floor; they forgot the rain and their companions; indeed, they forgot all the world except each other. Each had kissed before, William rather more than Marianne, but neither had experienced anything like the passion that ran through them now. It seemed to Marianne as if they merged into one creature, with one mind and one desire.

Then, slowly, reluctantly, the kiss ended. They drew a little apart, both breathing fast. For a long moment, their looks were rapturous. Then William stiffened and began to struggle upright again. "I'm sorry," he choked out. "I shouldn't have… I didn't mean…" He finally got free of the riding habit and stood, holding out a hand to help her up.

"You didn't mean to kiss me?" inquired Marianne, who was much less flustered now than earlier.

"No!"

"Strange. You seemed to mean it." She knew what he was feeling, but she couldn't resist teasing him. To Marianne, it seemed that all had been settled between them in that kiss. There were a number of wearisome details remaining, of course, chiefly his offer and her acceptance, but each of them knew the outcome. The only important thing was what had just passed between them.

William, however, had no such certainty. He was, in the first place, raging with self-blame for giving in to the impulses he'd been fighting so hard. Whatever his intentions toward Marianne, he told himself, he'd behaved abominably. But of more concern was the next step. William wanted nothing more than to ask Marianne to be his wife and to resume, with that sanction, their previous activity. But he was aware of certain impediments.

Marianne MacClain—*Lady* Marianne, he corrected himself miserably—was the daughter and sister of an earl. Though the Wyndhams were a fine old family, they had never risen above a knighthood, and their fortune was merely comfortable, while Marianne's was known to be munificent. She could make a far more brilliant match. Moreover, and worse, William knew quite well that she'd refused a man last Season who had all the advantages he did not. What would she think when he proposed marriage? She might well laugh in his face. Or slap it, which was what he deserved after today. That Marianne had responded eagerly to his advances, and that she was smiling expectantly at him now, William was too miserable to notice. He could think only that he loved this girl with all his heart and did not deserve her. "I...I cannot apologize sufficiently for my unforgivable behavior," he stammered at last. "We should go. And put it from our minds. I swear to you I will never do such a thing again."

Marianne gaped at him, astonished and feeling the beginnings of bitter disappointment.

He misinterpreted her look. "I know it seems impossible to go on as if nothing had happened," he said. "But I do not see any alternative. I will, of course, keep out of your way after this."

"You...you..." Marianne couldn't think of an epithet harsh enough. She couldn't believe that he was rejecting her.

"You cannot hate me more than I do myself," replied William unhappily. "Come, let us go." He offered his laced fingers again, and Marianne was too hurt and angry to do anything but step up. This time, she mounted without mishap, and William followed suit. He pushed open the door and waited for her to ride through. The rain was somewhat less, merely a heavy shower now, and the water served to wash the mud from their clothes. They rode in silence to the lane and turned along it. They had not gone far before they met Susan and Tony coming back.

"Where have you *been*?" exclaimed Susan through the rain. "Tony insisted we come back for you. What took you so long? We might have found shelter by now and been out of this awful rain, if you had only kept up."

"Sorry," replied William gruffly, and he spurred his horse ahead.

"Anything the matter?" wondered Tony.

"Nothing whatever," snapped Marianne. "Can we go on now? I am soaked to the skin." And she followed William, at a distance, in his gallop.

Susan and Tony exchanged a bewildered look. "Well, why didn't they keep up, if they are in such a hurry?" asked Susan, and they turned their mounts to follow.

TWELVE

Several days passed without incident at the post-ing house. Ellerton regained strength slowly, but he was not capable at first of long conversations or sustained attention. Georgina established a quiet routine, sitting in the sickroom reading or sewing in the morning and afternoon, taking her meals in a private parlor downstairs, and sometimes walking near the inn for fresh air and exercise. After the second day, Jenkins was forced to sleep most of the day, as Georgina had predicted. Not even his devotion could erase the need for rest in the intervals of his night watches. Thus Georgina's days grew easier, and she once again felt truly useful to the baron. Though Jenkins would sooner have cut out his tongue than acknowledge her contribution, and though he slept as little as possible and hung about Ellerton's chamber, he told no more anecdotes about the baron's female admirers. He even, at the end of the week, admitted to the doctor that Miss Goring was a fair nurse. When Dr. Mason repeated this to her, Georgina had to smile, for she knew that Jenkins would be mortified if he discovered she'd been told. But her early antipathy to the man was giving way to amusement as they adjusted to each other, and Jenkins's unquestionable loyalty and unflagging industry in caring for his master impressed her. She had no intention of taxing him with his compliment.

A week and a half after the accident, Ellerton showed definite signs of improvement. He slept less, ate more, and began to complain of boredom. At this point, Georgina's task became far harder than Jenkins's, for Ellerton remained awake the whole day and rested peacefully most of the night. After one afternoon of complaints, she even considered asking the valet to change with her, but she could not bring herself to admit defeat, and when her annoyance faded she admitted that she didn't really wish it.

On Tuesday morning, when Georgina came into the room, the valet met her near the door. "He woke very early today, miss," he told her. "And a bit irritable."

Since Jenkins had never before voiced even so mild a criticism of his employer, Georgina prepared herself for a difficult day. The valet looked very tired, she noticed; his eyes were reddened, and his face haggard. "You should get a good long sleep," she whispered sympathetically.

This instantly brought back his suspicions. "I can look after myself, thank you, miss." And with a little bow, he went out.

Georgina shook her head and went to her armchair. Ellerton appeared to be drowsing, so she picked up her book from the table and opened it. But instead of reading, she found herself gazing at the far wall and musing over her situation. It really was ridiculous, she thought, the way she and Jenkins vied for supremacy. There was no reason they should be rivals, for they both wanted the same thing. At the idea of rivalry, Georgina's lips curved upward. First Susan and Marianne had thought themselves rivals for the baron's affections, or Susan had seen it so, at least, and now she and Jenkins were being equally silly, though she claimed for herself Marianne's part. The contest was of Jenkins's creation. Amused, Georgina developed the comparison in her mind until finally the ludicrousness of it struck her so forcibly that she laughed aloud, at once stifling the sound and glancing at Ellerton to see that she had not disturbed him.

The baron was wide-awake, and watching her with an interested gaze. "What is the joke?" he asked, as if they were in the midst of a conversation.

Georgina flushed slightly. "I was only thinking of something."

"Obviously." He waited for her to tell him what.

She did not feel she could. It would mean exposing Susan and Marianne, and herself. "A private matter," she replied, and before he could object, added, "Have you had your breakfast?"

"Yes, I have. And I have been shaved and combed and fussed over until I am half-mad. And now I shall lie here in bed all day with nothing to do. I am abandoned wholly without amusement, and now you refuse to so much as share a joke." He made a piteous face.

Georgina hid a smile. He sounded more like a small boy than an elegant Corinthian. "You have had a number of visitors."

"Cruel, Miss Goring! Do you not know that there is nothing more infuriating than laughing aloud, then keeping the reason to yourself? It's nearly as bad as assuring someone you have a secret which you can on no account reveal. Perhaps worse."

"I begin to better understand the old saying about idle hands," responded Georgina. "They might better say idle minds give rise to mischief. I don't believe you care a whit for the joke; you're merely lightening your boredom by rallying me."

"Miss Goring!" But though he pretended shock, an arrested look in his blue eyes showed that she had scored a hit. "I'm thinking of nothing but this joke, I promise you.

I daresay I shan't be able to put it from my mind. I shall become obsessed and develop brain fever, I suppose."

"You are feeling better, aren't you?" commented Georgina. She had not seen him so lively since the accident.

"On the contrary, I am worse. I begin to find this room and this bed intolerable. I shall ask the doctor for a pair of crutches today and get out a bit."

"But he said you mustn't move for two weeks, at least," replied Georgina, alarmed.

"He doesn't know my iron constitution." Ellerton smiled a little. "You needn't look so worried, Miss Goring. I said I meant to ask the doctor, and I shall abide by his decision. I fancy he was being overcautious."

Georgina nodded, realizing that her concern was exaggerated by her own reluctance to end this interlude just as he was improving and able to talk. This was inexcusably selfish, she scolded silently.

"And so, what about the joke?" he continued when she did not speak.

"Do you never give up?"

"Never!"

"Even though I have told you it was a private matter?"

"That is what one always says to silence awkward questions. Is it really true in this case?"

"Yes!"

"Ah. Well, then, I mustn't inquire further."

His expression was so comical that Georgina burst out laughing. "I have never met a man so curious, or so determined in his curiosity. I was thinking about Jenkins." She stopped, sorry to have revealed this much.

"It is true," he replied. "Curiosity has always been my

besetting sin. It often gets me into trouble, but on the other hand, it has helped me learn a great many useful things." He paused. "Jenkins, now. I should be happy to know something amusing about him. He is such a solemn fellow. Some mornings, when he comes in with my coffee, I'm quite cast down by his dolorous manner."

Georgina laughed again. "It's really nothing. You make me ashamed to tell it. I was merely thinking of Jenkins's jealousy over the nursing. He so hates to let anyone help."

"Ah. Yes, he is rather like a mother hen."

This comparison was so apt that Georgina had to smile. "You and he are not dreadfully at odds, I hope?" added the baron.

"Oh, no. We have reached a truce."

His eyes gleamed appreciatively, and Georgina was certain that he understood more than she'd said. "What do you think of him?"

"Mr. Jenkins?" She was surprised.

"The same."

"Well, I... Nothing, really. He seems a very good servant, and he is devoted to you."

"Come, come, you expressed a much more natural opinion a few moments ago. What do you think of him as a specimen of human nature?"

This reminded Georgina of a conversation they'd had some time ago. "I am not in the habit of considering people as 'specimens,' Baron Ellerton."

"No? I'm not so sure. I think you are as avid a student of the subject as I." She started to object, but he forestalled her. "Watching your face as you thought of your 'joke,' I distinctly observed some of the same delight in oddity. I'm convinced you share my interest in unusual personalities. That's one reason I insisted upon hearing it. As well as my insatiable curiosity, of course."

"I don't think of my friends and acquaintances as 'oddities,'" answered Georgina stiffly, recalling more of that talk and his characterization of her.

"Of course you don't. Why so haughty? There is nothing ill-natured or wrong in what I say. Indeed, it was just such an impulse that allowed us to make each other's acquaintance in the beginning."

When he had rescued Susan and Marianne, at the first ball, thought Georgina. He was interested only in her "oddity." The thought hurt surprisingly.

"Why else are you here, after all?" he finished, and his words so echoed Georgina's thought that she gaped. "Come, come, do you claim that you weren't taken with the unusual, and ridiculous, elements of this situation? I certainly would have been, had I not been knocked unconscious. A mere chit, who looks as if she couldn't stand in a high wind, takes over my phaeton, wrecks it, consigns me to a sickbed, and comes away without a scratch. And then I, who have some little reputation both as a whip and as a man of the world, am left to be rescued by this girl and her friends. If I were not the victim, I should call that the most amusing story I've heard in years."

Georgina had to laugh.

"There, you see? How is your charming cousin, by the by?"

"Very well."

"I had no doubt of it. Enjoying the Season, I suppose?"

She nodded, trying not to laugh again.

"Having forgotten all about her little contretemps with my phaeton."

"Of course not! Susan is…" Georgina hesitated, remembering her cousin's rapid dismissal of her mistake.

"Precisely," said the baron, as if making the final, conclusive point in an argument.

"We have done everything possible to give her a proper sense of her, er, overexuberance," answered Georgina stiffly.

"A fine word for mayhem and near-murder," he responded admiringly. "What will you call it when she does manage to kill someone, I wonder. By the by, I hope *I* succeeded in ridding the world of that hellish cat?"

Georgina was forbidding herself to laugh again. "Daisy? No, he's fine. He found his way home all alone."

He was staring incredulously. "Daisy? I am referring to a very large, ginger-colored animal with the character of a Tothill Fields assassin."

Georgina nodded, her laughter escaping.

"Its *name* is… No, you needn't tell me. Miss Wyndham christened it, of course."

"She was very young."

"That girl was never young," declared the baron, his eyes twinkling.

"I…I shouldn't laugh." She strove for control.

"Why not? Does this strike you as cruelty?"

This brought her up short. "No," she replied after a moment. "But it is…"

"Yes?" He looked politely interested.

"Well, if Susan were here…"

"I should speak just as I have, and no doubt a lively discussion would ensue."

"Lively, indeed!"

"I am fascinated by human nature, not contemptuous of it, Miss Goring. And I pride myself on understanding its foibles."

This gave Georgina much to ponder, for it was true that she felt an answering impulse in herself when he spoke of his "study." She had resisted her own bent in this direction, feeling it was a sign of false superiority, but now she began to wonder. Unfortunately, Dr. Mason called just then, and the conversation was dropped. It remained vivid in Georgina's mind, however.

———————————

Ellerton was refused crutches, but the doctor did say he might be carried to a sofa downstairs for part of the day, and he seemed satisfied with this concession. In the afternoon, this was accordingly done, and a party of visitors arrived soon after to inquire about him. Georgina, as was her custom on such occasions, retreated to her own room. She had no wish to be found sitting at Ellerton's side by members of the *haut ton*. It was enough that she was vaguely known to be helping with the nursing. And the baron was unlikely to need her now.

She was just about to put on her hat and go out for a short walk when there was a tap on her door. Opening it, she found Lady Marianne MacClain in the corridor, hands clasped around her riding crop. "How do you do?" said Georgina warmly. "I have not seen you for several days. Are the others here as well?"

"No, I rode out alone." Her hands twisted on the crop. "With a groom."

Georgina was surprised at this. When William and the

others had come the last time, Marianne had not accompanied them. And though she had thought nothing about it at the time, this solitary visit made it appear more significant. Looking closer, she thought Marianne showed strain. But she said only, "I was just going walking. Would you care to come, or shall we remain here?"

"A walk would be nice," answered Marianne.

"Oh, but you are wearing riding dress, of course. You will not wish to—"

"It's quite all right," interrupted the other, more sharply than Georgina had ever heard her speak. She looped the trailing folds of her habit over her arm and turned toward the stairs.

Georgina said no more until they were outside the inn and strolling along the grassy lane that wandered out behind it, leading, as she had previously discovered, to a small village about a half mile away. Then she ventured, "A fine day."

Marianne merely nodded.

"Your family is well?"

"Yes," was the curt response.

Having established to her own satisfaction that something was wrong with Marianne, Georgina fell silent. They were not very well acquainted, but Marianne had come a good distance to see her, and that argued some sort of appeal. Georgina wished to help if she could. "The baron is much better," she offered. "He is allowed to lie on the sofa downstairs, and he has callers today."

"Ah," was the only reply.

Not Ellerton, then, concluded Georgina, conscious of a feeling of relief. "How is Tony? When I saw him last he had just purchased the most astonishing waistcoat."

Marianne smiled a little. "He has another, even more brilliant."

"No, how could it be? I had to shade my eyes against the last." They laughed together, and then Georgina suddenly realized why she must have come. "Susan hasn't fallen into another scrape, has she? I know I'm imposing dreadfully on your good nature in asking you to take her about, but—"

"No, no, Susan is very well. She is enjoying the Season hugely and has done nothing wrong."

Her tone implied that others were not experiencing such enjoyment, and Georgina glanced sideways at her, trying to discover the reason. "I suppose William is watching over her," she said, simply to fill the silence.

"Undoubtedly!" snapped Marianne, bitter and derisive. "He should be very good at that."

"What is it?" asked Georgina, unable to ignore her tone. "Have you quarreled with William?"

To her astonishment, Marianne burst into tears.

At once Georgina was all efficiency. She took the other girl's arm and hurried her toward a spot she had found some days previously. It was a grassy nook amidst a grove of beeches near the road, invisible to the casual passerby and pleasantly warmed by the sun. Once there, she urged Marianne to sit on a fallen log and settled beside her, her arm about the younger girl's shoulders.

Gradually Marianne's tears abated, and when she began to search for a handkerchief, Georgina was ready with her own.

"I beg your pardon," said Marianne tremulously when she had blown her nose. "I didn't mean to cry."

"It doesn't matter in the least," replied Georgina. "But what's the matter? *Is* it William?"

Marianne gazed at the grass, sprigged with tiny pink and blue flowers. "I came to see you because I could think of no one else, but I don't believe I can tell you after all."

Georgina watched her face, perplexed. "You needn't tell me anything you don't wish to, of course, but I shall keep your confidence. And I should be happy to help, if I can."

"Oh, no one can *help*," responded Marianne.

Silence fell between them. Georgina wondered what she should say. Marianne began to cut off the grass tops with her riding crop.

"I must speak to someone!" she blurted out finally. "Mama doesn't listen properly, and Ian and Alicia won't be home for months. I thought of Lady Goring, but I'm not at all acquainted with her, and besides, if I called I might see… him. But I am so miserable, and I don't know what to do!"

"Tell me," commanded Georgina. "No one else shall hear of it." Her sympathy blotted out any awkwardness she might otherwise have felt at advising this polished young woman.

Haltingly Marianne began the story of her encounter with William during the storm. As she talked, the words seemed to flow more easily, and by the end she was speaking in a breathless rush. "So I suppose he thinks me some sort of horrid *fast* creature," she finished. "But I have never done such a thing before. Never! Ian used to scold me about wishing to…oh, go to a masquerade, or dance too often with the same partner, but with William—Sir William, I mean—I was just…I can't explain it to you. I love him!"

This last rose to an anguished cry, and it was obvious to Georgina that Marianne had been accusing herself and indulging in agonies of remorse since the day this had

happened. It was equally clear that her brother's early stric-
tures had made her sensitive on such matters. Georgina was
amazed to discover that the girl she had thought so self-
possessed and at ease was prey to these doubts. And she was
delighted to know that she *could* be of help. She had known
William most of his life, and she felt confident in interpret-
ing his actions. She'd noticed his initial interest in Marianne,
and its development into something deeper. The story she'd
been told confirmed her suspicions, for William was not
the sort of man to give way to his impulses unless they were
very strong and acceptable to his highly developed code of
honor. He loved Marianne, Georgina was certain.

"William is an admirable character in many ways,"
Georgina began. "He has a strong sense of responsibility, for
example. I have always thought Susan had something to do
with that." She smiled, though Marianne did not respond.
"He is kind and loving and almost wholly without conceit.
Unfortunately, the latter trait sometimes causes him to
underrate his own abilities or attractions, and to fail to get
what he wants because of diffidence in asking for it."

Marianne's woeful expression began to shift, and her
blue eyes sharpened.

"I've seen it happen more than once," Georgina continued, "even over quite important things, though none this
important, of course."

"Do you mean…?" began Marianne, and stopped.

"I believe William loves you as much as you do him, but
I imagine he can't quite bring himself to say so. I know he
would blame himself for the incident you described, berat-
ing himself for taking advantage of you."

"Any man with sense could have seen that I—"

"Ah, but in this area, William's usual good sense deserts him, the more so as the matter becomes more serious. And you must remember, Marianne, that there are differences in your rank and fortune—"

"Who cares for those?" she interrupted impatiently.

"William," responded Georgina. "And he would also remember your reputation."

"My...?" Marianne's eyes clouded with doubt again.

"As the girl who refused the most brilliant match the *ton* had to offer," finished Georgina, teasing a little.

Her face cleared. "But that was entirely different. Lord Devere was... I didn't love him!"

"William wouldn't be sure of the difference."

"What idiots men are!" But Marianne's misery had dissipated.

"They do seem very dull at times," agreed Georgina.

"But what am I to do? I utterly refuse to propose to *him*!"

Georgina smiled. "Indeed, you should not. Shall I speak to him?"

"You mean, tell him to offer for me? No!"

"I believe I could be a bit more subtle than—"

"If he can't muster the courage to ask me himself, then that's that."

"But don't you think—"

"No." Marianne jumped up, all her confidence and vitality restored by Georgina's assurances. "I have no patience with him if that's what he thinks. He ought to be able to *see* how I feel."

"Well...but, Marianne—"

"Promise you won't say anything."

"I have promised, but—"

"Promise again!"

Georgina met her eyes for a long moment, then sighed. "I promise."

"Good. And thank you. I must be starting back to town now. I will be late for dinner as it is." Marianne turned back toward the road.

"Won't you think it over and come to see me again?" asked Georgina, hurrying to keep up with the other's long strides.

"There is nothing to think about."

"But…"

Marianne stopped abruptly, causing Georgina to collide with her. She turned and grasped both Georgina's hands, gazing earnestly into her face. "I thank you for being such a good friend," she said. "But there is nothing more to be said on this head. I hope you will simply forget it."

"I couldn't!"

"Well, put it from your mind, then. I intend to."

Georgina frowned, trying to think of some argument to sway her.

"And now I really must hurry. Will you be all right if I go on?"

"Of course," she responded automatically.

"Good-bye, then." And with a wave, Marianne departed, nearly running. In her haste, she did not remember that she had also meant to talk to Georgina about Baron Ellerton.

Georgina followed more slowly, pondering what she'd learned and racking her brain for some way to make it right. Her promise bound her to reluctant silence, but mightn't Marianne thank her if she broke it? Her forehead creased with this dilemma, Georgina returned to the inn.

THIRTEEN

ELLERTON'S VISITORS WERE STILL WITH HIM WHEN Georgina returned, so she went directly upstairs and sat down in her bedchamber to think. She'd always prided herself on her honesty and trustworthiness, but the current problem seemed to bring these into conflict. If she was honest with William in a matter which could decide his life's happiness she would betray Marianne's trust. And though she felt that such a betrayal might be best for both in this situation, she could not make up her mind to it. Marianne had been angry, and revealing her confidences might simply make her more so. She might make matters worse, Georgina thought, by sending William to make an offer that Marianne refused out of pique and annoyance at her.

There seemed no satisfactory solution. Georgina was called down to dinner in the same state of mind, and ate abstractedly, paying no attention to the remarks of the landlady when she served, and thereby almost offending that kindly woman. She finished without any idea of what she'd eaten and returned to her room in the same state. She did not go to the baron. Jenkins would be with him by now, serving his dinner and later readying him for sleep. Georgina's duties ended with dinnertime.

She tried to read, but her thoughts kept coming back to her two young friends and the question of the best way to help them. Considering both their characters, Georgina thought they might suit one another very well. The match would be a bit unequal in the world's terms, but not unduly so. Marianne would rouse William's liveliness and sense of fun, and William would provide a bulwark and useful channels for her energy. Smiling at her solemn wisdom, Georgina said aloud, "And they are obviously in love, which of course counts for a great deal."

But this brought her no closer to deciding what to do. At last she concluded that she must talk to Marianne again, since she was forbidden to speak to William. Perhaps, when her temper had cooled, she'd be more amenable to Georgina's suggestions. Thus, just before going to bed, Georgina wrote a note to be carried to the MacClain house first thing the following morning, asking Marianne to visit her again. This much settled, she was able to put the matter from her mind and fall asleep.

The following day dawned beautifully clear, without even the scattered clouds that had dotted the sky yesterday. Georgina woke to a breath of cool, verdantly fresh air from her window, and as she rose and dressed and went down to breakfast she felt much more optimistic. Something would happen to make things right, she couldn't help believing, and when she gave her note to one of the stableboys to carry to town, she smiled so broadly that he was led to tell his fellows that the "nursing lady" was not so Friday-faced after all.

Ellerton was alone in the downstairs parlor when she sought him out. Jenkins had seen to his needs and helped carry him down before going off to bed, Georgina was told when she inquired. "He looked dead beat," the baron added. "I've told him over and over that there is no need for him to sit up all night. I'm on the mend and unlikely to take a fit and wander off. But he won't listen. Sometimes, you know, I feel that I exist for the sake of my servants, rather than the other way about." He smiled to show that this was a joke, and when Georgina didn't respond, added, "You are far away this morning."

Again, she didn't seem to hear, and Ellerton examined her face more closely, realizing that he'd become accustomed to their daily conversations, and looked forward to them. Georgina's viewpoint was, like his own, interestingly slanted, and at the same time different enough to make her insights fascinating. He'd met his match for the first time. She shared his interest in human nature, but she saw what he did not and understood things he missed, adding to his knowledge and deepening his perceptions. Indeed, he realized, Georgina Goring was his counterpart, a thing he had not really expected to find in a woman. The fact had somehow crept up on him during these days together, and emerged abruptly full blown.

Georgina, becoming conscious of the silence, looked up, and said, "What?"

He merely smiled and shook his head.

"I'm sorry. I was thinking about something."

"Evidently. And something of compelling interest. What?"

"I can't…" Georgina hesitated. She could not, of course, tell him the whole story, but might she not give the outlines in order to ask his opinion? She'd come to respect his judgments about people, for he seemed to sense things that she did not. "Two friends of mine have had a falling-out," she began haltingly. "They are, I believe, very dear to one another. Indeed, I think they might marry. But this…misunderstanding has separated them. One confided it to me, after making me promise that I would never speak of the circumstances, and when she had done so, I could see that it was nothing more than a muddle. I wished to speak to…

my other friend, but she absolutely forbade it. It seems such a shame. I mean to talk to her again, to try to change her mind, but… What would you do?"

She raised clear gray eyes to his, her confidence in his perspicacity evident, and Ellerton felt an unexpected pang in the region of his heart. For a long moment he could only gaze at her delicately etched features, framed by pale blond curls and so full of sincerity and concern. Then, seeing her begin to frown, he replied, "I suppose I would speak to the second friend."

"Even though you had sworn not to do so?"

"Some promises are unreasonable."

She pondered this. "I don't believe I would want those who made promises to me to think so," she answered finally.

"You implied that the happiness of two people rests on your actions," he responded.

Georgina nodded slowly.

"Do you think a moral scruple should stand in your way, then?" Ellerton felt more interested in her answer than in the problem.

"It's not only that. M… my friend might be so angry at my interference that she would refuse him. Or I might put it badly, and ruin everything."

"That, I cannot allow," he said. "But it is true that when one begins to take a hand in others' lives, the outcome is uncertain."

"Have you ever done so?" she asked, curious.

"Once or twice."

"And you regretted it," she accused.

He shrugged. "I must admit I did. But neither case was as clear-cut as yours seems to be."

Georgina looked down. "I don't believe such things are ever clear-cut. I think I must do as I had decided already." She sighed.

"Perhaps I could help," he offered.

Georgina raised her head, surprised. "You? How?"

"Well…" He couldn't think of a way. He'd been moved to offer by her disappointment. It seemed very important that he justify her confidence in him. "I don't suppose you would tell me the whole story, and allow me to speak to the man?"

She smiled. "But in that case, I may as well tell him myself. I'm still betraying a confidence."

"I had hoped you might overlook that." He smiled, and after a moment she smiled back. "You're very scrupulous," he added.

Something in his gaze held Georgina silent. It made her throat tight and her breath constricted.

"Indeed," he added, "I don't believe I've ever known a person so concerned for others and at the same time so conscious of their foibles. An admirable combination. It allows you to be compassionate without losing your sense of the ridiculous. I must strive to emulate you. I tend too much to the latter side."

This did nothing to restore Georgina's powers of speech. That the polished Baron Ellerton would want to be like her was too astonishing an idea. Georgina had always seen herself as a bit clumsy.

His blue eyes started to twinkle. "I shall, however, strive to maintain my perspective."

"It is just so…strange," Georgina blurted out. "That *you* should say such things to me."

"That *I*? What do you mean?"

"Well, you are so...grand. I mean, I am awkward in company, and...oh, I don't know. You see?"

"I'm not sure that I do." His expression was wry. "But I believe I've been insulted."

Georgina shook her head, aghast.

"To be called 'grand.' It calls up visions that make one shudder."

"I didn't mean it that way. Not that you look down your nose, but..."

"Thank God for that, at least."

"You are just so...so..." Georgina paused, with no idea how to finish this sentence or repair her gaffe.

"I see I must make a determined effort to convince you of my sterling worth," he said, half-serious, half-teasing. "And I find I have a strong desire to do so."

"I think your character is..." began Georgina, ready to say more than perhaps was wise to repair her mistake. But at this inopportune moment, Jenkins entered the room.

The valet looked from one to the other of them suspiciously in the charged silence that followed his appearance. "I came to see about luncheon, my lord," he said. "And I believe Miss Goring's is waiting downstairs. What would you like today?"

"Don't you ever sleep, man?" was the baron's reply.

Jenkins drew back, startled.

Georgina, embarrassed by his hostile scrutiny as well as her own emotional state, turned and fled, flinging, "I must go," over her shoulder. Both men watched her, Ellerton annoyed and Jenkins indignant.

Georgina took her time over her meal, using it to regain her composure and rehearse the scene just past. Baron

Ellerton had been amusing himself, she decided—not exactly at her expense, but he had meant nothing by it. He had probably thought she would laugh with him, and the next time, she would. And it was probably time that she thought of returning to town. It was obvious that Ellerton would recover completely; indeed, he would soon be able to travel to London himself. She'd repaid Susan's carelessness to the full, and if in the process she had suited herself, it was now clear that she'd gone far enough. She could no longer trust her emotions, and it would be wise to leave before she made a worse mistake than today.

Having come to this very sensible conclusion, Georgina immediately felt dispirited. She rose from the table determined to walk a little before going back upstairs. She was reluctant to face the baron again. But she'd just gotten her hat and stepped outdoors when she was hailed from the road and turned to find Susan, William, and Tony riding up, grinning and waving.

"Hallo!" called Tony. "We've brought you another cargo of books. I don't know how you get through so many of them so quickly." A mass of tangled brown fur shot out from behind his horse and raced toward Georgina. "Here, now, Growser," shouted Tony. "Sunday manners!"

Though this did not stop the dog, he did not, as Georgina expected, throw himself upon her. He merely ran round and round barking joyfully and wriggling with apparent delight at seeing her again.

"We thought he would like the exercise," said Tony, dismounting nearby. "Here, sir, to me." Growser jumped up and sought to lick his master's face, reducing Tony to a desperate defense of his primrose pantaloons.

William and Susan also climbed down, handing all three horses to an ostler. Georgina noticed a basket over Susan's arm. "You haven't brought Daisy!" she exclaimed.

Susan looked thunderous, as if she'd heard this before. "Yes. Why shouldn't I?"

"Well, don't take him inside. Baron Ellerton will wring his neck."

"I should like to see him try!" retorted Susan.

"So should I," seconded Tony appreciatively.

Susan turned toward the inn, disgusted. Tony followed, keeping a grip on Growser, and Georgina fell in beside William. "How are you?" she said.

"Well," he replied in a voice that implied the opposite to one who knew him.

"Are you enjoying the Season still?"

"Susan is having a splendid time," was his evasive answer.

Georgina saw that she would get nothing from him without direct confrontation, and since she couldn't yet bring herself to this, she let it drop. They came into the inn and the leading pair started for the stairs. "The baron is in this parlor," said Georgina, stopping before the closed door. "He is much better."

"He can walk already?" exclaimed William.

"No, he is carried. Let me just see if he has finished..." But as soon as she opened the door, Growser was through it.

They heard, "What the devil?" from inside, and all four hurried after the dog.

Ellerton was alone in the room. Growser stood with his front paws on the sofa cushions, examining him with scientific curiosity. The baron seemed torn between laughter and surprise. "Ah," he said when they came in, "this, I suppose, is another of Miss Wyndham's pets. What does he do? Eat one's waistcoats?"

"Growser is Tony's dog," protested Susan.

"Ah," said Ellerton again.

"And he don't bite," Tony assured him. "Though as for waistcoats…" He stopped, seeming to contemplate some past incident.

The baron burst out laughing. "Remove him from my sofa, at least. Have you forgotten I am an invalid?"

As Tony pulled the dog away and pointed him toward the far corner of the room, William said, "You look much better, sir."

But Ellerton was not attending. His eyes were fixed on the basket over Susan's arm. "Do not tell me that is—"

"I brought Daisy because he needed some fresh air," interrupted Susan defiantly. "He is not allowed out in London." They all watched, fascinated, as she set the basket on the floor and opened the lid. At once, Daisy popped out, then stretched enormously on the parlor carpet.

"At least he didn't come through his attack on me unscathed," commented the baron, noticing a number of scratches in the cat's ginger fur.

Daisy turned his yellow eyes on Ellerton and went very still. The two stared at each other, and Georgina braced herself to move if Daisy leapt. However, after a while, the cat merely turned disdainfully and stalked over to join Growser.

"You're the first person I've ever seen stare him down, Baron," said Tony.

"I was thinking of my neckcloth," responded Ellerton gloomily, causing Georgina to laugh.

"Daisy was just frightened," put in Susan. "It wasn't his fault."

"I don't blame your *cat*," answered the baron, fixing her with a stern eye.

Susan straightened and looked resolutely at the wall above his head. "I know it was my doing," she stated, as if giving a memorized speech. "I was very wrong, and I came today to beg your pardon. I will never do anything like that again."

"You will never get the chance with *me*," responded Ellerton. "But let us forget the whole matter. I accept your apology."

Susan looked both relieved and annoyed at his manner.

"Why don't you all sit down," suggested the baron. "I'm developing a stiff neck looking up at you." They all quickly found chairs. "And so, how are you getting on? Is the Season up to your expectations?"

Susan chatted for a while about the parties she'd attended and the people she'd met, occasionally seconded by Tony. It gradually became apparent that William was not speaking at all. Ellerton, noticing this, caught Georgina watching the boy with great concern. His incipient boredom dissipated, and his eyes narrowed in thought. At the first pause in the conversation, he asked, "Where is Lady Marianne? Doesn't she usually accompany you on these visits?" He had heard as much from Georgina.

"Oh, she had another engagement," answered Susan lightly. "She is very busy." There was a hint of puzzlement in her voice, and this, combined with her brother's distinct start when Lady Marianne's name was mentioned, told Ellerton what he wanted to know.

"She's always flitting about someplace or other," added Tony. "We scarcely see her these days."

"I see her," protested Susan. She turned to Georgina. "Marianne has done just as you asked. She always invites me to accompany her and her family."

Georgina nodded, a little surprised that Susan would make a point of reassuring her.

"Well, William and I scarcely see her, though I live in the same house, eh, William?"

"I'm sure Lady Marianne has many important things to do," answered William, his voice expressionless.

Ellerton, certain now, merely smiled and turned the subject.

The three stayed for nearly an hour, the conversation sustained mainly by Susan and Tony, with questions from Georgina and, rarely, Baron Ellerton. Daisy and Growser lay in remarkable quiet in the corner. When Ellerton marveled at this, Tony simply shrugged, saying, "*I* don't understand it."

Finally Susan rose and said they must go. "I promised to be back at three," she told Georgina. "I am to have a new ball gown, and I must go for a fitting."

Tony hooted, but the two young men also stood.

"Do you need anything, Georgina?" asked William.

"No. I shall be returning to town soon, I think, and I have all I need until then." This was difficult to say, but, she told herself, necessary.

Ellerton turned to stare at her, but his quick movement went unnoticed in the round of farewells. The party was starting through the doorway when he recalled himself to say, "Wyndham, could I speak to you for a moment?"

They all stopped and turned again, surprised.

"A small private matter," added the baron, his expression bland.

Looking puzzled, William stayed behind as the others filed out.

"If you would just shut the door," said Ellerton. Totally bewildered, William did so. "Good. Now, I have something to say to you, which you may not wish to hear from me. Nonetheless, I think you will be grateful for the information."

"If it is about Susan—" began the younger man.

"It is not."

William stared at him, unable to imagine what Ellerton could have to say to him that required a closed door and such a serious tone.

"I know of no subtle way of leading up to this," the baron went on, feeling more awkward than he had expected. "So I will simply say it. You are in love with Lady Marianne MacClain."

William's mouth dropped open.

"And she is in love with you."

The younger man's blue eyes bulged with disbelief.

"You have had some sort of quarrel. I don't know the details, and don't care to. But if you have any sense at all, you will make it up and offer for her. This isn't a time for pride."

William made a strangled noise in his throat.

"You may think it odd that I bring up this matter…"

"She…she didn't *tell* you?" choked William, aghast at the idea that this elegant near-stranger knew of his lapse.

"I have not spoken to Lady Marianne."

"But how…?" This seemed to William some sort of

magic, and he had not sufficiently gathered his wits to take in what he'd heard.

"That doesn't matter. Be assured that I am telling you the truth. And don't, for God's sake, be a fool. Marry the girl!" Ellerton felt both ridiculous and compassionate. He could fully understand how shaken William must be, yet now that he'd done what he set out to, he wished the boy would leave and put an end to this uncomfortable conversation. Ellerton was not accustomed to the role of mentor, and he did not find it easy.

"Sir," said William, regaining some measure of his composure, "I have no idea how you—"

"Nor are you likely to," interrupted the baron, his impatience to have this over now overriding politeness. "I've said what I meant to; there's no more to discuss."

"But I—"

"In fact, I'm rather tired," he added cravenly. "If you will excuse me."

William hadn't the address to do more than bow and take his leave, but he returned to his friends with his mind in turmoil. The baron's assurance that Marianne loved him was just sinking in, sweeping aside the mystery of how Ellerton had known anything about this matter. And the possibility was so thrilling that William lost himself in the realms of fantasy, forgetting to bid Georgina good-bye and failing to respond to the remarks Susan and Tony addressed to him. Fortunately, they were soon involved in one of their endless disputes, and took no more notice of William than he of them.

FOURTEEN

FOR WILLIAM, THE JOURNEY BACK TO TOWN PASSED IN A daze. He went over and over Ellerton's remarks, pausing always at "she is in love with you." The phrase made him want to kick his horse to a gallop, whoop his happiness to the skies, and throw his hat into the air. The fact that he could do none of these things without lengthy explanations to his companions reduced him to a state of trembling tension, which transferred to his mount and caused it to shy and toss its head at the least excuse.

He wanted only to find Marianne and speak, yet when he thought of calling on her, some of his former nervousness returned. How could Baron Ellerton really know her feelings? He couldn't believe the man would have spoken to him if he wasn't certain. But it remained inexplicable. William had thought Marianne was avoiding him because of his loose conduct. He'd concluded that she was angry, but it now seemed that she might be hurt. This idea goaded him to near-frenzy. He had to see her at once.

They'd reached the streets of London by this time, and were nearing the section where both the Goring and MacClain houses lay. William looked around, then said, "Let us go this way. We will pass Tony's house and can leave him there."

Tony looked surprised. "I thought you and I were to go on to Renfield's lodgings, to see about that horse of his."

"Oh." William had forgotten about this previous engagement. "I believe I shall put him off. I'm...a little tired."

Susan gaped at him. "Are you joking? Besides, I want

to get home as soon as possible. It's shorter that way." She pointed to a street that indeed led more directly to the Goring house, without passing Marianne's.

"We must be polite and accompany Tony," tried William, feeling himself on weak ground.

The other two were predictably amazed. Tony customarily rode home alone from their joint outings. "What's the matter with you?" asked Tony. "You've scarcely said a word the whole day, and now you seem to have gone off your head."

"There's nothing the matter," retorted William, and before they could object further, he turned his horse's head and moved in his chosen direction.

His friends hesitated, Susan appearing ready to go her own way without him, but finally they followed, shaking their heads and frowning.

It was not far to the MacClain town house. William approached it as he might a five-barred gate on the hunting field, but drew up short when he discovered that Marianne was actually before him, being helped down from a showy carriage by a pink of the *ton*.

For a moment he was transfixed. Susan and Tony, coming up behind him, greeted Marianne and her escort, whom they had met before. The driver bowed and began an elaborate salutation; Marianne seemed immobile.

"I must speak to you!" blurted William, his blue eyes fixed on Marianne.

Her escort, cut off in mid-phrase, drew himself up and stared.

"It is very important," added William, conscious of nothing but her.

Susan and Tony were gaping as well by this time.

"As you see," managed Marianne in an unsteady voice, "I am engaged with Mr. Ottington."

William turned his gaze on her companion. Ottington, who had been ready to resent this high-handed intrusion, saw something in Wyndham's eyes that made him shrink back. "Just returning, actually," he stammered. "Been driving in the park. Harmless, you know. Must be getting on." He grasped Marianne's hand before she could offer it, bowed again, and turned to his vehicle. In another moment he was driving away, leaving behind a startled, silent group.

William dismounted. "Would you see Susan home, Tony?" he requested.

"I thought *you* were escorting me home?" protested his friend, more bewildered than put out.

"Please," replied William, throwing him a speaking glance.

"Have you gone mad?" said his sister. "I have never seen you behave so oddly in your life."

William simply made a dismissive gesture, his attention focused on Marianne. Tony bent to take the rein of Susan's horse. "Come on."

"But I don't—"

"Let him be," advised Tony. He had the sense that something significant was going forward, though he was not clear just what.

Marianne watched the two ride off, and William watched her profile. When they disappeared around a corner, and she turned, he said, "Shall we go inside?"

"This is very inconvenient," answered Marianne. "I am going out to dinner, and I must change—"

"It won't take long. Please, Marianne."

She eyed him. His expression was unsettling. A dreadful suspicion entered her mind. "Where have you been? Have you been talking to your cousin?"

"Georgina? No." William was surprised by her evident concern. "We have been visiting the baron, but I barely spoke to Georgina."

"What do you want?" responded Marianne, more composed.

"To talk with you for five minutes."

"Go on, then."

"We cannot talk in the street."

"Why not? I cannot imagine what you may have to say to me that cannot—"

"Marianne!"

His tone made her stop abruptly, and sent a shiver down her spine. "Very well!" She whirled and rang the bell. The door was opened so quickly that those more capable of observation might have suspected an eavesdropper. But William and Marianne were beyond such considerations. William thrust the reins of his mount into the footman's hand and strode after her into the library.

"Well, what is it?" she asked when he had shut the door behind him. "I did not think we had anything more to say to each other."

Now that he had a clear field, William found that his tongue clove to the roof of his mouth. She was so beautiful, and so obviously angry with him, that he couldn't think how to begin. "Shall we sit down?" he managed feebly.

Marianne glared at him, then sat in an armchair before the fireplace. He moved slowly to the chair opposite, marshaling his thoughts. There was a short silence.

"I really must go upstairs," said Marianne. She was mystified by his reticence, following so soon after his insistence on coming in. When she had first seen him ride up, her heart had begun to pound, and when he had demanded to speak to her, a flame of hope had risen. It had taken all her self-control to assume cool indifference, but she was very glad of it now. Had he come simply to offer another idiotic apology?

"I'm finding it difficult to begin," said William, "perhaps because I know what a fool I've been, and I am afraid to repeat my mistakes."

This was so interesting that Marianne unconsciously dropped her indifferent pose.

"The other day, on our ride, I...I did behave badly," he went on.

Marianne stiffened again.

"Partly in giving way to my feelings, and partly in not then telling you of them." He swallowed. "Frankly, I was a coward. I was afraid to tell you that I love you and wish with all my heart to make you my wife. I thought you would surely refuse."

Marianne went very still.

"I was overwhelmed by the disparity of our positions, you see. You could make a far better match from a worldly point of view, and indeed, I knew that you had refused a brilliant alliance, so I..." he ran down. As he stated the case, he nearly succeeded in again convincing himself that his suit was hopeless.

Marianne felt a wave of inappropriate giggles rising in her chest. When he said he loved her, she'd felt as if a great burden had been lifted from her soul, leaving joy in its wake. But as he went on, tangling himself further and further in rationalization, her feelings threatened to erupt in laughter. This, she knew, would be inexcusable, but she could not resist saying, "Do you *wish* me to refuse you?"

"What? No!"

"You are arguing against yourself so insistently."

"I wasn't. I didn't mean… It's just that I am so conscious of the inequality of—"

"But why mention it? *If*, that is, you truly wish to convince me."

William looked at her, pained. He had not imagined, when he heard that she loved him, that his proposal would be so difficult. He almost wished he had not spoken at all. "I wish with all my heart to marry you," he replied. "I can say no more than that."

Taking pity on him, and unable to restrain her own happiness any longer, Marianne smiled. "Yes."

"What?" He seemed uncertain he had heard correctly.

"Yes," repeated Marianne, "I will marry you."

"But…but…"

"There! I said you did not mean it."

William jumped to his feet in distress. "Marianne! I did. I do! I was just…"

"When a man apologizes so profusely for kissing one, after all…" She shrugged and raised her eyebrows.

This was too much. William took one step forward and grasped her elbows, jerking her to her feet. Then his arms slid around her and pulled her against him as his lips met hers in a passionate kiss.

Before Marianne could really respond, he drew back, holding her by the shoulders at arm's length. "There! I shan't apologize for *that*."

She gazed at him, her laughter swept away by very different feelings. "Good."

"In fact, I shall do it again." And he did.

This time, Marianne had ample time to put her arms around his neck and second his efforts wholeheartedly. Their bodies pressed closer, and both lost themselves in sensation, forgetting the rest of the world. An eternity seemed to pass as they wordlessly communicated a host of things that neither had yet said aloud.

Finally they drew apart again, though not far. Marianne smiled up at him.

"After all, a man may kiss his promised wife," he said.

"He is practically obliged," she answered.

William eyed her. "Has anyone ever told you that you joke at the most inappropriate times?"

"Heaps of people," was the cheerful reply. "Since I was tiny."

He smiled. "And have you never thought they might be right?"

"No. They were usually such *solemn* people."

"Ah." He frowned. "Do you think I am too solemn?"

"Do you think I am too frivolous?"

"You are perfect!"

Marianne laughed at last. "And so are you, in a different way."

"I suppose we can learn from each other. But I shall never be a jokester, Marianne." He looked doubtful.

"No, but you will become much better at *taking* a joke, I'm sure."

"So I am to be your bobbing block?"

"Naturally. I shall devote all my time to discovering ways to mock you."

William frowned, then saw the teasing twinkle in her blue eyes and smiled again. "You will certainly not lack opportunities," he replied ruefully.

"William! I was only funning. I'll never mock you." She hesitated. "Exactly."

"And what 'exactly' will you do?"

She met his gaze squarely. "Be your wife, and love you with all my heart."

There could be only one answer to this, and William gave it very willingly. It was nearly twenty minutes before the couple emerged, beaming, from the library and stood before the front door together.

"I will call on your mother at ten tomorrow morning," William said, holding her hand and gazing fondly down on her.

Marianne grinned. "I will prepare her for your visit."

"Do you think she will need bracing?"

"I think she will need to be told beforehand what is afoot, or she will pay no attention to what you are saying." She laughed a little.

After a moment, William followed suit.

"I will write to my brother by the next post. I suppose he and Alicia will come racing back to see what I'm up to."

William looked concerned. "Shall I write to him also? I could explain my situation and the—"

"Nonsense. Mama is my guardian."

"I hope to be friends with your brother, however," he chided gently.

"Oh, Ian will *adore* you!"

He laughed again. "Why do I feel that is not a compliment?"

"It is. More or less."

William looked inquiring.

"Ian and I have not always agreed, and I still rather enjoy startling him. I can't help but regret a little that we shall agree completely on *you*."

"Shall I lose my fortune at hazard or fight a duel so that he will disapprove of me?" Marianne looked pensive. "Stay! That was my own feeble idea of a joke."

She dimpled. "I know. And a promising one. The thought is tempting, though."

"Not to me!"

"Oh, well, you would probably do it backward. Your dice would never fall wrong, and you would challenge the greatest blackguard in England and rid the country of him, earning general thanks."

"Marianne!" He was half-laughing, half-scandalized.

She wrinkled her nose at him. "I *must* go and change. I can't have them waiting dinner for me."

He nodded. "Until tomorrow, then."

"Yes."

Seeing that the hall was empty, he kissed her lightly again and took his leave. Marianne walked slowly up the stairs to her bedchamber, a dreamy smile making her even more lovely than usual.

FIFTEEN

ALL WAS FORMALLY SETTLED BETWEEN MARIANNE AND William later the next day. There could be no objection to the Wyndham lineage or fortune, and Lady Bentham made none. She had satisfied herself of Marianne's happiness in a private talk, and she asked nothing more. The newly engaged couple spent a happy hour drafting a notice for the *Morning Post*, and an even more agreeable period discussing their future and bidding each other a very fond farewell. It was settled that William would come to dinner the following evening and become better acquainted with Lady Bentham and her husband.

These arrangements complete, Marianne had the leisure, as she was getting ready for bed, to wonder again how their reconciliation had been effected. She had forgotten, in the general excitement, to press William for information, so she determined to rise early and visit Georgina, the most probable agent of the change.

She arrived at the posting house by ten, having left home right after breakfast, and she found Georgina again setting out for a walk in the countryside.

"Baron Ellerton has visitors," she replied when asked about her patient's progress. "I have not seen him since yesterday, but he is mending quickly now. Dr. Mason gave him crutches."

"Good." Marianne's reply was perfunctory. "May I come with you once again?"

"If you are certain you don't prefer to go inside."

Shaking her head, Marianne fell in beside the older woman, and they walked for a while in silence. Georgina had just formulated her argument about William when Marianne said, "I came partly to bring you some good news."

"Yes?"

"William and I are engaged."

"What?" Georgina stopped and clasped her hands together. "Oh, Marianne, that's wonderful. But how did it come about? When we spoke last time…"

Marianne, who had been carefully watching her face for signs of previous knowledge, was disappointed. She would have sworn that her revelation was a complete surprise to Georgina. "He came to me yesterday afternoon and apologized." She grinned. "Indeed, he rather *over*apologized. And then he made an offer."

"I am so glad! But what can have caused William…that is… Never mind." Georgina realized that her puzzlement over William's move was hardly flattering. Yet her knowledge of William's character made her wonder what had impelled him. He was too modest to have acted without urging, she was sure.

Marianne laughed. "That is exactly what I came to ask you. In fact, I am tempted to accuse you of interference." She was watching the other's expression closely again. "Not that I could scold you too harshly for it, since it brought me such happiness."

Georgina shook her head, frowning. "I didn't speak to him. I thought of it, and I wished to, but I could not make up my mind to betray a confidence."

Marianne believed her. No one could feign such perplexed ignorance, she decided. "Did you mention my story to anyone else? But no, you would not."

"No," said Georgina, then abruptly remembered her careful conversation with Ellerton.

"Well, perhaps William did it on his own," continued Marianne, oblivious now of the arrested look on her companion's face. "I like that even better. One doesn't particularly like to feel that one's affianced husband had to be goaded to his proposal."

Georgina made a vaguely affirmative sound, absorbed in her own thoughts.

Marianne was now equally abstracted. "We are to be married at the end of the Season. William is taking me down to meet his mother in two weeks, when his brother will be at home as well. I wrote to Ian, too. He will be astonished by my prudent choice." Turning to share this mild joke, she finally noticed Georgina's distance. "What is it? Have you thought of something?"

"Umm? Oh, no, nothing. I was just thinking how you will like Anabel, and she you." Georgina did not intend to share her theory. The suspicion that Ellerton had taken this kindly task on himself had affected her deeply, and she wanted to assimilate the fact herself.

"William's mother? I hope she will. I am a little uneasy about that visit, actually."

This captured Georgina's full attention. "But why?"

Marianne looked at the ground. "You may not have heard—the talk of last year has died down now—but my father was…a notorious rake. I told William; he doesn't care. But his family might…"

"Anabel won't give a snap of her fingers for your father," Georgina assured her. "And neither will Christopher—her husband, you know. They will judge you as you are, and they will love you at once."

"Do you think so?"

"I am positive."

Marianne heaved a sigh. She had been more concerned about this than she realized.

"Will you be married in London?" asked Georgina, to divert her.

She nodded. "Scotland is too far, and besides, most of my friends are here." She went on happily detailing the plans that had been made, and Georgina again relapsed into her own thoughts.

Ellerton might have worked out who she meant, Georgina decided, especially considering William's transparent unhappiness during his visit. She remembered then that the baron had kept William back to speak to him privately, and her suspicion became a certainty. Baron Ellerton had brought William and Marianne together because of her talk with him.

For some reason, this knowledge filled Georgina was a warm glow. She was merely pleased, she told herself, that her cousin and her friend had surmounted the barriers to their happiness. But she could not deny that the *means* of their reconciliation was particularly gratifying. The baron's intervention had been so disinterested and so benevolent; she rejoiced to think of him in such terms. The doubts she had sometimes felt about his capacity for feeling—when his interest in others had seemed merely intellectual—dissolved. He was a thoroughly admirable character, she told herself blissfully. It was at this point that Marianne mentioned the baron's name, effectively capturing Georgina's attention again. "What?" she said, looking up.

Marianne looked self-conscious. "Don't be offended. I only wish to help. And I daresay you know everything I'm going to say very well, and have considered it already."

"I don't know what you're talking about," admitted Georgina, who had lost the thread of the conversation.

Marianne bit her lower lip. "You mean that I have no business giving you advice. That is true, of course. I just do not want to see you…perhaps embarrassed by a mistaken impression."

"Marianne, I vow I don't know what you mean."

The younger girl looked at her. "I am talking about Baron Ellerton, of course."

Georgina simply frowned.

"Oh, come. It was obvious when you determined to stay and nurse him, even after his servants arrived, that you… felt an unusual interest in him. I only wanted to say that he is much pursued, and you should not, well, form false hopes or…" Marianne broke off in confusion, wishing she'd never begun. She felt ridiculous admonishing this woman who was both years older and much more reserved than she.

Georgina felt as if she'd fallen from the heights of fantasy to a most unwelcome reality. Her joy in Ellerton's kindness was overwhelmed by the truth of Marianne's assertion, and all her doubts came rushing back. Whatever the baron did, it had nothing to do with her. She had, perhaps, piqued his interest with her tale of thwarted love, and he had indeed shown his quality in untangling the situation, but Georgina's part in it was mere informant, just as her relationship with Ellerton was no more than mild friendship, if that. He was, naturally, grateful for her help, and they occasionally shared a moment of amused understanding, but this was no basis for the rush of feeling Georgina had experienced a few moments before. She was, she thought unhappily, doing just what Marianne sought to warn her against. She was building upon her artificial intimacy with Ellerton when it was in fact a temporary, and meaningless, coincidence.

"Oh, how I wish I hadn't opened my mouth," exclaimed Marianne. "Of course you know what you are about. I mean... I was just—"

"It doesn't matter," interrupted Georgina, her voice sounding flat in her own ears. "You needn't worry about me."

"No," agreed Marianne, relieved that Georgina seemed neither angry at her nor unduly upset by her remarks. She must have been mistaken, she told herself. Georgina did not care for Baron Ellerton after all.

Her duty done, Marianne gladly turned the subject to more pleasant things, and they finished their walk in further discussion of her plans. By the time she took her leave some half hour later, Marianne had nearly forgotten about the baron. She rode back to London immersed in her own happiness, so abstracted that her groom more than once had to warn her of a hazard in the road.

Georgina reentered the inn to hear that Ellerton's visitors from London had departed and that he had asked for her. But she did not go to him immediately. She slipped upstairs to her own bedchamber and sat down in the armchair near the window, looking out over the garden behind the inn and trying to regain her customary calm.

But instead of growing more composed, she became steadily less so. In Marianne's presence, Georgina had held her feelings in check, but alone, she could give them free play. Indeed, she could do nothing else, for they were too strong.

She had been exceedingly stupid, she thought miserably. She had ignored her own inner warnings during these days away from society, and she had unconsciously assumed that Baron Ellerton was feeling as she did—content and happy in her company and increasingly drawn to her, as she was to him. Despite Jenkins's cautionary tales, and her own common sense, she had fallen in love with him.

This revelation brought tears to Georgina's eyes. How could she have been so foolish? She'd always prided herself on the sharpness of her intellect, but in this she had acted directly against its warnings. She had no one to blame but herself.

The best thing to do, that sensible part of herself declared, was to leave this place. Back in her aunt's town house, with Susan's antics and William's joyful plans to occupy her, she would no doubt soon forget the baron. Her earlier youthful infatuation had passed off in a matter of months when she had determinedly turned her attention elsewhere. When she saw Susan's stepfather now, she rarely even thought of the time she had fancied herself in love with him. This would be the same.

But another part of her remained stubbornly unconvinced. This was *not* the same, it insisted. This love was not built on the imaginings of a schoolgirl, and though its foundation might be equally illusory, the result was not. She would not forget Ellerton, ever.

A knock at the door made Georgina jump, her heart pounding. It was a moment before she could call, "Yes?"

Her maid looked in. "His lordship is calling for you, miss. Should I tell him that you're resting?"

Georgina rose and came forward. "No, I'll go down now." She would have to see him eventually, she told herself as she followed the girl downstairs to the parlor, and thinking was merely making her more agitated. She did not admit that his asking for her had raised a tiny hope.

The baron was reading one of her books when she came in, stretched out on the sofa with a mug of ale nearby. In the moment before he looked up, Georgina gazed lingeringly at his face. He was more than handsome to her now, she thought. She could see there all the qualities she admired.

He raised his head, and their eyes met. Georgina found it suddenly difficult to breathe. "Ah, there you are," he said, his voice very cool. "Where have you been? Packing your things?"

This took Georgina by surprise, and she merely looked at him.

"You did say yesterday that you would be leaving soon," he added. "So when I didn't see you today, I assumed you were making ready to go."

"You had visitors," blurted Georgina.

"Yes, of course." His tone implied boredom, but in actuality, Ellerton was furious. He'd been taken by surprise by Georgina's statement the previous day. He had not thought of her leaving, and his first reaction was denial. He did not wish her to go. And it was somehow worse that she had not discussed the matter with him first, but had simply presented it, in company, as a fact. And then she'd disappeared. Jenkins had brought his dinner and, as usual, remained with him through the evening and night, and at the hour when Georgina customarily joined him after breakfast, a pack of chattering Londoners turned up. Ellerton had sent them on their way as soon as he decently could, but even then, Georgina had stayed away. When he was forced to send for her, the baron's temper worsened further. "Well, do you intend to tell me your plans?" he went on, some emotion in his voice now. "Or were you going to simply depart and leave me to discover it for myself?"

"I didn't… I wasn't…"

"Not, of course, that you have any particular obligation to me. You have done a great deal too much already. Jenkins and the others can look after me quite well."

His manner seemed to confirm Georgina's worst fears. He didn't want her here, she concluded. When he'd been too ill to care who attended him, it hadn't mattered, but now he was weary of her constant presence, and using her own reluctant words as an excuse to be rid of her. The idea was very painful, but she refused to show it. "It is time I was getting back to town," she agreed, her voice shaking only a little. "Susan needs me, especially now that William is to be married. He is engaged to Lady Marianne, you know."

This news diverted the baron briefly. "Is he?"

"Yes." Georgina gathered all her courage; whatever her own feelings, she was determined to thank him for his part in that affair. "That was your doing, I think. I am very grateful to you."

"You figured that out, did you?" He looked at her more kindly, impressed yet again by her powers of observation and quick understanding.

"It could have been no one else. It was so kind of you."

"Merely pursuing my interest in human nature," he answered lightly, and smiled. For a moment the conversation hung in a delicate balance. The established sympathy between them worked to dissipate the discord. But then the baron recalled his grievance. It seemed monstrously unfair that she should leave because of his "kind" act. "And so you return to London to help with the wedding?" he asked sharply.

"I will certainly give what help I can," she replied unhappily. "Though it is Susan who will need me most, I imagine. The MacClains will be too busy to take her about."

"Ah." He couldn't argue against this, though had he known how much Georgina regretted her words, he might have done so. "When do you mean to leave?"

Somehow, Georgina thought miserably, she had maneuvered herself into a corner. While part of her protested violently, she responded, "This afternoon, unless you wish me to stay a day or two longer."

"No, indeed," he said through clenched teeth. "Jenkins will take things in hand."

"He'll be delighted to," added Georgina with a spark of wistful humor.

"He will."

She stood in silence before him. She could still change her mind, a part of her argued. She could find some excuse to stay. But the voice of reason was stronger now that he had, as Georgina thought, encouraged her to go. She would not hang about like one of those women the valet had described so vividly, waiting for the least crumb of attention, forcing herself on Ellerton when he couldn't get away. The fact that she loved him was humiliating enough without playing out such a pathetic charade. "I...I should pack." she said forlornly.

The baron was too wrapped up in his own resentment to hear the tone. "Of course," was his cool reply.

She turned to go.

"Miss Goring."

"Yes?" Georgina scolded herself for the eager hope she heard in the word.

"Since I suppose we will not be seeing each other for some time, I should thank you once again for the help you have given me."

Her spirits fell as quickly as they'd risen. "It was nothing. I was…that is, Susan caused your accident, so it seemed only right."

"Nonetheless, I do thank you." Inwardly he cursed the heedless Susan. The woman cared for nothing but her damned cousins, he thought. Let her go to them!

Georgina made a dismissive gesture, as if to physically put off his thanks. She hesitated before turning toward the door again. He'd seemed to imply that she was not to come back here. "Well," she ventured, "good-bye."

"Good-bye, Miss Goring." Ellerton's voice habitually grew more distant with intensity of emotion, so that by this time he sounded scarcely interested.

Georgina waited one more instant, wishing to speak but having nothing to say, then turned again and went out. Ellerton gazed at the empty doorway for a long time after she left it.

SIXTEEN

GEORGINA'S PACKING DID NOT TAKE LONG. MOST OF HER clothes were still in London, and Susan and William had been carrying books back and forth for her so that she had only a few in her possession. Her greatest problem was explaining to a startled Lucy the reasons for their sudden departure. The maid was full of questions for which she had no good answers, and finally she sent her down to ask the landlord about hiring a chaise simply to be rid of her.

But Lucy was back almost at once. "He says it's all right," she told Georgina. "They're harnessing up now."

"Oh." This was what Georgina had requested, but she realized then that she'd had some lingering hope that she would be forced to stay by lack of a vehicle. She raised her chin. "Good. You can take the dressing case down now. And ask someone to fetch the other things."

"Yes, miss. I swear I had no idea we were going so soon. I—"

"I decided rather quickly, yes, Lucy. Go on now."

In what seemed to Georgina a remarkably short time, all was ready. The innkeeper urged her to eat a bite of luncheon before she set out, but she wasn't hungry. She allowed him to press a packet of sandwiches on her for Lucy's sake, and then urged the maid to climb up. At the last moment, she nearly balked and went to Ellerton, but the interested gazes of the landlord, ostlers, and others in the yard changed her mind. She was very close to tears, and she did not want to break down before all these curious strangers. Thus, she got in the chaise, and the driver signaled his team. Georgina did not even feel comfortable twisting round to watch the inn out of sight.

Inside the private parlor, Ellerton had no such qualms. Stretched out on the sofa, he had a clear view of Georgina's departure through a front window, and was secure in the knowledge that none could see in as well as he saw out. This was the only gratifying circumstance, however, and he was very pleased to see that Georgina did not look happy as she left.

But this pleasure was short-lived. When the chaise had disappeared around a bend in the road, and even the sound of its wheels had died away, Ellerton lay back on his pillows with a sigh. His anger was fading, and with Georgina gone, he had the leisure to consider his actions. Why had he flown into such a rage? It was inevitable that Georgina return to London in time, and surely he was not so selfish as to wish to keep her to provide amusement for himself now that he was better. He had visitors often, and the doctor was talking of letting him return to his own house.

Yet these reasonable assertions did nothing to dispel the regret he felt at her leaving. He remembered some of their conversations, a smile curving his lips, and suddenly envisioned her face as he had sometimes seen it, vivid with laughter. A most unusual woman, he concluded, with qualities one rarely found in anyone, male or female. He would look forward to seeing her again, in town.

But when Ellerton imagined that scene—a crowded drawing room, loud with chatter and smoky with candlelight—his heart sank. That was not what he wanted, he realized. He wanted to continue as they had been, alone, quietly talking and laughing over shared observations, near enough to accidentally brush hands. Without warning, he was filled with blinding desire for Georgina Goring. All his senses came alive with memories of her, a series of glowing, sensuous pictures flashing through his mind. At first, he was too astonished to do more than lie still, eyes wide, breath quickening, and then, in an instant, he saw that he loved her. His body had been too weakened by injuries to respond until now, and he had mistaken his feelings for something milder. But at this inopportune point, when she was out of reach, perhaps forever, he saw the truth. This was the woman he had searched for all his life, and he had sent her away.

But as he struggled to sit straighter, jarring his broken ribs, and started to call for Jenkins, Ellerton was shaken by a highly uncharacteristic doubt. She'd given no sign of feelings like these, he thought. She'd been performing a duty, and she had gone as soon as it was done. Ignoring his own role in her departure, the baron hesitated. He'd been ready to force Jenkins to hire a carriage and accompany him to London, and damn all doctors. But now he was uncertain. What if she should refuse him?

This was a novel thought for the much-sought-after Baron Ellerton. All his efforts had been directed toward avoiding entanglement for years; it was odd to be not only contemplating marriage but also wondering whether his suit would be acceptable. And yet she *had* stayed, he told himself, and she had seemed to enjoy their times together.

Ellerton had a very unusual afternoon. He spent it arguing first one side and then the other of his dilemma, unaware of Jenkins bustling blissfully about his room or the other sounds of an active posting house. He could recall no other time in his life when he had felt so indecisive, and he did not care for the feeling at all. It had driven him nearly to distraction when Jenkins came in yet again and announced a visitor. "Sir William Wyndham, my lord."

William was directly on his heels. "The others are coming, sir," he blurted as soon as he was inside the parlor. "I rode ahead so that I could thank you for speaking to me the other day. You may have heard that Marianne and I are to be married." At Ellerton's nod, he grinned and shrugged. "And it is all your doing. You were dead right. One can't let anything keep one from the girl one loves. I shall never be able to repay you for telling me that."

The baron was gazing at him fixedly. "Perhaps you will," he said slowly.

"What?" William looked mystified, but willing.

Ellerton considered a moment, then nodded. "I must get to London at once," he declared. "And you can help me. This damned leg won't let me ride. It must be a carriage, and slowly, I suppose."

"But I thought the doctor—"

"The doctor says you aren't to travel for at least a week, my lord," interrupted Jenkins indignantly. The valet had left the room when William arrived, but he had come back with a tray in time to hear Ellerton's request. "He said he can't guarantee that you'll heal properly if you bounce about on the road just now," he went on. "And you won't while I'm alive!"

"Mason is being overcautious," snapped the baron. "I feel much better."

"And didn't he say you would?" replied Jenkins. "And that you'd likely get restless and try to move before you should. No, my lord, I won't allow it."

Ellerton looked to William.

"I...I wouldn't want to do anything that would prevent your recovery," stammered the younger man, torn between gratitude and responsibility. "If the doctor says—"

He was interrupted by the arrival of Susan, Tony, and Marianne, full of high spirits and teasing him about his neck-or-nothing riding on their approach to the inn. It was some minutes before this died away, time enough for the baron to stifle his rage and William to conclude that he had done the right thing. He could not, he decided, endanger Ellerton's health, no matter what he owed him.

"Where is Georgina?" asked Marianne then. "She will laugh at me for riding out twice in one day, but William convinced me." The engaged couple gazed fondly at one another.

"She has gone back to London," was the curt reply. "You must have passed her carriage on your way."

"What?" They all looked astonished.

"She didn't tell us she was coming," accused Susan. "And we *didn't* see her. She would have called out."

"It was probably that 'shortcut' you led us into," answered Tony. "Wasted half an hour, and made us miss her. I *told* you that—"

"It did not!" protested Susan. "It was much quicker than last time. But I suppose Georgina kept to the main road."

"Of course she did." Tony was contemptuous.

"Well, we will see her at home," retorted Susan, and turned her back on him.

Marianne was frowning. "She said nothing this morning about going." She looked at Ellerton, her earlier concern returning twofold.

"A sudden decision," he answered in an indifferent voice. "But you must allow me to wish you happy, both of you."

This successfully diverted William, who never liked to think the worst. He led Marianne in a discussion of their wedding plans, and the question of Georgina was allowed to drop. Ellerton could see that Marianne was not satisfied, but he had no intention of allowing her to find out the truth. This minor matter occupied only a small part of his attention, as did his visitors' chatter. His whole mind was bent on the burning question of how he was to get to London and see Georgina. A letter would not do, he had concluded. He must see her and take his chance. William's echo of his own words had tipped the balance of his indecision. He could not allow Georgina to slip away from him through his own inaction.

Ellerton felt imprisoned during the next half hour. He was surrounded by jailers, with the best intentions in the world. How could he elude Jenkins and find aid in getting to town? He would not be at all surprised to learn that Jenkins had alerted the inn servants to his plight. They would refuse to help him, no doubt. And he could not travel without assistance; he was not so foolish as that.

"They should let him do as he likes!" exclaimed Susan Wyndham at that moment, in response to some remark of Tony's.

Ellerton had lost the thread of the conversation, but this statement captured his attention. He eyed Susan speculatively. She might well have sympathy with his powerlessness, and she owed him a very large debt. Some of the tension left his expression as he began to plan his campaign.

When the four young people rose to take their leave,

Ellerton was ready. "Miss Wyndham, could I speak to you for a moment?" he asked. "Miss Goring left a message for you."

"For me?" Susan looked pleased to be thus singled out. "Of course." She waited as the others filed out, Marianne frowning. When William shut the parlor door, she gazed inquiringly at the baron.

"I fear that was a ruse, Miss Wyndham. What I wish to say to you does not concern your cousin." Though he realized at once that this was untrue, he pushed the thought aside. This must be left as uncomplicated as possible.

"If you are going to scold me again for driving your phaeton—" Susan began.

"I am not. It has nothing to do with that either. I need your help, Miss Wyndham."

"Mine?" She looked mystified, and a bit intrigued.

"I must go to London at once, and the servants here refuse to allow me to do so because of the doctor's orders." He had decided to be frank.

"The doctor is afraid you will hurt yourself more?" asked Susan.

"Yes. But he has said I may travel in a week, and doctors are always overcautious."

"That's true. When I had the measles, they made me stay in bed for days after I felt fine."

"Exactly. I will not be hurt, and it is vital I get to town."

She surveyed him speculatively. "Why?"

"That need not concern you. I think you owe me your aid, Miss Wyndham. I would *be* in London now if not for you."

Susan grimaced, then shrugged. "Oh, very well. What do you want me to do?"

For a moment Ellerton could not believe it was so easy; then he recovered and launched into his plan. Susan listened closely, nodding from time to time and seeming unconcerned with anything other than understanding what she must do. "You have it?" finished the baron.

"Yes. I'll come right after breakfast."

"Splendid! You are an unusual girl, Miss Wyndham."

She grinned impishly at him, and went out.

SEVENTEEN

ONCE HIS PLANS WERE MADE, ELLERTON RELAXED AND concentrated on carrying them through. His desire to see Georgina was undiminished, but he knew that certain steps must be accomplished first. His main problem was Jenkins, and he began at once to work on it. He kept his valet running here and there on various errands through the evening, attempting, without seeming to, to wear him out. Then he forced himself to wake after a few hours' sleep and find new services his valet could perform. Ellerton had been sleeping soundly through the night since the end of the first week after his accident. Indeed, he had repeatedly told Jenkins that it was unnecessary for him to sit up. Now he was glad the man had resisted, for it gave him the opportunity to ensure his lack of alertness the next day.

By early morning, the baron was satisfied, and he managed a few hours' sleep during the time when Jenkins must be busy with the morning routine. When his valet brought the breakfast tray sometime later, Ellerton even felt a bit guilty, for Jenkins really did look exhausted. And it was with real sincerity in his voice that Ellerton urged him to go to bed.

"Perhaps I will, my lord," agreed the other, "for a few hours. If you should want anything, you can always—"

"I shall be fine. Go on."

Picking up the tray to return it to the kitchen, Jenkins nodded. "I'll look in on you before luncheon, my lord."

Ellerton made an airy gesture. He mustn't be too emphatic or Jenkins's easily aroused suspicions would surface. The valet went out, and he felt some of the tension ease. That hurdle seemed safely past. He'd had Jenkins shave him, and he was fully dressed, as he always insisted on being lately. There was nothing to do now but wait for Susan to arrive, and hope that she hadn't botched it.

This time seemed very long to Baron Ellerton. He was accustomed to making his own arrangements and acting for himself, and in this vital matter he would have vastly preferred doing so. But as he had no alternative, he tried to school himself to patience. His success was limited. Do what he might, scenes of disaster continued to form in his brain—Jenkins discovering them as they were on the point of leaving, Susan failing to secure a carriage and avoiding telling him so, and more disagreeably, his injuries worsening irreparably because of the journey. Though he did not think the latter probable, the worry would intrude, and more than once he wondered if he was doing the right thing. But the pressure to see Georgina and settle things between them, for good or ill, was stronger than this concern. All his faculties were focused on getting to her; indeed, the one scene he did not visualize was that with her. The disaster of her refusal he could not contemplate.

At last, after what seemed hours to Ellerton, when he looked out the window at the sound of a carriage, it was Susan, and not some unknown traveler. He saw the girl get down from a hired chaise, speak briefly to the driver, and enter the inn. He swung his uninjured leg to the floor and prepared for the ordeal of moving.

In the next moment, Susan was looking round the door, her green eyes gleaming with mischief. "Are you ready?"

"Yes. Is the corridor clear?" Ellerton didn't want to meet anyone. None would oppose him like Jenkins, but there might be some dispute, and he did not wish to attract attention and the chance of someone recalling the doctor's orders.

Susan looked, then nodded.

"You will have to help me. The crutches are over there." The doctor had provided a pair of crutches, but as he had commanded they not be used for three days, they had been placed in the far corner of the room, where Ellerton could not reach them.

Susan fetched them quickly and helped the baron lever himself up and onto them. He tried them awkwardly, nearly falling. "Here," said Susan, "lean on my shoulder on one side. That will be steadier."

This worked better, and they made their way out of the parlor and into the hall, going more slowly than Ellerton would have liked. The strong wish for speed, combined with his inability to achieve it, was maddening.

"Does it hurt?" asked Susan, betraying more worry than either of them had expected.

"No," lied Ellerton. In fact, his leg was signaling distress, though the pain was not enough to seriously concern him. It was hardly more than the ache in his ribs when he breathed deeply.

They reached the front door and started outside, only to be nearly knocked over by an entering ostler. The man looked considerably startled to see Ellerton walking. The baron himself had to smile. He must look ridiculous, he realized, supported by a pair of sticks and a ravishingly pretty redhead.

They were halfway across the innyard to the chaise when the voice of the innkeeper hailed them from behind.

Ellerton cursed softly. "The ostler must have told him," he said to Susan.

"Sir," repeated the innkeeper, bustling forward to them. "Should you be up and about? It seems a mite soon to be—"

"I'm taking him for a drive," interrupted Susan in her customary positive tone. "He needs fresh air."

The man looked doubtful.

"The doctor thinks it will be good for me," added Ellerton, silently apologizing for the lie. He liked the landlord.

"Ah. The doctor does." He nodded wisely. "That's all right, then. But I hope you won't be late, my lord. I've found a brace of partridges for your dinner."

For the first time, Ellerton realized that he would not be coming back to the inn. He would not make the journey twice, but would go on to his own London house. And it seemed ungrateful to go off this way without a word. He glanced up at the inn. All here had been very kind.

"Is your leg hurting you?" asked Susan in a pointed tone, as if to remind him that they risked further discovery standing here.

"Lord, yes, I shouldn't keep you on your feet," exclaimed the innkeeper. "Have a pleasant drive." And raising a hand in farewell, he turned away.

"Come on!" added Susan.

The baron allowed her to urge him to the chaise. If his purpose was not so important...he thought, then shook off this hesitation. It *was* important, important enough to risk his own health. He could not be deterred by politeness.

"Can you climb up?" said Susan.

Ellerton looked at the chaise steps. "I shall have to," he replied.

But at that moment, the landlord reappeared with two of the ostlers behind him. "I don't know what I was thinking of," he said, and Susan and the baron froze. "You'll never get up into that carriage alone. Jem and Bill here will lift you."

Susan let out her breath. Ellerton nodded. "Thank you."

At last they were both inside, and Susan leaned out to signal the driver. Ellerton, his injured leg propped up on the seat opposite and swathed in blankets and cushions, still couldn't help wincing a little as they started off, but the first jerk was succeeded by a smoother movement, and he decided the bouncing would not be too bad.

"I've told him to go slowly and carefully," said Susan.

"Thank you." Ellerton sat back and let himself relax, for the first time at leisure to examine his surroundings. His eye fell on a basket in the opposite corner. "Is that... Tell me you haven't brought that hellish cat?"

As if in answer, the lid of the basket popped up and Daisy's ginger-furred head appeared. He focused gleefully malevolent yellow eyes directly on the baron.

Ellerton groaned.

"Daisy is under strict orders to be good," said Susan, fixing the cat with an admonitory glance. "But he hates being shut in the house all the time, you know."

"I do not understand," answered Ellerton, "why someone, most likely your parents, has not strangled you ere this. To bring that animal, after all that has passed, it is..." He stopped, for once at a loss for words.

"He won't bother you," retorted Susan. "And I don't think you should speak to me so when I am *helping* you."

The baron looked at her, and she grimaced. He put his head back on the seat cushions and closed his eyes.

There was a silence. Daisy could be heard emerging from his basket and establishing himself on the plush seat.

"You haven't told me why you must be in London," Susan said then.

Ellerton opened his eyes. "And I don't intend to."

"I should think that after all I have done—"

"You would be mistaken." His tone was extremely discouraging, but Susan merely frowned and bit her lower lip in thought. Another silence fell, in which could be heard a peculiar rasping noise. "I hope you are prepared to pay for the upholstery," added Ellerton. "Your cat is destroying it."

"Daisy!" Susan leaned forward and disengaged his claws from the plush. Holding them in one hand and shaking a warning finger, she said, "You will be shut in your basket if you do not stop it."

With every appearance of sullen rebellion, the cat subsided onto the seat. The baron suppressed a smile.

"Where are we to take you?" asked Susan then, her voice carefully casual. "Your house?"

Ellerton went very still, cursing himself for having overlooked this detail. He had to go directly to the Goring house to find Georgina, yet how could he explain this to Susan without revealing his purpose, which he absolutely refused to do. He could not even leave the girl and go on, for she lived at his destination.

Susan was gazing curiously at him.

"You will see when we arrive," he responded curtly. "Now please be silent. I slept poorly, and I should like to try to make it up while we drive."

She obeyed, but she also smiled at her triumph over him. Where they were going would tell her a great deal about his goal, she concluded. For Susan had no intention of ending this adventure without discovering what that might be.

Ellerton did not really expect to sleep, and he did not, though he kept his eyes closed to discourage Susan from talking. Indeed, his impatience built with every tedious mile, and he longed to command the driver to whip up his horses and return to town at the breakneck pace he had left it on that ill-omened drive that now seemed so long ago. But his leg made that impossible, and he had to endure the whole journey at a near-walk. He tried to pass the time by thinking of what he would say to Georgina, but this merely intensified his frustration, and he came close to anger at her for leaving him in the first place before he caught himself, remembering that it was his own fault.

Finally, after what seemed an age, Susan said, "We are in town now. Where am I to direct the coachman?"

The issue could no longer be avoided. Ellerton faced it squarely. "Your grandmother's house."

She gaped at him. This was not what she'd expected. "Our house? But why?"

Ellerton braced himself mentally. "It is very important that I speak to your cousin. She left before I could do so."

"But Georgina was at the inn for days." Susan was frowning at the floor, trying to work this out.

"Nonetheless. Will you tell the man?"

Starting, Susan leaned out and gave the directions; then she turned back to gaze at him. "This doesn't have anything to do with me, does it?"

"Nothing whatsoever," he assured her cordially.

She abandoned her notion that he might be going to complain of her conduct to her grandmother. It had not been a satisfying theory in any case. "Why didn't you write Georgina a letter?" she asked.

"I wished to speak to her," he answered, wishing fervently that the driver would go a bit faster. Only their arrival would silence her, he knew.

Susan frowned at the floor once again. She could not imagine what important matter Ellerton would have to discuss with Georgina.

It was at this moment that the baron was visited by inspiration. His crutches had been laid across the two seats in the middle of the carriage, where it was widest, and the tips rested very close to where Daisy curled. Glancing quickly at Susan, and seeing that she was wrapped up in her thoughts, Ellerton grinned wickedly and took hold of one crutch, unobtrusively poking Daisy sharply in the side. In the next instant, his hand was withdrawn and he was gazing innocently out the chaise window.

Daisy reacted predictably to this insult. He sprang up and glared all around. Then, the absence of visible foes not deterring him in the least, he leapt across the vehicle to fasten his claws in the plush covering the wall between the two passengers' heads. Yellow eyes glittering, he hung there, plotting his next move.

"Daisy!" cried Susan.

"Watch it," exclaimed Ellerton at the same moment, for the cat had leapt again, coming perilously close to landing on his injured leg.

From that point, chaos reigned. Daisy jumped from one wall to another, eluding his mistress's furious grabs with apparent ease. Despite a number of close calls, he never hurtled out the open windows or fell to the floor, but he did jar the baron's leg more than once, eliciting a groan and clenched teeth, along with a conviction that he had made a mistake in provoking the animal.

At last Susan managed to throw both arms around the cat and hamper his movements with her skirts. Ellerton thought she would be scratched to ribbons, but to his surprise, Daisy did not touch her. In fact, he allowed himself to be scolded soundly and stuffed back into his basket, the lid securely fastened over his head. That accomplished, Susan sank back and let out a sigh of relief. Both of them were panting from the battle.

"He doesn't scratch you?" asked the baron curiously.

"Oh, no."

"But why not?"

The girl seemed surprised. "He wouldn't."

"I can't imagine that there is anything that beast 'wouldn't' do."

Susan seemed almost shocked. "He would never hurt *me*. We love each other." She paused, then added, "We are very much alike, you see."

That Susan should echo a conclusion he himself had reached surprised Ellerton again. He looked at her with new interest.

But Susan had already dismissed the subject from her mind. "Are you going to tell me what you wish to speak to Georgina about?" she asked flatly.

"No," he replied with equal bluntness.

"I think it is very unkind of you, after I have helped you this way."

"I would not have required help, if it had not been for your earlier antics."

This was unanswerable. Susan scowled and turned toward the window. "Here we are."

The chaise was indeed drawing up before Lady Goring's house. Ellerton saw with relief that the street was empty. He hoped to make this visit quietly, though of course Lady Goring's servants must inevitably know of it.

"Fetch two of your grandmother's footmen," he said to Susan when they had come to a stop. "I fear I cannot climb down." The jolting of the ride had made his leg feel tender and tired.

Susan met his eyes. "What if I won't?"

"I beg your pardon?"

"What if I won't get them—unless you tell me what you are doing here?" Her green eyes glinted.

"Then you would be very sorry indeed," replied Ellerton in an ominously quiet voice.

Susan hesitated, then wrinkled her nose. "Oh, very well!" And catching up Daisy's basket, she jumped out of the carriage. The baron let out a long sigh. He'd had no idea what he would do if she balked.

In a few minutes, Susan reappeared with help, and Ellerton was gently lowered from the chaise and carried into the library just off the front hall. At his signal, Susan dismissed the servants. He thought she might make another attempt to pressure him when he asked her to fetch Georgina, but she did not, and shortly thereafter Ellerton heard steps approaching down the stairs and Georgina herself appeared in the doorway.

"Baron Ellerton! What are you doing here? You should not have—"

"I had to speak to you," he broke in. "Please come in and shut the door."

Astonished, she obeyed, and outside in the hall, a slender, red-haired girl slipped down the stairs and applied her ear to the door panels.

EIGHTEEN

By the time she had taken a seat opposite him, Georgina had somewhat recovered from her amazement. "You were not to travel," she said. "Oh, I hope you have not hurt your leg. The doctor said—"

"It couldn't be helped," interrupted the baron again. "It was imperative I speak to you."

"To *me*?"

"Yes." He had pondered his beginning, and he was prepared, indeed eager, to press ahead. "You left the inn abruptly." She started to protest, and he held up a hand. "At my, er, instigation, I admit. Do you know why I spoke to you in that way about going?"

Georgina shook her head. Something in his voice had made her heart begin to pound, and she was not certain she could speak aloud.

"I was angry. You had said the previous afternoon that you were going, without a hint to me of your intentions, and that made me very angry." He paused. "Because I did not wish you to go, you see."

"I...I never meant to, really," breathed Georgina.

"No?" His eyes were fixed on her face.

"No, I just...that is..." She could not explain her feelings and doubts to him. "I knew I would have to go eventually. I didn't *want* to."

Ellerton had seen what he hoped for in her expression. "Neither of us wanted it, then," he replied. "And why was that, I wonder?"

The teasing note brought Georgina's eyes to his again.

She saw there everything she had wished for, and despaired of. Unexpectedly, she smiled. "Perhaps because we enjoyed each other's company."

"Far more than that." He did not smile yet. "I love you, Georgina. I realized that when you had gone. Will you be my wife?"

She couldn't dissemble. "Yes," she answered, and felt as if a great bubble of joy had burst in her chest.

"Damn this leg!" exclaimed the baron savagely, making Georgina start. "I cannot get up, you know." His mouth twisted. "Will you come here?"

She rose and went to kneel beside his armchair, on the side away from the footstool where his leg was propped. Her smile reappeared.

But Ellerton's joy in her acceptance was lost in frustration over his state. To be unable to move, to take the woman he loved in his arms, was intolerable. He felt both enraged and humiliated. "Damn!" he said again.

Georgina did not ask him what was wrong. She knew, and knew too that speaking of it would merely make it worse. Instead, she leaned a little forward and slid her arms around his neck, bringing her face very close to his. Then, tentatively, she kissed him.

It was not an expert kiss. Georgina had had no experience in such matters, and she was, in spite of her insight, a bit unsure of herself. But it was enough. Ellerton's arms tightened around her, pulling her into the chair with him, and he kissed her in turn, teaching Georgina more about the subject in a moment than she had gleaned in all her years. Elated, she gave herself up to his embrace.

Somehow, the awkwardness disappeared. Georgina's

feet came to rest beside his leg on the footstool, and she rested against the length of his body in the wide chair, arms entwined about his neck. Ellerton's hands roamed at first gently, then more urgently along her back, firing Georgina with feelings she'd never imagined. It was as if all they had felt for each other, misunderstood and thwarted till now, burst out to submerge them in passion.

When at last they drew a little apart, both were panting and a bit taken aback by the violence of their feelings. They simply gazed for a long moment; then Ellerton laughed shakily. "You know, my one concern was that we were too much friends to feel great passion. Clearly, I was mistaken."

She nodded, still breathless.

"And I have never in my life been so happy to be wrong," he added, smiling down at her.

Georgina nodded again.

"Have you nothing to say?"

"I love you," she murmured. "I…I am so happy, I don't know what else to say."

This, evidently, sufficed, for Ellerton bent to kiss her once again, and they were oblivious of all else for a prolonged period.

"Perhaps we should, rather, be thankful for my accident," he said after a while. "I don't think I could answer for my restraint otherwise."

"*I'm* not thankful," declared Georgina. Her pale blond hair had come loose from the knot on top of her head and was curling about her face. With her color heightened by emotion, she was achingly beautiful.

He laughed. "Then I am!"

Georgina made a face at him, and raised her lips to

kiss him, showing the great strides she had made in this endeavor in only twenty minutes. His hands slid caressingly along her sides, and she shivered with pleasure.

But Ellerton drew away first. "You really must sit here," he said, indicating the chair arm. "What has become of the quiet, steady woman who nursed me through my injuries?"

Georgina grinned. "I believe you have swept her completely away." She offered her lips once more, but he looked stern and pointed to the chair arm. Still smiling, Georgina extricated herself and perched on it.

He took her hand. "The change really is, er, startling."

She shrugged. "You have only yourself to blame." Then, more seriously, she added, "And it is not such a change, I think. One can know nothing of another's feelings until one comes close. I suppose many of our acquaintances feel things we don't imagine, because we don't know them well enough."

"I will not admit they are as extraordinary as you," he responded.

She bent to kiss him. Somehow, though neither knew how, Georgina resumed her previous place in the chair, and they forgot all else once more. Then she moved an arm unexpectedly and jarred his injured ribs, eliciting a quickly stifled groan. In an instant she was up and sitting on the arm again. "Your ribs, I forgot!"

"It's nothing. I'm all right." Some of his chagrin had returned. "One feels damnably ridiculous trying to make love from an armchair."

"You could never be ridiculous," she objected.

The sound of the bell made them both stiffen. Then Georgina said, "They won't bring anyone here. Gibbs will take them to the drawing room and inquire."

But in the hall, Susan scowled. She had been able to hear enough to utterly fascinate her, and the interruption was infuriating. Yet she did not wish to be discovered by the servants in her present position. Grimacing, she dashed to the front door and flung it open.

Tony Brinmore stood on the step, considerably startled by the violence of his welcome and the presence of Susan rather than a footman. He opened his mouth to speak, but she gestured him in and whirled.

Mystified, Tony entered, closing the door behind him. Susan had returned to her post. "What are you—?"

"Shhh!"

Frowning, he took a step closer. "What are you doing?" he whispered.

"Baron Ellerton is proposing to Georgina," she hissed.

"Nonsense."

"Shhh!"

"You must have got it wrong," he murmured. "No sign of that when we were out—"

"Listen for yourself," whispered Susan. "And do be quiet!"

Unhesitatingly Tony joined her. From within, he dimly heard Baron Ellerton say, "When shall we be married?" and Georgina's voice reply, "Before William and Marianne, I think. We mustn't interfere with their plans."

"Well, by Jove," exclaimed Tony.

"Shhh!" said Susan again, exasperated.

They resumed listening, but there were indications now that Georgina was about to emerge. Susan jerked upright. "Come on," she hissed. "In here." And she dragged Tony further down the hall and into the back parlor. They stood silent for a moment, listening, and heard Georgina walking upstairs.

"Well, what do you know about that?" said Tony then. "I never suspected it, did you?"

Susan looked scornful. "Of course."

"You never said anything," he retorted skeptically.

"I'm not a gossip!"

He gaped at her, but decided not to contradict. "We've had a regular rash of offers hereabouts lately," he said instead.

She nodded thoughtfully.

Tony was struck by a sudden idea. Without thinking, he said, "Maybe you and I should join in, eh?" The moment the words were out of his mouth, he regretted them. Indeed, he was aghast. He began to stammer a disjointed retraction.

"Are you mad?" said Susan. "Marry you? I wouldn't dream of it."

Weak with relief, he agreed with her. "Terrible idea. I believe I *was* mad. Must have been."

"Come on," said Susan disgustedly. "Let's go and twit Baron Ellerton on his engagement. He will be sorry he wouldn't tell me what he meant to do." She grinned wickedly. "And I must remind him that he is to be my cousin now."

Tony, who would have gladly followed her anywhere short of the altar at that moment, walked behind her into the hall.

ABOUT THE AUTHOR

Jane Ashford discovered Georgette Heyer in junior high school and was captivated by the glittering world and witty language of Regency England. That delight was part of what led her to study English literature and travel widely in Britain and Europe. Her books have been published all over Europe as well as the United States. Jane has been nominated for a Career Achievement Award by *RT Book Reviews*. Born in Ohio, she is now somewhat nomadic. Find her on the web at janeashford.com and on Facebook, where you can sign up for her monthly newsletter.

If you're interested in the earlier adventures of Susan Wyndham and Lady Marianne MacClain, you can find them in Jane's books *First Season* and *The Impetuous Heiress*, respectively.

Can't get enough Regency romance? Read on for a
sneak peek of *An Inconvenient Duke* by Anna Harrington,
available from Sourcebooks Casablanca February 2020!

An Inconvenient Duke

ONE

May 1816
Charlton Place, London

Marcus Braddock stepped out onto the upper terrace of his town house and scanned the party spreading through the torch-lit gardens below.

He grimaced. His home had been invaded.

All of London seemed to be crowded into Charlton Place tonight, with the reception rooms filled to overflowing. The crush of bodies in the ballroom had forced several couples outside to dance on the lawn, and the terraces below were filled with well-dressed dandies flirting with ladies adorned in silks and jewels. Card games played out in the library, men smoked in the music room, the ladies retired to the morning room—the entire house had been turned upside down, the gardens trampled, the horses made uneasy in the mews...

And it wasn't yet midnight. God help him.

His sister Claudia had insisted on throwing this party for him, apparently whether he wanted one or not. Not only to mark his birthday tomorrow but also to celebrate his new position as Duke of Hampton, the title given to him for helping Wellington defeat Napoleon. The party would help ease his way back into society, she'd asserted, and give him an opportunity to meet the men he would now be working with in the Lords.

But Marcus hadn't given a damn about society before he'd gone off to war, and he cared even less now.

No. The reason he'd agreed to throw open wide the doors of Charlton Place was a woman.

The Honorable Danielle Williams, daughter of Baron Mondale and his late sister Elise's dearest friend. The woman who had written to inform him that Elise was dead.

The same woman he now knew had lied to him.

His eyes narrowed as they moved deliberately across the crowd. Miss Williams had been avoiding him since his return, refusing to let him call on her and begging off from any social event that might bring them into contact. But she hadn't been able to refuse the invitation for tonight's party, not when he'd also invited her great-aunt, who certainly wouldn't have missed what the society gossips were predicting would be the biggest social event of the season. She couldn't accept and then simply beg off either. To not attend this party would have been a snub to both him and his sister Claudia, as well as to Elise's memory. While Danielle might happily continue to avoid him, she would never intentionally wound Claudia.

She was here somewhere, he knew it. Now he simply had to find her.

He frowned. Easier said than done, because Claudia had apparently invited all of society, most of whom he'd never met and had no idea who they even were. Yet they'd eagerly attended, if only for a glimpse of the newly minted duke's town house. And a glimpse of *him*. Strangers greeted him as if they were old friends, when his true friends—the men he'd served with in the fight against Napoleon—were nowhere to be seen. *Those* men he trusted with his life.

These people made him feel surrounded by the enemy.

The party decorations certainly didn't help put him at

ease. Claudia had insisted that the theme be ancient Roman and then set about turning the whole house into Pompeii. Wooden torches lit the garden, lighting the way for the army of toga-clad footmen carrying trays of wine from a replica of a Roman temple in the center of the garden. The whole thing gave him the unsettling feeling that he'd been transported to Italy, unsure of his surroundings and his place in them.

Being unsure was never an option for a general in the heat of battle, and Marcus refused to let it control him now that he was on home soil. Yet he couldn't stop it from haunting him, ever since he'd discovered the letter among Elise's belongings that made him doubt everything he knew about his sister and how she'd died.

He planned to put an end to that doubt tonight, just as soon as he talked to Danielle.

"There he is—the birthday boy!"

Marcus bit back a curse as his two best friends, Brandon Pearce and Merritt Ripley, approached him through the shadows. He'd thought the terrace would be the best place to search for Danielle without being seen.

Apparently not.

"You mean the duke of honor," corrected Merritt, a lawyer turned army captain who had served with him in the Guards.

Marcus frowned. While he was always glad to see them, right then, he didn't need their distractions. Nor was he in the mood for their joking.

A former brigadier who now held the title of Earl West, Pearce looped his arm over Merritt's shoulder as both men studied him. "I don't think he's happy to see us."

"Impossible." Merritt gave a sweep of his arm to indicate the festivities around them. The glass of cognac in his hand had most likely been liberated from Marcus's private liquor cabinet in his study. "Surely, he wants his two brothers-in-arms nearby to witness every single moment of his big night."

Marcus grumbled, "Every single moment of my humiliation, you mean."

"Details, details," Merritt dismissed, deadpan. But he couldn't hide the gleam of amusement in his eyes.

"What we really want to know about your birthday party is this." Pearce touched his glass to Marcus's chest and leaned toward him, his face deadly serious. "When do the pony rides begin?"

Marcus's gaze narrowed as he glanced between the two men. "Remind me again why I saved your miserable arses at Toulouse."

Pearce placed his hand on Marcus's shoulder in a show of genuine affection. "Because you're a good man and a brilliant general," he said sincerely. "And one of the finest men we could ever call a friend."

Merritt lifted his glass in a heartfelt toast. "Happy birthday, General."

Thirty-five. *Bloody hell.*

"Hear, hear." Pearce seconded the toast. "To the Coldstream Guards!"

A knot tightened in Marcus's gut at the mention of his former regiment that had been so critical to the victory at Waterloo yet also nearly destroyed in the brutal hand-to-hand combat that day. But he managed to echo, "To the Guards."

Not wanting them to see any stray emotion on his face, he turned away. Leaning across the stone balustrade on his forearms, he muttered, "I wish I could still be with them."

While he would never wish to return to the wars, he missed being with his men, especially their friendship and dependability. He missed the respect given to him and the respect he gave each of them in return, no matter if they were an officer or a private. Most of all, he longed for the sense of purpose that the fight against Napoleon had given him. He'd known every morning when he woke up what he was meant to do that day, what higher ideals he served. He hadn't had that since he returned to London, and its absence ate at him.

It bothered him so badly, in fact, that he'd taken to spending time alone at an abandoned armory just north of the City. He'd purchased the old building with the intention of turning it into a warehouse, only to discover that he needed a place to himself more than he needed the additional income. More and more lately, he'd found himself going there at all hours to escape from society and the ghosts that haunted him. Even in his own home.

That was the punishment for surviving when others he'd loved hadn't. The curse of remembrance.

"No, General." Pearce matched his melancholy tone as his friends stepped up to the balustrade, flanking him on each side. "You've left the wars behind and moved on to better things." He frowned as he stared across the crowded garden. "This party notwithstanding."

Merritt pulled a cigar from his breast pocket and lit it on a nearby lamp. "You're exactly where you belong. With your family." He puffed at the cheroot, then watched the smoke curl from its tip into the darkness overhead. "They need you now more than the Guards do."

Marcus knew that. Which was why he'd taken it upon himself to go through Elise's belongings when Claudia couldn't bring herself do it, to pack up what he thought her daughter, Penelope, might want when she was older and to distribute the rest to the poor. That was how he'd discovered a letter among Elise's things from someone named John Porter, arranging a midnight meeting for which she'd left the house and never returned.

He'd not had a moment of peace since.

He rubbed at the knot of tension in his nape. His friends didn't need to know any of that. They were already burdened enough as it was by settling into their own new lives now that they'd left the army.

"Besides, you're a duke now." Merritt flicked the ash from his cigar. "There must be some good way to put the title to use." He looked down at the party and clarified, "One that doesn't involve society balls."

"Or togas," Pearce muttered.

Marcus blew out a patient breath at their good-natured teasing. "The Roman theme was Claudia's idea."

"Liar," both men said at once. Then they looked at each other and grinned.

Merritt slapped him on the back. "Next thing you know, you'll be trying to convince us that the pink ribbons in you horse's tail were put there by Penelope."

Marcus kept his silence. There was no good reply to that.

He turned his attention back to the party below, his gaze passing over the crowded garden. He spied the delicate turn of a head in the crowd—

Danielle. There she was, standing by the fountain in the glow of one of the torches.

For a moment, he thought he was mistaken, that the woman who'd caught his attention couldn't possibly be her. Not with her auburn hair swept up high on her head in a pile of feathery curls, shimmering with copper highlights in the lamplight and revealing a long and graceful neck. Not in that dress of emerald satin with its capped sleeves of ivory lace over creamy shoulders.

Impossible. This woman, with her full curves and mature grace, simply couldn't be the same excitable girl he remembered, who'd seemed always to move through the world with a bouncing skip. Who had bothered him to distraction with all her questions about the military and soldiers.

She laughed at something her aunt said, and her face brightened into a familiar smile. Only then did he let himself believe that she wasn't merely an apparition.

Sweet Lucifer. Apparently, nothing in England was as he remembered.

He put his hands on both men's shoulders. "If you'll excuse me, there's someone in the garden I need to speak with. Enjoy yourselves tonight." Then, knowing both men nearly as well as he knew himself, he warned, "But not too much."

As he moved away, Merritt called out with a knowing grin. "What's *her* name?"

"Trouble," he muttered and strode down into the garden before she could slip back into the crowd and disappear.

TWO

Danielle Williams smiled distractedly at the story her great-aunt Harriett was telling the group of friends gathered around them in the garden. The one about how she'd accidentally pinched the bottom of—

"King George!" The crux of the story elicited a gasp of surprise, followed by laughter. Just as it always did. "I had no idea that the bottom I saw poking out from behind that tree was a royal one. Truly, doesn't one bottom look like all the rest?"

"I've never thought so," Dani mumbled against the rim of her champagne flute as she raised it to her lips.

Harriett slid her a chastising glance, although knowing Auntie, likely more for interrupting her story than for any kind of hint of impropriety.

"But oh, how high His Majesty jumped!" her aunt continued, undaunted. As always. "I was terrified—simply *terrified*, I tell you! I was only fourteen and convinced that I had just committed high treason."

Although Dani had heard this same story dozens of times, the way Harriett told it always amused her. Thank goodness. After all, she needed something to distract her, because this evening was the first time she'd been to Charlton Place since Marcus Braddock had returned from the continent. The irony wasn't lost on her. She was on edge with nervousness tonight when she'd once spent so much time here that she'd considered this place a second home.

"A pinch to a king's bottom!" Harriett exclaimed. "Wars have been declared over less offending actions, I assure you."

Dani had been prepared for the unease that fluttered in
her belly tonight, yet the guilt that gnawed at her chest was
as strong as ever...for not coming to see Claudia or spending time with Pippa, for not being able to tell Marcus what
kindnesses Elise had done for others in the months before
her death. But how could she face him without stirring up
fresh grief for both of them?

No. Best to simply avoid him.

"Had it been a different kind of royal bottom—say, one
of the royal dukes—I might not have panicked so. But it was
a *king's* bottom!"

She had a plan. Once Harriett finished her story, Dani
would suddenly develop a headache and need to leave.
She would give her best wishes to Claudia before slipping
discreetly out the door and in the morning pen a note of
apology to the duke for not wishing him happy birthday in
person. She'd assure him that she'd looked for him at the
party but had been unable to find him. A perfectly believ-
able excuse given how many people were crammed into
Charlton Place tonight. A complete crush! So many other
people wanted their chance to speak to him that she most
likely couldn't get close to him even if she tried. Not that
she'd *try* exactly, but—

"Good evening, Miss Williams."

The deep voice behind her twined down her spine.
Marcus Braddock. *Drat it all.*

So much for hiding. Her trembling fingers tightened
around the champagne flute as she inhaled deeply and
slowly faced him. She held out her gloved hand and lowered
into a curtsy. "Your Grace."

Taking her hand and bowing over it, he gave her a smile,

one of those charming grins that she remembered so vividly. Those smiles had always taken her breath away, just as this one did now, even if it stopped short of his eyes.

"It's good to have you and your aunt back at Charlton Place, Miss Williams."

"Thank you." She couldn't help but stare. He'd always been attractive and dashing, especially in his uniform, and like every one of Elise's friends, she'd had a schoolgirl infatuation with him. And also like every one of his little sister's friends, he'd paid her absolutely no mind whatsoever except to tolerate her for Elise's sake.

Although he was just as handsome as she remembered, Marcus had certainly changed in other ways. The passing years had brought him into his prime, and the youthful boldness she remembered had been tempered by all he'd experienced during his time away, giving him a powerful presence that most men would never possess.

When he released her hand to greet the others, Dani continued to stare at him, dumbfounded. She simply couldn't reconcile the brash and impetuous brother of her best friend with the compelling man now standing beside her, who had become one of the most important men in England.

Harriett leaned toward her and whispered, "Lower your hand, my dear."

Heavens, her hand! It still hovered in midair where he'd released it. With embarrassment heating her cheeks, she dropped it to her side.

She turned away and gulped down the rest of her champagne, not daring to look at the general for fear he'd think her the same infatuated goose she'd been as a young girl. Or at Harriett, whose face surely shone with amusement at the prospect of Dani being smitten with England's newest hero.

No. She was simply stunned to see all the changes that time and battle had wrought in him. That was all.

But then, Marcus Braddock had always been the most intense man she'd ever known, with brown eyes so dark as to be almost black, thick hair to match that curled at his collar, and a jaw that could have been sculpted from marble, like those Greek gods in Lord Elgin's notorious statues that Parliament had just purchased. Broad-shouldered, tall and confident, commanding in every way…no wonder she'd not been surprised to learn of all his promotions gained from heroism on the battlefield or to read about his exploits in the papers. Only when she'd learned that the regent had granted him a dukedom alongside Wellington had she been surprised—not that he'd been offered the title but that he'd accepted it.

"You seem well, Duke." Harriett had the audacity to look him up and down from behind the quizzing glass she wore on a chain around her neck. But her seven decades of age gave her the right to take liberties that few others would deign to claim, including so shamelessly scrutinizing the new duke when she should have done it surreptitiously. The way Dani was doing.

She gave him her own once-over while he was distracted with her aunt, deliberately taking him in from head to toe and finding him more impressive than ever. Despite her nervousness at seeing him again, a smile pulled at her lips. Only Marcus Braddock could appear imperial standing next to a papier-mâché statue of Julius Caesar.

Harriett finished her examination with an approving nod. "Life in London must be agreeing with you."

His mouth twisted with amusement. "I feel as if I've just been put through a military inspection, Viscountess."

Harriett let out a sound halfway between a humph and a chortle. "Better grow used to it, my boy! You were the grandson of a baron before, but now you're a peer. A duke, no less. Privacy has just become a luxury you cannot afford."

Although his expression didn't alter, Dani felt a subtle change in him. A hardening. As if he'd already discovered for himself the truth behind her great-aunt's warning.

"Lovely party." Harriett waved a gloved hand to indicate the festivities, the rings on her fingers shining in the torchlight. "So kind of you to throw it and invite all of London."

Dani blanched. Of all the things to say—

"Couldn't invite the best without inviting the rest," he countered as expertly as if the two were waging a tennis match.

Her eyes gleamed mischievously. "And which are which?"

"If you don't know—"

"You're part of the rest," the viscountess finished, raising her champagne glass in a mock toast.

In reply, he winked at her.

Harriett laughed, tickled by their verbal sparring match. "You happened by at exactly the right moment. I was just telling everyone about the first time I met His Majesty. Have I ever told you—"

"If you'll pardon me, Viscountess," he interrupted politely to avoid being caught up in the story. *Smart man.* "I'd like to ask Miss Williams for the next dance." He turned toward her. "Would you do me the honor?"

Dani's heart slammed against her ribs in dread. Being

with him like this, surrounded by a crowd of friends and acquaintances where the conversation had to be polite and impersonal was one thing. But dancing was something completely different and far too close for comfort. There would be too many opportunities to be reminded of Elise's death, for both of them. *This* was exactly what she'd hoped to avoid.

"My apologies, Your Grace." Dani smiled tightly. "But I'm not dancing tonight."

His expression darkened slightly. Clearly, he wasn't used to being refused. "Not even with an old friend returned from the wars?"

Especially not him. "Not at all, I'm afraid."

Something sparked in the dark depths of his eyes. A challenge? Had he realized that she'd been purposefully evading him? The butterflies in her belly molded one by one into a ball of lead as he smiled at her. "Surely, you can make an exception."

Dear heavens, why wouldn't he let this go? "I haven't been feeling myself lately, and a dance might tire—"

"Danielle," Harriett chastised with a laughing smile. Beneath the surface, however, she was surely horrified that Dani was refusing not just an old family friend and the man of honor at tonight's party but the most eligible man in the entire British empire. "One dance will not overtax you."

Without giving her the chance to protest, he insisted, "If you grow fatigued, I promise to return you immediately to your aunt." Marcus turned the full charms of his smile on her and held out his hand. "Shall we?"

Now she knew what foxes felt like when they were cornered by hounds. With no more excuses for why she couldn't dance, the only way to avoid him now would be to flat-out cut him in front of his guests. *That* she would never do.

Marcus didn't deserve that. Truly, he'd done nothing wrong, except remind her of Elise.

She grudgingly nodded her consent and allowed him to place her hand on his arm to lead her away.

Once they were out of earshot of the others, she lightly squeezed his arm to capture his attention. "While it's kind of you to request a dance, it's perfectly fine with me if we don't take the floor. You shouldn't feel obligated."

"But I want to." He slid her a sideways glance that rippled a warning through her as he led her toward the house. "I was very happy to see that you'd attended tonight."

"I wouldn't have missed it." Although she'd dearly tried to do just that. Swiftly changing the topic away from herself, she declared, "This party is a grand way to celebrate your return as a hero. I'm certain that Claudia and Pippa are thrilled to have you home."

Regret surged through her as soon as the words left her lips, because her mention of them would surely only remind him of Elise's absence. She hadn't wanted to cause him more grief. After all, that was why she'd been avoiding him since his return. How could he not look at her without thinking of his sister's death? God knew Dani was reminded of exactly that every time she thought of him.

"And you—" she rushed to add before he could reply, pivoting the conversation in a different direction. "You must have missed England."

"I did," he said, although the way he said it sounded faintly aggrieved. "But I'm not certain England missed me."

"It did, a great deal." Part of her had missed him a great deal as well.

He chuckled at that, as if it were a private joke. "Very little, I'm sure."

Yet his amusement did nothing to calm her unease, which wasn't helped at all by the hand he touched briefly to hers as it rested on his sleeve. The small gesture sent her heart somersaulting. But then, hadn't he always made her nervous?

Yet he fascinated her, too. Something about him stirred her curiosity… Of course, she'd found his life as a soldier intriguing and had loved to hear Elise talk of his adventures. His sister had been so proud of him that she couldn't stop bragging, and Dani had soaked up all the stories, especially those few she'd been fortunate enough to hear him tell himself during rare visits home before the fighting grew so fierce on the Peninsula that he'd not been able to leave Spain.

"But you're right. I did miss my family, and I'm very happy to be back with them." Another brief rest of his hand on hers, this time with a reassuring squeeze. "Although I suspect that they're ready to toss *me* back over the Channel."

She shook her head. "Not at all."

He lowered his mouth to her ear so he wouldn't be overheard by the other guests. "Then why else would Claudia torture me with a party like this?"

"She's not torturing you."

"Oh?" As if offering irrefutable proof, he muttered, "A plaster model of Vesuvius is set to erupt at midnight."

She laughed, her gloved hand going to her lips to stifle it. Amusement mixed with surprise. Being with him was quite enjoyable, when he didn't remind her of how much she missed Elise.

"And you, Miss Williams? Are *you* ready to toss me back?"

Her laughter died against her fingertips at the way he asked that. Not an innocent question. Not at all a tease. A hardness lurked behind it that she couldn't fathom.

"Of course not." She smiled uneasily as he led her through the French doors and into the house toward the ballroom that had been created by opening the connecting doors between the saloon, dining, and drawing rooms. "Why would I want to do that?"

"Most likely for the same reason you've been avoiding me."

Guilt pierced her so sharply that she winced. *This* was what she'd feared during the past few months, why she hadn't come to Charlton Place—coming face-to-face with his grief over his sister and her guilt over avoiding him. She wanted no part of this conversation!

She tried to slip away, but his hand closed over hers again, this time pinning her fingers to his sleeve and refusing to let her go. Aware of every pair of eyes in the room watching them and not wanting to create a scene, she walked on beside him until he finally stopped on the far side of the ballroom near the musicians.

She pounced on this chance to flee. It was time for her headache to arrive. "If you'd please, General—" Remembering herself, she corrected, "That is, Your Grace—"

"Has your absence been because of Elise's death?"

She flinched beneath his bluntness. There would be no avoiding this exchange. This was the reason he'd refused to let her decline the dance.

"No," she whispered, unable to speak any louder past the knot in her throat. "It's been because of you."

THREE

Dani's pulse stuttered when his eyes flared in genuine surprise, then iced over. He demanded in a low voice, "What do you mean because of *me*?"

"I was the one who sent news of her death to you." She looked away across the dance floor as half of the couples moved off and more joined those who remained. "Why would you want to see me when I would only remind you of your loss?"

"You think me as weak as that?"

Never. Not him. "I think you…" How *did* she think of him, when he'd always paid her no more mind than a teacup? As his sister's friend and ten years younger, she'd expected no less, even as she'd admired him from afar. But now, seeing the man he'd become, she simply had no idea what to make of him. "I think you loved Elise a great deal. Even now, just speaking to me like this—it's making you grieve all over again."

His shoulders sagged almost imperceptibly. But she noticed. Given the hours she'd spent staring at him as a girl, of course she had.

"How could I bring that pain back into your home?" Or open herself again to fresh grieving? Or Claudia's? And sweet heavens, Pippa…did she deserve to be reminded that she'd lost her mother before she barely knew her, the same child who had already lost her father? "You've returned a hero, with a shining new future before you, and you've come back into your family's embrace. I didn't want to ruin that by reminding you of what you've lost. That is why I stayed away."

Tentatively, she placed her hand on his arm. She couldn't resist giving him this small gesture of reassurance. He deserved so much more from her, but this was all she could offer.

"I hope you understand." Her hand fell away to her side, yet her fingertips continued to tingle from the feel of the hard muscle beneath his jacket sleeve.

Not replying, he signaled to the master of ceremonies, who nodded and stepped onto the dais to speak to the lead musician. The violinist gestured toward the other musicians, setting them into a flurry of shuffling through their sheet music. Then they played the opening fanfare for the next dance—a waltz. Surprised murmurs went up through the crowd that the order of the dances had changed.

As Marcus gave her a low bow, Dani sank into an answering curtsy. But suspicion sparked in her belly for why he would order a waltz of all dances, when he now knew why she didn't want to be close to him.

The music settled into sweeping strains, and he led her into the waltz, taking them expertly into their steps.

A pinch of uneasiness tightened in her chest as she glided along with him, her full satin skirts swooshing around his legs whenever they turned. Every pair of eyes in the crowd that watched them dance past only served to remind her that life was now so very different for both of them than it had been before the wars, and so very complicated.

Yet knowing that didn't stop her from enjoying the waltz. How could she not, when he led her so skillfully around the room? A natural-born athlete, he made every move seem effortless. Dancing with him proved just as wonderful as she'd always suspected it would be during all those evenings as a young miss when she'd watched him partner with other women beneath the glittering chandeliers at so many otherwise forgotten parties. Although nervous suspicion still lingered inside her, so did pleasure, helped along by the hard muscles in his legs that she tried unsuccessfully not to notice every time they accidentally brushed against hers in the tight turns they were forced to make on the crowded dance floor. She couldn't help but follow yieldingly in his arms, couldn't help but ignore the rest of the world spinning around them.

When his lips curled faintly into a smile, a jolt of raw attraction sparked inside her so unexpectedly that it shocked the daylights out of her.

"You seem surprised," he said, amusement coloring his voice. "You didn't think I could waltz?"

He'd misunderstood her stunned bewilderment. *Thank God*, because she couldn't have borne the humiliation if he realized how her body tingled in response to his.

"I thought you'd be rusty in your steps," she dodged. "I didn't think you'd have had much opportunity to practice during the past few years."

"Not often, that's true. And my horse made for a damnably clumsy partner."

She laughed despite the fluttering butterflies in her belly. "Four left hooves?"

"The rascal kept wanting to lead."

Another laugh bubbled from her as he twirled her into a turn in the far corner of the room, then started a promenade back across the floor. How had she not remembered him being so witty? Brilliant, of course. Cunning even, from the stories she'd read of his battle exploits. But such a dry sense of humor was a welcome discovery, one that was helping to cut through her unease.

The worst was over between them, apparently. Hoping they could be friends, she teased, "Perhaps I should be partnering with the cavalry at society balls."

But he didn't laugh at her joke, instead forcing a tight smile as if distracted. Apparently, more lingered on his mind than the reason she'd been avoiding Charlton Place.

Well, if they were going to find a way to be friends, then she might as well be bold about it. "General, is something wrong? You keep looking at me as if..." She shook her head, puzzled. "As if you don't know what to make of me."

"Because I don't," he answered honestly, his brow drawing down into a puzzled frown. His bluntness was jarring, as was the sound of betrayal in his voice. "Because I simply cannot fathom why you lied to me about Elise's death."

Also by Jane Ashford

The Duke's Sons
Heir to the Duke
What the Duke Doesn't Know
Lord Sebastian's Secret
Nothing Like a Duke
The Duke Knows Best

The Way to a Lord's Heart
Brave New Earl
A Lord Apart
How to Cross a Marquess

Once Again a Bride
Man of Honour
The Three Graces
The Marriage Wager
The Bride Insists
The Bargain
The Marchington Scandal
The Headstrong Ward
Married to a Perfect Stranger
Charmed and Dangerous
A Radical Arrangement
First Season / Bride to Be
Rivals of Fortune / The Impetuous Heiress
Last Gentleman Standing
Earl to the Rescue